The Countess Angélique

In the Land of the Redskins

Volume One

By the same author in PAN Books

ANGELIQUE I: THE MARQUISE OF THE ANGELS
ANGELIQUE II: THE ROAD TO VERSAILLES
ANGELIQUE AND THE KING
ANGELIQUE AND THE SULTAN
ANGELIQUE IN REVOLT
ANGELIQUE IN LOVE
THE COUNTESS ANGELIQUE II: PRISONER OF
THE MOUNTAINS

The Countess Angélique

In the Land of the Redskins

Volume One

SERGEANNE GOLON

UNABRIDGED

Translated from the French by
MARGUERITE BARNETT

PAN BOOKS · LONDON

Originally published 1967 as *Angélique et le Nouveau Monde*
by Editions de Trévise

© Opera Mundi, Paris, 1967

First published as one volume in UK 1967 by
William Heinemann Ltd.

This edition published 1969 by Pan Books Ltd.,
33 Tothill Street, London, S.W.1

330 02249 0

2nd Printing 1969
3rd Printing 1969
4th Printing 1969

© Opera Mundi, Paris, 1967

Printed in Great Britain
by Richard Clay (The Chaucer Press), Ltd., Bungay, Suffolk

CONTENTS

PART ONE

Early Days

PART TWO

The Iroquois

PRINCIPAL CHARACTERS

Angélique, Countess Peyrac. An aristocratic French lady of the seventeenth century. After leading the people of her native province, Poitou, in the uprising against Louis XIV, she was condemned to death and obliged to flee France with her youngest child Honorine. She reached America, where she was reunited with her long-lost husband and her two sons, Florimond and Cantor.

Honorine. Angélique's illegitimate daughter, aged four at the time of the action.

Joffrey de Peyrac. A high-born Frenchman. His great learning and considerable fortune aroused the envy of King Louis XIV, who contrived his ruin and had him condemned as a sorcerer. After many adventures, he was reunited with his family and disembarked in America on the shores of Maine, where he planned to found a colony. The Indians called him Tekonderoga.

Florimond. Angélique's eldest son by Count Peyrac, aged 17.

Cantor. Second son of Angélique and Count Peyrac, aged 15.

Servants and followers of Count Peyrac on his expedition:

Hervé le Gaën : a Breton sailor.

Enrico Enzi : a Maltese diver.

Porguani : an Italian gentleman.

O'Connel : an Irish merchant.

Lymon White : an English Puritan, dumb as the result of having his tongue cut out.

Sam Holton : an English Puritan.

Clovis : a French blacksmith from the province of Auvergne.

Octave Malaprade : a French cook.

Jacques Vignot : a French carpenter.

Nicolas Perrot and François Maupertuis : French-Canadian trappers.

French Huguenots who fled France with Angélique:

Monsieur Jonas : a watchmaker from La Rochelle.
Madame Jonas : his wife.
Elvire : a baker's widow, whose husband was killed on the crossing to America.

French-Canadians:

Count Loménie-Chambord.
Lieutenant Pont-Briand.
Romain de l'Aubignière.
Baron Eliacien de Maudreuil.
Robert Cavelier de la Salle.
The Duke of Arreboust.
Eloi Macollet.

Iroquois Indians:

Swanissit : Chief of the Five Nations.
Outakke : Chief of the Mohawks.
Tahoutaguete.

Algonquin Indians:

Mopuntook : Chief of the Metallaks.
Piksarett : Chief of the Patsuiketts.

French Jesuits:

Father Masserat.
Father Sebastian d'Orgeval.
Father Philip de Guérande.

PART ONE

EARLY DAYS

CHAPTER ONE

'So we're together, then, he and I!'

This was the thought that kept fluttering around Angélique's head. She could not have said whether it came from within her own mind – for at that moment she felt herself quite incapable of forming any thoughts whatsoever – or whether it was rather something from outside herself akin to the buzzing flight of the mosquitoes and insects all about her. It came and went, began again, grew louder, then flitted away....

'So we're together, then, he and I!'

Her whole attention was focused on the task of keeping her horse safely pacing up a steep track, and Angélique could not have said that she was taking the slightest interest in the meaning of this buzzing sound which kept nagging at her.

'We're together! We're together!'

The phrase was repeated on two tones. One held a note of doubt, the other of affirmation. One was fearful, the other joyous. It formed a soothing accompaniment, a kind of leit-motif, to the weary tread of her mount.

The young woman who rode beneath the overhanging crimson maple leaves on this American autumn day was wearing a man's big felt hat with a feather in it; in the shadow of its brim her eyes looked as limpid as fresh spring water. To protect her hair from the dust of the trail, she had bound it up in a linen coif. She had given up riding side-saddle, and her long skirts revealed her legs in their close-fitting riding-boots right up to the knee. She had borrowed the boots from her son Cantor, who had been very willing to help her out. Her fingers, as they gripped the leather reins, warm and almost spongy from the pressure of her damp palms, were white at the knuckles from the strain of holding the horse's head turned towards the top of the hill, and preventing it from jibbing away towards the edge of the gorge on their left, whose deep shadows and rumbling echoes seemed both to fascinate and terrify the animal. Was it the void or the roar of torrential waters tantalizing the thirsty beast that made it so jumpy?

Her mount was a hardy mare, and very handsome too, but from the time they had set out, it had seemed utterly bewildered by what was being asked of it. That was hardly surprising either, when you came to think of it, for nothing could have seemed less suited for the noble pace of a horse than these twisting trails that snaked up and down the slopes and valleys, scarcely visible beneath the trees, losing themselves on scorched heathland or in swamps, vanishing into rivers along which the travellers had to splash for hours on end when the forest became impenetrable, clambering over crests and plunging into the abyss with a recklessness common to all paths which a man on foot will follow when he seeks the quickest possible route and when he has only his own bare feet to consider, and not the precious hocks of a horse.

The trail they were now following was carpeted with dry, slippery grass, burnt almost reddish brown by the sun. The horse kept on flattening it down, and its impatient hooves found nothing to grip on. Angélique held it with a firm hand, exercising careful pressure on the animal to keep it calm and force it to go on. She knew her mount by now, and even if it required a constant effort from her, she no longer feared that it would disobey her commands. It would do what she wanted it to do, and if, when evening came, she was left aching in every limb, that was another matter.

On and on they went. They were reaching the summit. The shadowy depths of the gorge, frothing with yellow and red foam tinted by the trees that leaned over the rushing waters, dwindled away below the trail, seemed to draw itself in between two slabs of enclosing rock and disappeared from view; then they found themselves on a kind of plateau over which there wafted a gentle resin-impregnated breeze.

Angélique breathed deeply.

Before her lay a forest of conifers: pine-trees, blue cedars, and shaggy spruces formed a dark army, shimmering with sombre, soft emerald green and blue-grey hues, embroidered by clusters of needles in tufts, posies, rosettes, and garlands which made up a finely stitched tapestry, tint on tint, green on green.

The ground had become stony again, broken by outcrops of hard shale, over which the horse's hooves clattered.

Angélique relaxed the grip of her hands on the reins and her knees on the horse's flanks. The persistent little thought fluttered about her again, mingling now with the welcome breath of the breeze.

'So it really is true, we're together!'

She halted and, as one does on waking from a dream, listened to the echo of it. She gave a start, raised her head, and her gaze sought out a familiar silhouette at the far end of the company of riders.

There he was at the head of the cavalcade, Count Joffrey de Peyrac, the great wanderer in the eye of the Eternal, adventurer of the two worlds, the man of dramatic destiny, who, having tasted of all life's glories and privations, today pressed forward, a grim horseman, drawing his company on behind him day after day, in a haughtily casual manner that occasionally appeared reckless, but always proved reliable.

How many times had Angélique said to herself when they came face to face with some obstacle: 'We will never make it. Joffrey shouldn't have risked it.'

Yet, even as she spoke, they would make their way one after the other, riders following trackers, porters following riders, through some burrow-like hole in the brushwood, through the tunnel of a mountain gorge, across the fast flowing current of a river, the shifting no-man's-land of a swamp, or the unknown fastness of a rocky hill across which the shades of night were falling. And they got through, they moved on, light appeared at the end, there was the shore, the shelter for the night. Each time it happened it seemed to have been neither possible nor predictable, and yet it happened. Joffrey de Peyrac never warned anyone of these surprises. He presented them as if they were the most natural thing on earth. Angélique still wondered whether he really knew where he was going or whether it was mere chance that kept bringing them through safely. They ought to have been lost and have perished a hundred times over, but the fact remained that no one had perished. And for three weeks now, those who made up the little caravan that had left Gouldsboro during the last days of September, had bowed to their destiny, carried along and intoxicated by the forest through which they were journeying, like pebbles swept along in the flood of a torrent, their complexions brown and roughened at the angles, their eyes faded by the brilliant light, the dazzling blues, the blue of the sky seen through the coloured kaleidoscope of the leaves, and the folds of their garments redolent with the scent of wood fires and autumn, resin and raspberry. In the autumnal heat the mist that hung over the lakes would evaporate in the early hours of the morning, leaving the surface of the water dazzling and limpid, and the undergrowth so dry that it could be heard crackling at a considerable distance.

In the evening, the temperature would suddenly fall almost unexpectedly, bringing a sudden chill that was a foretaste of winter, but there were still many trees decked in green, only just beginning to turn yellow. Then, as if by a miracle, a camp site would appear, just a little off the beaten track, to avoid the sandflies and the mosquitoes. Fires were lighted. The Indian women deftly cut long poles from the undergrowth, and in less than an hour the clearing was dotted with tepees covered with sheets of birch-bark sewn together or with great patches of elm-bark overlapping like rooftiles. At first Angélique had wondered how they had managed to strip these sheets of bark from the trees in such a short time. Later she noticed that Joffrey de Peyrac used to send a party ahead whose job it was to clear a path and sometimes even to blaze one, and also to prepare the camp site. On some occasions, there was no one waiting for the cavalcade at its destination, but in that event the men would dash off in various directions, and, as lively as a dog unearthing a bone, they would lift up big strips of moss in various places in the wood, or roll away rock from the entrance to some cave, to reveal an abundant cache of elm-bark piled up ready for the traveller and supplies of buried maize.

It was primitive but adequate. For the three white women, Angélique, Madame Jonas, her niece Elvire and the three children accompanying them, a drill tent was erected. The ground was covered with pine branches and bearskins, which also served as blankets. It was very cosy in these tents and a good night's sleep could be had provided one was not accustomed to feather-beds and eiderdowns, which was certainly not the case for Angélique and her daughter, who had experienced many far less comfortable lodgings in the course of their adventures.

The unchanging fair weather made their journey easier. At least they did not have to dry out rain-drenched garments. Hunting and fishing provided them with tasty food every evening, to supplement their commons of dry biscuits and bacon which they had brought with them from Gouldsboro.

But, as the days, then the weeks passed, their cautious advance disguised extreme lassitude. Angélique felt it especially this morning, when her horse's hooves began to clatter over the stony ground. The noise seemed to be amplified by the grey trunks of the pines, and by contrast emphasized the silence in which they were advancing. She noticed that for several days now Cantor's guitar had been silent, as had the cheerful voices of Maupertuis and Perrot bandying jokes or swapping advice. The company kept steadily on but no one spoke any longer. It was weariness perhaps, or the instinctive cunning of those in peril, who at every step are on their guard and try to be as inconspicuous as possible. That morning, Honorine had asked to ride behind Angélique for the first time since they had set out. Up till then she had foisted her company on each of the riders in turn, and indeed she had been much sought after, for she was a most entertaining companion. She had even got herself carried on the greasy shoulders of some of the Indians, with whom she claimed to have had some very interesting conversations.

But today she wanted her mother. Angélique could feel her asleep against her back. When the terrain became difficult the child ran the risk of slipping off, but Honorine had been brought up on horseback, and had been rocked all her childhood by the stride of horses making their way through dense forests, and in her sleep she instinctively tightened her grip around her mother's waist.

The trail vanished into a patch of grey sand, intermingled with pine needles, and the velvety surface deadened all noise once more. The sounds of breathing, the creaking of the saddles, the snorting of the horses as they drove off the flies, all mingled with the sighing of the wind that whispered softly through the pine-trees like the distant roar of the sea. The trees were very big now; straight, pale-grey trunks shot high up in the air, stretching out their horizontal branches with architectural precision. These were trees worthy of having been planted by the hand of man. They reminded one irresistibly of the cathedrals, and of the great parks on the Ile de France and at Versailles.

But it was only a park created by untamed nature, sown spontaneously at the wild will of the winds, the soil, and frail seeds, and which today, for the first time since the dawn of the world, was echoing to the sound of horses' hooves. The tall American pines watched the horses go by. They had never seen one before.

The animals sniffed the fragrant air. Their senses told them there was something unusual about this first meeting with the giants of an unexplored world, but, like the civilized creatures of noble English and Irish blood that they were, they overcame their apprehensions.

A pine-cone came tumbling down from branch to branch, one of those round bristly fruits, open like a water-lily and rimy with white resin. Angélique started at the noise, her mount shied and Honorine woke up.

'It's nothing,' said her mother.

She spoke softly. There were squirrels up there in the trees, watching them as they went by.

They had been walking now for nearly an hour on this flat ground amidst the grey colonnade of pine-trees.

The land began to slope down gently towards the valley, and with it went pines then firs then, as they slid down the slope, birches appeared again, and aspens with their leaves still almost green, then elms, already golden brown, rugged oaks with clusters of huge brown or wine coloured leaves, and finally the entire gamut of the maple family, of which Angélique had never encountered so many different varieties. It was these maples that gave the autumn its loveliest colours, ranging from honey via hectic red to burnished gold.

Shortly before plunging into undergrowth hung with purple, they caught sight on their left of a vast horizon rimmed with dark mountains. These were the first mountains they had seen, for although up till now they had appeared to be constantly going up- or downhill, since they had left the coast, the travellers had merely been crossing a vast peneplain, furrowed by sudden gorges, watercourses and lakes.

The mountains they saw did not seem very high, but there were many of them and they seemed to go on for ever, rolling away into the distance like a long, gentle swell, with blue upon grey and grey upon blue, until they melted into banks of similarly coloured clouds that crowded the far sky.

At their feet, in the foreground, spread a valley, pink-tinted beneath a light mist. It was vast, calm, serene, and devastatingly empty.

Angélique suddenly felt overwhelmed by the panorama she had glimpsed, for it had brought sharply home to her the scale of the world in which she found herself. It represented, so to speak, the discovery, all illusion past, of the true extent of a virtually impossible task. She began to doubt whether she had ever lived anywhere else, whether she had ever been among a crowd of people, amidst other women, at Court, at Versailles, whether it were possible that, somewhere in the world, there were cities thronged with people and the busy hum of men, nations where human beings lived huddled together, over-crowded and turbulent. It all seemed inconceivable. They were now transported back to the beginnings of the world, the pride of silent matter: water, earth, rocks, swamps, and clouds, leaves and sky. And for her, everything had fallen silent. Gone now were the noisy scenes of the past, where she had played out her brilliant but solitary destiny as a beautiful young woman hemmed about by desire and peril. It was as if a red theatre curtain had fallen, from behind which she could hear laughter, sniggering, and cackling.

Angélique shuddered and drew herself up in her saddle, with a sensation of nausea:

'I almost went to sleep. How stupid of me, I could have broken my own ribs and dragged Honorine with me. You're all right, aren't you, Honorine, my love?'

'Yes Mummy.'

'It's all this red too. . . .'

They were moving forward in a blaze of scarlet, through a grove of maples that the autumn had turned red from head to foot, for the fallen leaves already formed a thick carpet and made it almost impossible to pick out, in the midst of the foliage, the black trunks and branches that supported all this panoply. The light filtering through the leaves took on all the brilliance of a blacksmith's forge, the radiance of stained glass. Three bold, rapturous black-and-white magpies hopped from branch to branch, chattering clamorously.

'Oh, that's all it was! It sounded like Madame de Montespan.' Her rival at Versailles was far away, and the thought of her was like something out of a colourful nightmare. All that was no more real and substantial than an empty fruit-skin crushed between one's fingers. The Court, King Louis XIV's passion for her, Angélique. The curtain had come down. All that lay be-hind her. That was how she felt about it. And before her lay the desert and the man she had found again. Everything was beginning once more.

She had felt something analogous to this a long time ago, when she had crossed the desert of Mahgreb with Colin Paturel: a transformation of her whole being, a break with herself. But it had not been at all the same thing; for then she had been fleeing from the desert, and Colin Paturel had merely crossed her path. Whereas now the desert to be crossed would never end, and she was tied to the man she loved.

They were together.

And this thought around her and within her suddenly raged with conflicting feelings, an unspeakable joy and then a sudden chill of fear, as if a chasm had suddenly yawned beneath her feet. A feverish shudder ran through her body, leaving her feeling inwardly shattered. The fear sprang from the words she had uttered almost unconsciously, speaking of herself as 'tied', or saying that the desert was never-ending. She looked down at her hands as they held the horse's reins, and found them familiar. They were slender and long, and many a man had kissed them without suspecting their hidden strength. It was that strength, practised over the years, which now made it possible for her to handle heavy arms, to knead dough or to wring washing as she performed her heavy household tasks, and to master a restive horse.

They were clean-cut, those hands, very much her own, and they bore neither dress rings nor a wedding ring. They were her hands!

Angélique trusted them, they were her most faithful friends. But as for the rest of her, at times she felt a weary, childish weakness. Her heart and her mind were in a turmoil, she felt so highly-strung, her laughter was close to tears, a single word could cause her dismay, joy, plunge her into uncertainty, perplexity, and she felt a feeling of oppression mounting within her, nameless and without purpose, that began to overwhelm her just as the clouds across the plain, piled above the valleys, had begun insidiously to swell and invade the clear sky.

Everything had gone too quickly, and now everything was going too slowly.

It had been too swift, too staggering, the joy she had felt that morning when he had taken her hand in front of them all and said: 'I would like to introduce to you my wife, the Countess of Peyrac.' It had been too dazzling, too painful, like a flash of lightning, that moment when she had caught sight of her sons, alive, and had realized that they were really there.

It had all been too violent, too exhausting, the joy of those nights when her body, restored to life again, had rediscovered the urgency of desire.

It had been like a whirlwind that gripped her and ravished her. The red-hot brand of joy and happiness had touched her, had penetrated her, but she was not yet capable of severing herself from all that she had been for too long, that other woman born in travail, that woman branded with the seal of the King, the Rebel. That was why she sometimes found herself a widow again, alone with all her old irrational reflexes.

. It was at times like these that the reality of her situation would strike her like a gunshot, leaving her in a state of shock and stupor.

'But it's true. He is here. We are together.' Joy and fear mingled within her, and she would almost faint.

Rather than face these moments of awareness that burnt or froze her in turn, Angélique found it preferable in the end to allow her mental energy to lapse, to sink into a kind of torpor favoured by the slow laborious progress of her horse. There was nothing really dangerous about the journey, but everything was unexpected. Attention remained on the alert, thought slumbered, grew vague, and seemed unwilling to consider anything beyond the narrow track, its winding course, its rise and fall, its signs and smells, refusing to dwell on anything beyond tangible and immediate marks, stones, leaves, grassy patches to cross or skirt, and what lay all around them ... and that was nothingness, nothingness, nothingness, as far as the eye could see, nothing but silence and a dead earth wrapped in a shroud of crackling leaves.

'But I've always had too much imagination,' Angélique told herself. 'I would dream ... I would settle down among the pictures of my own imagination, and find that I liked it so much there that I had great difficulty in coming back to a different and often disappointing reality. If I begin to let my imagination play on the idea of a vast hostile desert behind those interminable clumps of trees, I will wear myself out before we get there. ... Much better for me to wait till I find out what this country really is and not to think about it. Oh, all this red...!' she murmured with a shake of her head. 'How could one ever dream of such splendour? Could one have dreamt that such colours existed?' she asked herself, with a feeling of sudden exhaltation, drawn out of herself by an impulse of admiration that plunged her into a state of almost supernatural bliss, eyes wide open, gloating on the rippling colours, in which light and shade vied with one another to give to each subtle shade all the splendour of a jewel. Red, saffron, and pink stood out against the bronze sackcloth of the undergrowth and blackberry bushes from which emanated a warm perfume of blackberries and honey. Angélique thought she saw something move beside a near-by tree-trunk and discovered two black bear cubs climbing up the tree, the claws of all eight paws gripping the bark. As the horse went by they turned their snouts curiously to watch, with a look that was both artful and guileless.

She nearly woke Honorine to show them to her, for they were so funny.

But she reflected that the mother-bear might well be in the offing, and she checked the pocket of her saddle to make sure that the pistols Joffrey had given her were still there.

Some distance behind her Master Jonas's horse came out from under a double scarlet archway. As if bent double beneath the weight of the incandescent leaves, the watchmaker's back had grown round. He too must be half-asleep, and Angélique kept an eye on him as he set out across the track covered with dead leaves. If the mother-bear were to make a movement over there in the undergrowth, the horses would certainly take fright. But nothing happened; Master Jonas and his horse passed under the gaze of the bear cubs, which took considerable interest in watching this apocalyptic animal whose four-footed lower half looked like the original and whose upper half, surmounted by a kind of black cone – the baby bears did not know it was called a hat – gave out a loud snoring noise as it went by.

Master Jonas and his wife had asked the Count de Peyrac if they might join his expedition rather than remain in Gouldsboro. With their niece Elvire, the baker's widow and her two young children, they formed the Huguenot contingent of the company, Angélique's personal acquaintances. The rest of the party, among whom were Italians, Germans, Englishmen, and possibly Scots, she still did not know properly and even found it hard to distinguish one man from another. She reproached herself for this uncertainty, which was by no means her way; for she had always shown a degree of curiosity about her fellows which inclined her to get to know them quickly. But they were Peyrac's men, not hers, and both sides were biding their time.

The only one to stand out from the crowd was still the Canadian trapper, Nicolas Perrot, more generally capable, useful and indispensable than ever; he had a way of appearing at the opportune moment whenever she needed something done. He walked, by choice, with the tireless, silent gait of the Indians, his gun resting butt upwards on his shoulder. He often went on ahead to clear the trail and prepare the site for the evening camp. Angélique had the impression that this calm, mysterious young man could well have familiarized her with everything that frightened her, but he would no doubt have been astonished to know her thoughts since his surroundings were so everyday to him : a tree was a tree whether red or not, a river was a river, a redskin a redskin, the important thing being to decide very quickly whether one was dealing with a friend or foe. A friend was a friend, an enemy an enemy, and a scalp a scalp; one of the best things in life was a halt round a well-packed peace-pipe, one of the most disagreeable an arrow through one's heart.

In this respect he was a simple man, and the mystery in him derived only from knowledge he possessed of strange and unaccustomed things. He was quite unconscious of it himself.

She was sorry that he was not near her now. She would have asked him the names of some of the plants she saw along the track; for she knew some of them but not all. She would have asked him how they managed to feed horses in a land with no fields, no clearings, with nothing but the dense undergrowth, dead leaves, fallen branches, and no grass. She sensed that this problem of the horses must be worrying him. He had already explained at considerable length to her that in this area, the only means of communication were the rivers, and the only means of transport little Indian birch-bark canoes which one carried on one's head over the rapids and refloated on calmer waters farther on. 'But of course, with horses and women. . . !' he would say with a shake of the head.

The forest was coming to an end in a blaze of sunset hues between the walls of rock which widened out to form a sort of gorge. Water came bounding down the hillside to meet them, but this time the slope was not difficult to climb. Before going on her way, Angélique halted this time and turned round to look back over the cavalcade emerging one by one from the ravine, some on horseback, others on foot, as if they were climbing out of a well.

She noted their weary demeanour; all of them, even the young men, seemed to be overcome by fatigue and heat.

Honorine, the little four-year-old, was sleeping with her

arms around her mother's waist, leaning against her back. At the spot where the child's plump cheek rested on her, Angélique could feel a hot damp patch. The slightest point of contact was almost unbearable in this intense heat, for the air was bone dry and quivering.

Sweat ran down the back of her neck and made her clothes stick to her skin. In spite of her broad-brimmed hat the back of her neck was sore.

One of the men in the party came up to her and greeted her with a vague salutation as he went by. He never even raised his head, and his dragging footsteps raised a little trail of dust behind him. Angélique looked back again. She could not see her younger son, Cantor, and felt slightly anxious about him.

The men filed by one after another, bent double beneath the weight of their burdens.

Some of them, strangers to her, were speaking English together. They glanced briefly as they went by at the young woman sitting on her horse at the edge of the path; some of them greeted her, but none stopped.

During the course of those three weeks, all Angélique had managed to gather as she watched these men, chosen by Count Peyrac to accompany him on his expedition into the backwoods of the American continent, was that they were not a talkative lot, that they were shy, unsociable men, of tremendous stamina and passionately devoted to their leader. They were rough fellows and it did not take much penetration to suspect that each one of them had his secret to hide. Angélique was not unfamiliar with this breed of men, and she knew that they are not easy to tame.

Later on she would see about establishing some contact with them. Meanwhile her task – and it was such as to demand all her strength – was to dominate a restive horse and to look after her little daughter and the handful of Huguenot friends who had accompanied her.

In spite of the fact that she had long been accustomed to riding through forests, up hill and down dale, she had had some anxious moments. She remembered her husband's dubious expression when she had begged him to take her with him, and now she was beginning to understand. The life of adventure that awaited them in the backwoods of the province of Maine, where Count Peyrac had decided to work the gold and silver mines, would be full of unknown unforeseeable difficulties, like the trail they had been following for so many days.

Indian men and women passed her too, leaving a musky smell behind them in the sweltering atmosphere. They had joined the caravan when it had reached the banks of the river Penobscot. They were members of a small tribe of Abenaki Indians, the Metallaks, who, after a trading expedition to the coast were returning to their normal hunting grounds beside Lake Umbagog. They had asked for Count Peyrac's protection on their journey, fearing possible encounters with the Iroquois, their cruel hereditary enemy, who often ravaged their lands during their warlike excursions in the summer season.

Monsieur Jonas, the watchmaker from La Rochelle, stopped beside Angélique, holding his horse by the bridle. He took off his hat, carefully wiped its brim, then his forehead, then his glasses.

'Goodness! What a steep slope! And to think that there are twenty more like this to climb every day!'

'I hope your wife is not finding the going too hard?'

'I asked one of the men to help her during the climb. One false move and I fear my poor wife might well break her neck in one of these cataracts. Ah, here they come!'

The worthy lady from La Rochelle caught up with them. The young Breton Yann le Couennec, one of the men from the *Gouldsboro*, was obligingly leading her horse. Madame Jonas was crimson in the face, but cheerful.

So far they had stoically faced all risks involved in their decision to go with the Count, and Madame Jonas, a strong sprightly woman in her fifties, had shown great endurance as a horsewoman.

'What a change it is from the back shop in La Rochelle,' she would say. And she had gone on to explain to Angélique that, as the daughter of a farmer, she had been brought up almost entirely in the country.

'Have you seen Cantor?' Angélique asked her.

'Yes, he's giving Elvire a hand; she's not especially good on a horse. Poor child! I wonder what on earth induced her to ask to accompany us, with those two sons of hers, rather than remain at Gouldsboro. Of course it's true that she is our niece and that we are all the family she has left!'

Cantor appeared at the edge of the ravine and Angélique felt a glow of pride on catching sight of his sturdy youthful figure leading with a firm hand the horse to which a young woman and a little boy of six were clinging.

Elvire seemed frightened and admitted that it was above all the noise of the waterfalls that upset her. Now she would be able to continue unaided. She thanked Cantor politely and asked whether anyone had seen her elder son Bartholomew, who was eight. Angélique reassured her, saying that Bartholomew had gone ahead with Florimond, who had taken charge of him, and that the child refused to leave his side.

The group from La Rochelle set off again and Cantor stared after them, shaking his head as they walked off.

'If it wasn't for me, I don't know how that poor girl would get on,' he said in a tone of scorn tinged with pity. 'To encumber oneself with women and children on a trip like this is sheer madness. I don't mean you, Mother ... you are my father's wife, and it is only natural that you should come with us. But you must admit that to travel in a caravan in an unknown land is a very different thing from dancing in the salons at Versailles!'

'Yes indeed, Cantor, yes indeed ...' Angélique agreed, suppressing a smile, for the boy spoke so earnestly, 'and I admire your endurance: you're carrying a heavy load and are on foot, whereas we women and children are on horseback!'

'Pooh! It's just a question of habit! We are no milk-sops!'

'Aren't you feeling a bit weary nevertheless in this dreadful heat?'

He straightened up, refusing to admit the slightest trace of fatigue. She guessed that he was not being entirely open with her; for even the toughest of the men in the party occasionally complained of the length and severity of the day's march. She noticed that he had grown thinner, and that he had rings under his eyes, which were the same shade of green as his mother's. Once again she asked herself why Joffrey was forcing them to keep up this almost inhuman pace. Was he putting them to the test, trying to find out what he could expect from each of them? Was he trying to prove to himself that the women and children in no way hindered his plans? Or did he have some secret reason that forced him to press on towards a goal which to Angélique was still vague and unprecise?

'What about you, Mother, how are you? Is that horse still playing you up?' Cantor inquired, forcing his chapped lips into a smile.

He already had the solid frame of a young man, but beneath

the layer of grime and sweat, his soft pink cheeks were still those of a child. And it was these fresh, beardless cheeks that reminded Angélique of the chubby little page he had once been, singing for the Queen at Versailles, and she wanted to stroke his curly hair, to smile tenderly at him, to draw him to her and press his head against her hip, the head of her boy restored to life again, the son she had at last re-discovered, and who now stood before her, miraculously alive. . . .

But she restrained herself, knowing that adolescents feel shy about expressing emotion, and after many years of separation, her son's heart was a closed book to her. She was longing for the time when the caravan would finally come to a halt beneath a permanent roof, when the weariness she now felt would vanish and she would be able to establish closer contact with her family, to gather them about her, her husband her two sons, and to get to know them better once more in the tranquillity of everyday life.

This journey was a barrier separating them from her, she felt. Each one of them had to fight his own separate battles, obsessed by the thought that he must not be the one to slow the others down.

In answer to Cantor's question she said that everything was going fine, that Wallis seemed to have calmed down and to have grown more obedient.

'It was asking an awful lot of you,' Cantor said anxiously. 'Florimond and I could see that the mare was a handful, and we were worried when we saw that you had taken her over. We kept on thinking that she was going to hurl you down a precipice or that you would never manage to force her through a difficult bit of the way. . . .'

'And do you boys think that I have not managed too badly?'

'Oh yes, you have managed very well,' said Cantor patronizingly, in order to conceal his surprise.

'You ride very well,' he admitted, stressing each word.

'Thank you very much. I needed that encouragement to help me to keep it up. I was very nearly going to give up this morning. It's so hot.'

'Would you like a drink of water?' he suggested helpfully. 'I filled my flask at the foot of the cascade and it's still cool.'

'No thanks, but I'll give Honorine some.'

'It's not worth it. She's asleep,' said the lad quickly, withdrawing the flask he had held out.

He fastened it and hung it on his belt again.

'I'm going on ahead. Once we're through this wood, we'll have another shelf of rock to cross and I must help poor Madame Elvire,' and he strode off.

Angélique guided her horse back on to the path. She was watching Cantor, thinking that he was handsome, that he was being kind and thoughtful towards her and that she would have no difficulty in winning his confidence again, but she had been aware for some time that he did not like Honorine.

She gave a sigh and bowed her head a little.

Would she ever have the courage to talk to her two big sons about Honorine? What would she say to them? It was perfectly understandable that the two lads should wonder about the half-sister their mother had brought them from the Old World!

Which of their mother's lovers was her father? This thought must have sometimes crossed their minds. How had they both reacted in their heart of hearts to these disturbing revelations? What did they think of their father who had forgiven her and made the child welcome?

Honorine represented the essence of everything they wanted to forget; the cruel past with its separation and its inevitable betrayals. . . .

'Should I have left her at Gouldsboro?' Angélique asked herself. 'Abigail would have looked after her with loving care.

'No, I could never have done that! I know that you would have died if you had been separated from me, my poor little bastard child,' she told herself, looking over her shoulder at the little round head pressed up against her so trustingly. 'And could I ever have forgotten you, could I ever have lived happily after once again casting you out of my life? Poor little child of fate, thrown on the world with such violence and horror!

'No, I could never do that.'

Why was it that Honorine, that very morning, had absolutely insisted on returning to her mother? Wasn't it revealing? Whenever the child felt anxious about something, she would always seek out Angélique.

Up till then, she had been gay and very sociable. What manner of danger might they have to face today that made her feel the need for protection? Would there be difficulties along the trail? Would there be a thunderstorm? A tornado?

Would they run into Iroquois?

For the entire duration of the trip, the Indians, whether friend or foe, had been almost invisible. Perrott and Maupertuis explained that the tribes had gone off to the coast to sell their furs, and that ships lay waiting for them loaded with brandy, hardware, and pearls. The travellers passed abandoned camp sites full of purple willowherb and honey-coloured pumpkin flowers with bold-shaped leaves cupping the morning dew.

These were the last traces of a semi-settled way of life which would soon disappear altogether as the trees closed more and more around them. The numerous Abenaki tribes, the indigenous race in Maine, had nomadism in their blood.

At the beginning of the journey they had first encountered Metallaks, who had joined the white man's caravan.

But apart from these they had seen no one, neither Iroquois nor Abenakis. And this absence of human contact, which for a long time had seemed a guarantee of safety, now began to weigh heavy on their weary hearts.

On their right, the mountains came into sight again across a wide stretch of scorched ground where fire had destroyed the trees, thus opening up a wider vista.

Angélique glanced hopefully towards the mountains, for she knew that at the foot of the Appalachians lay the outpost of Katarunk which belonged to Count Peyrac and was the destination for which they were heading. They were to spend the winter there, before going on in the spring to the mines which lay farther on. The mare went on across the soot-coloured plateau. A strong smell of burnt wood and resin hung in the air like incense.

In the crackling drought of this Indian summer fires broke out easily. It only took one spark to unleash an army of roaring flames that devastated and devoured the forest with the insatiable appetite of a ferocious dragon, driving before them the panic-stricken animals, and only coming to a halt when they reached the edge of a cliff or a stream, with an infernal hiss. For a long time after they had passed, the clear air still smelt of smoke which gave the vast forest spaces their characteristic and specific savour.

Here the fire was of recent origin; for the horses stirred up warm ashes with their hooves. Branches left black marks on anything that brushed against them, and the stumps of trees and tree-trunks that were still standing were burnt-out and dead. Through their bristling spikes, the valley glittered with the pink and mauve of its innumerable lakes. They reached the edge of one of these lakes to find that the fire had burnt right up to the water's edge and that there was not a single blade of grass left for the horses to eat.

They skirted the lake through the ashes until they came to a ford which the horses crossed, picking their way gingerly over a dam of boulders. The land rose steeply on the other side, and they climbed up the banks in the cool of firs and other trees untouched by the fire. These were not yet the foothills of the mountains, but a kind of island that rose in the middle of the valley, a rampart of rocks left stranded amidst the lakes, that must once have been rivers or formed a single fresh-water sea. After crossing this spur dark with pines and cedars, they began to descend again and soon another shimmering lake appeared, through the garishly yellow branches of a clump of young birch-trees.

Beneath a pearly sky, the mirror-like expanse of water sparkled in the noonday sunshine. Opposite them lay a hill steeped in gold and blood, its leafy masses reproduced in the depths of the waters.

The lake was extraordinarily limpid, unlike those they had encountered up to now, which always seemed to be thick with algae and moss. Here the grey sand was visible through the luminous water.

'I would like to paddle in that water,' exclaimed Honorine.

There were signs of an impending halt. Some way ahead, behind the willows, men were shouting and horses snorting. One of the trappers who had gone ahead reappeared and waved an arm to tell those who were still on their way down that there was to be a short rest. For those who might have missed his sign, he gave a guttural cry, to which the Indians who were bringing up the rear and were still some distance off among the trees, replied.

Angélique slid off her horse and helped Honorine to clamber down.

The little girl immediately removed both shoes and stockings and, drawing up her skirts, ran into the water.

'It's very cold,' she called, laughing with delight.

The horse had had a drink and had begun to crop the grass which, although scant, was still green along the little beach. As it grazed with lowered head Angélique stroked its neck, which, in the brilliant sunlight, resembled the sumptuous colours of the forest.

'Don't you worry, old girl,' she said softly. 'Look, there is plenty for you to eat. One day we shall find some big wide-open spaces for you to gallop over. We shall soon reach our destination.'

The mare twitched her ears as she ate and one had the impression that her breast was heaving with great repressed sighs. Horses do not like forests. Angélique remembered the war in Poitou and the long rides she had had to make with her supporters through the farthest corners of the Druidic forests. It was not the sense of danger, of a lurking enemy, that had made their horses so nervy, but rather the silence peculiar to the forest, a silence made up of numberless sharp, menacing sounds, and of the play of light and shade among the tree-trunks and the branches, giving rise to phantasmagoric visions, unleashing superstitious imaginings and adding to the real perils men face the fear of spirits and demons.

The great forestlands of North America were perhaps less grim and forbidding than those in which Angélique had spent her childhood. These forests were studded with vast blue lakes, and the crystal-clear atmosphere, vibrant with a dryness that even the winter mists could not dispel, made all outlines so clear-cut that they lacked mystery. This was no haunted forest.

Angélique was standing beside the lake. She did not want to let go of Wallis's bridle, for once, when left to graze, the mare had suddenly rushed off into the undergrowth as if to break out of some magic circle. She might easily have impaled herself on broken branches or broken her legs in potholes, and it had taken the Redskins, who knew the thick undergrowth like the back of their hands, all their skill to find her again.

The young woman felt the blood beating through her temples, and the back of her neck ached. She was deafened by the strident calls of cicadas.

Seeing that the mare appeared perfectly calm, Angélique took the risk of tying the end of her bridle to a branch of a young tree, then walked down to the water's edge to scoop up a little water in her hand and raise it to her lips.

An exclamation behind her stopped her in her tracks. The great Sagamore Mopuntook, Chief of the Metallaks, was making signs to her not to drink. Still in sign language, he explained that higher up there was a spring whose water was better to drink and that his braves had stopped there to quench their thirst. He invited her to join them there. She pointed to her horse, signifying to him that she could not move away from where she was. He understood her and with an imperious gesture told her to wait. Shortly afterwards he returned with a squaw bearing a wooden bowl full of water from the precious springs. The only trouble was that the bowl had contained a maize gruel and possibly other concoctions as well, and had only been cleaned by being scraped with fingers and nails; so the water in the bowl was already beginning to grow unappetizingly cloudy.

Angélique nevertheless forced herself to put it to her lips and swallow a few mouthfuls. She had already had occasion to notice that the Red Indians were extremely quick to take offence.

The great Chief waited solemnly, watching her drink, and undoubtedly he expected her to express lively appreciation of the remarkable water he had taken the trouble to offer her.

She found his smell, the strong smell of a male animal, covered from head to foot with bear grease, decidedly off-putting.

His smooth chest was tattooed in blue and black. Two serpents outlined his powerful pectoral muscles and a bear's-tooth necklace cast spiky shadows across it.

He was a chief, a Sagamore, as one could tell from the eagle feathers and the bushy racoon tail he wore in his hair that was pinned up in a bun at the back of his head.

From all along the edge of the lake came the noisy splashes and the happy shouts of men enjoying the diving and the cool water.

Florimond came up to greet his mother as he did during each halt along the way. He almost burst out laughing when he saw the delicate situation she was in; he intervened tactfully:

'I am terribly thirsty, Mother. Might I be allowed to drink some of that wonderful water you have been fortunate enough to taste?'

Oh, Florimond! What a thoughtful boy he was!

Angélique passed him the calabash with a sense of relief, but once again Mopuntook stopped her with an exclamation of horror. There followed a discussion to which they summoned Nicolas Perrot to act both as interpreter and diplomat.

'If I understand correctly,' said Florimond, 'a greenhorn like me is not worthy of the privilege of drinking from the same spring as his honourable mother?'

'Yes, that's part of it. . . .'

'It is not rather that there is a certain element of contempt for women in this ban our great chieftain has just mentioned?' Angélique asked.

'No, on the contrary. In offering you the best water he could find, the Sagamore wanted to pay tribute to the Woman, the Mother in you. Women are greatly revered among the Indians.'

'Really?' replied Angélique in surprise, glancing at the slave girl standing with lowered eyes behind the Chief.

'I know this seems too difficult to grasp, Madame. You have to have visited the sacred valley of the Iroquois in order to understand . . .' the trapper replied.

He handed the bowl back to the Indian with a great flow of words which seemed at last to satisfy him.

'And now, my boy, what do you say to a plunge in that cool water?'

'Hurray!' cried Florimond.

They vanished behind a curtain of willows and alders whose long leaves drooped down towards the surface of the water, and shortly afterwards they were swimming vigorously, their heads breaking the surface of the shimmering lake.

Angélique would have given anything to have been able to do likewise.

'I want to swim too,' said Honorine, beginning to strip off her tiny garments.

Madame Jonas and Elvire joined them with Elvire's two little boys, Thomas and Bartholomew. They agreed to allow the three children to splash in the water.

They danced about naked near the bank making great splashes and shouting for sheer delight.

A group of outraged wader-birds rose up out of the bushes with a noisy beating of wings.

Some tufted ducks with flame-coloured and violet crests on their heads, showed their annoyance by cackling loudly as they swam off leaving a wake behind them across the shimmering surface of the lake.

Angélique gave a sigh of envy as she looked at the cool water. But she remained beside her horse, a victim of her duty. And that was how Joffrey de Peyrac found her when he appeared on the little beach at the edge of the lake.

CHAPTER TWO

HE WAS still holding the sextant with which he had just taken their position. He handed it to Octave Malaprade, the sailor from Bordeaux, who had escorted him carrying his leather writing-table and parchment. The man sat down beside a rock to put away the instrument and the maps in the portable desk that had been entrusted to him.

Angélique watched her husband as he strode forward through the brilliant light that was made even harsher by being reflected back from the water. His tall figure seemed to look even more solid. Amidst these almost too lovely evanescent surroundings, in which everything seemed dulled by the heat, he stood out hard and real. He seemed to move across this fascinating landscape unconcerned by the disturbance he brought into it. The utter indifference, even latent hostility of the countryside which Angélique did not like, seemed to make no impression on him.

The gravel crunched beneath his leather boots, as he strode across it with heavy tread.

'He still limps a little,' Angélique thought to herself. 'Aboard the Gouldsboro one noticed it less, because of the movement of the ship, but here on land one does.'

'What sudden thought made your eyes sparkle like that?' asked Joffrey de Peyrac.

'I just noticed that you still have a slight limp.'

'And you are pleased?'

'Yes!'

'Women really are an unpredictable lot! All the efforts I made to give you back a husband in presentable shape have only succeeded in stirring up regrets for the past! Or even arousing suspicions! I wouldn't put it past you to wonder whether this is not a case of assumed identity.... They tell so many entertaining stories of that sort, during those long evenings in the country districts, back in France. It is never easy to play the part of a man brought back from the dead! In the end I shall begin to wish I had my short leg back again.'

'It is only that I loved you the way you were then!'

'And you are not quite sure that you love me the way I am now?' he said with a roguish smile.

Then, without awaiting her reply, he greeted Mopuntook.

He always treated the Indian Chief with ceremonious politeness. He had removed his feathered hat and his thick hair glist-
ened in the sun with a metallic sheen. Steely lights shone on his
tight curled, typically Gascon hair, still almost jet black
although beginning to shine with silver at the temples. His
southern ancestry, with its admixture of Spanish and Saracen
blood, made his face look as dark and sun-baked as that of the
Redskin he was addressing. There was a paler area over his
cheekbones left by the mask he sometimes wore. His bushy
eyebrows had an easy graciousness above his magnificent eyes,
but his profile was still sharp, broken by the sinuous curve of
his lips, which stood out provokingly aggressive and sensual.

His lips were strong and wide, like fine silk but scarcely
tinged with pink beside the tanned skin of his face. They
trembled, they tightened, or parted over his shining teeth. They
seemed to lead their own life in his extraordinary face in
which every element seemed to contribute to the total aristocratic impression. He had the vast strongly-lined forehead of
the man of intelligence, the delicately arched browline of the
man of birth, and there was fire of spirit in the depths of his
dark eyes. His nose and chin were strong and rugged, those of a
conqueror, a man from the mountains, accustomed to hold his
head high, to watch the eagle in his soaring; and between them
lay that slightly Moorish mouth, imperious, demanding so it
seemed, even when silent and impassive, the mouth of the man
of this earth, a sign of materiality amidst the sublimated
features, which enhanced its ambivalent and disquieting
strength. It was such a mouth that the sculptors of ancient
times gave to the images of their gods, without realizing that
their chisels were thus expressing all the lust for life and
pleasure of those early Mediterranean civilizations.

Whenever Angélique looked at that vibrant and sensitive
mouth set in that often severe and formidable face, she felt
suddenly overcome with the desire to lay it on hers.

She was now, for example, as he stood answering the Chief
of the Metallaks with gestures and a few Indian words. Then he
turned and gazed away into the distance towards the other
shore, trying to fathom who knew what mystery of this un-
tamable landscape.

For a moment he seemed far away, perhaps anxious after
their exchange of words. He was thinking and his mouth

quivered. As she watched him, Angélique felt her heart beat faster. She longed for those lips on hers, their tenderness then their passion. She devoured him with her eyes.

The heat of the ride had left his brow damp and a few drops of sweat ran across his temples and, without his being aware of it, trickled down the scars on his face. Angélique would have liked to wipe that lined face tenderly, but she did not dare. There were still spontaneous gestures she found it impossible to make, held back as she was by a kind of fear. She told herself that he had lived for so long without a woman at his side, completely unhampered. That he had been accustomed to considerable sexual and emotional freedom. Might he not find the daily attentions of a wife importunate?

Here, even more than on board his ship, she sensed the man's independence. It radiated from him like a halo. He was a man who had lived many lives.

A complex man beneath his apparent simplicity. And she must find her place in the complexities of this superior mind.

In the dazzling light she saw him as he was, a man who had reached the peak of his existence, in full possession of his strength, of his faculties, and of his experience of life. He was a complete, close-knit personality, a man without uncertainties, his character forged by his life of adventure, wars, death, torture, and passion. When he stood motionless like this, his breathing was almost imperceptible. She could see no tremor in his chest, held tight in a black velvet doublet, no movement of his waist tight-buckled in a wide leather belt, and the impression was mildly disquieting. She did not remember ever having noticed in him in the past this resemblance to the great cats when immobile just before pouncing. But in the past it had never occurred to her to observe him, to notice every detail about him, apart from the scar that had so frightened her. That was why she had so quickly forgotten his features after he had disappeared. What a scatterbrain she had been in those days! Life had taught her to read people's faces, to examine their physiognomy, to catch a fleeting thought in an expression. When one's life has hung by the thread of other men's decisions, these are things that one learns.

Once upon a time she had lived two years of her life beside this man, but she had never examined him as she did today. She did it with singular avidity. She found him even more compelling than she would have wished. His gestures, the in-

flection of his voice which she was beginning to find more
familiar again, intrigued and fascinated her; she could neither
explain nor resist her fascination. But perhaps there was nothing to explain. It was a case of an overwhelming natural
attraction that draws a woman towards her predestined mate.

Her heart would beat faster when he came near, his attentions gratified her, she grew anxious when he went away. But
above all she had still not grown used to not losing him any
more, not having to wait for him.

'How I love you, oh man that I fear!'

She stood and watched him, motionless. After his discussion
with Chief Mopuntook he raised his telescope to his eye and
examined the surrounding countryside. Then he folded it again,
handed it back to Malaprade, and again turned towards Angélique.

With his inimitable courtesy, that contrasted so sharply with
his *condottière*-like appearance, he took her two hands in his,
turned them over, lifted them to his lips, and gently kissed the
hollow of her palms, a furtive gesture accompanied by a glance
full of complicity from his warm eyes, which had suddenly
filled with a great tenderness as they rested on her.

'These lovely hands seem to me less sore than they were
yesterday. Am I to understand that your steed is proving more
docile?'

'Yes indeed. She is growing tamer. My wrists are no longer
stiff from holding her.'

'I entrusted her to you because I knew how strong you were.
You were the only person who could have managed her. I
myself have tamed the stallion, who is of the same breed as
her. We have a couple of other English horses, and the rest
come from Mexico.'

'Is this country suitable for horses?' she asked, allowing her
anxiety to show through.

'It will become suitable! Wherever man lives, there must
horses come. That is one of the cornerstones of a well-estab-
lished civilization. Did not the Huns bring their horses with
them? Did not Alexander the Great conquer India on horseback? And what about the Arabs in Africa? And the Iroquois
in South America?'

Mopuntook had gone off. He came back with some more
water and offered some to Honorine, still in the same questionable calabash. The child was quite unconcerned and laughed

and joked with the Indian as if they could understand each other. As she paddled in the lake she splashed him and the proud Metallak, far from being offended, crouched down at the water's edge to be on a level with the child, and went on chatting animatedly to her.

Joffrey de Peyrac had taken one of his pistols and was loading it. His patrician hands had a precision and swiftness of movement that stemmed from years of practice.

'Are your guns loaded too?'

'Yes. I checked them this morning and replaced the powder in the primer which had been spoilt by damp.'

'Good. In these parts it's just as well to have one's guns always at the ready.'

'But the countryside seems completely deserted, and wild animals would run away rather than attack us.'

'It isn't only wild animals I am thinking of. And deserted country can be misleading.'

He changed the subject.

'Not one of the ten horses we have brought with us from the coast has died. That is one victory already and we can count ourselves lucky to have managed the journey so successfully. It was something no one had ever dared to undertake, travelling across country instead of following the rivers.'

'I know. Nicolas Perrot told me so. But I had already realized that the horses were not here to carry us, but rather that we were here to get them successfully to their destination. And likewise the Indians are not escorting us, we are escorting them.'

'That's right. The Metallaks are frightened of meeting Iroquois, whose war parties are permanently on the prowl in their lands during the summer months. They have put themselves under the protection of our muskets, and reluctantly agreed in exchange to carry some of our baggage. And incidentally it's their womenfolk who do the carrying. America is not the Africa you knew, my love, swarming with slaves. White men are here on their own, their own masters, but also their own servants.'

'But there are black slaves in the English colonies in the south.'

'Yes, but not in the north. And that, incidentally, is why I chose the north.... And also because of the gold and silver mines,' he added as if suddenly remembering the true reason for his choice. Slavery has its advantages ... especially for the masters.

'I am sorry, my love, not to be able to offer you all the comfort I would have liked, for lack of domestic help. But here we have to do without either servants or slaves. For the Red Indians are anything you like but not slaves. If a Red Indian is forced to work for a white man he will die.'

'I am not concerned with comfort.'

She plucked up the courage to move closer to him, touched his sleeve and rested her cheek for a moment against his shoulder. She was frightened to show him much tenderness in front of his men.

'I am longing to have you to myself for a while. I always get the feeling that when I sleep far from you I have lost you again. When shall we reach Katarunk?'

'Perhaps soon .. perhaps never!'

She questioned him sharply:

'Are you expecting something to happen?'

'Nothing, darling! Just my old cautious habit! I shall not believe we have reached Katarunk until the gates of the palisade have closed behind us, and my flag is flying at the top of the mast to inform everyone that I am at home. My love, the more I look at you, the more wonderfully beautiful I find you. You cannot imagine how disturbing you are, when your eyes shine like that out of your reddened face, when your eyelids are ringed a little with weariness, when you are hot, and when you do your best not to appear tired.... I adore you.'

'How right you are! I am worn out and I am hot!' Angélique replied. 'And, believe me, the object of the exercise was not to seduce you; I would give my life to be able to take a dip in that cool water.'

'That shouldn't be difficult.'

He beckoned to Nicolas Perrot, who had come out of the water and dressed again.

'My good friend, may I ask you to watch over the reputation of the ladies? I have discovered a small creek near by in the shelter of the willow-trees where they could enjoy the pleasure of a bathe. All I ask of you is that you stand sentry at the mouth of the path that leads down to the creek and head off anyone indiscreet or unsuspecting who wanders that way. Place another sentry at the end of the promontory to keep the swimmers away too. We shall stay here for an hour or more.'

CHAPTER THREE

ANGÉLIQUE WAS absolutely delighted with the little cove, which was indeed as quiet and sheltered as could be wished. Her two companions hesitated. Bathing with nothing on, out in the open, no, really they never would dare! Angélique did her best to assure them that they could not be seen and that sentries had been sworn to guard them, but they could not bring themselves to bathe. But they decided to make the most of the privacy and removed their stockings and their head-dresses to cool themselves a little. Angélique left them and moved farther along the shore, where she threw off her clothes behind a clump of trees and looked out jubilantly across the smooth surface of the lake all golden in the sunshine.

As soon as she was undressed she stepped cautiously down the sloping shore. The water was indeed very cold and it took her breath away. But after a while she began to feel the full benefit of the icy water on her burning skin. She walked on until the water came right up to her neck, letting herself slide backwards into it with a sigh of satisfaction. The water covered the sore skin on the nape of her neck. She shut her eyes. The sensation of cold reached to the very roots of her hair, and she felt herself come to life again.

She kept herself afloat by moving her hands slowly. She could swim a little; for, during the summer months in Paris, she used to swim in the Seine, at the quayside. She had also bathed at Marly with the Court.

But the Seine was far away.

Angélique opened her eyes. A whole new world of light and shade, fresh and beautiful, appeared to her now, a world that was all hers. She rolled over a little and began to swim gently, her hair trailing out behind her in the water like pale seaweed.

She swam away from the bank, round a promontory, and on the other side discovered a bigger creek which no doubt formed one of the ends of the lake.

At the far end of this cove, beside a little beach, a huge red maple spread its great roots along the surface of the sand, amidst a bed of mauve asters. Above the maple-tree stood a cliff crowned with round grey rocks set above sumac bushes glowing red like hot embers. Then still more maples, but yellow this time, forming a veritable fortress of pure gold, glittering in the sunshine.

On her right, where the cove widened out, lay some little low islands covered with thick-leaved alders, glowing wild cherries, and black firs, giving a silken sheen to the opaline surface of the waters in which they were reflected. The low bank on the opposite side was topped with a colourful army of conifers and deciduous trees.

The scarlet cherry rubbed shoulders with the blue cedar, the purple beech stood out splendid against the emerald green of the great tufted pines, and the bushes ran like flames along the banks.

Near the shore, rounded rocks broke the surface of the water, which was now pale, now blue.

Angélique swam over to one of these rocks, hauled herself, with the water streaming from her, up on to the granite block, and examined the deserted landscape around her. Then slowly, as if in a drowse, or waking out of an enchanted sleep, she stood up, offering her white body, made golden by the light, to the warmth of the sunshine. She took her hair in both hands, wrung it out, and lifted it above her as if in homage, then, throwing her head back, her gaze lost in the seraphic blue of the sky, she raised her voice and chanted rather than spoke the words of rapture that rose unbidden to her lips.

'Thank you, O Creator, for this moment.... Thank you for the scarlet of the maple and the gold of the poplars, for the scent of the stag in the undergrowth, and the perfume of the raspberry.... Thank you for silence and ice-cold water.... Thank you for keeping me alive and well.. . Thank you, O Creator, thank you for the fact that I am in love. Thank you for my body.... Thank you for your gifts of beauty, youth, and life, O Creator.'

She dropped her hands again and held them open at her sides while her eyes drank in the beauty of the day.

'Glory be to thee, New World! New World!'

Then she slid swiftly down into the water again, supple as a siren....

Torn suddenly from her rapture, she felt her heart beat wildly.

She looked up towards the golden foliage above the grey rock in an attempt to solve the mystery.

'WHAT IS UP THERE? I heard a sound. I saw something black

move. . . . Who is there? WHO SAW MÉ?'

She stared intently at the dazzling fringe of trees against the deep blue of the sky. There was no sign of movement save the slow convulsive shudder of the trees in the light wind. But this apparent calm could not rid her of the sense of anxiety that had so abruptly assailed her.

'There were eyes up there just now; yes, eyes that pierced to my very soul.' And she shuddered violently. She suddenly felt desperately faint and was frightened that she was going to sink inertly under the clear water. But somehow she managed to swim to the bank, then, clinging to the bushes, made her way back to the cove where she had left her clothes. She dragged herself up on to the sand and lay there for a while to get her breath back. She found it hard to understand what had happened to her, but she was trembling all over.

Was it some unusual noise she had heard? Had she seen or thought she had seen something moving through the branches, as she stood naked on the rock, while the smooth surface of the lake sent back the reflection of her white body?

Whatever it was those could not have been human eyes. It had been something supernatural.

The members of the caravan were gathering over on the right side of the lake, where she could hear them laughing and shouting. The rest of the countryside was deserted.

Then she suddenly remembered some of the stories that Perrot and Maupertuis had told round the camp fire when they halted for the night, stories about strange happenings in the great forests of the New World, from which dark furies had not yet been exorcized, where missionaries, travellers, and traders had often sensed the presence of evil spirits and felt the breath of dread and black magic upon their faces. The wild monster lurking, the cruel soul of pagan peoples, that roamed at large and took on unaccustomed forms the better to lure men into its snares.

She told herself that it was probably the effect of the ice-cold water on her overheated skin that had made her feel so faint. But she also knew that something inexplicable had happened and that it had struck a chill to her heart. At the very moment when she had felt her whole being overflowing with love for this new land which was to be hers, a contrary force had intervened, casting her back once more into the darkness. 'Get you gone!' was its cry. 'You have no right to live here. You cannot be a citizen of this land.' This was the mysterious message that had struck her like a hurricane blast, only to disappear as swiftly as it had come.

She lay motionless on the bank, then suddenly sat up and stared fixedly again at a point in the forest beyond. Nothing stirred. Everything was still.

She got up and dressed quickly. She felt better now but her anxiety and distress remained.

This land had rejected her, this land was her enemy. She told herself that she possessed none of the qualities needed to face it, nor to face the life awaiting her beside an unknown husband.

CHAPTER FOUR

SHE RETURNED to the beach where the young Breton, Yann, was looking after her mare. Those with horses were already in the saddle and the caravan was beginning to get under way. Honorine was half dressed and still paddling. She held something in her hand, examining it with undivided concentration. It was the skin of a white ermine, that had been so beautifully cured that it looked like a supple, little live animal.

'Mopuntook gave it me.'

And she added as she came out of the water:

'We did a swop. He gave me this little animal and I gave him my diamond.'

'The diamond your father gave you at Gouldsboro?'

'Yes! That was what Mopuntook wanted. He is going to wear it in his hair when he dances. He'll look very handsome, you'll see!'

Angélique was already in such a state of nerves that this announcement of her daughter's made her feel the urge of hysteria.

'I really don't know what to think,' she said to herself, finding it very hard to keep calm. 'Joffrey did say that the diamond was less valuable than a head of corn, but all the same! And he gave it to her that evening when he said: "I am your father." She can be infuriating at times!'

She hauled her daughter unceremoniously up into the saddle, settled herself there too and, gathering up the reins, steered

Wallis away from the water and its green banks, and back on to the arid path under the flaming archway of the trees.

She rode on for a long time, quite unaware of how much ground she had covered. The end of the lake narrowed into a valley, and as they entered it through the open gates of the raspberry-tinted gorge, the deep blue dome of a distant mountain came into sight. The travellers began to pass through the valley, at first following the bed of the river, its crystal-clear water strewn with rocks; then bit by bit they were obliged to make their way up the steep side, as the river became a torrent and outcrops of rock appeared all round them.

They climbed up a path that still held a certain amount of clay, and on which the roots of the trees formed steps. A mule would have managed it comfortably but the aristocratic Wallis showed some apprehension.

As they rounded a bend, they came upon three snowy waterfalls whose roar filled their ears. The water spilled over three steep ledges in the black rock, crashing down into the bed of the deep-set river. Trees clustered along the precipice, almost covering it. It was like a well from which rose a ceaseless rumble and clouds of smoky, iridescent spray that wet the elm and ash leaves and made them glitter like a thousand tiny metal spears. The sky was invisible, the shadows, sepulchral, and yet light seemed to penetrate everywhere, pitilessly, stinging their eyes, etching the lines of the undergrowth as if it were copper, shining in ever-changing facets through the thicket, and further complicating with its deceptive patterns of light and shade the inexplicable tangle of trees through which the path wound its way. Angélique could no longer pick out the Indians ahead of her. The noise of the waterfall cut her off from the few echoes which, until then, had kept her aware of the presence of the others, even when the forest had grown too dense for them to see one another : the crackle of dead leaves, the dull thudding of the horses' hooves, someone calling, or a murmur of conversation borne to her on the wind. The thunderous roar of the waters seemed to shut her up in an uneasy, leaf-enclosed world in which she felt utterly alone. It was as though she were moving through a nightmare on the border of realms of dread, impenetrable forests watched over by dragons, fallen gods, or monsters, in which she could not even hear the sound of her own horse's hooves.

The noise grew deafening. Angélique saw the leaves dripping

wet through an emerald light, and felt the damp exhalation of the chasm on her lips.

A huge stone, a great round mass, broke away from the slope in front of her without a sound – which made its slithering fall all the more unnerving – and came to rest full in her path. As it lay there, this inert, hard block seemed to come to life under the spell of the greenish light. It swelled, it puffed itself up, like a big grey bubble, split open like a hideous fruit, with the slow movement of a blossoming plant. Then, out of the mass that was both rock and living creature, a cruel reptilian head reared itself and stretched out towards her wavering sickly from side to side.

Panic-stricken, Angélique's horse reared up to its full height. She did not hear its terrified whinnying but felt its fear in the spasms that coursed through the animal's body. She gave a cry, but her cry was lost. Honorine must have screamed too, unheard. The horse beat the air with its hooves and backed away. It was going to fall, dragging down both Angélique and the child, and together all three of them would roll in a tangle of saddle-bow, reins, and harness before plunging in a huddled mass headlong into the abyss.

With a superhuman effort, Angélique threw herself on to the horse's neck, and pulled herself forward almost up to its head, to force it back on to its four feet by the sheer force of her weight.

But this was not enough to save them; Wallis still continued to back down the fated slope.

Angélique knew perfectly well that the creature that they had seen was only a giant tortoise. But how could she convey this to her frantic mare? The shocking din of tumbling water was all around them and all other sounds seemed to have ceased to exist. She could not even hear the branches snapping, but she could see them breaking and the splinters flying. She saw the racing white torrent raging below her, coming closer and closer, rising to meet them, a dancing mass of foam spewed forth by some mythical monster, but she was no longer aware that the din that deafened them came from the unleashing of these rabid waters. For an instant, a large gory patch loomed beneath her gaze, the inverted reflection of an archway of leaves in the waters. For a fraction of a second she imagined she heard the sound of their fall, a confused tumble down to the bottom of the ravine. She even thought she felt herself falling, caught up in the roaring torrent.

A twig struck her across the forehead and tore her from this deadly sensation. The rocky ground was crumbling beneath Wallis's hooves, a few inches from the precipice, but it was still within her power not to yield to death. The thought of Honorine, whose tiny hands clung to her, galvanized her into action. It seemed to her that her whole consciousness and lucidity were centred in those hands. She knew what she must do. She relaxed the grip of her clenched fists on the reins and let them hang loose, giving the horse its freedom. Thus freed, the animal shook its head, astonished at the sense of relief. Then she dug her spurs into it until she drew blood, and the horse took a leap forward, slightly closing the gap between her and safety. She managed to steer the animal firmly back on to the path, where it stood, its legs quivering. They had been saved from their imminent fall, but the giant tortoise was still there, blocking the path.

'It's a tortoise! It's only a tortoise!' Angélique shouted, as if hoping her steed could understand her.

She could not hear the sound of her own voice and became aware of the pain in her wrists and legs, whose muscles had gone into spasm with the effort she had had to make to dominate Wallis.

Would no one come and help her to hold the animal, or at least get rid of the horrific creature that blocked their way? The Indians stood motionless around her. She might have taken them for statues, had it not been for the glitter of their almond eyes, which seemed to form a sombrely glinting mass about her. They watched her fighting, struggling within an ace of death, watched her with a wooden impassiveness which, even in such mysterious people, seemed decidedly odd. Then suddenly she thought she detected a hint of fear and wonder in their attitude. But they themselves did not seem altogether real, separated from her as they were by this solid wall of sound which made deaf and dumb ghosts of them. Nevertheless, their pungent smell of warm fat and carrion reached her nostrils, almost as if it were the smell of the tortoise, of the forest, or of the abyss.

Honorine was still there!

Angélique managed to turn round towards her daughter, and shouted to her to get off the horse. And in the end the child understood her.

With a sense of relief her mother saw her tumble down on to the dead leaves, then pick herself up and run towards the nearest Indian.

Now it was her turn to leap off the horse, but it was no easy task; for Wallis was doing her best to get away and bolt off through the bushes. She reared again and only just missed striking Angélique with her iron-clad hoof. Angélique sprang to the horse's head; holding it firmly with one hand and slapping it hard across the nostrils with the other, she gradually managed to force the animal back under the overhanging trees. Above all she wanted to get it away from the object of its terror.

The bit crunched between the mare's teeth. Angélique's neckerchief, her hands, and her sleeves, were drenched in froth from the horse's mouth, but she took not the slightest notice and went on striking the animal harder and harder.

At last Wallis appeared to calm down. Trembling, covered with froth, the mare allowed herself to be firmly tied to a tree; she ceased her agitation and rebellion, and her delicate head suddenly drooped towards the ground in a movement of surrender. Angélique almost felt like doing the same. There she stood, unspeakably dishevelled, her clothes covered with stains. But above all she must escape from this infernal noise, she must somehow get away.

She went back to the path and approached the tortoise. The Indians did not move a finger. They seemed rooted to the spot for all eternity. The tortoise's shell was as big as a small table, and its feet, covered with reptilian scales, were as large as a grown man's hand.

Angélique's anger was even stronger than the repugnance she felt towards this antediluvian monster, which, as she approached it, began to draw back its hideous head into its shell. Wedging herself against the shell, she pushed it with one heave out of the way. The huge thing began to slither down the slope, tipped over then rolled in leaps and bounds down to the bottom. And it, and not they, finally plunged into the river with a great splash.

Angélique sat down and, somewhat dazed, wiped her hands on some dead leaves, then went back to fetch her horse. She led the horse by the bridle up to the top of the slope, until they had at last emerged from the hollow in which they had almost died. She came out on to a plain covered with red bilberry bushes and small blue fir-trees. As if by magic, the roaring of the waters ceased, swallowed up in the depths of the gorge. They could hear the chirping of cicadas again and the song of birds and the wind. Now the travellers found themselves in a tall deserted valley at the foot of the mountains, the domain of a thousand lakes. A little river full of grey and pink stones meandered by on their right amidst its escorting throng of fiery red bushes. The Indians appeared again, talkative once more, and began to argue together with bird-like squawking noises.

Angélique could hear Honorine sobbing her heart out. She remounted her horse. She would have given anything to have been able to lie down among the bilberries and fall deep asleep, even if only for a short time. But Wallis would have been quite capable of talking advantage of her and making a final dash for freedom.

'Come on,' she said to Honorine. She lifted her up in front of her in the saddle, blew her nose for her, wiped her swollen face, kissed her and hugged her close. She felt stunned. Then she suddenly caught sight of Count Peyrac on horseback only a few paces away, with her son and most of the menfolk who had turned back.

'What's going on?'

'It's nothing,' Angélique replied, as pale as death. The twig that had struck her across the forehead had left a red line. With her filthy clothes, her snivelling daughter in her arms, her steed with blood coming from the corners of its mouth, she was acutely aware of how distressing a sight she must be to a man unaccustomed to being burdened with his family on his expeditions.

'I was told we had run into some Iroquois!' Joffrey de Peyrac went on.

Angélique shook her head. Fortunately the wind was dispelling the nauseating odour of the savages who had moved in close and were busy explaining in detail what had happened. Florimond and Cantor joined them, making full use of their knowledge of the Indian dialect.

'Mopuntook is absolutely convinced that there are Iroquois in the offing.'

There was a clicking of muskets being cocked at the mere mention of the name, and the Spanish soldiers took up position around the group of travellers.

Angélique was incapable of getting a word out, then at last she managed to speak.

'It was only a tortoise . . . a tortoise blocking the trail.'

And she briefly related what had happened. Count Peyrac frowned and gave the mare so angry a look that Angélique felt guilty herself.

Honorine's sobs redoubled.

'Poor tortoise!' she wailed. 'It was so stupid and so clumsy. And you pushed it over the cliff. You're horrid.'

Angélique nearly burst into tears herself. For on top of everything else she had just noticed that Honorine's feet were bare. She must have left her shoes and stockings beside the little lake where she had paddled. This was a disaster. Where-ever would they find more shoes and stockings for the child in this wilderness? It was the last straw. Had she not needed both her hands to hold her daughter and her horse, she would have looked for her handkerchief in which to bury her misery. As it was, she had to turn her head away to hide her over-brilliant eyes.

The Indians now seemed to be seized by a kind of hysteria and were noisily acting out their explanation to the whites, who plied them with questions in a babble of different languages, trying to understand what had happened. The Spaniards were demanding a chance to get at the enemy.

The Count drew himself up slightly in his saddle and called for silence.

The tone of his voice produced an immediate effect. The Indians obeyed him. When there was a certain expression on Joffrey de Peyrac's face, there was no choice but to obey. 'He would be capable of striking a man down on the spot,' thought Angélique with a shudder.

Joffrey de Peyrac laid a soothing hand on Honorine's head.

'Tortoises can swim,' he said gently. 'This one that frightened you has already climbed out of the water and is wandering along the edge of the river eating flies.' The child was consoled as if by magic.

Then the Count dismounted and approached the Sagamore to hear what he had to say. He was as tall as the Indian, and listened attentively to his explanations. The advent of Nicolas Perrot finally cleared up the misunderstanding.

Joffrey de Peyrac smiled, climbed back into the saddle and rode over beside Angélique.

'This is another example of the way their superstitious minds interpret things,' he said. 'For them the tortoise symbolizes the

Iroquois. Meeting a tortoise was an evil omen to them, an almost infallible sign that their most redoubtable enemies are prowling in the neighbourhood. Hence their dismay and fright when they saw the harmless creature, which is common enough in these parts.'

And Nicolas Perrot added:

'They also say that the emblem of the Iroquois rose up in front of the white woman in an attempt to kill her, but that she fought against it and refused to let it overcome her. The Metallaks consider, Madame, that from now on none of the Five Nations of the Iroquois will be able to prevail against you.'

'I accept their omen,' she replied, forcing herself to smile too.

'Come and ride beside me, the path we are on now is wide enough. We are coming out on to an Indian "trail" as the English call it, that runs along the crest of the Appalachians for hundreds of leagues. Don't leave my side, my love.'

Her husband's calm voice made her feel better. And she was happier at the idea of riding beside him. And yet she still felt intimidated by him, and wondered whether he were not angry at heart about an incident that had almost ended disastrously, although with his customary self-control he revealed nothing.

At the end of a huge pale-green lake that turned and twisted like a river, and whose shimmering surface ran between promontories bristling with straggling pine-trees like so many regiments of lancers, another deep, narrow valley opened up at their feet. The mountain opposite them was a mass of pink, red and orange-tinted crests, stippled here and there in blue and mauve by clusters of trees that had already lost their leaves, with an occasional patch of startling green. Something on the flowery mountainside, this embroidered and brocaded dome, caught Joffrey de Peyrac's eye, and he called a halt at the edge of the wood. They had reached a small open patch of bare rock from which they could scrutinize the surrounding country before plunging back under cover of the endless trees.

He called for his telescope.

A thin haze blowing up from the valley had softened all the colours, which looked washed out and appeared to melt into one another. The sky, now filled with clouds, was coming down to meet the mists rising from the land.

'In a few moments, we shall probably not be able to see any

more,' said the Count. And swiftly he handed his telescope to Angélique.

'You have a look and tell me what you think you see.'

At first she was surprised by the brilliant image that appeared in the circle of the lens. The trees looked so close, larger than life, and as if drawn one above the other with a bold brush, aiming at perfection of detail.

The tree-trunks, some black some white, seemed to bear aloft the brilliant masses of their foliage in accord with some rigidly fixed artistic convention. In the shadowy gaps for which provision seemed to have been deliberately contrived, she was astonished to see human figures moving. There was no mistaking the shimmering of the feathers that decked them in spite of the fact that from a distance they would escape notice, melting into the background of the autumnal hues of the forest.

'What do you see?'

'I can see savages; two or three? No, more! In fact there seem to be a lot of them.'

'Do you notice their hair?'

'Their heads are shaved and they have left a tuft of hair in the middle into which they have stuck their feathers.'

She lowered the telescope.

'Joffrey, the Cayugas wore their hair like that. . . .'

'Yes indeed!'

And slowly he closed the telescope.

'Does this really mean that your encounter with the tortoise had a hidden significance after all? I don't want to appear credulous, but it certainly looks as if we have run into a band of Iroquois. . . .'

Two or three of the men began to mutter among themselves, and slowly the members of the little caravan drew together, the escorting Indians mingling with the whites and staring with the same weary resentment in the direction of the low multi-coloured mountain where lurked unseen dangers.

'What rotten luck!' said the steward, Malaprade. 'We were almost within sight of Katarunk, and would soon have been greeting good old O'Connell, and enjoying all the blessings of civilization. Monsieur de Peyrac, I was going to cook you some *quenelles de volaille aux choux* as soon as we arrived, but it looks as if we're going to end up in quenelles ourselves now.'

'Nonsense!' said Florimond, 'don't be so gloomy, my good

friend. We will live to eat your hash, Malaprade. The Iroquois rather take advantage of their reputation in the north : people run away before they even set eyes on them. But I have seen some of them in New England, where they are known as Mohawks, and they don't seem any worse than the Mohicans. In the New York region they even lent a hand to the English against King Philip, a Narraganset Indian who from time to time massacres the white inhabitants of the frontier-lands.

'It all depends whether the Indians over there on the other side of the ravine take us for French or English. Either way, they won't have much time for the Metallaks accompanying us. Any member of the Algonquian race is, to their way of thinking, only fit either to become a slave or to be roasted alive. And the Metallaks know it. Look at them !'

They were indeed preparing for battle under the orders of their Sagamore.

Swiftly they laid the baggage on the ground. The Indian women and children vanished, as if swallowed up in the depths of the scarlet-leaved forest. The men hastily made themselves up with red, black and white powder, but mainly red. The bowmen checked the tension of their bow-strings, then the three feathers on each arrow, to check that they were accurately set.

Each man was equipped with an enormous tomahawk hooked over his left arm, and with his right felt for his scalping knife, which he then held between his teeth in order to put the finishing touches to his bow.

Several scouts slipped away like serpents into the yellow and red undergrowth, where, even when still close at hand, they became invisible although moving about.

The Chief and the main contingent of the braves formed up in close ranks in front of the whites.

All the Indians were aglow with a savage joy, as if the prospect of battle was what they most ardently desired.

The Europeans, with the possible exception of the young men, like Florimond, could scarcely be said to share their enthusiasm for the forthcoming battle. Their faces, dark tanned by long days on the march, wore expressions of weariness and anxiety. If it was indeed true that only a few more hours' march lay between them and the outpost where they would find the security of a palisade and the welcome if simple comfort of a few basic necessities, it was a bitter disappointment to be held up by an ambush, and to run the risk of being killed or wounded. Angélique glanced at her husband, awaiting his verdict.

'Let us wait,' he said. 'When the scouts come back, we shall know what is what. If these Iroquois look like attacking us, we shall dig in and defend ourselves; if they decide to ignore us, we shall treat them in the same way! I have warned Mopuntook that if he shows any sign of beginning the battle, without evidence of hostility from the other side, I shall not come to his assistance.'

They stood waiting, arms at the ready.

When the Indians returned they seemed disappointed, for, not only had the Iroquois not shown the slightest desire to attack the caravan, but it seemed highly likely that they had not even seen it, for they had literally melted away without leaving a single trace.

The Metallaks turned their stolid, grotesquely painted faces towards Angélique and shook their heads. The white woman had put the Iroquois to flight.

CHAPTER FIVE

'THERE'S THE Wolf, the Roebuck, the Bear, the Fox, and the Spider, but above them all is the Tortoise.'

Thus spoke Nicolas Perrot that evening at their encampment. The cold was beginning to edge over the top of the ravine and they all clustered round the camp fires.

A saffron-coloured haze had turned everything about them to gold; in the distance the mountain seemed to sink to rest, to settle down like a beast brought to heel, and at its feet they caught the glimmer of a long liquid path, the gentle, languorous waters of a broad river. . . .

Joffrey de Peyrac had pointed it out in the distance as they reached the encampment:

'That's the Kennebec.'

Like the Hebrews contemplating the promised land, so did de Peyrac's men rejoice, each in his own way. Some of them, the Jonas family for example, said a devout prayer of thanks to the Lord for granting them a glimpse of the end of their wearisome trek. Some exchanged great friendly thumps on the back, or threw their caps up into the air.... They were all the more delighted at the prospect of soon being in the shelter of a good strong palisade because of the glimpse they had caught of those frightening Indian shapes among the trees, and still more because the strange, though fortuitous, incident of the tortoise had left the whole caravan with a vague feeling of apprehension.

Mosquitoes buzzed all round them. Angélique sat with Honorine clasped sleepily against her, wrapped round with her heavy woollen cloak. From time to time her eyes would turn towards the shining line of the Kennebec winding its way gently across the plain. That was where Katarunk lay, their haven of safety!

'The Wolf for the Mohawks, the Roebuck for the Onondagas, the Fox for the Oneidas, the Bear for the Cayugas, and the Spider for the Senecas, but the Tortoise stands for all of them, the Five Nations of the Iroquois; it is their password and their Spirit Commander-in-Chief.'

Whenever Nicolas Perrot was deep in thought, the tanned leathery surface of his forehead wrinkled up and made his fur cap wriggle.

'The tribes in this region, the Abenakis, Etchemins, or Souriquois are accustomed to a nomadic existence. They have no sense of order or custom, no bread, or salt. But the Iroquois ... they are a superior people a great farming nation.'

'Anyone would think you were fond of them,' Angélique remarked.

The trapper gave a start.

'God forbid! They are demons, the scum of the earth. The Iroquois are the Canadian's worst enemy. But it is true,' he went on after a moment's reflection, 'that I have lived among them, and I cannot forget it. Anyone who has shared the life of the Iroquois will understand what I mean. For I have seen the Sacred Valley where reign the Three Gods worshipped by the Five Nations.'

'Three Gods?'

'Yes! The Maize, the Pumpkin, and the Bean,' Nicolas Perrot replied without a smile.

Honorine had fallen asleep. Taking care not to wake her, Angélique rose and walked over to the drill tent that was pitched every evening for the women and children. After wrapping up her daughter snugly in the furs, she went back outside again to help Madame Jonas who was busy cooking with Octave Malaprade.

The Appalachians were glowing purple in the light of the setting sun. They were mountains of gentle yet lofty lines.

The wind swept across the headland where they had pitched their camp in the hope that the continuous breeze would protect them from mosquitoes and sand-flies; another reason for selecting this promontory had been so that they could keep a better watch on the surrounding country.

Florimond and Cantor were busy cooking in the embers some fish wrapped in leaves which they had caught with their hands at one of the bends of the river.

Several haunches of moose were roasting on a spit, and the tongue, the choicest portion, simmered gently in a stew-pot with vegetables and herbs. There was boiled maize in another pot which Madame Jonas had taken off the fire and was beginning to serve out.

She was still slightly shocked to see the dirty Indians mixing shamelessly with the whites, and being the first to hold out their dirty bowls to her.

They were constantly interfering with everything, handling everything, meddling with everything with a quiet insolence; for was this not their home and were not these Palefaces after all under their protection!

The good woman pursed her lips and cast what she hoped were eloquent glances in the direction of Count Peyrac. She could not begin to understand how so fastidious a gentleman could tolerate the close proximity of these smelly people, a matter which also perplexed Angélique herself on occasion.

Now a cold blue light spread over the landscape, and the sentries walked back and forth along the edge of the forest. For a long time the only thing visible in the valley was the sparkling Kennebec.

It had been a day full of excitement, and one further stage of their journey had been completed. What did the following day hold in store for them?

Angélique looked around for her husband and caught sight of him standing a little way off, looking into the distance. He was alone.

She could tell from the way he stood that he was deep in thought.

Angélique had already noticed that when he withdrew from them all in this way no one ever dared interrupt his meditation.

A strange respect surrounded the leader in whom these very different men, most of them not at all amenable to discipline, had placed their trust.

The majority of them had observed with some jealousy and anxiety Angélique's advent in the life of the man they worshipped.

'Women! Everyone knows what they do to a man worthy of the name,' said Clovis l'Auvergnat, screwing up his narrow eyes. 'They take the guts out of him!'

'Not him though,' Yann le Couennec, the Breton, protested.

Then, with an admiring glance towards the young woman, he went on:

'Nor her, either!'

'Oh, you're an innocent, you are!' replied the man from Auvergne with a shrug. His drooping black moustaches gave a sardonic twist to his mouth.

Angélique had no difficulty in guessing what they were talking about. She herself had once been the leader of an armed band. And these men were not 'her' men.

A life of shared dangers and triumphs had brought them together round the Count de Peyrac. Personal, highly prized, indissoluble bonds, of which their manly reticence would never allow them to speak openly, bound each and every one of them to the man whom experience had taught them to consider their lord and their sole hope. Together they had fought Saracen and Christian, explored the Caribbean, and rode out storms. They had shared the booty with him and, with his encouragement, had caroused and revelled, living like lords whenever they put into port. Wine had flowed freely, there had been women for the asking, and their leader had distributed gold-pieces to them with open-handed generosity.

Angélique sometimes tried to imagine what kind of a life her husband had led during their years of separation.

More often than not she imagined him surrounded by his scientific equipment.

She saw him leaning over a globe or a map as his cabin swayed with the movement of the ship; or else he stood at the top of some Moorish terrace beneath the Cretan sky, examining the stars through a priceless telescope. But in that past, the moment would always come, of an evening, when a servant would enter and bring in a veiled woman, a Spanish beauty when they were in the Caribbean, or a half-caste Indian or Negress.

He would leave his work and welcome the woman with his inimitable charm, and would dance attendance on her, laughing and joking with her to coax from her all the sensual pleasure she had come to give him.

He was an individualist, a lone figure.

He was a complete man, in full possession of his powers and his faculties, entirely self-sufficient. And now she, Angélique, was claiming her place at this man's side. But when he stood motionless thus, absorbed and far away, she dared not approach him.

The night grew dark. As he sat by the fire Cantor began to play a Tuscan cantilena on his guitar. He had a delightful voice; for although it was already rich and firm, it still retained the soft inflection of youth. When he sang he seemed happy. But as far as her boys' inner thoughts were concerned, Angélique had simply not had enough time to talk to them and win their confidence. . . . That would have to wait until they reached Katarunk.

She felt a sudden pang of anxiety about her mare again, and before rejoining the others she walked down to the bank of the river where the horses had been put out to pasture.

Wallis had escaped! Her broken halter hung from the tree to which she had been tethered.

Angélique had a feeling that the horse could not be far away, and after climbing up the slope again to collect a bridle and bit, she walked along the bank of the river calling softly.

A misty moon was rising over the top of the black firs. A tawny owl screeched. Dormice coughed in the thickets, and the river, running almost dry, babbled over the stones.

She heard a snapping of branches and, turning in the direction of the sound, she caught sight of the mare in a patch of moonlight, cropping the grass in a small clearing; but when she reached it, the flighty animal had moved farther on.

By the time Angélique finally caught up with the creature at the top of a hillside, she realized that she had lost sight of the camp fires. But this was of no consequence; for she would make her way down to the river-bed again and follow the river downstream. After fastening the bridle firmly over the horse's nose she kept a tight hold on it and listened for the sound of running water from below.

As she stood there all alone in the depths of the dark night, she no longer felt afraid. The scent of this unknown virgin forest enveloped her in its pungent perfume, and once again she tasted the fleeting yet intense sensation of being alive, full of youth and strength, on the threshold of a new life which it was for her to build up from its very foundations. But she would find an ally in the great unmapped open spaces which they had reached after so many dangers. And she felt her heart swell with the same feeling of love towards this untamed land that she had felt earlier when bathing among the magical shimmering waters of the lake. It was at this moment that the strange noises began.

She could hear the distant call of a moose, the whispering of the wind, the dull roar of waterfalls in the depths of the forest, and, mingling with all these sounds, she heard the sound of hymn-singing.

CHAPTER SIX

Ave Maris Stella
Dei Mater Alma ...

THE WORDS of the hymn rang through the primeval night. Angélique stared up at the treetops as if expecting the sky between their branches to open and reveal a choir of angels.

A shudder ran down her spine, and she turned round warily. Behind her a pinkish glow like an anxious dawn showed over the edge of the cliff, casting dancing shadows among the pines.

Holding Wallis by the bridle, Angélique crept towards the edge of the ravine from which the sound of men's voices rose in a hymn.

Angélique found it hard not to imagine that she was back again in the forest of Nieul where the persecuted Huguenots had taken refuge to pray and sing psalms.[1]

She moved still closer to the edge and, leaning over, discovered a strange, incredible scene.

At the bottom of the gorge, the rocks were red from the

[1] See *Angélique in Revolt*.

56

glow of two great fires that had been lit by the river. A priest in a black soutane, his arms held aloft in benediction, stood facing a group of kneeling men.

He was standing with his back to her, but she could see the men's faces; some were dressed in suède and fur, while others wore blue uniforms with gold frogging, and Angélique noticed two noblemen among them with lace collars and cuffs.

They reached the last lines of the hymn and the singing stopped. Then the priest's voice rose up alone, clear and fervent.

'Queen of Heaven.'

'Pray for us,' the congregation murmured in response.

Angélique started back.

'They are French!'

'Tower of David.'

'Pray for us.'

'Arc of the Covenant.'

'Pray for us.'

'Refuge of sinners! Comforter of the afflicted.'

'Pray for us! Pray for us!' they replied in chorus after each invocation. There they were, trappers, soldiers, and noblemen, kneeling together, heads piously bowed, telling their beads.

'They are French!'

Angélique's heart began to beat wildly.

She would have thought herself in the grip of a nightmare in which she was reliving all the horrors of the Poitou war, had she not noticed behind the French, the copper-coloured figures of some half-naked Indians. Some of them were praying and singing with the white men and women, while others sat around a second fire scraping the last of their meal from the bottom of their wooden bowls with their fingers. The smell of food still hung in the air, and a medium-sized cooking pot had been laid to one side of the fire after its contents had been doled out.

The tall figure of a strapping, shaggy-haired Indian all glistening with grease bent over the glowing embers. As he stood up, he took an axe from the flames, and its red-hot blade flashed. Holding the weapon with care, the savage moved a few paces away from the circle of men. It was only then that Angélique sensed the presence of another naked Indian in the shadows, tied to the trunk of a tree.

Slowly and deliberately, as if he were doing the most natural thing in the world, the man with the axe pressed the red hot blade against the man's thigh. Not a sound passed his lips, only the sickening smell of burning flesh reached Angélique a few moments later.

She started in horror, choking back a cry, and Wallis shied, making the branches snap. Realizing that she would be seen, Angélique leapt astride the horse.

The savage, who had just replaced his axe in the fire, looked up and lifted his sinewy arm with its feathered bracelets towards the top of the cliff.

In a flash they were all on their feet, and glimpsed the figure of a woman with long hair, on horseback, outlined against the moonlit sky.

Then a terrible cry went up from their breasts:
'The She-Devil! The She-Devil of Acadia!'

CHAPTER SEVEN

'DID YOU say they shouted: "The She-Devil of Acadia"?'
'That's what I thought I heard.'
'Good God! Heaven forbid that they should have taken you for her,' Nicolas Perrot exclaimed, crossing himself. And Maupertuis did likewise.

'I do not know whom they took me for, but whoever it was they gave chase like madmen. One of them a giant of a man, almost caught up with me just as I headed Wallis into the river.'

'Did you kill him?' Peyrac asked sharply.

'No. I fired at his hat and he fell backwards into the water; they are French, I assure you, camping in the ravine on the other side of this very mountain where we are encamped.'

'If you would allow us to, Monsieur de Peyrac, we trappers, Maupertuis, his son Pierre-Joseph and I, could go and meet them,' said Nicolas Perrot.

'It would be a very odd thing indeed if we did not find some good friends and acquaintances among these people from Quebec, and we would be able to reach an understanding with them.'

'But don't forget, Perrot, that we have been condemned to

death by the Government of Quebec,' Maupertuis objected, 'and even excommunicated by his Grace the Bishop.'

'Pooh! That's all nonsense. People from the Saint-Lawrence always enjoy meeting old friends.'

So the two trappers, followed by Maupertuis's son, a half-caste of twenty by an Indian woman, disappeared into the dark bush.

The whole camp had been under arms since Angélique had returned and given the alert.

The soldiers and the other men were all at their stations, muskets in hand.

When the three trappers had gone off into the woods, Angélique turned towards Peyrac.

She found it hard to suppress a trembling in her voice and when she spoke to Peyrac her tone was a little sharp.

'You did not warn me that we might run into the French where we are going.'

'One always risks running into the French when wandering about North America. I've already told you that, although there are not many of them, they are very active, and travel about every bit as much as the Indians. They were bound to take an interest in us. . . .

'Come closer to the fire, darling; you are frozen. This unfortunate encounter has upset you. And once again it's the fault of that blasted mare of yours.'

Angélique held her hands out towards the flames. Frozen she was, frozen to the bottom of her heart.

Question upon question rushed to her lips. She wanted both to be reassured and to find out exactly how great the danger was.

'That was what you were frightened of, wasn't it? That was the reason you made us hurry so? You were frightened the French might make a raid into the land you want to settle, where you have already built your outpost.'

'Yes. Not far from Gouldsboro, my nearest neighbour, Baron Saint-Castine, from Pentagoet, who is in charge of the French outpost in Acadia, a man with whom I have always been on good terms, came to warn me that the Catholic Missionaries who are busy converting the Abenakis in Maine were concerned about my arrival near the source of the Kennebec, and had asked the Government of Quebec to send out an expeditionary force against me.'

'But what right have the French to object to your settling in these parts?'

'They consider this land part of Acadia and, as such, their territory.'

'Who in fact do all these uninhabited lands belong to?'

'To whoever shows the greatest enterprise. It's a no-man's-land. The Treaty of Breda, to which France was a signatory, gave it to the British, but they consider the forestlands too dangerous and don't care to leave the coastal strip to enforce the provisions of the treaty.'

'And supposing these Frenchmen from the north discover one day who you are, and who I am . . .'

'That isn't going to happen tomorrow . . . and by the time it does I shall be a great deal stronger than this wretched group of colonists the King of France has abandoned in the Antipodes. . . . No, have no fear, the arm of Louis XIV cannot reach us here. And in any case, even if he still dared try to get us here, we could fight him. America is a big country and we are free . . . so take heart, my love, and get warm . . .'

'What did they mean by the name they shouted out when they saw me: the She-Devil of Acadia?'

'They must have thought you were a vision. Castine and Perrot had warned me that New France has been greatly disturbed by the visions of a saintly nun in Quebec: she dreamed that a female demon was snatching the souls of the Acadian Indians, whether baptized or not, from the Church. This would explain their suspicion and excitement. And it may well also be the reason for their present expedition. . . . They say that the She-Devil, riding a mythical animal, a unicorn . . .'

'Ah! I understand,' Angélique exclaimed with a nervous laugh, 'when they caught sight of me: a woman, a horse . . . something unthinkable round here . . . and it fitted in with their vision . . .'

Peyrac seemed annoyed:

'It's stupid . . but it's pretty serious. This confusion in their minds could well cause us further bother. These people are fanatics.'

'But still, they can't attack us if we show no hostility towards them. . . .'

'Wait and see! Time will tell what they have in mind. This morning Perrot sent his Indian scout Mazok out on a reconnaissance. When he returns, he will be able to inform us about all likely movements in the area: the French, the Iroquois, or the Indian allies of the French who accompany them on their expeditions, Abenakis, Algonquins, or Hurons. Come to think of it,' he said suddenly, 'the savages we saw earlier on were in all likelihood only Hurons following the French. For, although the Hurons are sworn enemies of the Iroquois, they belong to the same race and observe the same customs, among others the way of doing their hair up in a single twist on top of their heads. But we did hear that there was also an Iroquois war party on the prowl in the region, and the French may only be here on their account, and we might ...

'You see, that's America for you. Wastelands which suddenly come to life and swarm with a vast number of different people, all sworn enemies.'

They saw some torches shining through the undergrowth, coming towards the camp. They could hear the sound of muskets being cocked and the smell of the tinder that some of the men had lighted.

But it was only the three trappers returning empty-handed.

Farther up the river they had indeed found traces of the French camp, as well as a half-roasted Iroquois prisoner tied to a tree, but not a sign of soldiers or Hurons.

In vain had they called at the tops of their voices:

'Ahoy there! You men from the Saint-Lawrence, where are you, cousins? Where are you, brothers?' Reply came there none.

And as for the Iroquois prisoner they had set free, burned as he was, he had managed to take advantage of a moment when their attention was diverted, had leapt up and vanished into the dark undergrowth.

Henceforth they would be surrounded by a varied throng of shadowy figures: French, Algonquins, Hurons, Abenakis, Iroquois, while the mysterious forest continued to murmur serenely in the sighing wind, with no other sound save those of distant waters and the belling of a rutting moose.

Joffrey de Peyrac left some of his men under arms and organized a twenty-four-hour watch, for he had no intention of being taken by surprise.

He advised Angélique to take some rest in the women and children's tent. He accompanied her to the tent and, as it was very dark, took her in his arms and tried to kiss her lips. But she felt too agitated and anxious to be able to respond.

She also felt resentful towards him at times like these for having journeyed apart from her and for not letting her spend the nights with him. But Angélique realized that the discipline of the caravan and the recent arrival of women in this world of men made this essential.

She remembered that when she had escaped from Meknes with the Christian slaves in Morocco, Colin Paturel, their leader, had banished her from his company in the same way, saying, 'This woman belongs to no one; we'll have no dalliance before we are safe and sound in Christian territory.'

There was a touch of the same severity in the way Joffrey de Peyrac insisted on mustering the women and children in the same tent, while the men were made to sleep apart, in threes, on mounds of bark.

He, the Chief, remained alone too, without special privileges, feeling that he owed it to the men under him.

He took and made his own the law of ancient primitive tribes which says that a warrior, on the eve of battle, or when faced with some particular danger, must shun women to keep his mind clear and his strength intact.

But Angélique did not share this strength. She was weak, she sometimes told herself, and needed him terribly. She never felt entirely secure when she was far from him, fearing lest she lose him again. The miracle of their reunion was still so recent.

Of course she knew that behind Joffrey de Peyrac's self-control and coldness lay a keenly sensual, passionate nature, and there was no mistaking his feelings where she was concerned. But sometimes she feared that she was nothing more to him than an object of pleasure, who charmed him no doubt, but whom he kept apart from his inner life, from his joys, his ambitions and his cares. As the days went by she realized that she was bound to a man about whom she knew little, to whom she nevertheless owed submission and devotion, and also that she would often find herself pitted against his iron will; for he had an unyielding, secretive, matter-of-fact side to his character, and had grown even more astute than he had been before. You never knew what he had up his sleeve.

She slept badly, expecting at any moment to hear shots or, at the very least, a noisy invasion by the French.

At dawn she heard a sound and slipped out of her tent.

Mazok the Indian loomed up out of the mist; on reaching the shores of America, after his voyage to France, he had resumed his loin-cloth and his leather moccasins. His plaited hair was full of feathers again, he carried his bow in one hand, and had a quiver full of arrows across his back.

He greeted his master and Joffrey de Peyrac who came forward to meet him.

Angélique joined the men and they told her the Indian's news.

For two days now the outpost of Katarunk had been occupied by a small detachment of French, accompanied by their allies the Algonquins and Hurons.

At first light, they broke camp. It was still cold, and a rainbow-tinted mist hung over the land, making it impossible to see more than three paces ahead.

Moisture hung in drops on all the leaves, and the whole forest was dripping.

One behind the other, leading their horses by the bridle, they left the clearing and plunged into the damp thickets. Messages were passed along the line in a whisper and the soaking wet children told to try to control their coughing. The dew was raining down on them and their stealthy march was wrapped in mystery. Little by little the mist grew less damp and, when the sun appeared, a pale yellow disc that burst into blossom above an invisible land, it was only a matter of minutes before the fog vanished, revealing a glistening, wet landscape, shining in the full radiance of its brilliant colours.

They were crossing an open space at that moment and orders were given to make haste for the shelter of an oak-grove a little below the trail, where they were instructed to regroup and halt for a while.

It gradually grew warmer beneath the branches of the great twisted oaks, with their sombre violet, almost black leaves. Acorns fell without a sound on the dry mossy ground. The horses had been grouped together and were tethered to low branches, and all continued to observe the strictest silence.

The four Spanish soldiers began to climb down to the bottom of the ravine, moving rather heavily and making the undergrowth crackle as they went, whereas Mopuntook's Indians seemed to melt into the bushes and reached the bottom first, quieter than ghosts, each man standing behind a tree of which he seemed almost a part. They appeared delighted at the chance of putting a hole or two into the skin of some French or Indian enemy. Hidden behind a dry brushwood hedge, the soldiers stuck their forked musket-rests into the pebbles of the river-bed and rested their arquebuses on them. These guns were far more powerful and carried three times farther than muskets, although they were less accurate, and more like portable culverins.

Angélique was wondering what she should be doing since it seemed evident that they were preparing to give battle, when Count Peyrac came towards her.

'Madame, I need to call on your skill as the best shot I have in my company; we're going to need it.'

He told Honorine to stay like a good girl with the Jonases and the other children and two men were detailed to watch the horses.

Then he took Angélique right to the edge of the cliff, where big rocks formed an overhang. It was an excellent look-out point from which they could see quite a long way up and down the river, as it ran below them in a deep cleft. The river was broad and in torrential flow even at this time of the year. There was a ford across it, but apart from the rocks that stood out of the water, allowing people to cross easily, almost without wetting their feet, the surrounding river was deep, and full of whirlpools that betrayed a treacherous river-bed. This was another of the ledges, or 'saults' as the trappers called them. which brought the level of the river down step by step to the lake, which they could see shimmering farther down the valley through the purple leaves.

'Sakoos Ford,' whispered Nicolas Perrot.

The ford was divided in the middle of the river by a small sandy island with a spinney on it.

The Count pointed this out to Angélique, and he showed her too the dark tunnel in the hedgerow on the opposite bank through which anyone following the forest path would come out on to the shore.

'Soon some men will come out there and begin to cross the ford; they will probably be the Frenchmen you saw yesterday evening and their Indians.... You will recognize them since you saw them face to face. When they reach the little island, but only when they reach it, I want you to fire to stop them crossing the second half of the ford.'

'The island is too far away for accuracy,' said Angélique with a frown.

'That is what the others said when I asked them to do this, but there is nowhere else we can stand. There is a cleft in the rock that prevents us from taking up a better position opposite the island, and we have not got time to cross the cleft; it would take several hours. So we must shoot from here and stop the head of the convoy so that no one can go to the outpost to raise the alarm. We must stop them, but you must not hit anyone, for I want no bloodshed.'

'You are asking something well-nigh impossible.'

'I know, my love, Florimond himself said he could not do it, and yet he claims to be a good shot. . . .'

The lad was there, looking dubiously at his mother and father, tempted to show off his skill, but honest enough to have doubts about his own capacities.

'Firing at the tip of the island, Father, that's impossible,' he cried. 'If you wanted it done as they started to cross the ford, that would be different. . . .'

'But at that stage some of their party would still be in the forest. I don't want anyone to escape. Some of our men are posted up-river on the bank, to catch anyone who does try to get away, but if there are too many of them, it will turn into a real battle and there will always be one or two who manage to escape. No, I want to get them all, or almost all, out of the wood, either in the process of crossing the ford or on the island, before we fire. Our Spaniards down at the bottom can then cut off their retreat completely on this side and they will be well and truly encircled.'

'But the island stretches right out in front of us. Stopping the head of the convoy at the very moment when it begins to cross the second half of the ford, at this distance, and without wounding anyone, would seem to me a very tricky business.'

'Do you think you can do it, Madame?'

Angélique had been examining the situation in minute detail, and she turned towards him.

'And what about you, Joffrey? . . . Are you not a skilled shot too?'

'At this distance, I am convinced your eyes are better than mine. . . .'

'If that's how it is . . .'

She hesitated. What he was asking her to do was extremely difficult. Sunshine flooded through the gorge.

On the other hand, she was pleased at the confidence the Count was showing her by this request, and pleased to be able to do something at last. Her sons and the men who had been posted near by looked at her in perplexity, astonished at the Count's action, and she welcomed the chance of proving to them that, when it came to wars and gunfire, she had seen as much, if not more than they, for all that they were pirates.

And as Joffrey repeated:

'Will you take up the wager, Madame?'

She replied:

'I will try.... What weapon are you giving me?'

One of the men handed her a musket which he had loaded, but she refused it.

'I want a gun I have loaded myself.'

They handed her Monsieur de Peyrac's own gun, which the Breton, Yann le Couennec, carried for him and kept in order. It was a flint musket which could fire two shots without being reloaded. It had a walnut butt, inlaid with mother-of-pearl. It was both light and strongly made, and Angélique put it to her shoulder with a feeling of satisfaction. She examined the powder, the bullets, and the primer they handed her, cleaned the double barrel, rammed the charge home once, slipped the bullets in and rammed again. Eyes full of curiosity followed her every movement.

When the primer was in position, she leant back against the stony ledge.

The slight feeling of excitement she knew so well was beginning to steal over her, the scent of guerrilla warfare! Down below in the sunlight, she could see the tip of the island, and the sparkling heap of stones at the beginning of the second half of the ford.

Her heart beat faster. That was what happened before the fighting began. But when the moment came, on the contrary, she would feel strangely calm, empty, petrified. She stood up.

'Have two loaded guns ready to pass me in case the first shots are not enough to stop them.'

Then she waited.

Less than an hour later the screech of a nightjar rang through the forest. It was so familiar a cry, that and the cooing of doves, that no one took much notice of it any more. But Nicolas Perrot seemed to read a particular significance into this call, for he leaned over a little towards Angélique and whispered:

'That's Mazok's signal.'

An Indian was the first to appear at the river's edge, a Huron, followed by a trapper whom Angélique had seen the day before in the ravine. Then followed an officer, several Indians and a very young Frenchman, a mere golden-headed boy, dressed in the blue frock-coat of an officer of the King beneath a miscellaneous collection of arms, an axe, a cutlass, and a powder-horn. His lace cravat was rather rumpled and carelessly tied, while his hat, which was all dented, was adorned with black and white eagle feathers which had absolutely nothing in common with the regulation plumes, even though the frogging of his revers, his cuffs, and his buttonholes did give his get-up some semblance of a uniform. He wore leather leggings and moccasins.

They saw him rush gleefully into the water at the edge of the river, give his face a splash, and shake off the foam. His commanding officer, the colossus whose hat Angélique had put a bullet through the day before, called him to order:

'Take it easy, Maudreuil! You're kicking up as much din as a charging moose.'

'Well, we are only half a league from Katarunk,' the young man replied cheerfully. 'Are you frightened of another meeting with evil spirits like last night? . . .'

Their voices were carried, clear and distinct, to the watchers by the echo in the valley.

'I don't know what I fear,' the lieutenant replied, 'but I don't like the look of this place. I always have thought it a real death-trap.'

He glanced up at the cliffs and his eyes seemed to be trying to penetrate the secret of the leaves moving gently in the breeze.

'Can you smell the Iroquois?' the young soldier asked with a laugh. 'You seem to have a particularly sharp nose for them.'

'No, but I do sense something else, I don't quite know what. Let's get a move on. The sooner we are on the other side, the better for us. Come on now. I'll go first. L'Aubignière,' he called to the trapper, 'bring up the rear, will you?'

And he began to cross the ford, springing with great supple strides from stone to stone.

Up on the cliff-top, where they were hiding in the trees, Nicolas Perrot touched Angélique's shoulder.

'For heaven's sake don't kill them,' he whispered. 'That one, the big fellow, is Lieutenant Pont-Briand, my best friend. The other is Three-Fingers of the Three-Rivers, and the youngest is young Baron Maudreuil, the finest lad in all Canada.'

Angélique blinked to show that she had understood. Yes, of course she would take every care of such precious enemies, but all these recommendations did not make her task any the easier.

The colossus whom Nicolas had called Lieutenant Pont-Briand had reached the island. There, he stood motionless once more, hands on hips, looking up, examining his surroundings like a suspicious dog. He appeared to be literally sniffing the air. He wore no hat, and his dark brown hair blew free round his head and shoulders. With the light behind him he seemed to be wearing a small reddish halo. He did not seem to sense anything odd, and with a shrug of his shoulders began to cross the island, followed by the Hurons who had already crossed the ford.

Angélique concentrated hard and steadied her gun against her shoulder. Then she began to follow Pont-Briand's silhouette with the tip of the gun-barrel as he moved on down the beach.

L'Aubignière, the trapper, known as Three-Fingers, was nearer to her, he was still on the shore urging on the savages who continued to pour out of the forest.

Pont-Briand had just reached the farthermost tip of the little island. He stopped for a moment and looked at his men, now engaged in crossing the river. Without realizing it, he was playing into the hands of those who watched him from the cliff-top; for soon the entire contingent of men would be assembled in the gorge, and that was exactly what Joffrey de Peyrac had wanted.

Then at last the lieutenant made for the second half of the ford.

The moment had come.

Angélique's entire concentration was fixed on that one point: the flat stone on which the man was about to place his foot.

Her finger pressed the trigger. The edge of the stone shattered, and the gorge echoed with the sudden roar of the explosion.

The French officer sprang backwards.

'Get down!' he shouted, as the Indians and the French on the island fell to the ground and crawled into the shelter of a few scant bushes.

But the lieutenant, instead of doing likewise, made a dash for the ford again. Angélique fired. He was already half-way across. Once again a stone exploded at his feet. They saw him lose his balance and fall into the water. It occurred to Angélique that this was the second bath he had to thank her for in two days; he had also fallen into the river the previous evening, when he had been chasing her through the ravine. She was sure she had not hit him.

'The other gun!' she snapped.

The lieutenant's head reappeared. He was struggling in the current and moving still farther off. Angélique put the gun to her shoulder again, aimed, and fired. The bullet ricocheted on the surface of the water, passing so close to him that it must have splashed him.

'Don't kill him,' Nicolas Perrot begged in a whisper.

'The devil take you!' thought Angélique, all on edge. Could he not see that the man would not be stopped, and how was she going to prevent this madman from reaching the bank unless she killed him?

She fired again. This time, the French nobleman seemed to get the point. Caught between the dangerous currents in the river and the running fire a few inches from his head, there was no longer room for hesitation. He swam back to the island, clambered up and, like the others, dragged himself into the shelter of a stunted alder.

Angélique was able to relax a little, while still keeping an eye on the ford. But no one else appeared keen to imitate the officer's reckless example, and it seemed very unlikely that anyone would now risk his life across so well guarded a stretch of water.

She relaxed and half sat up. Sweat poured down her brow which she wiped instinctively with her powder-blackened hand; then she took another loaded gun from the hands of one of her amazed sons, reassumed her firing position and continued her watch.

It was just as well that she did, for once again the lieutenant tried his luck, springing up like a jack-in-the-box...

A bullet ricocheted off the sand at his feet, and he promptly took shelter again. Meanwhile the surprise attack had been going forward on all fronts. When Angélique's first shot stopped the convoy, the Hurons who were half-way across the first half of the ford had tried to retreat into the cover of the forest, but shots rang out from the shore they had just left. L'Aubignière dived behind a tree and began to shoot back in the direction of the cliff.

The Hurons, encircled as they were by heavy fire on all sides, stood in the middle of the first ford, daring neither to advance nor to retreat. Even so one of them, with the customary audacity of his race, hurled himself into the tempestuous river, but as he reached the bank farther downstream, a little above the rapids, one of the Spaniards shot at him, wounding him in the leg.

Another of them managed to break away into the thicket, but the invisible enemy posted there by Peyrac was waiting for him, for there was the sound of a struggle followed by an exclamation of fury.

Then silence fell again, so complete that the strident chirping of the cicadas seemed to drown every other sound, even that of the rushing river.

The acrid smell of gunpowder filled the gorge.

Angélique gritted her teeth. She had forgotten where she was. It seemed to her that she was once again on the watch above some canyon in Vendée, in the heart of the forest of Poitou, and that the King's men were falling beneath her fire. Behind her clenched teeth there rose that ancient cry from her heart, which had so often risen to her lips: 'Kill! Kill!'

She began to tremble.

A hand was laid on her shoulder.

'There, it's all over!' said the calm voice of the Count.

She sat up a little, her face drawn, her gun smoking in her hand, looking at him as if she did not recognize him. He helped her get up, then gently wiped the black powder marks from her forehead with his handkerchief.

There was a smile in the depths of his eyes and something indefinable, half-way between pity and admiration, as he looked into her face, a woman's face of such rare beauty blackened with the sweat of war.

'Bravo, my love,' he said softly.

Why had he said bravo? What was he applauding? Her immediate success? Or was it her erstwhile struggle? Her frantic, despairing struggle with the King of France? Or was he applauding everything that lay behind the fantastic skill of those hands, resting on that weapon of death?

With great respect he took her lovely powder-blackened hand and kissed it.

Her two sons and Peyrac's men stared wide-eyed at Angélique. The trappers fired from the bottom of the gulley. Pont-Briand had guessed where they were from the movement of the leaves. A piece of the overhanging rock exploded right beside them.

'Now then, that's enough!' Perrot shouted at the top of his voice. 'Enough damage done already, my good folk! Stop this little game, will you? Pont-Briand, my cousin, calm down or I'll make you wrestle with me and I'll force your shoulders to the ground as I did on the famous feast of Saint Médard that you won't have forgotten!'

The trapper's stentorian voice echoed back and forth across the gorge hung with acrid smoke.

There was a silence, then a voice from the island:

'Who is that?'

'Nicolas Perrot, from Ville-Marie, on the island of Montreal.'

'Who is with you?'

'Friends, French friends!'

'And who else?'

Perrot turned to the Count with a questioning look, and Joffrey replied with a nod.

Then the trapper cupped his hands round his mouth and called:

'Hear me, good people of the Saint-Lawrence, hear my proclamation. Let me introduce Monsieur le Comte de Peyrac de Morens d'Irristru, Lord of Gouldsboro, of Katarunk and other places, and his company.'

Angélique thrilled to hear the Indian forest ring with that name which for many years had been condemned to the silence of disgrace and death. Joffrey de Peyrac de Morens d'Irristru! Was it written that this old Gascon name should be born again, should dare to live again, so far from its native place? But was this not dangerous?

She turned towards her husband, but the expression on his face revealed nothing.

He was standing at the tip of the promontory, hidden by the drooping branches of the pine-tree against which he leant, still observing the site of the encounter with the same attention, as if indifferent to all the shouting.

The smoke took a long time to clear, and sounds were deadened by the powder-laden atmosphere. Visibility was poor and prudence demanded that both sides should remain on the alert. Joffrey de Peyrac kept his loaded pistol in his hand.

At last someone stood up behind the bushes on the island. It was the tall man, Pont-Briand.

'Come down here unarmed, Nicolas Perrot, if it's really you and not your ghost!'

'I'll be with you in a moment.'

The trapper handed his gun to his servant and clambered down the slope to the edge of the river.

As he made his appearance on the narrow bank, in his suède clothes and fur bonnet, he was greeted with exclamations of enthusiasm. Both the French and the Hurons ran forward to welcome him. He shouted to them to go a little farther up the river, round the next bend where they would be able to cross by a simple bridge made of tree-trunks which the Spaniards had thrown across at a point where the two banks were only separated by a narrow gap. This crossing was rarely used, since the ford alone spared people several hours' detour by enabling them to avoid a very deep chasm in the rock. As soon as they had all joined forces, there was a great deal of strenuous back-slapping and noisy congratulations. The trapper and his compatriots greeted one another with great slaps on the shoulders and thumps in the ribs.

'Oh, brother! Here you are, as large as life! We thought you were dead!'

'We thought you had gone for good!'

'Gone back to the Iroquois!'

'We thought you had got used to living with savages and would end your days there!'

'That is in fact what almost happened to me,' Nicolas Perrot replied. 'I had intended to return to the Iroquois after I left Quebec three years ago. But I met Monsieur de Peyrac and changed my mind.'

The Hurons were very pleased to see Perrot. But some of them looked a bit sour and demanded blood-money, since one of their men, Anahstaha, had been wounded.

Perrot spoke in the Huron tongue:

'My brother Anahstaha should not have tried to slip like a snake between our fingers when our musketeers ordered him to stop. Let him who knows not the language of gunpowder not meddle with making war.... Come gentlemen, if you please,' he concluded, turning to the French officers, while the Hurons, subjugated by this familiar manly voice, sat down for a pow-wow and finally decided to let the Palefaces sort things out for themselves.

CHAPTER EIGHT

THE THREE men who followed Nicolas Perrot up the steep side of the mountain were not lacking in curiosity in spite of the discomfiture they had just suffered. For the name of Count Peyrac had already acquired some renown in North America. Few had seen him, but people talked a great deal about this enigmatic personality, from the coast of Massachusetts and Nova Scotia up to the borders of Canada.

Furthermore, since they had occupied the fort which the Count had built on the Kennebec with a military garrison, the French were in an embarrassing situation, and, had it not been for the presence of their friend Perrot, they would not have given much for their chances. As they went by, they caught sight of men posted behind the bushes, true buccaneers' faces from the four corners of the globe, who glared at them as they passed.

On reaching the top of the slope they came to a sudden halt, overcome with fear and astonishment.

In the shadows dappled with patches of light falling through the leaves, they had just caught sight of a rider, wearing a black mask, and seated on a jet-black stallion, as motionless as a statue.

Behind him they saw other men on horseback, and a group of women.

'Greetings, gentlemen,' said the masked rider in a muffled voice. 'Please come closer.'

In spite of their courage, they found it hard to recover their self-possession.

They greeted him nevertheless and, as the tall lieutenant seemed incapable of uttering a single word, it was the trapper Romain de l'Aubignière, known as Three-Fingers of the Three-Rivers, who spoke up. He introduced himself and added:

'Sir, we are here at your disposal to parley with you,

73

although your method of opening the discussions seemed to us a trifle ... explosive.'

'Was yours any less so? I have heard that you took it upon yourselves to occupy my outpost on the banks of the Kennebec.'

L'Aubignière and Maudreuil turned towards Pont-Briand.

The lieutenant ran his hand over his brow and came back to earth. 'My lord,' he said with spontaneous deference – a fact which later was to astonish him – 'my lord, it is indeed true that we have been instructed by the Government of New France to proceed to the source of the Kennebec in order to find out all we can about your movements and your intentions; we had expected you to arrive by river and were awaiting you in the hope of being able to open discussions with you with a view to reaching an understanding.'

A slight smile appeared at the edge of Peyrac's mask, for the lieutenant had said : 'we were expecting you to come by river.' Their arrival overland, on horseback, had taken the French unawares.

'What about my Irishman, what have you done with him?'

'Oh! do you mean the fat red Englishman, the funny one?' exclaimed little Baron de Maudreuil. 'He led us a fine dance. Although he was all alone up there, anyone would have thought there was a whole garrison inside the fort. The Hurons wanted to scalp him, but our colonel said they weren't to, so we just put him in the cellar to cool his heels, after stringing him up like a sausage.'

'God be praised!' said Peyrac. 'I could never have forgiven you the death of one of my men, and the issue between us would have had to be settled by fighting. What is the name of your colonel?'

'Count Loménie-Chambord.'

'I have heard of him. He is a great soldier and a very worthy man.'

'Are we your prisoners, sir?'

'If you can guarantee that no treachery awaits us at Katarunk, and that the sole purpose of your expedition is to parley with me, I shall be happy to treat you as friends rather than hostages, as my adviser, your countryman Monsieur Perrot, suggests.'

The lieutenant bowed his head and seemed to reflect for a time.

'I think I can guarantee that, Monsieur,' he said at last. 'I know that, even if your movements were causing anxiety in certain circles which viewed them as an incursion of the English into our territory, there were others, and in particular Governor Frontenac, who were interested in the possibility of an alliance with you, that is to say, with a compatriot who would not seek to harm New France.'

'If that is the situation, I will agree to meet Monsieur de Loménie before embarking on pointless hostilities. Monsieur de l'Aubignière, may I ask you to go to your colonel and tell him of my arrival with the Countess of Peyrac, my wife.'

He beckoned to Angélique to step forward, and she urged her mare out of the shade and came and stood beside her husband. She did not feel much inclined to show any particular friendliness towards them after the fright they had given her the previous evening, but the expression that came over their three faces when they noticed her and saw her coming towards them brought a smile to her lips.

All three recoiled as one man and their lips formed a strange word which could be easily read although it remained unspoken : 'The She-Devil! The She-Devil of Acadia. . . !'

'Madame, may I introduce these Canadian gentlemen?'

'Gentlemen, Countess Peyrac, my wife. . . .'

With an ironic expression he watched the varied emotions in their faces.

'The Countess told me of your encounter yesterday evening. I think you must have given one another quite a fright. I can understand that the appearance of a white woman on horseback in these parts must have caused you some surprise, but as you see, what you saw was no vision. . . .'

'But it was,' exclaimed Pont-Briand with true French gallantry. 'Madame de Peyrac's beauty and grace are such as to make us wonder whether our eyes are not deceiving us and whether we are not in fact witnessing a vision or apparition.'

Angélique could not help smiling at this amiable retort.

'Thank you for your courteous words, Lieutenant. I regret that our first meeting was a somewhat rough-and-ready one. I owe you a hat, I believe!'

'Almost a head, Madame. But what matter! I would have welcomed death from so lovely a hand.'

And Gaspard de Pont-Briand, bending his knee, bowed with

courtly elegance. It was quite obvious that Angélique fascinated him.

The caravan had set off again in some disorder.

Now that they had reached agreement, they fetched the wounded Huron so that he could be carried on horseback, but he was afraid of the strange animal.

Baron Maudreuil introduced their chief, a man called Odessonik, resplendent with his bears' teeth trappings and with feathers stuck in his top-knot. For those unfamiliar with Indians it was difficult to tell one from another, but Angélique felt sure that this was the warrior she had seen the previous evening torturing the Iroquois prisoner with such thoroughness. The Hurons had grown friendly and curious now, and thronged about them, anxious to see the new Palefaces. Their tufts of hair and feathers rising from their shaved scalps danced a saraband around the riders.

'They frighten me,' said Madame Jonas. 'They look far too like the Iroquois. They are all so much of a muchness.'

The Protestants were terrified. They felt, possibly even more than Angélique, the unfortunateness of this meeting with the French Catholics and soldiers, the very people they had fled from in La Rochelle at such risk. They kept quiet, hoping that the two officers would not notice them.

Actually, the interest of the latter was centred on two things: Peyrac's masked face, which they found utterly intriguing, and Angélique's. In spite of the fact that she was weary and dusty in the shadow of her big hat, Pont-Briand kept on asking himself whether her face was not in fact the loveliest in the world. She-Devil or not, her eyes shone with a strange light, and he found himself obliged to look away suddenly whenever he met her glance.

The emotional shock he had felt on seeing her astride her horse, a creature of flesh and blood and no vision, still made him catch his breath, and he showed a complete lack of interest in his present situation, which was in fact a rather delicate one. The farther they went, the more convinced he became that this woman who had loomed up out of the forest was the loveliest creature he had ever met.

Lieutenant Pont-Briand was a colourful colossus, a solid mass of muscle, to which his aristocratic ancestry alone was able to lend a certain elegance. Born to be a soldier and, what was more, compelled to be one on account of his position as youngest member of the family, he had a ringing voice and a hearty laugh. He was a brilliant swordsman, a man who could tear the end off a cartridge with a single rapid bite, an indefatigable marksman, a warrior of fantastic endurance; but although he was a man in his prime, having passed the age of thirty, he seemed still to have the mentality of an adolescent.

This explained his relatively subordinate position for a man of high birth, since, while he could perform wonders under the orders of an enlightened leader, his impulsive nature often made it extremely dangerous for him to act on his own initiative. He had, nevertheless, been given the governorship of one of the most important French fortresses, the outpost of Saint Francis, and was extremely popular with the natives of his area. In spite of his strength and huge stature, he could walk through the forest as silently as an Indian.

Angélique was aware of his attentions and found them irritating. There was something about this sanguine man with the surprisingly feline step that immediately put her on her guard.

There were moments when she regretted the fact that they had not fought it out that morning. Her husband wanted to settle things by negotiation but her whole instinct and all her memories rejected the notion of conciliation with the French.

Meanwhile the flame-coloured mountain was subsiding and settling down like a tamed beast, and suddenly in the distance, set in the pass the mountain no longer defended, they caught sight of shimmering blue water. In under an hour they had reached the river.

From close to, the Kennebec looked a deep, metallic blue, like armour, and they were surprised to find themselves looking up into the pale sky to see what it was that caused the reflection in the water.

The clouds that had been heaped on the horizon had melted into mist; and the mist, joining with the river haze, had risen towards the heights, where, warmed by the sun's rays, it gave the sky the gentle hue of flax blossom. It was impossible to tell whether the wind would not once again blow the little puffballs into heavy, scudding masses.

But there was one piece of open sky, a limpid, brilliant blue, through which the sun shone in dazzling rays.

Angélique was delighted to catch the whiff of man-made fires.

Then, quite suddenly, she saw the fort.

Her face grew radiant and she stood up in her saddle.

It was set back from the bank in the centre of a clearing from which had been cut the heavy stakes for the palisade. This was rectangular in shape, and nothing appeared above it save the shingle-boarded roofs of two buildings with quietly smoking chimneys. All around the palisade, the land looked rough and chaotic, although green. It had not the symmetry of a garden, nor the rolling lines of a meadow, which was easy to understand once one realized that the stumps of the felled trees had not been cleared from the ground and that the few crops planted outside the palisade were coming up in the midst of gnarled roots and sawn-off stumps. Still, these were the first crops they had encountered during their long trek through the forest, and Angélique's dry lips broke into a smile. She liked the place. After so many wanderings she would be pleased to have a settled home at last.

Pont-Briand was looking at her.

She was oblivious of his stare. She was completely engrossed in what she saw from the top of the hill, an area over which seemed to hang a golden mist composed of mingled smoke and dust.

It was only a remote outpost, without clear boundaries, and looking ridiculously small in the heart of this limitless forest, but for one who had travelled for many a long day without seeing the slightest trace of any human handiwork save a few wretched wigwams, and one or two birch-bark canoes left to rot in some creek, the sight of this piece of land brought promise to the traveller of many missed comforts in a less primitive world.

The river widened out in front of the outpost to form a kind of big peaceful lake across which canoes glided swiftly, light as dragon-flies, some making for a small near-by island, others skirting the banks, while still others set off to join a whole flotilla of light skiffs that lay motionless, side by side, at the southern extremity of the semi-circular beach.

It was still hard to make out the men paddling the canoes, and those who must be moving about on the shore, but the impression was one of movement, like the agitation in an ant-hill which tells one, when still some distance away, that it is inhabited and not deserted.

Farther down, Angélique could see a beach of grey sand and big pebbles, on which had been erected a number of birch-bark tepees, from whose cone-shaped tops white wisps of smoke rose sleepily. The site had clearly been chosen because it was protected from the unpredictable mountain winds.

A long cry heralded the arrival of the caravan, and the Indians, scattered about the outpost, converged in their direction, chattering loudly and uttering ear-splitting whoops as they began to climb the slope to meet them. L'Aubignière must have warned them of the arrival of strange Palefaces, mounted on horseback.

After calling a halt, Joffrey de Peyrac examined the outpost and the beach from his horse.

'Monsieur de Maudreuil!'

'Sir?'

'Is that not a white flag I see flying at the central masthead?'

'Yes indeed, sir! It is the oriflamme of the King of France.'

Peyrac raised his hand to his hat, removed it, and held it at arm's length in a respectful salute, which, for those who knew him well, had a hint of exaggeration about it.

'I bow before the Majesty of him you serve, Baron, and am honoured that he should visit my house in your person.'

'And in that of my superiors,' young Maudreuil retaliated, looking anxious.

'I am delighted at the prospect. . . .'

He put his hat on again. His manner was so lordly that even his friendliness seemed dangerous.

'Nevertheless, custom demands that when a lord returns to his own land, it should be his flag that flies from the masthead. Perhaps you would run ahead, Baron, and give orders to this effect; for it would seem that nobody has thought of this. O'Connel will know where to find my flag.'

'Certainly, my lord,' the young Canadian replied, dashing off along the stony track.

He raced past the Indians as they came up the hill, dived into a spinney and ran on to the fort. Shortly after, the gates were opened, and a blue flag with a silver escutcheon was hauled to the top of the flagpole.

'The arms of Rescator,' Peyrac said softly. 'Theirs may be an obscure glory, perhaps even a dubious one, but surely, Madame, the time has not yet come to strike them without a battle?'

Angélique did not know what reply to make.

Once again she was disconcerted by her husband's attitude.

For her part, she felt that the French had not been entirely straightforward in saying that they had come to Katarunk without hostile intentions. The occupation of a military out-post had never been regarded as evidence of great friendship. But their position had been reversed. Peyrac had arrived, taking them by surprise. And among his friends he numbered Perrot and Maupertuis, men who had been long years in Canada and were held in the highest esteem.

But for all this they were standing on a powder-keg. Angé-lique was horrified to see the host of Indian warriors, the allies of the French troops, who climbed up the hill towards them giving blood-curdling whoops; although, for the time being at least, these were merely cordial manifestations of amusement and welcome.

Joffrey de Peyrac continued his examination of the port and the esplanade through his telescope.

Facing them, the two big gates in the palisade stood wide open.

The soldiers had lined up on either side of the gates as if for an inspection, and a little in front of them stood an officer in full dress uniform, no doubt Loménie-Chambord, whose name had been mentioned to him.

He folded his telescope, bowed his head, and appeared to be deep in thought.

He knew that this was his final opportunity to answer force with force. Once this moment had gone he would be in the lion's mouth.

He and his men were about to mingle with a changeable band that could from one moment to the next turn into ferocious enemies.

Everything would depend on the good faith of the colonel, and on his influence over his men, in a word, on the wisdom of the man with whom Peyrac was about to find himself face to face, the man who represented the King of France.

He looked again. Through the telescope he saw the dis-tinguished figure of a man who stood, hands behind his back, apparently waiting fearlessly on the arrival of the master of Katarunk announced to him by Maudreuil.

'Let's go,' said Peyrac.

He asked those on horseback to line up behind him, placed the Spaniards in their breast-plates at the head of the column with their arms, followed by Florimond and Cantor bearing his banners, then his men, each carrying his musket and a piece of lighted touchwood.

Indians loomed up on all sides, intensely curious. Nicolas Perrot, struggling with every language he knew, greeted them, and at the same time asked them to be a little quieter, for the horses, alarmed by the sudden din, the hurly-burly of plumes, painted faces, bows, and brandished tomahawks, had begun to neigh and to shy. At last the procession got under way, and soon Wallis's delicate hooves were treading along the river's edge between a double line of soldiers. Peyrac had asked Angé-lique to remain beside him. She felt embarrassed by Honorine's bare feet, and would also have liked to tidy her own hair, but it was as much as she could do to keep her horse walking slowly in parade step. After the loneliness of the vast open spaces, they were now the cynosure of the eyes of a noisy, feathered, brown-skinned crowd of strong-smelling people, all wanting to see and touch them.

Perrot, the trappers, and the Sagamores, chieftains of the various assembled tribes, shouted in vain to keep the more frenzied members of the crowd away from the horses. Wallis of course reared up, her hooves lashing out at some of the greasy heads. Then she bolted at a gallop down to the river's edge. Angélique managed to bring her to a halt and force her back, quivering but docile and magnificent before the aston-ished gaze of the hysterical mass of Indian spectators, who were whooping with delight. Apart from this incident, which was clearly regarded as a welcome interlude, the arrival of Count Peyrac and his followers at Katarunk took place as protocol demanded.

He sat motionless before the open wooden gates, his wife beside him, his companions behind, while the two Canadian drummer-boys, in their blue military uniform, came forward to meet him, drums rolling. Behind them at a slow march came six soldiers and sergeants to form a guard of honour, im-maculately turned-out in spite of its small size and the speed with which it had been organized.

The colonel came forward, dressed in the blue frock-coat with gold frogging worn by the officers of the Carignan-Salière regiment, adorned with chamois-leather revers on sleeves and collar, and big guilloched buttons.

He was a distinguished-looking man of about forty; he wore knee-boots, and his sword at his side was tied with a white sash, which, for a soldier in the field, showed a determination to keep his turn-out up to regulation standard. His short pointed beard, a trifle old-fashioned, suited his distinguished face with its fine, handsome features; his tanned cheeks and forehead made his calm, grey, penetrating eyes look pale in comparison.

What struck Angélique about him was above all the gentleness that seemed to emanate from him, like a kind of diffuse, inward light.

He was not wearing a wig, but his hair was well cared for.

He saluted, one hand on the hilt of his sword, and introduced himself.

'Count Loménie-Chambord, leader of the lake Megantic expedition.'

'A great name!' Peyrac replied, bowing his head. 'Monsieur de Loménie, am I to understand that the position of my modest outpost here has simply served as a secure place to bivouac? Or must I consider your presence here, along with your native allies, as a seizure of my territory?'

'A seizure! Heaven preserve!' the other man exclaimed. 'Monsieur de Peyrac, we know you are French, although not a representative of the King, our master; but no one in Quebec would dream of considering your presence here as damaging to the interests of New France – far from it! At least, that is before you have given us cause to think so.'

'That is precisely my view of the matter, and I am delighted that we have removed any possible misunderstanding between us. I shall in no way harm the interests of New France, neither by my work, nor by my presence beside the Kennebec, provided no one tries to harm mine. That is an undertaking that you may give in so many words to your governor.'

Loménie bowed again without replying. Although his career brought him considerable experience of delicate situations, the one in which he found himself involved on this occasion seemed to him the most astonishing of all. People had indeed begun to tell all sorts of tales throughout Canada about this French adventurer, of obscure background, who was prospecting for precious metals, manufacturing gunpowder, was a friend of the English to boot, and who, for more than a year, had decided to stake out claims somewhere in the vast, undeveloped depths of French Acadia. But their actual meeting had proved a far livelier event than could ever have been imagined.

This fantastic story must be reported to Quebec and was indeed of unusual interest. A group of Europeans had arrived from the south, on horseback, not by water, travelling through regions which had never before heard the sound of a horse neighing. There were women and children among them. And their leader was a masked rider, slow-spoken and gruff-voiced, who from the very outset had adopted a position of command and authority – as if two hundred armed savages, allies of the French, and ready to rush into action at the slightest sign, had not been there at all, bearing in on him and his tiny party on all sides.

Count Loménie liked courage, he liked the grand manner.

When he looked up again, there was a respect and a sudden, spontaneous warmth in his eyes. 'Perhaps this is what falling in love at first sight is like, if it can apply to friendship. . . .' he thought.

He wrote these words many years later to Father Daniel de Maubeuge in a letter dated September 1682, which was in fact never finished. In it he described his first meeting with Count Peyrac, and in spite of the lapse of time, he remembered every detail, with admiration tinged with sadness.

'That evening,' he wrote, 'beside a wild river in the midst of the wilderness we have tried in vain to win over to civilized Christian thought, I knew that I had encountered one of the most extraordinary men of our time. There he sat, on horseback, and I do not know, Father, if you appreciate just what the words "on horseback" signify, unless you have ever dragged your boots through the cursed, majestic country of the upper Kennebec. There he was, surrounded by his wife, children, young men, all of them having undergone great hardship, the women unaware of their own courage, the children contented, the young men daring and passionate. He did not seem to realize what a feat he had just accomplished, or perhaps he did realize it but cared little. I had the feeling that this man lived his life on a superior plane, but with all the simplicity that people bring to their daily actions. And I began to envy him. All this took place in a flash as I tried to penetrate the secret of his black mask.'

The drums continued their muffled rolling, which beat an accompaniment to no one knew what potential drama.

Loménie walked up to the horse and looked up at the masked rider. His simple greatness had made him loved by all around him. One could see from his calm, honest eyes that cunning and fear were unknown to him.

'Monsieur,' he said, coming straight to the point, 'I think that you and I shall never need many words to understand one another. I also think that we have just become friends. Would you be willing to give me a token of your friendship?'

Peyrac examined him carefully. 'I might. What kind of token do you have in mind?'

'A friend has no need to hide his face from his friends. Would you show us your face.'

Peyrac hesitated slightly, then a ghost of a smile flitted across his face and he raised his hands to the back of his head to untie his leather mask.

He took it off and put it away in his doublet.

The French showed considerable curiosity and stood silent examining his face, the face of a *condottière*, marked with the scars of battle. It was a face that told them they were up against no mean adversary.

'Thank you,' said Loménie gravely.

And he added with a trace of humour :

'Now that I can see you, I feel convinced that it was a good thing we reached an understanding with you.'

Their eyes met, then Peyrac burst out laughing :

'Monsieur de Loménie-Chambord, I like you.'

He leapt down from his horse, throwing the reins to one of his servants. Then he took off his glove and the two men shook hands vigorously.

'I too anticipate that our friendship will be to our mutual advantage,' Peyrac went on. 'I trust you found everything you needed here in Katarunk to refresh you after your campaign?'

'More than enough; your outpost is undoubtedly as well equipped as anyone could hope for. I must confess that my officers and I have ... er ... made some inroads into your stocks of excellent wine. Let it be clearly understood that we will pay you back, if not in wines of such high quality, which we would be unable to send you, at least by the advantage of our presence here in case of any threat from the Iroquois. They are said to be on the prowl in the region.'

'We took a prisoner yesterday, a Mohawk, but he escaped,' Lieutenant Pont-Briand interposed.

'We too ran into a party of Cayugas in the south,' said Pey-rac.

'That treacherous tribe has infiltrated the whole area,' Count Loménie sighed.

As he spoke his glance fell on Nicolas Perrot, and it became apparent that his eyes, which to Angélique had appeared so gentle, could also take on a look of great sternness. The look he gave to Peyrac's right-hand man would have made anyone other than this easy-going trapper wish the earth would open and swallow him up.

'Is that you, Nicolas, or am I dreaming? Count Loménie asked coldly.

'Yes it's me, my lord,' Perrot replied cheerfully, his face lighting up in a broad smile. 'Delighted to see you again ...'

And with a spontaneous gesture, he went down on one knee in front of the officer, took the hand that was not being offered him, and kissed it.

'I have never forgotten the marvellous battles you led us in in the past against the Iroquois, sir. How often have I thought of you during my travels ...'

'You would have done better to think about your wife and child whom you abandoned in Canada, without giving them any news of your whereabouts for the past three years.'

The unfortunate Perrot hung his head in confusion at this reprimand, and stood up with an expression on his face like a scolded child.

The French soldiers had broken ranks and hastened to hold the ladies' horses. They were now able to dismount, and to the accompaniment of much hat raising, they made for the gates of the outpost.

Seen from close to, it was in fact, as Peyrac had said, more a trading post than a fortified position to defend a strategic point. The palisade was scarcely taller than a man, and the only artillery it possessed consisted of four small culverins set at the corners facing the river.

Inside, the place looked more like a sheepfold, it was so crowded with people and miscellaneous objects. Merely to walk across it was quite an adventure. The first thing Angélique noticed were the carcasses of two black bears, slit open and hanging like monstrous scarlet water-melons, which the Indians were beginning to carve up skilfully.

'There, you see, we shall not need to touch your stocks of

venison,' said Monsieur de Loménie, 'hunting went well today and our savages have decided to hold a feast straight away. There are two more animals already cooking in the cauldrons. And with a good bag of bustards and turkeys, everyone will be able to eat his fill, and tomorrow too.'

'Could you tell me if the cottage is available?' Peyrac asked. 'I would like to put up my wife and daughter there, so that they can get some rest, and the women and children with them as well.'

'My officers and I had taken up quarters there, but we shall vacate it. If you can wait just a few moments... Maudreuil, go and check over the cottage!'

Young Baron Maudreuil dashed off, at the double as usual, while Peyrac informed the colonel that one of the members of his escort was the great Sagamore Mopuntook of the Metallaks. Loménie knew him by reputation, but had never met him, and congratulated him warmly, expressing himself in the Abenaki tongue with great fluency.

This great crowd of people moving around began to stir up the dust, which mingled with the smoke from the many fires. The breeze was so gentle here that it did not blow the smoke away. Angélique longed to get away from the noise. At last they managed to cross the courtyard, taking it stage by stage, little by little through a confused jumble of pots and pans, the guts of animals lying around in pools of blood, ashes, glowing fires, kegs and quivers, animal skins and feathers, muskets and powder-barrels. Angélique accidentally stepped on a kind of blue greasy substance which the Indians apparently used to paint their faces. Honorine almost fell into a cooking-pot, Elvire slipped on some slimy entrails, while her two sons were kindly invited by the savages to partake of some raw bear's brain, a delicacy reserved exclusively for men.

They finally reached the door of the house that had been set aside for them. Baron Maudreuil was just coming out, while an Indian of indeterminate race finished sweeping the floor with a broom of leaves. The young ensign had worked hard, and the room they entered was small, but cleared of all unnecessary clutter, and only the merest trace of the inevitable smell of tobacco and leather remained. A big pile of juniper wood had been placed in the central fireplace over a handful of bark, ready to be set ablaze as soon as they began to feel the chill of the evening.

CHAPTER NINE

ANGÉLIQUE COULD not help giving a sigh of relief as soon as the door shut behind them. She collapsed on to a wooden stool standing near by, and Madame Jonas sat down on another. The place was poorly furnished.

'I hope you are not too worn out, my dear?' Angélique asked, thinking sympathetically of the fact that the plucky woman was over fifty.

'Well, you know, the journey itself was all right, but my head is splitting with the noise all that mob made. In this country you seem either not to·see enough people, or too many....'

'How do you feel, Elvire?'

'I'm scared, I'm awfully scared!' the young widow replied. 'All these men are going to slaughter us.'

Master Jonas took a peep out of a crack in the window by lifting one of the pieces of hide serving as a pane, which had come unstuck. His serious, good-natured face revealed that he too was frightened.

Angélique kept her fears to herself, in an attempt to reassure them.

'You must not worry. Here we are under the protection of my husband. The French soldiers have nothing like the power here they have in France.'

'Still they gave us some very queer looks. They must have discovered that we are Huguenots!'

'They must also have noticed that some of our men are Spanish and some even English, whom they regard as far worse enemies than you. But we are a very long way from France, as I said.'

'Yes, that's true!' the watchmaker agreed. He was watching the Indians swarming round the house.

'Don't they look just like the masked carnival figures that you see at home at shrovetide. Some of them have their noses painted blue, their eyes, eyebrows, and cheeks black, and the rest of their faces red. What a masquerade!'

The little boys went over to the window and looked out too. Angélique took off her right boot and scraped the sole with a penknife to remove the remainder of the blueish paint clinging to it.

'I wonder what ingredients they use to make these paints. The colour is very fast. It would be wonderful to paint one's eyelids with before going to a ball. . . .'

Then she took off her stocking to look at a bruise on her ankle which had been hurting her for some days.

The door burst open and there stood Lieutenant Pont-Briand on the threshold, petrified as he realized that he had forgotten to knock.

'Please forgive me,' he stammered, 'I was bringing you . . . some candles.' In spite of himself he could not take his eyes off Angélique's bare leg and foot resting on the hearthstone.

She pulled down her skirt and gave him a haughty look.

'Please come in, Lieutenant, and thank you for your kindness.'

The lieutenant was accompanied by two men carrying the baggage. As they deposited the bags and the tawed leather trunks in a corner, the lieutenant himself placed candles in brass candlesticks on the table, with a pitcher of beer and some drinking mugs, talking incessantly to cover up his blunder.

'Do take a little refreshment, ladies. I have no doubt your ride must have been long and difficult. My comrades and I are full of admiration for your courage. Do not hesitate to tell me if there is anything I can do to make you more comfortable. I will bring you anything you ask for. Monsieur de Loménie-Chambord has instructed Monsieur de Maudreuil and me to place ourselves at your disposal, while he receives Monsieur le Comte de Peyrac. I would advise you, if possible, not to budge outside this evening; there are a lot of Indians here and they have decided to hold a celebration. They could be a nuisance. Tomorrow, most of them will be going on their way and you will be able to get to know the place better. In any event, do not let any of them in here and keep your eye on your possessions. It is not so much on account of the Abenakis or the Algonquins that I say this, but because there are a lot of Hurons among them and, according to a well-known Canadian proverb: who says Huron says thief.'

As he spoke he gave an occasional bold glance towards Angélique. But she was paying little heed to his words and was waiting impatiently for him to leave them. She was weary. She ached all over. Although primitive, the outpost of Katarunk would have delighted her had they been able to arrive as masters of the place. As it was, notwithstanding the protestations of friendship they had received, their situation was far from agreeable. The place was still not their own, and she could see what turn events were going to take. Her husband would be entirely taken up by his self-invited guests and forced to keep an eye on them. For a start, she would not see him that evening, and she would indeed be lucky if he did not set off the following day on some reconnaissance goodness knows where, leaving her in this stinking hole full of cheeky Indians whose language she could not even speak.

With a sudden unconscious movement she threw off her big hat which felt too tight across her forehead and, throwing back her head, she closed her eyes and ran her hand over her brow, which was beginning to ache.

Pont-Briand fell silent and his heart rose into his mouth. My goodness, she was lovely! So lovely she took your breath away.

Angélique looked at him, thought he looked thoroughly stupid and had to restrain a shrug.

'Thank you for your kindness, sir,' she said somewhat coldly, 'and please believe me when I say that my companions and I have not the slightest desire to mingle with these savages, nor any intention of losing our few possessions to gratify their acquisitive instincts. My daughter is already without shoes. She left them beside a lake. And I cannot begin to imagine how I shall ever get hold of a pair of shoes to fit her.'

Pont-Briand stammered out that he would take care of that. He would ask one of the Indian women to make some moccasins for the child and tomorrow she would be shod. He backed over towards the door, snatching up some items of uniform that had been left lying on a bench, and found himself on the doorstep with his mind about as sharp and unsteady as if he had drunk three glasses of Canadian rye brandy.

'By jove!' he muttered between his teeth, 'what's up? Is something actually going to happen in this god-forsaken country?'

Love began to stir in him like a serpent. He felt it stealing over him with an inner shudder. It was like the excitement one felt when hunting or fighting, and he could not understand it. But life had acquired a new savour for him and, as he crossed the courtyard, he lifted his face to the sky and gave a wild whoop, an explosion of sheer uncontrolled delight.

'Why are you giving your victory cry?' asked some of the Indians near by.

He launched into an imitation of their syncopated dance round the camp fire, their war dance, with brandished tomahawks and arrows. The Indians laughed. They in their turn began to dance too, interspersing their movements with sudden strident whoops that rent the air above them.

'What a din!' Angélique sighed.

The noise sent horrible shudders down her spine, and she took Honorine in her arms and clasped her wildly to her. The threat of violent death hung everywhere, infesting the very air they breathed. She could taste it on her tongue. How could she explain what she felt? That was America – violent death surrounded you wherever you went but you had the right to live and defend yourself.

'Madame,' Elvire called, 'come and see. There are two rooms beside this one, three in fact, with beds in them, and each one has a fireplace. We shall be very comfortable here.'

The tiny bedrooms had been built around the central chimney as if round a pillar, which made it possible for each room to have its own fireplace. The chimney itself was pretty rough, and appeared to have been constructed with stones from the river bonded together with mortar made of sand, lime, and gravel. The rustic beds, some with posts made of logs, which had not even been stripped of their bark, had moss-filled mattresses but were made with comfortable looking woollen blankets and furs. The bed in the room on the right was a well-made piece of furniture, elegant but solidly built, with a tester and curtains of coarse brocade held back by cords. There was another less elaborate bed in the room on the left, also with curtains round it. The room at the back contained several low beds with logs for legs, but they were all covered with woollen blankets or furs. Elvire decided that she would sleep here with the three children.

The two Jonases would sleep in the room on the left and Madame de Peyrac in the one on the right. As a matter of fact, they had already automatically placed her trunk in there. There was something about the furnishing of this little rustic room, which was more akin to a woodcutter's hut than to a room in a farm-house, with its walls made of great logs that had hardly even been squared up, that told Angélique that this was the room that Joffrey de Peyrac had used himself the year before when he had stayed at Katarunk. As she drew back a curtain that covered some roughly-made shelves she discovered a collection of leather-bound books with titles in Latin, Greek, and Arabic.

The other rooms must have been intended for his sons or for his right-hand man whom he always took with him. He regarded this place only as a camp, a road-post, a place for men to live among men; but she recognized his touch in the details, in his love of comfort, in a certain felicity he had always shown in his choice of the objects that surrounded him. The chandelier that stood on the vast table in one corner was of wrought brass. Its delicate curves were a pleasure to look at, although its beauty seemed strange and somewhat out of place in this hut in the depths of the woods. Unfortunately, no one had bothered to remove the mountains of wax which had trickled down on to it, as candle after candle had burned low during the past few evenings. The hearthstone was furnished with handsomely forged fire-dogs, but the floor was strewn with ash, and pieces of charred wood. Everything was in the usual untidy mess characteristic of the military. Young Maudreuil had obviously not had time to arrange for the cleaning of the bedrooms as well as the main room.

Angélique realized that the first thing to do was to set to work with a broom. There were some besoms, made of leaves or twigs, standing in corners, and the women set about trying to purge their quarters of all traces of the barrack-room. When they had finished, they decided that they liked their little well-sheltered house with its four fireplaces, in which the logs were soon crackling merrily. They were anxious to leave their mark on the place, to make it their own, to impress on it their personal habits of tidiness and cleanliness, so that they could feel well and truly at home, and no longer wanderers and vagabonds as they had been for the past three long weeks.

Once the door was well shut, and the latch well latched, they began to feel more and more at ease. Master Jonas sat down in front of his fire and set about drying out his shoes and stockings, which had been soaking wet ever since they had crossed the last marsh. Elvire undressed the three children and washed them.

After finishing her sweeping, Angélique looked round to see if she could not find some sheets for the beds. Leaning the lid of a chest back against the wall of her room she discovered a large mirror fixed to the inside. This too, she thought, was the hand of Joffrey de Peyrac. It was a friendly surprise, a mark of the unspoken bond between them.

'Oh, how I adore him,' she thought.

She stayed where she was, kneeling in front of the chest, looking at herself. She was resting. There was no linen in the chest, only some men's clothes. After looking them over, she stood up again and shut the lid of the chest. Those few moments in front of a mirror had made her long to change into something more elegant. She opened her own trunk. First of all she found a clean shift for Honorine. Fortunately, the children were sleepy, and they were able to put them to bed in the little back room where they were less likely to be disturbed by the noise from the courtyard.

Madame Jonas had found a big cauldron in the shed to hang from the pot-hook. Someone would have to fetch water, but not one of the three women felt she had the courage to face the crowds in the courtyard which they would have to cross to reach the well. Master Jonas said he would go, and he returned accompanied by a swarm of Indians who crowded round the doorway to see the white women. They would never have thought of carrying his load for him; for they considered it scandalous that a 'tcheno', an elderly man, should be given this chore to perform while his womenfolk stood idle. The little house came very near to being invaded by an excited horde of evil-smelling natives who refused to be put off.

'I have never met a more brazen lot than these barbarians,' said the watchmaker, dusting himself down and wiping his brow when at last the door had been closed and barricaded. 'Once they've decided to pick on you, there's no shaking them off.'

To avoid having to send him on a second expedition, the ladies decided to share out the precious water between them for their ablutions.

They hung the cauldron over the fire which was crackling merrily. And as they waited for the water to get hot, they sat round the fire and poured out some beer.

This time there were several light taps on the door, and Nicolas Perrot appeared with a large loaf of wheat bread, some cold meat, and some blackberries, raspberries, and mulberries in a small basket. His Indian servant carried in a supply of logs.

They were cheered by the food and took some to the children, who fell fast asleep before finishing the last mouthful.

'But what's all this about your being married and having a child, Nicolas?' Angélique asked. 'You never told us anything about it.'

'I didn't know,' the trapper replied hastily, growing very red.

'What do you mean you didn't know you were married?'

'No, I mean I didn't know I had a child. I left immediately afterwards.'

'After what?'

'After the wedding, of course! You see, I was forced into it. If I had not got married, I would have had to pay an enormous fine and at the time I was hard up. The trouble was I had been condemned for trading without a permit from the Governor of Canada, and they threatened to excommunicate me into the bargain for selling brandy to the Indians. So you see, I preferred to get married. . . . It was easier.'

'What had you done to the poor girl to be forced into that?' Madame Jonas asked.

'Nothing. I didn't even know her.'

'Really?'

'She was one of the King's Girls, and she had only just landed in Canada. I understand she is a nice respectable sort of a girl.'

'You're not sure?'

'I didn't have time to find out.'

'Do explain yourself a bit better, Nicolas,' said Angélique. 'We can't understand a word of what you are saying.'

'It is simple enough. The King of France wants to build up the population of his colony, so from time to time he sends over a boat-load of young women and all the bachelors in the place are forced to marry within a fortnight, under pain of paying a large fine, or even being sent to prison. So you see, when I was asked, I did it. But afterwards, off I went back to my savages. . . .'

'Did you find your wife as bad as all that?' Elvire asked.

'I've not the faintest idea, we didn't have time to get acquainted, as I said.'

'Enough time, though, to become a father,' Angélique remarked.

'But I had to. If she had complained that the marriage had not been consummated I would have been in for another fine.'

'So, the very next morning after your wedding night off you went without a backward glance. And have you never had any regrets these last three years, Nicolas?' Angélique asked, with feigned severity.

'As a matter of fact I haven't!' the trapper admitted with a sigh. 'But I must say that since Monsieur de Loménie gave me that old-fashioned look earlier on today, I do feel a bit uneasy. That man is the most saintly person I know. It's a pity he and I are not more alike,' Nicolas concluded with a wry smile.

In spite of the shortage of water, Angélique enjoyed her wash in front of the fire in her bedroom. She had brought with her two dresses which might have seemed unnecessarily elegant for these wild regions, but she had decided that, even if there was no one to admire her, she should still be able to take pleasure in her appearance. What was more, she did have her husband, her young sons and even Honorine to think of; in short it was a matter of prestige! Why should she not from time to time give them a glimpse of an elegant woman, like those in the faraway cities, where coaches pass along the streets, and where, behind every window, eyes peer and mouths exclaim 'have you seen Madame X's new dress?'

So she put on her silvery-grey dress, with the silver braid outlining the seams of the sleeves and shoulders, and a lawn collar and revers edged with fine silver lace. She freed her hair from her headdress and gave it a thorough brushing with the gold and tortoiseshell brushes from the exquisite toilet set her husband had given her before they left Gouldsboro. It gave her a sense of well-being to feel these luxurious articles in her hand.

Before they set off on their journey, Angélique had asked her friend Abigail Berne to trim her long hair.

Now she wore it at about shoulder length, where it made a golden frame round her face.

It was thick silky hair, that fell in broad waves and curled lightly at the ends, and she wore a slight fringe over her sunburned forehead.

There was something a trifle coquettish and provocative in the way Angélique de Peyrac made the most of her hair. For, although she was only thirty-seven, a few premature white hairs mingled already with the dazzling gold. But this did not worry her; she realized that their silver sheen gave an elusive charm to her astonishingly youthful face.

She bent over the mirror in the chest to fix a little pearl-studded diadem in her hair.

As she did so a shadow moved across the yellow parchment of the window and fingers came to rest on it, their tips making small round spots ringed with light, while the nails scratched lightly on the surface.

CHAPTER TEN

AFTER A MOMENT'S hesitation, Angélique lifted the wooden latch and drew one of the roughly-made shutters of the little window towards her.

A man stood leaning forward with an air of mystery and looking all round him as if fearing to be noticed. She recognized young Yann, the Breton lad who had been a member of the crew of the *Gouldsboro* and whom Monsieur de Peyrac had brought along with him as a skilled carpenter and a man capable of standing up to fatigue and hardship.

'Madame la Comtesse.'

'Yes?'

He smiled, looking a trifle embarrassed, as if about to make a joke, then suddenly he blurted out:

'Monsieur de Peyrac wants to shoot your mare Wallis. He says she is vicious and that he made up his mind yesterday to get rid of her.'

Then he disappeared. Angélique had scarcely had time to hear what he said, let alone to grasp its implications. She leaned out and called:

'Yann!'

He had vanished! The window was at the back of the house, near the palisade, and the space outside served as a storage space for a whole arsenal: muskets, arquebuses, bows and quivers, along with fur cloaks, leather jackets, and uniforms. There were enough savages wandering around for her call to attract their unwelcome attentions. She saw them turn at the sound and quickly shut the window again. Then, leaning on the frame, she began to think of what the young Breton had said, and the implication of his warning began to sink in. Almost at once, she felt the full force of the blow and her eyes blazed. So angry was she that her heart began to pound in her breast and she almost choked. She stumbled around the room looking for her coat, for it had grown quite dark. The very idea of killing Wallis, her mare, whom she had brought through to safety after such incredible difficulties!

It was by this sort of behaviour that men gave women the impression they did not exist, that they did not count! And it was a feeling that no human being worthy of the name, even if she were of the weaker sex, could endure without protest.

So Joffrey wanted to put down Wallis, did he, and without even telling her! Wallis, the mare Angélique had ridden until her back and her wrists were nearly broken, ridden with her life sometimes at stake! After all the work she had put in to calm her, break her in, force her to accept this uncivilized land, every square yard of which seemed to cause this hypersensitive animal insuperable terror and repulsion! There were some smells which neither the mare nor Angélique could stomach, the smell of the Indians, for example, or of the undergrowth in the eternal forest untamed by the hand of man. The mare was suffering in both body and spirit from the strange, unfamiliar world it had been compelled to face: the vastness of the country, its uncultivated wildness, the latent hostility of nature turned in on itself, and it almost seemed to suffer physical pain in setting its delicate hooves on the virgin land. How many a time had Angélique asked the blacksmith from Burgundy who was travelling behind her, to take a look at its shoes. But he could find nothing; the agony was all in Wallis's mind. And yet her mistress had succeeded, or almost....

She was about to sweep like a whirlwind through the other room, when she halted.

She must control her violent impulses a little in order not to get the young Breton into trouble. He had shown considerable courage coming to tell her what was going on when he had not been instructed to do so. Joffrey de Peyrac was a master whose decisions no one ever questioned.

Lack of discipline, and even mistakes, were dearly paid for under his command. Yann le Couennec must have hesitated a great deal before he acted.

He was a lad who showed a certain delicacy of feeling compared with his coarser companions. During the trek he had frequently made himself useful to Madame de Peyrac, by holding her horse's bridle on a slope, or by rubbing the mare down when they halted for the night, and the two of them had become firm friends.

So that evening when he heard that the Count had given orders to destroy the mare, he had decided to come and warn her. Angélique resolved to remain calm when she discussed the matter with her husband, and not to mention the young man's name.

She quickly picked up and wrapped around herself a purply-pink taffeta cloak lined with wolfskin which she had not yet had occasion to wear.

Madame Jonas threw up her hands when she caught sight of her.

'Are you thinking of going to a ball, my lady Angélique?'

'No, I am only going to visit the gentlemen in the other building. I have something of the greatest urgency to say to my husband.'

'No, you must not go,' protested Master Jonas. 'All those Indians... ! It is no place for any woman to be alone in the midst of all those savages!'

'I only have to cross the courtyard,' said Angélique as she opened the door.

The din outside struck her like a blow in the face.

CHAPTER ELEVEN

THE SUN had not quite set and a golden glow from the West bathed the scene in a diffuse, powdery radiance, a tinted haze of mingled dust, smoke, and steam.

The insipid sweet smell of boiled maize rose in a cloud from huge black cooking-pots suspended over the three fires. The soldiers were doling out the mush in big wooden ladles, and the natives crowded round the stewpots holding out their birch-bark or wooden bowls or even their hands cupped together to receive their steaming portion, without appearing in any way troubled by the heat.

Angélique reached the door of the main building, which was guarded somewhat casually by a sentry who was busy swapping tobacco leaves with the Indians for half a dozen black otter skins.

She did not bother to ask his permission to enter the room in which she hoped to find Count Peyrac. He was there, as she had expected, making merry with a motley crowd of men among whom she found it hard to pick out Count Loménie and his lieutenants. The main room of the outpost was so thick with smoke that it seemed almost dark inside, although they had already lighted the oil-lamps on the walls. But through the swathes of smoke their light was yellow and flickering like that of distant stars.

Opening the door helped to clear some of the haze, letting in a bit of fresh air and some light from outside. Angélique noticed that the room, which was fairly big, was occupied from the threshold, which consisted of two steps, right to the fireplace at the back, by a long solid wooden table, which was laden with steaming dishes, brass goblets and a few flagons of smoked glass, as well as a big pot-bellied earthenware jug running over with white froth and smelling of beer. After the smell of tobacco this sour smell was the strongest, followed by that of hot fat and boiled meat, and the more diffuse and complex scent of leather and fur; and over and above everything else, mingling with the other scents like a delicate, piercing counterpoint heard through the sounds of many other instruments, hung the subtle aroma of brandy.

The men had their pipes in their mouths, and a glass or goblet stood within reach of every hand. Their knives were being busily plied, cutting up pieces of meat, and their jaws were actively at work. Their tongues too; the noise of conversation in the raucous Indian tongue mingled with the smacking of lips as they seized their food, to form a continuous uproar in the background which, from time to time, was broken by a burst of laughter like a thunderclap. Then the eating and talking would rumble on again.

In the middle of the table she caught sight of Sagamore Mopuntook wiping his hands on his long plaits, and not far from him, the Huron Odessonik wearing the gold-braided felt hat belonging to Lieutenant Fallières. Angélique almost had the impression that she had burst right into an Indian camp. But the Indian chieftains were only guests, as was the custom, at the Palefaces' table, and it was in fact the Palefaces, however odd they might appear, who were busy feasting as dusk fell on that October day. They were celebrating a meeting all the more accidental for having taken place at an almost unknown spot on the continent, between people who, coming from different directions, had each secretly hoped to avoid the other party or to give it a thorough mauling. Beneath their apparant cordiality they were watching one another. Their inner tensions and conflicting ideas were not apparent. Count Loménie-Chambord was possibly sincere in saying that he considered himself fortunate to have encountered Count Peyrac under such peaceful circumstances, but Don José Alvarez, Peyrac's Spanish captain, looking sombre and disdainful as he sat between an Indian and a Frenchman, was irritated by the presence of these intruders in a land which the decisions of the Pope had, since the year 1506 and for all eternity, assigned to their Most Catholic Majesties the King and Queen of Spain.

The Irishman O'Connell, as ruddy as a tomato, was considering what sort of explanation he would give his master Count Peyrac when he asked him later about the invasion of the post. The two or three French trappers who had come with Peyrac from the south of Dawn-East hoped they would not have to give any account of what they had been up to during the previous year to their trapper friends from the north; some, like L'Aubignière, had made their way to the trading post on the Kennebec with the vague idea of meeting the new fur dealer, not with the idea of running into soldiers and officers of his Majesty Louis XIV's army.

As for Eloi Macollet, a very old man who, a couple of months back, had escaped from the loving care of his daughter-in-law in the village of Levis near Quebec, and had paddled off into the depths of the forest with the firm intention of never setting eyes on another human being, no, nothing but bears or moose, or at a pinch a few beavers, he was busy telling himself that America was no longer a country for folk with a taste for solitude. The land had been completely 'spoiled'. With his red woollen hat decorated with two turkey feathers pulled right down to his bushy eyebrows, the old man mulled over his grievances as he chewed away at his briar pipe; but the alcohol helped and by the time he had reached the third glass his eyes had regained their merry sparkle and he told himself that at least his daughter-in-law would never find him here, and that meanwhile it was quite enjoyable to find oneself among friends at a well organized 'napeopounano', or 'bear festival', which is celebrated, according to rite, exclusively in male company, after blowing tobacco smoke down the animal's nostrils and throwing a mouthful of meat and a spoonful of fat on the fire for luck.

Pont-Briand, who had killed the bear, had been the first to

taste it, cutting himself a piece from round the neck and distributing the rump, which was considered a real delicacy, among his friends. It was autumn, the season in which bears, having gorged themselves on whortleberries, are particularly tasty.

No sooner had the old man come to the end of this train of thought than he almost choked on a small bone and spat it out with an oath. He thought he had seen his daughter-in-law suddenly appear through the smoke. No, it was not Sidonie! But it was a woman standing on the threshold looking at them all.

A woman in a 'napeopounano'! What sacrilege! A woman in the heart of the wildest territory south of the Chaudière, a region no one likes to drop down to when coming from Saint-Lawrence, and up to which those who come from the shores of Acadia on the Atlantic never go, where in fact no one would go were there not from time to time a few heretics to scalp in New England.

The old man began to bellow inarticulately and to wave his arms about amid the wreaths of smoke and thick steam rising from the maize gruel. His neighbour François Maupertuis – can you believe it? That feller had disappeared the year before, and everyone thought he had frozen among the Mistassins – pushed him down on to his chair again, saying 'calm down, Grandad!'

The Sagamore raised a hand and, pointing to the woman, began to speak in solemn tones. He started to tell an involved story about a turtle and the Iroquois, saying that this woman had overcome the turtle and had the right to sit among the warriors.

So it was not a 'napeopounano' any more, the men's feast, but a 'mokouchano', and old Eloi needn't have bothered to come so far just to avoid meeting a piece of skirt, and in any case these Metallaks from Lake Umbagog were the most idiotic of all the Algonquins. Yes, of course they were hunters, for the region was a hunter's paradise, but they were still the most stupid of all Indians; for one could not even teach them to make the sign of the cross.

'Oh shut up you old dotard,' François Maupertuis bawled at him, pulling his hat down over his eyes. 'Aren't you ashamed of yourself, insulting a lady?'

Maupertuis's beard was trembling with indignation and excitement. He found Angélique tremendously impressive as she appeared through the blue haze of tobacco smoke, with her fair, shining hair gilded by the evening light as it streamed in through the open door. He scarcely recognized her. And yet he had come all the way from Gouldsboro with her, in the caravan. But she was no longer the same woman, with her hair hanging free and wrapped in that huge cloak that was the colour of the sky at sunrise. She looked as if she had stepped right out of a picture frame, one of those pictures you see in the home of the Governor of Quebec, with her hair over her shoulders and her white hand peeping out from a lace cuff and resting on the rugged wood. She appeared delicate now, no longer the tough horsewoman of the past week.

The trapper tried to go to her rescue, tripped over his stool and fell headfirst on to the cobbled floor. Clasping his battered nose, he swore at O'Connell's treacherous brandy, saying that the Irishman must add fermented barley and boiled roots to it to make it so strong.

Angélique, hesitating between laughter and fear, told herself that, all things considered, she had never seen so handsome a collection of men, even back in the days when she ran the Red Mask Tavern. And among these men, her own husband was by no means the least formidable!

He had not yet noticed her coming in, but was sitting at the far end of the table, smoking his long Dutch pipe as he talked to Monsieur de Loménie. Whenever he laughed, she caught the flash of his teeth clenched round the stem of his pipe. His profile stood out clear-cut and black against the dancing flames in the hearth.

There was something about the appearance of the room which reminded Angélique irresistibly of the past: the great Count of Toulouse entertaining his guests in the Palace of Gay-Savoir in the midst of gold plate and exotic dishes. There too, he had sat at the head of the table while behind him the flames in the vast chimney with its armorial plaque and sculptured pediment cast their cheerful, dancing light over velvet, crystal, and lace.

This scene was like a parody of those happy days. Everything seemed to have conspired to make Angélique aware of how both her husband and she had fallen over the years. Their table was no longer graced with elegant lords and ladies, but with all manner of men of a strain of coarseness produced by the lives they led – harsh, dangerous lives, lives given over entirely to the vicissitudes of warfare and hunting.

Even the distinction of Count Loménie seemed diminished in this unduly masculine atmosphere of tobacco, leather, game, alcohol, and gunpowder.

She noticed that he too had sunburnt skin, the teeth of a meat-eating animal, and the dreamy, fixed gaze of a tobacco smoker.

She realized that Joffrey de Peyrac had also become attuned to this rough world.

Life on the ocean with its tempests, unending battles, struggles to the death, daily fighting with sword or pistol in hand, for the success of one's ambitions, for the control of one's men, for the achieving of some object, or the conquest of nature at its most extreme – desert, ocean, or forest – had emphasized the adventurous side of his nature which, in the past, she had sometimes glimpsed beneath the elegance of the great lord and the measured gestures of the scholar. He had led men into battle through sheer necessity, but also because he enjoyed it, and he had made his life among men.

Angélique made as if to withdraw.

But Pont-Briand had leapt to his feet in his turn, and managed, unlike Maupertuis, to remain on his two feet and walk over to where Angélique stood. In any case, he was not drunk, having imbibed a mere two glasses of brandy to liven himself up.

'My compliments, Madame.'

He offered her his hand and helped her descend the two steps, then led her towards the middle of the table to find her a chair. She hesitated, resisting a little.

'Monsieur, I fear that my presence may offend the Indian chiefs. I am told that they do not welcome women at their banquets.'

The Sagamore Mopuntook, who was sitting close by, raised one hand and said something, which Pont-Briand immediately translated for Angélique's benefit.

'You see, Madame, the Sagamore is saying that you are worthy of a place among the braves for you have vanquished the emblem of the Iroquois. . . . So please do not hesitate to grant us the pleasure of your company.'

With a few vigorous shoves, he cleared a place in the middle of the table. Finding himself unable to catch Corporal Jeanson, whom he had pushed a little too roughly to one side and who was struggling to get up from under the table, he found a handsome young colossus, pushed him down beside Angélique on her right and seated himself on her left.

Pont-Briand's intervention and Mopuntook's speech had attracted everyone's attention; the buzz of voices ceased and everyone turned in Angélique's direction.

She would have preferred to sit beside her husband and tell him immediately why she had come. But she found it difficult to escape the peremptory welcome the lieutenant and his friends had given her. Her neighbour on her right leaned foreward and tried to kiss her hand, but he was seized with an uncontrollable fit of hiccoughs and missed his aim, excusing himself with a smile.

'Let me introduce myself; Romain de l'Aubignière! I think you must have seen me already. Forgive me, I am a little hazy. If you had come a trifle earlier ... but don't worry, I am still sober enough not to insult you by seeing double and thinking that there is another woman on this earth as lovely as you are. I can see one and that is enough. I assure you that you are the one and only ...'

Angélique began to laugh, but her laugh froze on her face as her eyes lighted on the young man's hands. The left hand had the thumb and middle finger missing and the right lacked the fourth finger. His remaining fingers were all swollen at the ends, some of them had no nails, only horn-like blackened skin in their place. When he had been introduced to her in the forest she had not noticed this disfigurement.

'Pay no heed, lovely lady,' L'Aubignière said gaily. 'Those are only a few mementoes of the friendship of the Iroquois. It's not pretty, I must admit, but it doesn't stop me from using my gun.'

'Did the Iroquois torture you?'

'They caught me when I was sixteen, one autumn when I went out duck shooting on the marshes around Three-Rivers. That's why I am also known as Three-Fingers of Three Rivers.'

And, as Angélique could not help looking sympathetically at his terrible hands, he went on :

'They began by cutting three fingers off with some sharp shells. The remaining thumb was burned in an Indian pipe, and as for the others, they tore off the nails with their teeth, and burned some of the other fingers.'

'And you didn't break down?'

It was Florimond's voice. His tousled head appeared over the

103

soup tureen, and his eyes were glistening with excitement.

'Not a whimper, young man! Do you think I'd have given those wolves the pleasure of seeing me writhe and twist in pain. What's more, I should have been condemning myself to death, and by the hands of the women as well. What shame! When they saw I had the endurance of a brave, they adopted me and I spent over a year with them.'

'Do you speak Iroquois?'

'Possibly better than Great Chief Swanissit of the Senecas himself. . . .'

And he added suddenly with a glance round the room that seemed to take in more than met the eye:

'It's him I am looking for here.'

He had black eyes set in a brown face. His hair was brown and curly and hung down on his suède Indian jacket with its leather fringes. Round his head he wore a headband embroidered with tiny beads and with two feathers fixed at the back. It must have been the ribbon in his curls which gave his face an effeminate and almost childlike look, in spite of his burly shoulders and above-average height.

'If it's Swanissit you are looking for, my lad, anyone would think you were trying to dodge him; for last month he was up in the north on Lake Mistassin, with some of his tribe,' said Count Loménie. 'We heard that from two savages from the mountains who fortunately managed to escape from them before they reached their village.'

'And I assure you he is here,' replied L'Aubignière striking the table with his fist. 'He has come down to join Outakke, the great Mohawk leader. We captured an Iroquois the other evening. We made him talk . . .

'Wherever Outakke is you will find Swanissit. Scalp those two heads and that's the end of the Five Nations of the Iroquois.'

'You're out to avenge your three fingers,' said Maupertuis with a laugh.

'I'm out to avenge my sister and my brother-in-law, and the relatives of my neighbour Maudreuil here. For the past six years now we have been on the trail of that old fox Swanissit to do his hair for him.

'Patience, Eliacien,' he said, turning to the little Baron beside him. 'Some day you will hold Swanissit's scalp in your hand, and I shall hold Outakke's.

'When I was with the Iroquois,' he went on, 'Outakke was my brother. He is the most eloquent man I know, the most cunning and the most vindictive. He is something of a medicine man and in close touch with the Spirit of Dreams. I both love him and hate him. Put it this way : I respect him for his courage, but I would gladly kill him because he is far and away the most vicious animal a Frenchman could ever run into.'

'Are you ever going to give this lady anything to eat, cousin?' Eloi Macollet interrupted crustily.

'Yes, yes, Grandad, keep your hair on. Madame, I do apologize. Pont-Briand, couldn't you do something about it too?'

'Yes I am, I am looking for some morsel in this revolting stewpot which would be fit to grace the fork of a pretty lady, but . . .'

'What about this, the bear's foot? It's the tastiest bit. You've no idea at all, Pont-Briand, my friend. It's easy to see you're a new arrival.'

'Me? I have been fifteen years in Canada!'

'Are you or aren't you going to give her something to eat?' the old man asked again in a threatening growl.

'Yes, yes, here it is.'

They drew the enormous dish towards them with its gelatinous dark rounds of meat swimming in amber-coloured grease. Romain de l'Aubignière thrust his mutilated fingers into the dish without fear of being burnt. He skilfully removed the boiled meat from the sharp claws, each one resembling a tiny, cruel, curved stiletto, which had been slightly softened by cooking, but still clinked as he piled them on the table.

'Our friend Mopuntook would make himself an elegant necklace with these, to wear round his hips or round his neck. Here, Madame, is a piece you will be able to taste without the risk of Maskwa – his lordship the bear – leaving one of his defensive weapons stuck in your throat.'

Angélique carefully examined the piece of bear meat her neighbours had insisted on placing so courteously on her plate, covering it with the greasy sauce. She had come here to discuss the question of the mare with her husband and found herself caught up in an almost official banquet. She kept on glancing towards her husband, who was sitting quite a distance from her at the far end of the long table, but because of the smoke and the movement of the guests, she was unable to catch his eye and could scarcely make out his expression. She was aware that from time to time he seemed to look somewhat enigmatically at her. She decided she must make an effort of politeness towards the somewhat tipsy Frenchman who had invited her to sit beside them and who might take offence if she disdained their offering.

She did not feel hungry, but after all she had done more difficult things in her life than eating bear meat; so she put a piece in her mouth.

'Have a drink!' said Pont-Briand. 'You must have something to drink to wash all the fat down.'

Angélique took a drink and nearly fell over backwards.

The entire table was following her every gesture in complete silence like hunters on the watch.

Fortunately Angélique had learnt to drink at the French court and was able to put a good face on things.

'I am beginning to understand why the Indians call your alcohol firewater,' she said when she had regained her composure.

They all burst out laughing and filled her glass again in delight. Then suddenly everyone turned back to his food and the roar of conversation broke out again.

Angélique caught sight of Octave Malaprade, the cook, who had appeared at the end of the room with some roast poultry. Remembering her friends the Jonases, she made as if to stand up, with the intention of asking him to take something across to the little house. But Pont-Briand held her back with such force that her forearm was quite bruised.

'Don't go,' he said in a voice full of urgency. 'I couldn't bear it.'

At the other end of the table Count Loménie noticed Peyrac, who had half risen from his feet in anger. He intervened.

'With your permission, Count,' he murmured, 'I shall set Madame de Peyrac free and bring her to the place of honour. Don't worry, I shall look after her. Let us avoid a scene.... They are drunk.'

Angélique suddenly saw the French Colonel bowing before her.

'Madame, allow me to lead you to the place which is rightly yours as lady of the manor.'

As he spoke he gave Pont-Briand a brief but peremptory glance, ordering him to release his grip. Taking Angélique by the arm, he led her most gallantly to the far end of the table,

which was unoccupied, seated her there and sat down himself
at her right hand. Angélique now found herself still farther
from her husband, but she could see him at the other end,
facing her, and it was just like their Gay-Savoir days. The
Colonel was very attentive towards her and had her brought
some roast turkey with a few braised vegetables.

'This food is more to the taste of a young woman freshly
arrived from France.'

She protested for, all things considered, she had not found
the stewed black bear so unpleasant a dish. She could see that
she would have no difficulty in getting used to it.

'But there is no need to force nature pointlessly,' said
Loménie. 'You will see, here in the autumn we have a great
deal of the kind of game to which our European palates are
accustomed. We might as well make the most of it. Monsieur,'
he said to Malaprade, 'Madame de Peyrac would like a nice
supper taken over to her friends in the little house. Would you
be kind enough to see to it?'

And he told the cook to put in a flask of good wine with the
food.

However drunk Lieutenant Pont-Briand might have been, his
Colonel's intervention was enough to sober him up again.

'I don't know what came over me,' he whispered woefully to
L'Aubignière.

'You must be mad!' the other replied uneasily. 'Mad or
under a spell . . . you watch out! The She-Devil of Acadia may
not be a myth after all. . . ! This woman really is too beautiful. . . . What if she were the Devil? Remember what Father
Orgeval said?'

Sitting beside Colonel Loménie-Chambord, Angélique was
beginning to relax.

Her husband was facing her, as of old. She could see him at
the end of the table, through a haze, and, as in days gone by
when he had begun to fall in love with her, she could feel his
searching gaze upon her. It gave her a feeling of euphoria, a
desire to shine and to join in everything that was going on
around her. She felt happy. The alcohol was beginning to make
her feel slightly hazy, and she was forgetting why she had
come. The courtly charm of the Colonel was having its effect
on her, and the instinctive attraction she had felt towards him
from the first was changing into a feeling of confidence.

The simplicity of his manners and his clear-cut precise

gestures went hand in hand with a gentle, winning grace in which Angélique's observant mind could not help seeing the man accustomed to talking with women. This did not, as people all too often think it does, take the form of paying elaborate compliments, but he possessed that rarer quality of knowing how to talk to women in a way that is familiar to them and puts them at their ease, and which, in brief, without any attempt to charm them, reassures them and wins them over. He intrigued her, for there was something uncommon about him.

He told her all about the northern territories, the three French cities on the Saint-Lawrence, and of the many tribes that swarmed around them; and when she asked him about the Hurons, he confirmed that they were in fact of Iroquois origin. They had broken away from their kinsfolk in the Sacred Valley a long time ago, after some dispute or other, and had henceforth regarded the Iroquois as ancestral enemies. It was from the mouths of the Hurons that the first French explorer Jacques Cartier had learnt the name of the Iroquois, a word signifying 'cruel vipers'.

The talk always came back to the Iroquois. Angélique's immediate neighbours were happy to join in a conversation on a subject they knew something about and which seemed to interest them. They were tremendously impressed by her manner, which was that of a great lady. Even here everyone had a feeling that she had once sat at the King's table. They had not the slightest doubt that she had ruled at Court amid an admiring throng of men. They sensed that she had been the darling of princes. . . .

They watched her every movement, the way she crossed her supple hands, and rested her chin on them, the way she would look the person who spoke to her straight in the eyes as she listened to him, or, on the other hand, lower her long eyelids reticently; the way she nibbled absent-mindedly at her food, grasped her goblet and emptied it unceremoniously in one draught, and suddenly burst into irrepressible laughter that stirred their vitals.

That evening the motley specimens of mankind gathered together at Katarunk had a glimpse of an unfamiliar paradise.

This woman sitting at their table represented heaven on earth, spring in midwinter, beauty come among them, rough as they were, smelling of leather and grease. She was a ray of sunshine piercing the fog of tobacco smoke, and her smile fell like balm on their hardened hearts.

They felt like heroes, strong in resolution, nimble of wit, and words came effortlessly to their lips to describe the lands they had known, or to express their point of view.

Romain de l'Aubignière spoke of the Sacred Valley of the Iroquois, of the pink light that bathes the hillside covered with rows of long bark houses with rounded roofs, and the smell of green maize: '. . . Few are they that come back alive from that valley. . . . Few are they that come back with all their fingers. . . .'

'I did,' said Perrot spreading out his hands.

'Oh you, they treat you as if you were a medicine man. You must have made a pact with the devil, old chap, to get away unscathed. . . .'

'It is a strange fact that the mere mention of Frenchmen sends the Iroquois into a furious rage, which surely proves that they are especially prone to possession by evil spirits,' said one of the trappers called Aubertin. 'They seem above all to fear the power of the religion the French bring with them. Look at the way they treated our missionaries! We can never consider ourselves safe from them, even in the depths of winter. Wasn't it in the middle of February that they attacked your domains, Maudreuil, and yours, L'Aubignière, and scalped your parents and your servants, setting fire to everything? Those who were left wounded died of exposure. . . .'

'Yes, that was what happened,' confirmed Eliacien de Maudreuil.

A sombre glow came into his blue eyes, as if grief lay heavy in them like molten lead.

'It was Swanissit who did that, with his Senecas, and ever since he has scarcely stopped ranging the countryside spreading terror wherever he goes. I am not going to let him go to earth again before I have his hair.'

'And I shall have Outakke's scalp,' said Romain de l'Aubignière.

Mopuntook raised his hand and stood up to speak, and everyone listened to him in solemn silence.

The Palefaces had learnt from the savages never to interrupt a man when he was speaking and to listen to one another respectfully. Everyone present appeared to understand what the chief of the Metallaks was saying. Loménie, realizing that

Angélique was interested, leaned towards her and quietly translated what the Sagamore was saying.

'We are surrounded by the Iroquois, who prowls the land like a ravenous prairie wolf. He wishes the destruction of the children of the Dawn. We encountered him on the borders of our lands, and he spoke to us of war. But the white woman faced him without fear and hurled him down into the waters. Now the Iroquois has lost his strength. He knows it, and will seek peace with us.'

'Pray God you're right,' Perrot replied.

'The old tortoise story again,' Angélique said to Loménie. 'At the time, I must admit I was frightened, but it never occurred to me to see such mystical significance in the incident. Was it really as important as all that?'

She took a sip of brandy and got a whiff of apples from the bottom of the glass.

Loménie watched her with a smile.

'I think you are beginning to feel less anxious already,' he said. 'You have reached the stage when the horror stories you hear every day have little more effect on you than the latest titbits of local gossip. You will see, you get used to this life very quickly.'

'It may be due to this excellent brandy, and to your kindly encouragement,' she said, with an affectionate glance. 'You know exactly how to handle women.... Oh! please don't misunderstand me. I mean that you have a particular manner, which is rare in a soldier, of building up a woman's self-confidence, of reassuring her, and giving her the impression that she really matters. Where did you acquire these skills, Monsieur de Loménie?'

'Well,' replied the Count, not in the slightest embarrassed, 'I suppose it was during the years I worked for Monsieur de Maisonneuve.'

And he told her how he had come to Canada at the time that gallant nobleman was founding Ville-Marie on the Isle of Montreal. At that time young couples were arriving from France along with the King's Girls sent over to marry the colonists. He, Loménie, had been given the task of meeting them on the banks of the Saint-Lawrence, advising them and helping them to get used to their disconcerting new way of life.

'At that time we were a constant object of Iroquois attacks and there was not a man among us who did not run the risk of losing his scalp on his very own doorstep. The settlers harvested their crops with their guns at their side. The King's Girls they sent over to us were for the most part nice, agreeable, well-behaved girls, but they knew very little about running a house or working in the fields. Mademoiselle Bourgoys and I were responsible for teaching them.'

'And who was Mademoiselle Bourgoys?'

'A saintly young woman who had come over from France for the sole purpose of teaching the settlers' children.'

'All alone?'

'Alone at first under the protection of Monsieur de Maisonneuve. Our Governor did not consider it possible at the time to bring over an order of nuns to so remote an outpost. More often than not we all lived together in the fortress. Mademoiselle Bourgoys tended the wounded, did the washing, taught the women to knit, and mediated in their little squabbles.'

'I would like to meet her,' said Angélique. 'Is she still in Canada?'

'Yes indeed! Over the course of the years she has found companions to help her in her task and she is now head of a small group of women who teach about a hundred children in Ville-Marie and in the outlying villages around Quebec and at Three-Rivers, and for my part, since Montreal is now self-sufficient and Monsieur de Maisonneuve has been recalled to France, I re-enlisted under Monsieur de Castel-Morgeat, the military governor of New France. But I shall not easily forget the time I turned master cook in order to teach the new arrivals from France some recipes to keep their husbands happy.'

Angélique laughed at the picture of this army officer wearing a blue overall, busy teaching the rudiments of family cooking to the village lasses or orphans from the poorhouse whom the Board of Administration had been generous enough to get off their hands by sending them overseas to get married.

'It must have been marvellous for them to have you to welcome them and to enjoy your company. The women must have been mad about you, weren't they?'

'No, I don't think so,' said Loménie.

'You surprise me! You are so charming!'

Loménie laughed, realizing that she was becoming a trifle tipsy.

'Didn't it all lead to a great deal of jealousy?' Angélique asked.

'No, not at all, Madame. You see, we were a very pious community with a strict code of behaviour. Had it been otherwise, we should never have been able to live as we did on the frontiers of Christianity. I myself am a member of a religious order; I belong to the Knights of Malta.'

Angélique gaped in utter astonishment.

'Oh, how silly I am!' and then she added rapturously:

'A Knight of Malta! How wonderful! I am so proud of the Knights of Malta. It was they who tried to buy me back when I was sold as a slave in Crete.... At least they did their best to. But the price went too high for them. I shall never forget the fact that they tried, though. And when I think of all the stupid things I have said to you! How will you ever forgive me!'

And she threw back her lovely neck and burst into peals of laughter.

Everyone including Loménie looked at her, enchanted. Her teeth flashed through the semi-darkness of the smoke-filled room and her eyes were like two stars. Her laugh made them disturbingly aware of a female presence among them.

Peyrac clenched his jaw. He had watched her, fascinated, overcome by her charm, but now he felt anger welling up inside him at the display she made of her charms, the way she looked at people and giggled, and the somewhat coquettish manner she had adopted towards Loménie. It was quite obvious that she liked him, and in any case she had had too much to drink.

But, by Jove, how lovely she was!

The laugh made men's hearts turn over with happiness.

No, he could not possibly be angry with her for being so beautiful and attracting everyone's attention. She had been born to dazzle....

But, damn it! he would know how to remind her tonight that she belonged to him and to him alone!

Clovis l'Auvergnat, the sinister gnome in the woollen cap, suddenly appeared beside Peyrac with a musket under one arm.

'I am off to shoot the mare, sir,' he whispered.

Peyrac took another look in Angélique's direction. Even if she was behaving a trifle giddily he could certainly trust Loménie.

'Right, I'll come with you,' he said standing up.

CHAPTER TWELVE

ANGÉLIQUE GAVE such a start that Loménie, caught by surprise, put out a hand as if to support her.

'It's nothing,' she stammered, 'but, I wonder . . .'

She had just noticed that her husband's place at table was empty and she sprang to her feet.

'Forgive me, but I must go . . .'

'Already, Madame? We shall all be heartbroken, could you not stay a little longer?'

'No, no, I must have a word with Monsieur de Peyrac . . . and I see that he has gone. . . .'

'At least allow me to accompany you.'

'No, thank you very much all the same. Please stay with your friends. I can manage perfectly well. . . .'

But Loménie behaved as any gentleman should towards an attractive woman whom he suspects to be slightly inebriated. Without hesitating, he nevertheless helped her to the door, opened it and left her only once he felt sure that the outside air had helped her, that she could stand on her two legs and was only a few yards from her room.

As soon as he had left her, Angélique rushed away across the courtyard. It was even more crowded than before. Night was falling, mingling with the thick smoke, and in the blue misty cold the red flowers of the camp fires blossomed beneath the cauldrons.

But the sky above the fortress was limpid and cloudless like a great golden dome.

Angélique pushed her way roughly through the crowd to the gate in the palisade. She caught sight of her husband walking down the slope towards the lower fields beside the river and at his side she saw the stocky shape of the blacksmith from Auvergne carrying a musket.

She rushed after them.

It was no easy matter to pick a way among the treacherous tree-trunks, which were themselves all entangled with runner beans.

Angélique tripped and tumbled to her knees, swearing like a trooper. But the shock of her fall sobered her up a bit. Once back on her feet again she was careful to keep an eye where she trod. She was trembling all over with impatience, fearing to arrive too late.

She could see the silhouettes of the horses, black shadows against the dazzling sunset, as they cropped the scant grass where it grew through the dried mud.

At last she was within earshot.

'Joffrey! Joffrey!'

The Count turned round.

Angélique was panting when she reached him.

'Are you going to kill Wallis?'

'Yes...! Who told you I was?'

Angélique refused to reply. She was beside herself, choking with rage. The darkness of the earth and the brilliance of the sky both hurt her eyes. She could not see Joffrey de Peyrac's face, for he had the light behind him, and she felt as if she hated this black, opaque figure of a man as it stood there before her like a rock.

'You have no right to do it,' she cried. 'No right. Without even warning me. I brought ... Yes, I brought that animal here, I put up with all sorts of difficulties and exhaustion. And now you are going to destroy it all at a single stroke.'

'I am astonished, my dear, that you should come to the mare's defence. She has proved herself to be both vicious and intractable. By panicking in front of the tortoise, she nearly killed you and your daughter. And by breaking her halter in the evening she forced you to go and look for her under circumstances which could have involved us in a nasty incident....'

'What does all that matter? It's for me to decide. It's nothing to do with you....'

Her breath still came in gasps and her voice trembled.

'You gave her to me to see if I could get her here and I did. It was only because the noise of the waterfall prevented her hearing my voice. And she can't stand the awful smell of those Indians. Neither can I, incidentally. I understand Wallis. It's not her fault, it's the fault of this country. And you were going to kill her without even telling me! Oh, I shall never be able to get on with the man you have become.... It would have been better if I'd...'

Angélique choked. She felt as if she was going to burst into tears, and she turned away and ran off as fast as her legs would carry her in such a state of nerves that she managed to cross the dark, uneven field without tripping once.

She finally came to a halt through lack of breath, and found herself beside a small stream glittering with the reflection of the sunset.

She had run off instinctively in the direction of the light, where the plain and the mountains still glowed with the red of the now set sun. She had turned her back on the night and the noise of the camp, and now in the silence the sound of her own breathing seemed disproportionately noisy to her, as if amplified. It seemed as if the entire grandiose and taciturn landscape had suddenly stood still to harken to this solitary woman regaining her breath.

'I really must be completely drunk,' she told herself. 'They'll never catch me drinking their wretched Canadian brandy again! Whatever did I say to Monsieur de Loménie just now? I even think I told him I was sold as a slave in the market in Crete! How absolutely dreadful! And what about Joffrey? How could I have spoken to him like that? And in front of one of his men, too. It had to be Clovis too, the worst of all! Joffrey will never forgive me. But why, why is he so ... so ...?'

Words escaped her. She still could not see quite straight. She breathed deeply and her heart began to beat fast. Her great purple cloak billowed in the wind.

On the horizon small pearly-grey clouds stretched out to form a mass that melted into the summits of the Appalachians. Towards the west the mountains were gradually disappearing in a saffron haze, while the plain stretching out at her feet was growing darker, but it was a darkness steeped in light reminiscent of the fugitive glint of quicksilver; it stretched out, mile upon mile, dotted with a thousand lakes of unbearably brilliant gold. Beneath this cloth, beneath this veil spread by the approaching night, Angélique caught a glimpse of the true nature of this land, abandoned to trees and waters, everlastingly renewing itself yet sterile, and the slow panorama of the mountains as they vanished into infinity made her want to groan like a soul in pain. Not a single puff of smoke made its way slowly skywards to betray the presence of a human being somewhere in all this wilderness! It was a dead land!

She fell to her knees, overwhelmed by it all.

Close beside her some leaves beside the stream gave off a mild, slightly bitter smell which she recognized. She seized one of them and crushed it in her hands.

'It's mint, wild mint!'

And she buried her face in her hands, breathing in the heady, familiar perfume which reminded her of the thickets she had known in her childhood. She felt a kind of exultation as she revelled in the smell and sighed as she ran her sweet-smelling hands over her cheeks and her brow.

She threw her head back. The wind caught her hair and rustled interminably through the woods with their crackling autumn leaves. The earth was growing darker and darker, and the sky had become pale yellow. A star appeared, white and trembling.

Angélique looked round slowly and tasted the wind on her lips.

But when her eyes reached the edge of the wood, a few paces from where she knelt, she turned her head away quickly, and went on examining the distant mountains, her mind a blank, wondering whether she was dreaming. What was it she had seen sparkling through those motionless tree-trunks?

Was it a pair of eyes?

She glanced twice again in the same direction and each time looked back at the dark plain whose lakes continued to sparkle like great sheets of gold interspersed with brown islands.

When she looked the third time her eyes no longer returned to the plain.

There was no doubt about it. There was someone standing just a few feet from her. A tree had become a man, a column of flesh and blood amidst the tree-trunks, but of the same dark impassive colour.

A Redskin stood there looking at her, mingling so intimately with the shadowy forest and standing so completely motion-less that it was well-nigh impossible to pick him out from the surrounding trees. He stood among them as if among his peers. He lived the same vegetable life, with its unseen pulsations, born of the earth, a prisoner of their roots and, like them, the secret, silent, and proud witness of wind and weather. A tree with living eyes. Two agate eyes in the smooth bark.

The sulphur-tinted light filtering through the branches fell on his shoulders, his arms and his hips, throwing his powerful muscles into relief.

He wore a glistening white bear-tooth necklace around the base of his extraordinarily long neck, which was broad as well and very muscular, hung on either side with spherical scarlet-coloured earrings. His face was short and round, but sharply angular, and his nose, his cheek-bones, and deep-set eye-sockets stood out strongly above a broad sardonic mouth.

His ears were wide-set, large and pointed at the top, and seemed not to belong entirely to the rough-hewn head, but to have been added as an afterthought, with their pendants as ornaments.

Out of the middle of his forehead grew an enormous tuft of hair that thickened until it reached the top of his shaved skull, there to sprout into a tuft of eagle feathers, and black and white skunk tails.

He wore his hair like a Huron.

BUT HE WAS NOT A HURON!

Of this, Angélique was certain. It was this chilling conviction that made her scrutinize the Indian, who was a mere six paces from her, with all the attention one concentrates on a dangerous animal.

But at the same time something inside her refused to accept the face as human, since it did not stir. It was as motionless as a rock, and even the brilliant eyes lost their life, so fixed and motionless they were.

She suddenly felt convinced that the face did not exist, and that her eyes had deceived her.

Then the wind brought his smell to her, the animal smell of an Indian smeared all over with rancid bear fat, impregnated with tobacco and blood, possibly hiding half-dried scalps in the folds of his leather belt.

That smell was certainly real and made her leap to her feet in horror. Still the Indian made no move and she began to back away slowly. Soon she could see him no longer for dusk was falling and darkness had spread over the earth.

Then she turned and ran back towards the fort, fearing that she might feel an arrow strike her between the shoulders.

Astonished to find herself still alive, she reached the outpost without difficulty and found herself back in the midst of the Indian encampment. She was about to give the alarm, 'Iroquois in the offing' but refrained from doing so; she no longer felt certain about what it was she had seen. And yet it had not been a Huron. The Hurons had lived for too long under the shadow of the French, following in their tracks, participating in their wars, camping on the outskirts of their townships, eating their leftovers, praying to their God.... They were little jackals, always in groups. They never prowled through the woods like that, as solitary and wild as wolves.

Here were the Hurons, dancing, with their little bells, their plumes and their medallions all a-quiver and, as she went by, they thrust out their dirty hands in an attempt to touch her cloak.

She crossed the threshold of the camp, then the compound, and soon shut the cottage door behind her.

The entire excursion outside the palisade, her meeting with the Indian, all the comings and goings through the shadowy silence, broken by the soughing of the wind and other unidentifiable noises, had had the incoherence of a nightmare. Angélique felt like a person in a dream who, while conscious of certain events, has forgotten who he is and what he seeks. She remembered that she had run first to the right, then to the left through the dusk, as if trying to escape some intolerable menace, that she had thought she had found peace on plucking the wild mint, that she had looked at a tree and had seen that it was not a tree but an Indian, then, on examining the Indian, she had seen that he was not human but the very epitome of hatred, and now she was no longer sure that she had really seen any of these things at all. In the big room the embers were dying in the grate. There was no one there. The impression of unreality continued and for a while Angélique could not remember exactly what it was she had hoped to find. A sound rising and falling hypnotically, going on and on endlessly, brought her back to herself again. She gave a shudder, unable to understand what was producing the noise that broke the heavy silence at regular intervals. Then at last it dawned on her – it was merely Master Jonas snoring in the next room.

Angélique took a deep breath and laughed at herself. Her friends had gone to bed, making the most of their well-earned rustic comforts after weeks of trekking. Everyone was fast asleep, including Honorine, no doubt. On the table she saw a pile of bowls that had been washed up, a witness to the Protestant housewife's concern to leave her house tidy before going to bed. The washing-up bowl was drying in one corner of the room and they had carefully mopped up the water spilled on the floor and cleared away the remains of the meal from the rough wooden table.

A candle set in a candlestick had been placed ready for her

with a stick of touchwood beside it. She struck a light and, candle in hand, entered the room on the left. This room, which she had left several hours earlier, was also empty, but someone, possibly Elvire, had discreetly removed her travelling clothes and her boots to clean them, had tied up the curtains of the rough bed and turned down one corner of the blanket as if in preparation for a restful night. Angélique mentally blessed the helpful young woman and knelt down before the fire to stir it into a blaze again.

Her nimble fingers, skilful at all manner of tasks, snapped the twigs and piled up the logs automatically, avoiding the long juniper spikes as she threw a handful into the flames to produce a pleasant smell. The fire crackled and roared up the chimney.

Angélique thought about the man she had glimpsed through the trees beside the stream. She thought about the French who had come from the northern territories, from the cold waters of the Saint-Lawrence, to lie in ambush for them, maybe to strike them down. She thought of her two sons and of their youth so difficult to understand. She thought of Honorine. Would there always be this insurmountable barrier between her daughter and herself which neither of them seemed able to cross? She thought too of her husband and was torn between her desire for him to come to her and her wish to be left alone.

She continued to feel a sense of oppression, but was unable to say precisely why. She held out her hands to the flames.

The flames danced and crackled, and Angélique clung to the things she knew, the things she could still bend to her will, like fire, and wild mint. . . .

The latch lifted and, seeing Joffrey de Peyrac's tall form on the threshold, she was overcome with joy and a hunger for him which sent the blood coursing through her veins, as she said to herself:

'He has come back. He won't leave me. . . . He knows that I need him. . . . And he needs me. . . . How lucky that our bodies understand one another. . . .'

CHAPTER THIRTEEN

ON ENTERING the cottage, Joffrey de Peyrac had felt a sudden fear that she might not be there. Earlier beside the river she had run away from him so tempestuously; at the time he had considered running after her but had feared that might make her still more angry.

In any event, before joining her he had to post his sentries for the night, sentries of his own to keep an eye on the French sentries. There was to be one of his men to each group of Frenchmen or Indians. Throughout the night, Cantor would play his guitar for the soldiers and sing them some of the local songs.

'*Alouette, gentille Alouette ... Alouette, je te plumerai ...*'

The question was, who would pluck whose feathers! Florimond would come and relieve him in the early hours of the morning and, if the soldiers finally decided to go to sleep, Florimond could do likewise, but he was only to doze. These were the orders.

Octave Malaprade was to put himself at the disposal of the officers after they had got to bed, and Yann le Couennec would take over from him, ready to spring into action at the slightest move on the part of these gentlemen.

Throughout the night Perrot, Maupertuis and his son were to go from wigwam to wigwam among the Algonquins, Hurons and Abenakis, chatting with the Indian chiefs, smoking a pipe or two with them, and reminding them of old times.

For they were all good friends, were they not? But it was just as well not to lose sight of one another for a single moment.

At last Count Peyrac was free to return to the cottage and the thought had suddenly flashed through his mind that she might be there no longer.

He had lived so many days, so many years, without her, with the pain of her absence eating into his heart; now they were reunited the idea sometimes seemed incredible to him, and he would begin to doubt whether she was really there or had disappeared once more.

She had become a shadow, a memory, a bitter, torturing

memory as in the days when he had thought of her in another man's arms or dead in the Moroccan desert.[1]

He contemplated the empty first room with dismay. Then, seeing a light through a crack in the door on his left and hearing the crackling of a fire, he strode across the room and found her there, kneeling before the hearth, her golden hair spread over her shoulders, looking at him with those unforgettable wide eyes.

He pushed the door to silently and turned the clumsily-made key in the lock.

Then he walked slowly towards her and leaned against the hood of the pebble chimney.

Nothing could separate them, they were both thinking at that moment. Nothing, as long as the mere sight of one another filled them with so urgent a desire to be together, to make love.

She was thinking that she would accept anything in order to have the joy of knowing him there, beside her, standing firm on his long sinewy legs with their high black leather boots.

He was thinking that in order to have the right to take her in his arms, to put his lips on hers, to caress that full, supple form, he would forgive her anything. . . .

She looked up at him and saw that he was half smiling.

'I think that what I had to drink made me very foolish to-night,' she said softly, genuinely abashed. 'Please forgive me for saying more than I really meant. You didn't shoot Wallis, did you?'

'No, I wouldn't dream of distressing you in that way. Still, she is a dangerous animal and I am very angry with her for the dangers she caused you. . . . But I admit that I blundered badly in not warning you of my intention to shoot her; that was a mistake unworthy of a man who once claimed to be a master of the Art of Love. I hope, Madame, that you in your turn will forgive me. For far too long now I have ceased to show women the consideration I used to give them in Toulouse. The Mediterranean teaches one bad habits in that respect; association with compliant, mindless courtesans makes one forget that women are thinking beings. One is tempted to despise them as playthings, objects of pleasure or slaves. . . . Where did you run off to this evening to cool down after you left me?'

[1] See *Angélique and the Sultan*.

'Up on the hills over to the west. I found a stream with wild mint growing by it.'

'Do be careful! It is extremely unwise to go so far from the camp. There is danger everywhere and I cannot be sure of anyone. Please promise me you won't do it again, my love!' Once again a pang of fear shot through Angélique's heart.

'I'm frightened,' she murmured.

Then, looking him full in the face, she summoned all her courage and went on:

'I am frightened. I disappoint you, don't I? I told you I would never be afraid, that you could bring me with you and that I would be strong and a help to you and now . . .'

She wrung her hands in anguish.

'Nothing is going as I expected it to. I don't know whether it is I who have got off on the wrong foot. . . . Everything appals me. I keep on wondering what we are doing in this frightening, dangerous wilderness full of enemies on the prowl. I feel that these enormous distances can only separate us, that this is no life for us, and that I do not have, or no longer have the necessary qualities to cope with it.'

And she repeated:

'I disappoint you, don't I?'

She hoped he would reply immediately, that he would accuse her, that he would unburden himself.

But he remained silent as she watched the firelight play over that tough, furrowed face in which she could read nothing.

'No, you don't disappoint me, my love,' he replied at last. 'On the contrary, I am pleased to know that you are neither gullible nor oblivious of the true nature of things. But what precisely are you frightened of?'

'I don't know,' she replied with a helpless gesture.

For there were too many things and, had she been asked to put them into words, would she have been able to say that the things that made her so uneasy were vague, imprecise things, like the sensation she had had of someone looking at her through the trees? And would she have told him about the Indian she had glimpsed that evening?

She shook her head.

'It's a pity,' he said, 'it might have helped us both for you to know precisely what it is that is frightening you.'

He drew a leaf of tobacco rolled into the shape of a cigar from a pocket in his jerkin. He occasionally relinquished his pipe in favour of something else. She liked to see him smoke as he had in the Gay-Savoir days, and she hastened to pass him a piece of burning twig.

Slowly he puffed the smoke out from between his lips.

'The thing I am frightened of above all,' she went on hesitantly, 'is to find that I have been completely mistaken, and that I am incapable of ever getting used to this land, or to its people. . . . Or even to you,' she added with a smile to soften her words. 'Wives are a nuisance, aren't they, my lord?' And in the smile she gave him he could read the full weight of her passion for him.

He gave a little nod :

'Yes, indeed, a wife can be a nuisance when one is unable to look at her without wanting to make love to her.'

'That is not what I meant.'

'But I did !'

He paced up and down the room in a cloud of blue smoke.

'It's true, my love, you are a terrible nuisance to me. I must keep cool headed and yet when you come near me, no matter what time of the day it is, your nearness excites and disturbs me. I have a terrible urge to go off alone with you, to take you in my arms and kiss you and kiss you, to listen to you speaking to me alone, to look at you. But I have other things to do and I find it very hard not to regard them as of secondary importance whenever you appear. Your voice sends shudders down my spine, and the sound of your laughter leaves me quite distracted. I forget where I am . . .'

In spite of everything he had succeeded in making her laugh, and her cheeks were beginning to recover their colour.

'I don't believe you. You are talking nonsense.'

'Nonsense, perhaps, but it happens to be true, and I take none of it back. What is more, I haven't finished yet. Yes, a wife is a nuisance when not a single man can look at her without marvelling at her beauty and when, however far into the wilderness you take her, she stirs up enemies around one. At Gay-Savoir in Toulouse, I was the master, I was known, held in high regard and feared. Few would ever have dared to set themselves up as my rival. Here, things are not the same at all, and I shall have to teach the people of Dawn-East and those of New France that I am no complaisant husband. I can foresee duels, ambushes and shows of force involving much bloodshed. But who cares ! I would not exchange all the torments your presence causes me for the often bitter peace of my solitude.'

He came back and stood towering over her, leaning against the chimney; she sat with upturned face and hands folded in her lap, unable to take her eyes off his dark, admiring face.

'I am greatly impressed by your maturity,' Peyrac continued gently. 'You were an inexperienced little girl when I took you; your mind was as virginal as your body. How much you have been moulded by others since then! You are not the product of my love as I had dreamed you would be, a somewhat Utopian dream in any case, even if we had remained together. But time has passed, and today, you are yourself, that is to say a woman in the fullest sense of the word, a woman with all her mystery. A woman who no longer seeks her own reflection in another in order to know herself. A woman standing alone ... who belongs only to herself, who has made herself what she is. And it is that fact that sometimes puts a distance between us.'

'But ... I belong to you,' she said timidly.

'No, not yet, not completely. But that will come....'

He drew her to her feet and, putting his arm round her shoulders, led her over to a map which he had pinned up on the rough wooden wall.

He pointed to several places.

'There ... towards the north and east, that's New France. In the south you see New England. To the west we have the Iroquois. And I am there, in the middle, with a mere handful of men, do you see? There is only one way open to me, to make allies. As far as New England is concerned, it's already done. As for New France, our meeting with Colonel Loménie-Chambord was providential, because it may lead to an alliance.... As for the Iroquois, a year before I sailed for Europe I sent them plenipotentiaries and presents. The Cayuga attack makes me fear that my efforts have been in vain, but, all the same, we must wait and see. Any declaration of war, any fighting would be disastrous to me at the present moment. We must bide our time, consolidate our position. If we manage to get out of this hornets' nest alive, I wager that one day we shall be stronger than the lot of them. And now come, my love, it is time to think of serious matters.'

Laughing, he turned her to face him, clasped her against his powerful chest, then gently let his hand wander over her shoulder, the back of her bowed neck, and the rich curves stretching her bodice, under her arms.

'The Iroquois won't come tonight, my love. And the French will sleep, for they have been drinking, singing, and making merry. Their plans to massacre us can wait till tomorrow. One night! Who cares about tomorrow provided we are granted one night more.... One night is a whole lifetime!'

He tilted her chin up with his fingers and kissed her proffered lips insatiably. Then he buried her proud, lovely head in his shoulder, and clasped her tightly to him again.

'We are new-made creatures, darling. And so is the world around us. In the past we lived in our palaces, surrounded by riches, and we thought ourselves free. Yet our every act was judged by a thousand cruel, pitiless eyes, the eyes of a petty, jealous society that had run its course and whose bonds held it fast on every side. I was the living proof that it was no easy matter to be different from others in the Old World. Here it's another matter.'

Then very softly, with his lips in her hair, he added:

'And even if we should die, maybe tomorrow, maybe in dreadful torment, at least it would be together and no longer for some futile, pointless reason.'

She felt his hand on her hips, through the stuff of her dress, then suddenly she felt it gliding over her naked breasts, and she saw stars everywhere. Yes, he was right, nothing else mattered, even if they were to die tomorrow, even a terrible death.... She was his, subject to his male strength. He had undone her dress, and pulled the top of her shift down over her arms.

'Let me undress you, my darling. One needs to be able to breathe feely when one's heart is gripped with fear of the French and the Iroquois. Now, isn't that better...? Let me ... It is so long since I had the pleasure of unlacing these complicated European clothes. In the East, the women offer their bodies without giving a man any sense of mystery.'

'Oh, don't talk to me about your slave-girls any more!'

'But you only stand to gain by the comparison.'

'That's as may be! But I hate them.'

'I adore you when you're jealous,' he said, tumbling her on to the rustic bed.

And a thought flashed through his mind as it had through hers earlier, about how lucky they were that their bodies were so well adjusted to one another.

CHAPTER FOURTEEN

IN THE enclosed darkness of their bed where, surfeited with delight, their bodies lay resting, Angélique dreamed a dream. The Iroquois she had glimpsed that evening rose up out of the forest and fixed her with his cruel eyes. The dusk had given way to day and the sun, glittering on his oily chest, transformed it into a brilliant gold breast-plate. His face stood out sharply in the light and the tuft of hair on his scalp, decked with feathers and blown upright by the wind, looked like the crest of a strange bird. He was standing over her brandishing a tomahawk, about to bring it down on her head. He struck her a furious blow but she felt nothing; then she suddenly noticed that she was holding the dagger that the Polak – the woman who had been her friend at the Court of Miracles, when she had lived among thieves and outlaws – had given her. 'I know how to use it,' she remembered, and she in her turn struck out at him, a swift, sharp blow. And the Iroquois melted away like a cloud.

She tossed about so much in her dream that the man lying beside her woke.

'What is the matter, my love?'

'I killed him,' she murmured.

And she fell back to sleep again.

He struck a light from the flint, and lit a candle on a little shelf above the bed. They had drawn the linen curtains round the bed to protect them from the chill of the night.

In the impenetrable darkness, under the cold pall of mist that had formed over the remote little outpost, presaging the coming of winter, they were alone, as alone as if they were the only people in the world.

Leaning on one elbow, Joffrey de Peyrac lowered the candle to look at his sleeping wife.

She seemed to have fallen back into a deep sleep again. Her outstretched hand had fallen back on the bed and her lips, which a moment before had murmured 'I've killed him', were slightly parted over her light breathing. Cradled in the hollow of their coarse mattress of moss and dried grasses, her body took on a new fullness. As she lay beside him in the abandon of her superb nakedness, the curves of her back appeared more opulent, her breasts heavier, and her beauty had a statuesque quality that her liveliness of manner prevented one from noticing during the day.

In her sleep, she had the full, fruitful curves of an ancient goddess. Her smooth face kept its secrets. Not a trace remained of the expressions which it sometimes wore, appearing as suddenly as flames, revealing for an instant Angélique's secret soul. Nothing of that infinite variety of astonishing feelings: hatred, for example, like that she had felt when she raised herself up that afternoon, her musket smoking in her hand, and he had seen her delicate jaw thrust forward as she repeated in a kind of incantation through her clenched teeth: 'Kill! Kill!'

Nothing remained either of the seductive charm she had displayed that evening, laughing with the men. During the feast, silent and apparently detached, he had allowed jealousy to eat his heart out, wanting as he did to know everything about her; for he had the scholar's obsession with the truth and had never refused to face the facts.

Might it not be better to be a little blind when love with its imperious demands had crept into his very heart?

For his part, what more did he want than what he already possessed? Nothing. He had everything, danger, the struggle, victory and success, and every night this woman's body was his and his alone, in all its lush sensuality.

One of his Angélique's arms was thrown back like a pale flexible stem opening out above the dark, heady calyx of her armpit.

What more could he ask for himself? Happiness? But this was happiness! The earth had given him all it had to give. But what about her? Who was she? What innocence, or what calculation lay hidden in this fleshy envelope, which seemed the quintessence of every feminine charm? What open wounds lay concealed behind the serenity of her face?

Peyrac brushed her still cheek with his hand, brushed her soft skin. If only with the same caress he could reach her unquiet spirit, he might soothe the hurt he sensed within her. He might make her well again. But she confided so little in him, and when she slept, she seemed still farther from him. She was alone. It was as if the veil that hung over those fifteen years of separation were parting, revealing her as she had been, passionate and vulnerable, swept along by the turbulence of a broken life. Separated from him she had become a flower uprooted by the wind, the wildly oscillating needle of a compass that has lost its North, a heart bereft. He was beginning to understand how true had been her protestations when she had said: 'When you were not there I did not live, I merely survived. . . .' Her life of adventure had served merely to stifle her hunger, to enable her to defend herself.

Although constantly besieged by men, although sometimes carried away by her own emotions, the lengthy periods of continence she had suffered as a woman without a husband, had made of her a woman whose body had grown solitary and often frustrated.

The violent repugnance she had felt over the past few years for love in any of its physical manifestations had changed her without her knowing it, had left a strange mark upon her. They had to begin all over again, to start afresh. But he was the lover she needed. She lay there beside him, a woman who had known many a lover, and yet she seemed possessed of a kind of virginity which he found most attractive, an incorruptible amazon whose unapproachability made her conquest all the sweeter.

He kissed her soft shoulder tenderly, almost religiously, and as she gave a little shudder, he drew away and buried his face in her hair as it lay spread out, smelling of wind and forest.

Her scent was the scent of the lands they had travelled through and, by that adaptability to circumstance so many women have, she already seemed completely different from the woman he had known in La Rochelle.

The sun had turned her skin golden, and her gestures had taken on a primitive languor. These wild lands had already enfolded her in their mystery.

What would come to pass between her and this wild country?

True women are incapable of remaining outside things; they must enter into them, become involved in them, make them their own.

For his part, neither the Mediterranean, nor the Atlantic, nor the Caribbean had affected him. He would leave his mark on North America, but America would leave no mark on him. . . . Very little at any rate.

But what about her? What would be Angélique's reaction to the New World?

Sleep, my mysterious darling. Sleep! I shall not leave you. I shall stay beside you to defend you.

Outside, a night bird hooted, and its lugubrious velvety cry rang out several times through the night. There was an answering bark of dogs, and Peyrac heard the Indians calling to one another from their birch-bark wigwams. Then silence fell again.

Joffrey de Peyrac sat up. His arms were ready beside his bed, a loaded pistol on the table and his musket leaning against the foot of the bed.

Then he lay down once more, stretched an arm out towards his sleeping wife and drew her to his breast.

One night is a whole lifetime.

In the chill mists of the night in which the great round orb of the moon looked like a watery silver sun, up there on the hillside, in the heart of the dark forest, the Iroquois stood naked and alone, watching the fort, and his catlike eyes glittered between the branches.

CHAPTER FIFTEEN

T H E D A Y dawned and the previous day seemed a long time ago. That autumn day in Upper Kennebec which might have echoed to the sound of fratricidal musket shots between the Palefaces had ended peacefully.

This morning, all round the little outpost, smoke rose from all the birch-bark shelters in pure white arabesques into a blue sky.

Angélique, with that recuperative capacity women have, awoke happy, her fears gone. The bed in which he had slept beside her still held the shape of his beloved body and reminded her of the moments of forgetfulness and intensity of living that he had given her. It was like a miraculous dream, and she reached out her hand to touch the empty place beside her to convince herself of its reality.

She remembered that she must busy herself about the house and have an excellent meal prepared.

Angélique was a wanderer. Ever since her days in Toulouse life had driven her from one place to another until she had grown accustomed to feel at home anywhere. She needed very little to create the homely atmosphere she needed around her: a good fire, warmth, a few oddments in a bag, a few comfortable clothes, and Honorine's box of treasures. She had liked all the different places she had lived in, but had grown attached to none of them. The tiny room in the rue des Francs-Bourgeois where she had lived with her two little boys held more pleasant memories for her than the Beautreillis mansion where she used to hold such elegant receptions. She had not as many happy memories of her suite of rooms at Versailles as she had of the chimney-corner in La Rochelle, where she used to sit with old Rebecca of an evening, 'picking' a crab they had cooked in the ashes. She even remembered with contentment the stable in the Abbey of Nieul where she had slept with her child, and where the singing of the monks had brought her an extraordinary peace.

Yet, ever since she had found her husband and sons again she had developed a nostalgic desire to have a house of her own, in which she could make them at home and look after them. The natural urge that women have always to go on rebuilding their nest after it has been destroyed was not dead within her. So this morning her head was full of ideas, which she had decided to put into action without even waiting for the French to depart.

She found the Jonases in the next room, peering through the cracks in the little window to see what was going on in the courtyard.

'Dame Angélique, we are not at all happy,' they said, lowering their voices and glancing all about them as if expecting to see the devil himself rise up through the floor. 'It appears that a missionary has come to say Mass for the French soldiers. . . . A Jesuit. . . .'

As they uttered this last word their eyes nearly started out of their heads and Angélique found it difficult to repress a smile.

There had been a tragedy in these people's lives. As Huguenots of La Rochelle they had sent their two little boys of seven and eight off to school one morning and the children had never come home. They had heard later that the two Protestant children had been imprudent enough to stop and watch a Catholic procession as it went by; for they were curious to see the embroidered chasubles and the gold monstrances. Some worthy souls had seen in their interest irrefutable proof of their desire for conversion and had taken them off to the Jesuits. At that very moment a cart-load of Protestant children who had been removed from the care of their parents was on its way out of the city, and the two little lads had been loaded on to it along with the others. All attempts to find them or even to find out what had happened to them had proved fruitless.

It was not hard to understand the Jonases' fright today. Angélique herself had shared the countless dangers the French Huguenots had lived through, forced as they were to flee a kingdom in which persecution of their sect was growing worse with every day, although she herself was a Catholic, had been brought up in a convent, and one of her brothers, Raymond, belonged to the Society of Jesus.

'You must not get all upset,' she told them. 'We are not in La Rochelle any more. I shall go and see what is happening, but I am quite sure that there is nothing very sinister about this worthy missionary.'

In the courtyard she found something which she certainly had not expected, but which in itself was in no way alarming, namely a portable altar in carved wood gilded over.

Some tall Indians covered in medallions were busy securing it in a wooden packing-case which two slaves lifted up on to their shoulders. Their chief was a tall, thin, supple man, draped in a black bearskin and holding a lance in his hand. His sharp profile with the upper lip standing out over two prominent front teeth gave him the appearance of a sarcastic squirrel.

As she went by, Angélique thought it wise to greet him but he did not return her greeting. Shortly afterwards they left the outpost.

After their departure the courtyard appeared almost deserted. There were still a few traces of the feasting of the night before : ashes and cold logs lay where the three fires had been, and a yellow dog sniffed at some scraps of meat, nibbling at them without much sign of appetite. There was not a bone left behind and every container from the big stewpot down to the bark bowls had been cleared away.

With his red woollen cap pulled down to his eyebrows old Eloi Macollet was sitting smoking on a bench in the sunshine, leaning against the wall of the cottage. He gave her a sidelong glance, like an Indian, and he too appeared not to have heard her greeting.

In a corner down by the store, she found Honorine and Elvire's two little boys rapt in admiration while the youngest of the drummer-boys practised on his drum. He was a puny-looking lad who could hardly have been more than twelve or thirteen, and he literally disappeared beneath his three-cornered hat and his blue military capote. But his skinny wrists seemed to be uncommonly strong and agile, and when he began one of his impressive rolls you could no longer see his drumsticks.

'He has promised to teach us,' said Honorine in great excitement.

The drum was taller than she was but she had not the slightest doubt that she would rapidly master the instrument.

Angélique went off again and shortly bumped into Octave Malaprade.

'Madame, we are not savages,' he told her, 'and we cannot go on living on bear fat. I must think up a menu to include some good Christian food. Could you help me?'

He had been the cook on board the *Gouldsboro* and behaved more like a steward than a run-of-the-mill cook. The inhabitants of Bordeaux are great gourmets. His sing-song Médoc accent which gave his speech a slightly southern touch, called forth memories of *agapes de cèpes à la crème* and succulent steaks coated with the famous *sauce au vin rouge et aux échalottes*, as it is eaten in the taverns of Bordeaux.

In this barbarous country there was no question of their being able to create such masterpieces, but with the imagination of a true artist, Malaprade was already beginning to see how he could make the best of what local products there were.

Angélique and he entered the storehouse together. He told her that he had already taken an inventory of the little cellar, which held only barrels of wine, beer, and flasks of brandy.

Angélique would have been astonished to learn that, while she was busy inspecting the stores, she was at the same time irresistibly and quite extraordinarily filling the thoughts of two men as different from each other as Loménie-Chambord the Knight of Malta and his lieutenant, Monsieur de Pont-Briand.

The latter, accompanied by Romain de l'Aubignière and Second-Lieutenant Fallières, was walking back from the esplanade where Mass had just been celebrated.

He caught a glimpse of Angélique before she vanished into the doorway of the storehouse, and stopped dead in his tracks.

'That woman! Oh! that woman!'

L'Aubignière gave a sigh of exasperation. 'Are you still at

it. . . ? I had hoped that after you had slept off your brandy you would stop making such a bloody ass of yourself!'

'Shut up! You don't know what you're talking about. Are you incapable of seeing that you only meet a woman like that once in a lifetime? Granted, she's lovely, but there's more to her than that. To put it bluntly, one has a feeling with her that she enjoys a good lay and does it well.'

'And you saw that all in a flash, did you?' replied the trapper ironically. 'What do you want to go and fall for a white woman for? You've got Chief Faronho's daughter, and all the savages you want at Fort Saint Francis, where you live like a king!'

'I like the Indian women,' said little Fallières. 'It's funny . . . they've no hair! They're smooth all over like children.'

'Well, I'd jolly well like to feel some hair again . . .'

'Shut up, you lewd lout. You're out of your mind.'

'I've had enough of savages. I want some white skin! A woman who reminds me of the ones I used to lay in the Paris brothels when I was a young man. We didn't half have fun!'

'Well, get back to your Paris then! Who's stopping you?'

L'Aubignière and Fallières burst out laughing; for they knew perfectly well why Pont-Briand kept on re-enlisting with the colonial regiment instead of returning to France. He suffered from sea-sickness and his first crossing had left him with such terrible memories that he had sworn never to set foot on a ship again.

'No need to go back to Paris if I find what I want here,' he growled, looking defiantly at his two comrades, who had grown serious again. The trapper laid a hand on his arm.

'Listen, Pont-Briand, it's no go, old chap. You're forgetting Count Peyrac. Believe me, he has his reputation too; Castine tells me that he is pretty fond of women and can have Indian women or whoever he wants whenever he feels like it. He is a man who likes a good lay as well, and who does it well. Anyway, well enough to keep a woman happy enough not to care much about others. You only have to see the rapturous way she looks at him. Believe me, you have no chance in that direction. And as for him, he's not going to give up his handsome wench!'

'Wench! But she's his wife,' young Fallières protested, shocked at the coarse, off-handed way the two men had spoken about a woman whom he, from the moment he set eyes on her, had regarded as a great lady, as fascinating as she was inaccessible.

'His wife! That's what *they* say! For a start, they're neither of them wearing wedding rings!'

Pont-Briand was one of those men capable of a total disregard for the obvious, which enables them to bend the facts to suit their purpose and keep their conscience clear. He managed to convince himself more and more strongly that Angélique was free, only too ready to think of her as one of those lovely creatures condemned by common law that the Kingdom of France was accustomed to unload on the colonies, and who could always be picked up in the Caribbean islands. If Peyrac had appropriated her, why shouldn't he? His friends left him and he remained leaning against the palisade, smoking, his eyes glued to the door of the storehouse through which she had vanished.

On the other side of the courtyard Count Loménie-Chambord, seated in front of an upturned barrel he was using as a desk, was reading a letter from Father Orgeval. For it had not been the head of the Acadian mission who had celebrated Mass that morning at Katarunk but one of his assistants, Father Lespinas, and he had brought the Colonel a letter from his superior.

The sun blazed down from a pale-blue sky. It was a day that was to be filled with a multitude of small happenings, which, added together, became something like the light mists of a summer's day building up little by little into thick storm clouds or even a hurricane.

Anxiety and uneasiness lay just below the surface; people haltingly sought contact with one another without daring to come out into the open. Count Loménie, the leader of the Canadian mission, read his letter:

My dearest friend,

It is a great source of sorrow to me not to be able to see you. As I was about to set out to meet you, something unexpected – I might almost say supernatural – happened, which so upset me and brought on such a raging fever that I had to break off my journey and make for the little village of Mobedean, which I reached with considerable difficulty. I am still unable to leave my bed and I still lie here shivering. But I must find strength to write to you.

Our faithful Abenakis, the Patsuiketts and their Chief have come down from the upper reaches of the Connecticut to this village, and are only waiting for a sign from you to join your troops in your holy campaign to exterminate not only the Iroquois in the region but the group of undesirable foreigners who are trying to settle there. You could wind up your campaign with a double victory, and today, which is the feast of the Archangel Raphael, I could not help thinking of you as I read the words of the gradual: 'Raphael the Angel of the Lord took hold of the demon and put him in chains...'

When strength is sustained by grace, it has no need of a thousand wiles or a thousand battles to achieve its ends.

Loménie understood full well what his childhood friend, the Jesuit, meant. Peyrac in Upper Kennebec was 'a contemptible, heretical Englishman penetrating in the heart of our land once the way is opened up for him'.

'Now he is chained and powerless,' Father Orgeval wrote, 'thanks to you.'

Loménie tugged thoughtfully at his beard. There was a mis-understanding.... It did not seem to have occurred to the Reverend Father that Count Peyrac and his men might not have been arrested. Apparently he couldn't imagine that they might have come to some sort of understanding.

But why had he not come to Katarunk himself, after meeting Pont-Briand, Maudreuil and L'Aubignière two days before? Did the incident of the woman on horseback, whom, in the dark-ness, they had taken for the apparition of a she-devil astride her mythical unicorn, justify his sudden departure?

It was he, Father Sebastian d'Orgeval who, in the spring of the previous year, had asked for help against the foreigners settling in Acadia.

Loménie almost decided to embark and visit the Jesuit lower down the river. He could be there that same evening and would come back two days later. But he thought better of it, realizing that he should not leave his men nor his Indian allies. Their situation was unstable, explosive, and his presence here indispensable to avoid any incident which might touch off the powder barrel.

'I am anxious to hear your news,' the Father went on. 'If only you knew how pleasing it is for me, my dear friend, my *dear brother, to know that you are near. . . .'*

Beneath the deliberately cold, peremptory tone of the Jesuit, one had a glimpse at this point of the warmth of affection which was his great charm and the delight of those he counted as his friends. Loménie was one of them, their friendship going back for many years, in fact to their school-days. It was the friendship of two children who had grown up close to each other beneath the dark vaults and the miserable cold of the dawn with its smell of ink and incense, the murmuring sound of the Mass and the recitation of lessons. Sebastian d'Orgeval, a quiet sensitive boy, had found the hardships of life as a boarder hard to bear. Loménie was a contented, gentle, happy lad, and he supported and protected his friend, driving away the shadows that weighed on his childish soul which might well, without this friendship, have been broken. Many a young child goes into a decline and wastes away in the infirmary of a boarding-school.

Then came adolescence and their roles were reversed; Sebastian d'Orgeval developed magnificently, burning with a sombre fire, enduring every manner of mortification and hardship with unshakeable courage, and encouraging Loménie, who was strong but less fervent, to follow him along the path to saintliness.

Their theological studies had separated them, but the two friends had met again years later in Canada. Loménie-Chambord had been the first to disembark, with another Knight of Malta, Monsieur de Maisonneuve, and they had founded the settlement of Montreal. Indeed, this had influenced his friend the Jesuit's decision to come to Canada. Loménie's letters had aroused a passionate vocation for the conversion of the Indians in d'Orgeval, who at the time was teaching philosophy and mathematics in the Jesuit college at Annecy.

Father Orgeval had done wonders in the ten years since he came to New France. He knew the whole country, every tribe, every dialect, and had experienced everything, even the torments of martyrdom. Loménie considered his own colonial service to be of little merit and relatively unimportant beside that of his friend. He felt inferior, and sometimes reproached himself for having allowed his passion for a military career to overshadow his religious vocation in which he believed he should have been more single-minded. So he was always touched to the bottom of his heart, when, in the letters they exchanged, a word or a phrase brought him closer to the friend whose exceptional qualities had come to inspire him with a kind of veneration. Now, as he leaned on his desk, he thought of Orgeval's high forehead with its thick tuft of auburn hair. Orgeval had an immense forehead, which was an indication of his extraordinary intelligence.

'This child will never live with a forehead like that,' the teachers in the seminary used to say. 'His intelligence will kill him.'

Blue eyes shone out under his bushy eyebrows, astonishingly clear and deep-set; his features were nobly cut and his nose, which had been broken by the Iroquois, in no way detracted from the impression they made; his broad, full mouth was framed by a beard like that of Christ. This impressive looking man bore the most crushing of burdens with the utmost serenity.

Loménie imagined his pen running swiftly across the piece of birch-bark which he used as parchment, although the hand that held it was shaking with fever. This hand was strangely swollen and pink, the result of terrible burns, and some of its fingers were too short, like those of a leper, while others were blackened by flames and still others stubbed at the ends where the nails had been torn out. His courage under torture had so impressed the Iroquois that they had allowed him to live. When he had recovered from his terrible burns, Father Orgeval had escaped and, after a journey fraught with peril, had reached New Holland and set sail for Europe. In spite of his mutilations, the Pope had granted him permission to celebrate Mass, and the great Jesuit had preached at Versailles and in Notre-Dame de Paris, to a congregation reduced to tears among whom ten ladies had fainted.

On his return to Canada he had been sent to Acadia, a province hitherto neglected on account of its remoteness and the dangers it was exposed to from its proximity to the British territories. On reflection, it would have been hard to find a man more suitable and better prepared for this difficult mission which had so many hidden facets. The presence of Father Orgeval on the banks of the Kennebec and the Penobscot, which were both important waterways, took on a political significance. He had received his instructions from the King in person.

'*Without you, without your help, my task would be an in-*

*tolerably heavy one, and I will not disguise from you the fact
that for many a long week now I have been troubled by a
terrible sense of foreboding. . . .'* the Jesuit's letter went on.

Loménie himself had also been troubled by a sense of foreboding. The weather, which was dry and, when the sun shone,
scorching hot against the icy background of winter, accounted
for much of his anxiety. For sparks would sometimes flash
from the ends of a person's hair, and run crackling over his
clothes, irritating like an infestation at the slightest movement.
There are certain times in certain seasons when everything
seems ready to burst into flames. Towards the end of winter or
at the end of summer, one has a feeling of being surrounded by
evil spirits. It is the time of sunspots, a time of tragedy, of
petty meannesses or bloody disasters. In the towns, a husband
whose wife has deceived him will kill his rival, and in the
depths of the forest a man will slay his best friend for the skin
of a beaver or an otter.

The Governor of Quebec remonstrates with the Bishop because he has not burned incense to him on the feast of Saint
Louis, alleging that it was not only his own feast day, but also
that of the King of France whose representative he is. A wine
merchant empties a whole crate of expensive bottles out of a
window on to a sailor who owes him money; little Indian boys
in the seminary leap over the walls and run away back to the
forest; nuns in their convents are tormented with passion, while
at night a devil wanders at large, twitching the feet of the most
saintly among them, banging the shutters and raising up before
their appalled gaze visions of naked women with flashing eyes,
mounted on apocalyptic unicorns. . . .

Count Loménie-Chambord himself remembered one of the
phrases in the prophecy of the She-Devil of Acadia.

'A very beautiful naked woman rose up out of the waters
astride a unicorn . . .'

A very beautiful woman . . .

He became aware of the fact that he had never stopped
thinking about Angélique de Peyrac. It was as if her face, her
presence, were stamped like a watermark over the entire letter
he was reading, and he felt intuitively that Father Orgeval, as
he had written, had also had her constantly in his mind,
although he had never met her. The martyr missionary knew
everything from a distance.

Count Loménie-Chambord slipped his hand quickly into the

pocket of his military cloak where he encountered his rosary beads. Their contact did him good and he felt calmer again. He must not lose his head. Sitting down at his barrel, he wrote his reply to Father Orgeval:

> ...For the moment a temporal rather than a religious policy seems to be indicated. Let me explain.... Warfare does not seem to me to be the only desirable course of action when what one is seeking is peace and it seemed wise both in the interests of Canada and in those of the King.... Monsieur de Peyrac has already given us proof of his good-will by supplying French outposts along the coast of Acadia during the winter.... Furthermore, as L'Aubignière, Pont-Briand, and Maudreuil had fallen into his hands yesterday, we were forced to parley and to give an undertaking. We should certainly not have succeeded in overcoming his company except with great bloodshed and this in any case did not seem to me essential ... I am confident in the good faith of this man....

When he had finished he swiftly sanded the wet ink. His orderly blew on the end of a touch-stick to melt the red sealing wax with which the Count closed the folded letter. While the wax was still soft, he pressed his seal into it: two sable towers on a field of gules, surmounted by a sun of or.

Absorbed and preoccupied as he was, he paid no heed to the Indians who were running hither and thither, for he had grown accustomed to their childish excitability.

CHAPTER SIXTEEN

ACCOMPANIED BY Octave Malaprade, Angélique was finishing her inventory. In the stores at Katarunk there were ample supplies of maize, and salted meat in two well-stocked largish wooden chests; there were also pieces of dried meat hanging from the rafters and even some hams that did not look like wild pig. O'Connell had been going in for pig-breeding, Malaprade said:

'The Irishman in whose charge Count Peyrac left the outpost during his last journey, told me that he raised some pigs brought over from Europe. Four or five of them are still grazing in the forest and we must bring them in to the camp before the first snows. We shall fatten them up for a while with scraps and kill them for Christmas. We should get about five hundred ells of sausages from them, three hundred pounds of pickled pork, with luck ten good hams and a hundred ells of black and white blood-pudding. That should be enough to see us through the winter even if the game gets thin on the ground.'

'That all depends on how many we have to feed, Monsieur Octave. If we have to keep a whole garrison going as we are now . . .'

The man pulled a face:

'That is not the intention of Monsieur le Comte. He told me so only this morning. If I am to believe the information I was kindly given this morning, the gentlemen from Canada and their savages will be leaving us tomorrow at crack of dawn.'

'O'Connell is the big fat red-head, isn't he? He never seems to be there when he's wanted and when one does see him he always looks a trifle bewildered.'

'Yes, he gets a bit bewildered by the intense activity of the Canadian gentlemen and above all of the Jesuit Father who called here this morning. O'Connell has gone off down the river with the Abenaki Indians as far as the mission, where he hopes to go to confession and receive the blessing of the great missionary himself. Now I am a good Catholic, Madame, but I reckon that just at present the most urgent task is to find out how we stand for stores. Winter is coming on and it's no joke wintering in these latitudes even when one has considerable supplies in hand.'

'Have you already spent some time here?'

'Yes, I strung along with Count Peyrac last year.'

As she chatted on with her newly-acquired steward, Angélique continued to list the stocks of food. There were large quantities of dried berries and even some dried mushrooms. The berries were only supplementary items, but by no means negligible when, towards the end of the winter, their weary bodies had grown tired of salted foods and preserves. She remembered the theory propounded by old Savary the traveller, who maintained that there were fewer cases of scurvy on long sea journeys if, failing fresh fruit, a handful of dried fruits was eaten daily.

'We shall soak some in water and put them into tarts or pies.

Oh, I know what I need, Octave; I would like some white flour to make a cake or, at least, a good cob of bread. We haven't had any for days.'

'I think there are a few sacks,' Malaprade replied.

Angélique was delighted with her find. But Malaprade frowned when he examined the contents of the sacks.

'We have no more than twenty pounds of white flour left. The rest is barley or rye flour. And, what's more, this was bought in Boston, so it's poor quality badly-ground wheat. Nothing but dust . . . the British, really, they haven't a clue.'

'Never mind, we shall still have a good loaf of bread tonight and we'll use some spruce beer to raise it. . . .'

Octave Malaprade took a calabash and put enough flour in it for their luxurious project. As he went along he wrote down the list of supplies on a piece of birch-bark stretched between two pine twigs. He noted three big round cheeses, barrels of sauerkraut, kegs of oil and pots of fat, dried peas, and beans, and on some swinging bails a whole array of neatly stocked marrows and pumpkins.

'We must eat those quickly,' said Angélique. 'These vegetables, which are apparently plentiful in America, soon spoil.'

'That's where you are wrong, Madame. Here, marrows will dry without losing any of their flavour and they can be used far into the winter months, although as food they are rather insipid and none too easy to digest.'

Their tour of inspection had cheered them both, and Angélique felt she would be able to make herself useful in the days to come in dealing with problems of a familiar nature.

But alas! The very next moment she was brought face to face with the realities of her new life. As they left the stores they encountered a crowd of Indians clustering round the door in silence. They had some difficulty in forcing their way out. Malaprade, thinking the Indians might be bent on pilferage, quickly closed the wooden door behind him and fastened the latches.

'If they manage to get in here they will eat us out of house and home! But what do they want? What's got into them?'

He knew a few words of the native language, but his questions received no reply.

Lieutenant Pont-Briand elbowed his way through the crowd to reach them, grabbed Angélique by the arm and set his impressive frame as a rampart between her and the evil-smelling onslaught of the Indians.

'Don't be upset, Madame. I noticed that you were in difficulties. What is going on?'

'How should I know? I don't understand what they want.'

The Indians turned to the lieutenant, shouting all at once with looks that spelt either anguish or ecstasy.

'The legend of your encounter with the tortoise, which is the sign of the Iroquois, has been passed on from wigwam to wigwam during the night. They want to know from your lips whether the Iroquois is really vanquished and whether you have reduced him to bondage. . . . You see, in their eyes, symbols and dreams are more important than life itself. But have no fear, I shall make sure that you are spared their curiosity.'

He spoke firmly to the Indians and they consented to wander off, still talking animatedly among themselves.

Pont-Briand was glad of this opportunity to approach Angélique and to assume the role of her protector. He was aware of the scent of her skin, but she saw through him and disengaged herself from the hand on her arm.

'Madame, I should like to ask you a question.'

'Ask away then.'

'Were you really the infernal marksman that gave me such a rough time yesterday? They tell me it was you, but I find it hard to believe.'

'Well, it's true. Believe me, never have I had to deal with so pig-headed a man. I really thought I would have to break your arm to get you to stop, since I had orders to stop you reaching the other bank. You know, Lieutenant, I think you find it very hard to grasp my precise status,' she added with a meaningful look. He gathered that she found his attentions too pressing, and out of place. But he could not bring himself to leave her. Since he had after all come to rescue her from an awkward situation, she stayed to talk for a few moments more, then, with a reserved nod and smile, she left him.

He felt shaken and giddy, as if he were drunk. The air before him trembled and her flashing smile danced before his eyes. What a lot had happened during the past two days! His whole world had been turned topsy-turvy; everything seemed to have a different flavour, a different colour. But why had Loménie refused to fight Peyrac? He, Pont-Briand, would have been the first to lay hands on her, thus acquiring the right to take her as his captive to Quebec ... to convert her. Have I not also the right to lead a lost soul back to heaven...? That way, I could have installed her in my house.

What evil spell had that great black devil with the masked face cast on them all to make them, French Canadians, as gentle and docile as a lot of sheep?

Beware, old chap, beware of evil spells! And what does it matter after all, he told himself, if she is the She-Devil of Acadia and if she does come from hell! I'd be happy to join her there!

CHAPTER SEVENTEEN

WHATEVER APPEARANCES may have suggested, the day dragged slowly on and everyone remained tense.

'What is to become of us?' moaned Madame Jonas tearfully. The arrival of the Jesuit had proved too much for her courage. 'Fetch your children inside, Elvire, they will slaughter them.'

Over the past few days Angélique had developed a considerable admiration for Peyrac's companions. The men showed an admirable spirit of discipline, and by remaining calm as they did, they manifested their confidence in their leader. Yet there were foreigners among them: Englishmen, Spaniards, Frenchmen on the run, men who might well have expected to be treated as enemies by those who awaited them at Katarunk. Even so they had entered the fort, heads held high, behind Count Peyrac, and the French had not protested. They had even all made merry together, laughing and singing companionably.

But they kept a constant wary eye on one another. Peyrac had a talk with Monsieur de Loménie, then went and greeted the chieftain of the Algonquins and the Hurons, taking them gifts of tobacco and beads.

The men worked together, and swopped stories.

'I wish they'd go! My goodness, how I wish they'd go to the devil!' Angélique thought.

Meanwhile, one must keep up the little game, keep a wary eye on everything and show no trace of fear or impatience.

She tried to create an everyday, humdrum atmosphere, making a show of settling down among her possessions. But it was difficult, for everyone's nerves were on edge.

Once when she had gone over to the well and was busy hauling up the big wooden, iron-banded bucket, she called Cantor who was standing near by.

'Would you give me a hand, my son?'

To which he replied arrogantly:

'What do you take me for? That's women's work!'

Angélique felt herself turn pale and, reacting automatically, seized the bucket and hurled the entire contents over him.

'That should freshen up the ideas of a great warrior like you, who considers himself too high-and-mighty to help his mother carry a heavy load.'

She hooked the bucket on to the chain again with a clatter and let it down the well, tight-lipped with anger. Cantor was soaked from head to foot and his eyes flashed angrily at her, but Angélique gave him as good as she got.

This furious exchange of glances appeared to strike old Eloi Macollet, who alone had witnessed the scene closely, as wildly funny. He came up with a great toothless grin on his face.

'Bravo, that's the way to bring up the young!'

A crowd of Indians, who had been lolling around doing nothing, rushed up roaring with laughter at the young man in his wet clothes, telling one another what they had seen from a distance and coming to take a closer look at Angélique; they hooted with laughter as if she were undoubtedly the funniest animal in creation. . . . They hustled so close round her that she almost let the full bucket fall down the well and nearly fell in herself.

'Back! Back!' said Macollet. He thrust them back with a few sharp words. 'I'll give you a hand, ma'am. I like to see women with spirit, I do. Oh, these youngsters nowadays, they have to be teached, and that's a fact. They don't know nothing, they don't. I'll carry your bucket for you. There's no shame in that when it's for a lady of your station. And I'm good deal more of a warrior than that little whipper-snapper. . . .'

'Hey, just look at him paying court to a lady,' Cantor shouted at him, his voice breaking in fury. 'You giving lessons in manners, that's a nice one! You who can't even take your cap from your skull, even with ladies present or even at Mass. I saw you this morning, when the priest was saying Mass.'

'My cap is my cap,' the old man replied. 'But if you're as easy to please as all that, I'll take it off for you, my lad.'

'No, don't,' L'Aubignière and Perrot shouted simultaneously. They had been passing by and rushed towards the old man, grabbing his two arms. 'Don't you look, Madame. He has the most hideous skull in the whole of New France.'

'He was scalped when he was a young man,' Perrot explained.

'Near Montreal,' added Macollet by way of explanation.

'It's a rare thing for anyone to survive such an operation. But he did! It was Mother Marguerite Bourgeois who saved his life. But the result is not nice to look at, and he is better with his cap on. Keep still, Eloi.'

'No, I want to give that little varmint a lesson.'

But Cantor had run away to hide his vexation and change his clothes.

The day dragged slowly on under a brilliant sky, and still more slowly a few of the Hurons and the Algonquins began to leave the camp. They had been told that there would be no war and had been given handsome gifts by way of compensation for their disappointment.

Peyrac kept an eye on them from a distance and every time one of the canoes left the shore and began to paddle up-stream, he felt a sense of relief. His shrewd glance travelled from the black wall of fir-trees in the north, to the meandering curves of the river that flowed like a golden snake through the kingdom of the trees then went on its way towards the south-east. For the time being the spectre of war was departing, leaving these vast uncivilized lands to go back to their customary daily round of hunting, fishing, sleeping and smoking.

The beach was humming with activity again, but this time it was the harmless hustle and bustle of a market day. The natives of the small local tribes, Metallaks, Narrandsouaks and Sokokis, were also preparing to leave, unmindful of the events that had passed them by so closely and of which they might well have been the victims, like all small neutral nations that lie between two opposing, powerful forces.

A thin, happy shout rose through the clear evening air and Joffrey de Peyrac turned in the direction from which it had come. It was little Honorine playing with her friends Bartholomew and Thomas, the little Huguenot boys from La Rochelle.

Peyrac watched her for a moment. She seemed happy, her cheeks were pink and covered in dust, and she had that look of health and rapture seen on children who are left to their own devices the whole day long.

His heart stirred with tenderness towards her. He felt strangely attached to this little illegitimate child, an attachment arising out of the rich complexity of feelings that lie concealed in a manly heart, feelings which they rarely have occasion to bring into play, and among which one would find first and foremost a sense of justice.

Looking at this tiny creature, so particularly weak and unprotected, that had received nothing when she came into the world, not even her mother's love, he felt that in exchange, since she had been placed under his protection, he must give her everything.

He always kept an eye on the child, and could see that Honorine was delighted, now they had reached Katarunk, to be in her own home with her own family, among people who did not merely tolerate her, as they had in La Rochelle where her mother had been a servant. Here she took first place, first place of all, as she had decided in her little head with its bulging forehead, for was she not the daughter of Count Peyrac?

She was the daughter of the man they called my lord as they bowed before him, of the man who was the arbiter of life and death, of peace and of war. Therefore, since she was the daughter of so great a leader, she must be the most important person after him, and her pride in her high rank was apparent in her exhilaration and the little shrieks of joy she gave, for all the world like an inebriated swallow.

All was well. He smiled. Yes, she was the daughter of his choice, for she had been free to choose, had chosen him, and her faith in him was unshakeable.

PART TWO

THE IROQUOIS

CHAPTER EIGHTEEN

THE SMOKY evening had come, with its accompaniment of red fires and lights shining through the cold blue darkness.

The little cottage was suddenly rent by a piercing, hysterical scream.

Angélique was busy setting bowls on the table for the children's supper.

The scream came from the room on the left, her own room, which Elvire had entered a few moments before to turn down the bed.

Angélique thought:

'Here we go, the massacre is beginning!'

And she rushed in with her hand on the butt of the pistol that never left her side.

In the middle of the room stood an Indian holding by one wrist Elvire, who was half-crazed with fear. The Indian was even more hideous and terrifying than the one she had seen the day before on the hillside. His pitted face, disfigured by small-pox, was daubed with soot, as were his naked limbs and body. A scrap of dirty red cloth held his hair so high on the top of his scalp and made it look so dishevelled that he looked just like a porcupine. You could smell him throughout the room.

She thought: 'He's an Iroquois!'

He had placed his other hand across Elvire's mouth and, after a struggle, she fell to the floor in a faint.

Angélique slowly raised her gun, hesitating. The Indian's eyes flashed and he uttered a few stifled words which she did not understand, but which she guessed from his gestures meant that he wished her to be quiet.

'Don't move,' she said to the Jonases who were standing in the doorway.

Seeing that they were not raising the alarm and that silence had fallen on the cottage again, the Indian put his hand to his filthy loin-cloth and took out a small object which he held out towards Angélique. He signalled to her to approach him, realizing that if he made a move towards her she would be frightened. She stepped carefully forward. The object he handed her was a cornelian ring and she recognized the seal engraved on the red stone as that of Rescator, her husband's seal.

Then something he had said the previous evening came back to her.

'I've got some of the Iroquois leaders on my side.'

She looked questioningly into the savage's slanting eyes.

'Tekonderoga, Tekonderoga,' he repeated in his hoarse, monotonous voice.

'Peyrac?'

He nodded vigorously.

'Nicolas Perrot?' she asked again. He gave a further nod and a glow of satisfaction lighted up his horrible face.

'I will take him this ring . . .'

The Indian clamped his greasy hand down on her arm.

He kept on repeating a certain word on a threatening tone, and she understood that he wanted her to remain silent.

The Jonases were clinging to her.

'Don't leave us alone with this devil. . . .'

'Well, you go then, Monsieur Jonas. Tell my husband that . . . someone wants him. When he sees the ring he will certainly understand. Don't speak to anyone. It seems to me that this Indian is trying to tell us to keep his visit a secret.'

'He's an Iroquois, I am sure he's an Iroquois,' Madame Jonas stammered, falling to her knees beside her unconscious niece.

The Indian, tense and on the alert, still held Angélique by the arm.

When Count Peyrac and Perrot appeared in the doorway, he released her and greeted them with hoarse welcoming noises.

'Tahoutaguete!' exclaimed Nicolas Perrot.

And after a warm exchange of greetings with the savage:

'It's Tahoutaguete, the deputy Chief of the Onondagas,' he said.

'Then he's not an Iroquois?' Madame Jonas asked hopefully.

'Yes he is! and one of the most ferocious too . . . he's a very important man among the Five Nations. Ah, good old Tahoutaguete, how good it is to see you again! But how did he get in?'

'Down the chimney,' said Elvire in a quiet voice as she came round. 'I was in here turning down the bed-cover when he just landed in the fire as silent as a devil out of hell.'

'Yes indeed! I can see that from here.'

Peyrac seemed pleased as he looked at the Iroquois.

'He has brought me back the ring I entrusted to him. It was intended to help me recognize their messenger if one day their Council agreed to parley with me.'

'It looks as if the day has come,' said Perrot, 'but they've chosen their moment badly. If ever any of those Hurons, Algonquins, or Abenakis, or any of the French wandering around out there suspected that there was an Iroquois here, and especially if they knew it was Tahoutaguete, I wouldn't give a bean for his scalp.' Then turning to the Jonases, he went on : 'Now listen, you others, you are to go into the next room and get on with preparing your meal. If anyone should come in, say nothing and try to forget you have ever seen this man.'

'That will be difficult,' Elvire murmured as she got up.

Angélique had fetched a bowl of stew and Joffrey de Peyrac handed it to the Iroquois with a twist of tobacco as a token of hospitality, but the savage backed away, refusing vigorously to touch the gifts.

'He says he will neither eat nor smoke before we have conveyed our decisions to the Grand Council of the Five Nations.' The Iroquois went over to the hearth and knelt down. He gathered together the glowing embers that he had scattered in his fall and threw a few small twigs on top of them. Then he took a pouch from his belt that contained some very finely ground yellowish flour and, after tipping a little into the palm of one hand, he uttered a single word as he held his hand out towards Nicolas Perrot.

'Water,' said Perrot.

There was a jug of fresh water standing in one corner and Angélique handed it to Perrot who poured a few drops into the savage's hand.

The man stirred the water into the flour with his forefinger, producing a not very appetizing-looking, transparent dough which he ate in tiny mouthfuls. When he had finished his frugal meal he gave a belch, wiped his hand on his moccasin, and began to speak.

Nicolas Perrot crouched down in the same position opposite him, and listened to him, patiently and amicably, without revealing any of his feelings, as he translated word for word what the savage was saying. Joffrey de Peyrac sat on a stool between them both.

Angélique sat down on the bed in the shadows. These were the words that Tahoutaguete spoke, apparently heedless of the dangers that surrounded him, a lone Iroquois, in the very heart of the enemy camp, to the man his people had nicknamed Tekonderoga, that is to say Man of Thunder:

'Ten moons ago you, Tekonderoga, whom we call Man of Thunder because it appears you can cause mountains to explode, you sent us gifts and two necklaces of wampum. It escaped nobody's notice that these porcelain beads were of inestimable value, the kind one exchanged between great nations, on the occasion of great treaties. So Swanissit made some investigations concerning the Paleface who sought alliance with the peoples of the Long House and cared enough to pay a considerable price for it, such as had never been paid before.

'You had also given me your ring and I spoke on your behalf. And what about the other presents, I asked Swanissit, were they to be disregarded? There were gunpowder, bullets, lengths of red cloth which neither rain nor sun could fade, and cooking-pots that rang beneath your fingers, made of metal so black and so strong that we did not like to use them for our everyday food, but kept them for our dead; there were axes and cutlasses so glittering that one could see one's face in them, and finally, a handful of shells so rare that I know not on what solemn alliance wampum we would ever dare to sew them; and finally, a gun that needs no touch-stick, that hides its spark in its entrails, with a butt inlaid with mother-of-pearl; Swanissit has carried it with him ever since, and it has never betrayed him.

'Furthermore, you promised us a magic powder to fertilize our crops, and you invited us here to Katarunk, to conclude a pact of alliance.

'When he had seen all these things, Swanissit pondered in his heart, and he called together the Council of Mothers and the Council of Ancients and told them that they must reach an understanding with a Paleface who took orders neither from the English, the French, nor the Black Robes, and who was, furthermore, a generous man.

'For Swanissit is very old, as I am myself, and we both know that the peoples of the Five Nations are not alas! what they were. Interminable wars have weakened us, and we spend too much time on fur-trading to the neglect of our crops, so that when winter comes, we are decimated by famine. The young men are for ever longing to be on the warpath to avenge their dead and the insults suffered, but Swanissit said, "Enough of death, or the Iroquois people will cease to be a great people held in awe. Thanks to this heaven-sent, powerful Paleface, we have an opportunity of a breathing space to gather our strength again; for one day he will be stronger than the French in Canada and will unite all the people in peace, as it is sung in our Song of Hiawatha."

'Thus spoke Swanissit and the greater part of the Nation harkened to his words.

'We therefore came to meet you, O Man of Thunder, but what did we find at Katarunk? Our enemies waiting to kill us!'

Nicolas Perrot was not at all impressed by this show of indignation. Sending a delegation to the Man of Thunder had not been the sole purpose of their voyage.

'On your way to Katarunk, did you not make a little detour to the east?' asked Perrot mildly.

'Yes, indeed, we had a small account to settle with some of the Iroquois on the Saint-John river.'

'And did you not also burn down some of the villages in that area and massacre their inhabitants?'

'Pooh! Only a few of the red scum the French make such a fuss of but who in fact don't know how to plant an ear of corn or a grain of sunflower seed.'

'Right then! Let us say that on your way back from your campaign on the Saint-John river you decided to come via Katarunk to meet the Man of Thunder....'

'And what did we find?' Tahoutaguete repeated in anger and despair. 'Was it you, Tekonderoga, who prepared this trap for us to fall into? All our worst enemies assembled here! And I don't mean only those Huron and Algonquin traitors who covet our scalps so that they can sell them at considerable profit in Quebec. But there is also that Colonel Loménie who has made a promise to his crazy God that he will kill us all before he dies, for it is true that nothing can harm him in battle; then there is Pont-Briand who walks silently on the warpath, a Paleface whose approach one cannot hear, although he is as heavy as a bison on the plain; and who else is with them? Oh, how can I bear the sight of those scoundrels? Three-Fingers who was my brother among the Onondagas, and Maudreuil who was a son to Swanissit. They are there, talking of vengeance, they who acted with such treachery! Did not

Three-Fingers kill two of our brothers when he escaped from our village, after we had shared the same cooking-pot for over a year. As for Maudreuil, he was a little boy when Swanissit took him in. He was handsome, and a good hunter, and our hearts were filled with sadness when we were forced to exchange him for two chieftains the French had taken prisoner. And now he too has forgotten the kindness we showed him, and the warmth of our hut, and here he is today telling everyone that he seeks to avenge the death of his family, his father, his mother, and his sisters whom Swanissit had killed. Nor is this true, for Swanissit has never scalped either a woman nor a child with his hands; and Maudreuil knows this better than anyone else. It was the Palefaces who taught us to kill women and children and what can we, the Elders, do if our young warriors have begun to imitate them? As for me, I am old, and I too shall die in the tradition of my forefathers, without ever having killed a woman or a child.

'When I went to Quebec, how many a time did I hear the French say: "as two-faced as an Iroquois" ... but who has been the more two-faced, us, or those who, like Maudreuil and Three-Fingers, betrayed the laws of adoption by which we had given them security instead of death? Vakia Toutavesa!'

Several times he repeated: 'Vakia Toutavesa', which means: 'It makes me shake and quiver to the very marrow....'

'And what about Black Robe Etskon-Honsi who is at Mobedean with all his preachers and his altar of gilded wood? Why did he come? Did he come to do the Magic?

'And what of Piksarett, the chief of the Patsuiketts, one of our worst enemies, who has the scalps of at least thirty of our brothers hanging on the door of his wigwam? What did he come here for?'

'The Abenakis have made peace with the English and with the Paleface Tekonderoga,' said Perrot.

'But not Piksarett. Piksarett is not an Abenaki like the others. He would break any treaty for an English or an Iroquois scalp! He hears only one voice, the voice of Black Robe. He proclaims that baptism is good for the Abenakis and that it is the God of the Palefaces that brings them victory. Black Robe has him in his power, and Black Robe seeks the destruction of the Iroquois.'

'But Black Robe is not in command of the armies. It is Colonel Loménie's decision whether we fight or not. And the

Colonel also wants to make peace with Tekonderoga.'

'But will he manage to hold back his friends the Abenakis? They have been after us now for several days.... They even captured Anhisera, the chief of the Oueiouts, and they half cooked him the other evening. He managed to escape and make his way back to us. We are living in holes in the ground and dare not approach your house, for it has been made foul by the presence of these jackals and wolves. Was it you, Tekonderoga, who laid this trap for us?' he repeated in solemn tones.

With Nicolas Perrot acting as go-between, Peyrac explained briefly that he himself had been caught unawares by the French incursion, and that at the moment he was trying desperately to get them to return home before any trouble occurred.

Contrary to what one might have feared, the Iroquois plenipotentiary appeared not to doubt his word in the matter, although he still seemed worried. He had already sensed the truth but the situation was none the less serious for his people.

'We could escape from them more easily if we were on the other side of the river, but we can no longer cross the river. There are too many people around between Katarunk and Mobedean.' Then he crouched even lower and plunged into meditation.

'We are being hunted in the forest,' he went on. 'Do you think we shall be able to escape the dogs on our heels for long?

'Tekonderoga, if you are truly powerful, give us a guarantee that we can cross the Kennebec in safety.... Protect us against those coyotes.'

'I think I can get Colonel de Loménie to agree to that,' said Peyrac. 'You haven't done anything reprehensible in the region, have you?'

'We were coming to see you.'

'Be patient until the day after tomorrow. The allies of the French are beginning to take to the river and heading up north. Most of them will have gone by then and you will be able to send a peace delegation to Katarunk.'

Tahoutaguete's face, which looked like a great earth-covered tuber, wrinkled under the effort of reflection. Then he stood up.

'I think that will be well,' he said. 'If our peace terms are rejected and we are unable to cross the river, at least we shall have fewer enemies to fight. Did you say that the tribes are heading north?'

'At least we can hasten their departure as much as possible,' said Perrot.

'Now my hardest task yet remains,' said the Indian. 'I have to convince Outakke, the chieftain of the Mohawks, that he must come to terms with you. You know that every one of the chieftains of the Five Nations has to give his consent before any action can be taken. Well, Outakke will hear none of it. He says that one can expect nothing but treachery from Palefaces, and that not a single exception to this rule exists. He is for war and war only. He wants to launch an attack with his braves on the Patsuiketts, while we attack here.'

'That is madness, and you know it, Tahoutaguete, and Swanissit knows it too. Can't he convince Outakke?'

'You know Outakke,' the man replied sceptically, 'his skull is harder than granite. And he said a terrible thing to Swanissit, which was that he had learned in a dream that you, Tekonderoga, Man of Thunder, would bring about Swanissit's death, Swanissit the great chieftain of the Five Nations.'

'I?' exclaimed Peyrac half standing up, in a burst of anger worthy of the best Indian tradition. 'Is that wretched Mohawk chieftain whom I have never even seen accusing me of treachery?'

'How could you possibly be the cause of Swanissit's death since you are seeking alliance with him? That was Swanissit's reply to Outakke. But we are not easy in our minds, because we know full well that Outakke is friendly with the Spirit of Dreams.... We also know that he is a great liar for he told us that he had overheard the Algonquins saying at one of their camps that your wife had triumphed over the symbol of the Iroquois at the Moxie waterfall, thus proving that you are planning our downfall.'

Tahoutaguete's little bloodshot eyes went from Peyrac to Angélique where she sat in the shadows. They felt that he was hoping for some kind of words of hope, but that the two serious objections that chief Outakke had presented had gravely shaken his own confidence in the Paleface, the Man of Thunder, whom he had warmly supported at the Council.

'Do the Iroquois want my wife to die?' asked Peyrac. 'Had you and Swanissit and the others decided suddenly to appear before her so that her frightened steed might hurl her and her child into the abyss? No, you did not seek that. But that was what the tortoise did. So you see, I don't hold you and yours responsible for what the tortoise did any more than you should consider my wife, who moved it out of her path to save her own life, responsible for wishing to harm the Five Nations? You know as well as I do that the tortoise is a capricious, dreamy animal, and that the spirit of your ancestors that slumbers within him does not always guide his actions.'

This piece of subtle logic seemed to please Tahoutaguete who, after passing it back and forth several times through the convolutions of his Indian brain, gave his approval by nodding his head several times.

'I always did think that Outakke was a little mad. His hatred leads him astray. Now Swanissit, he is a wise man. He wants to save the Five Nations and has seen that you could help him.'

'I shall help him,' said Peyrac, laying his hand on the Indian's.

He thought it pointless for the moment to ask for explanations of the Cayuga attack in the south.

'Return to the forest and tell Swanissit that he must continue to trust me. I shall do my best to hasten the departure of most of the Indians who are camping around my outpost, and I shall try to obtain a truce from the French officers to enable your braves to cross the river. In two days' time we shall let you know whether the French agree to the truce and whether your chieftains can come to Katarunk in safety.'

The Iroquois messenger rose and, after applying more soot to his face with a piece of charcoal; for his disguise had enabled him to move unseen through the night, he pushed the burning logs to one side with his moccasin and swung himself lithely up into the chimney.

They stood motionless for a long while, waiting for the shouts that would have told of a band of savages hot on the trail of the enemy. But nothing happened.

'That's odd!' said Nicolas Perrot, scratching his head beneath his fur cap. 'What a business! I have the impression that there's going to be one devil of a mess-up before long.'

'I thought that the hostile chieftain Outakke had been seized by the French during a banquet to which he had been invited and that he had been sent to France and sentenced to penal servitude!'

'Yes, he was! But he came back. Monsieur de Frontenac

obtained his release and permission for him to return.'

'How ridiculous!' Peyrac burst out. 'Will people in high places never learn that you pay dearer for a mistake than for a crime, and that when one has gone so far as to commit such a crime as that of kidnapping a guest invited to one's table, and of sending a great Iroquois chieftain to ply an oar in a galley on the Mediterranean, one might at least have enough political courage to carry things to their logical conclusion and let him die there. How could they ever have been so naïve as to imagine that once he was back in his own country he would not immediately become their most implacable enemy? How could one ever expect him to forget the way he had been treated?'

'Who is this man Outakke?' Angélique asked.

'A great Iroquois chieftain, of the Mohawk nation,' Perrot explained. 'He has led a most unusual life. As a child he was adopted by Monsieur d'Arresboust, who paid for him to be educated at the seminary in Quebec. Unlike the other Indian boys he was a serious lad and good at his studies. Even now he still speaks excellent French, which is a rare thing among the Indians. But when he grew up he disappeared and it was discovered that he had become one of the most ardent instigators of hatred for the French among his people. He himself tortured some of our missionaries with almost unbelievable refinements of cruelty. The fact is that this man Outakke is a wild animal.'

Angélique recalled the impassive face with the scarlet earrings which she had glimpsed at the edge of the wood, from whose eyes had shone such fierce hatred.

'What is he like?' she murmured. 'I mean what does he look like?'

But no one heard her....

CHAPTER NINETEEN

OUTAKKE, CHIEF of the Mohawks slipped through the sunny forest, treading silently between the branches.

Heedless of brushwood, roots, or intermingled branches, he strode on through the thick rampart the forest erects against living creatures, passing through it as a spirit might pass miraculously through a wall; nothing halted his progress, or the rapid pace of his tough, close-knit calves, the skin of which he had once slit open in order to remove fat so that only his tireless muscles might remain to thrive and develop alone.

He was crossing the Abenaki forest, an enemy forest, but one he knew, for he had ranged all the forests, ever since he was a young brave, tracking down Hurons, Algonquins, and Frenchmen.

On he went, crossing streams, rivers, skirting lakes, climbing abrupt cliffs, following the crests of the mountains with their jutting rocks and stunted pines. Then he came down again into the darkness of the overhanging leaves where the trees glowed purple and gold.

He thought of his brothers, the chieftains of the Five Nations, whom he had left behind, crouching like frightened rabbits as they listened to the words Tahoutaguete had brought them from Katarunk. No, never would he join them in making peace with the Paleface.... For he was not to be taken in. He could be deceived no longer. It was in vain that he had tried to warn them. Oh foolish brothers! The Palefaces had made a mockery of him, even though he, Outakke, had seen them in a dream, their heads covered in blood.

They laughed at him when he reminded them that Tekonderoga's wife had pushed the sign of the Iroquois out of her way. And yet he, Outakke, had seen her in flesh and blood, in the falling dusk, seen the white woman kneeling, doing homage to the God of the Earth. No, she had not been praying as the Palefaces pray, shutting up their fervour within them and not allowing it to escape. She had prayed by crushing leaves of mint in her hands, lifting her hands to the sky, then rubbing them over her face, while she closed her eyes and her face was aglow in the setting sun. Ever since he had seen her he had felt a heavy weight of dread on his heart. Then he strode rapidly across an open space devastated by fire, and his eyes wandered over the wilderness of forest lands, mountains, strings of lakes, and winding rivers that made up the bleak yet splendid landscape of Upper Kennebec. He wondered if this area had ever known such traffic as in the past few days, in which the Man of Thunder had arrived with his pack of horses and his womenfolk, his soldiers dragging their cannons, and had joined the Canadians from the north with their red allies armed with bows, lances, and tomahawks, while from the south had come the Patsuiketts from Connecticut and the Etchimins, all of them Abenakis, and enemies of the Iroquois, along the blue-black Kennebec river. And at their head, leading their flotilla, had come Black Robe with the eyes of fire, the Jesuit Etskon-Honsi.

And finally this great crowd had converged on the outpost of Katarunk. What could be their object, if not to destroy the Iroquois?

Outakke plunged into the forest again.

He thought of the white woman who had encountered the tortoise along her path and who had not turned away.

And as he lifted his eyes towards the sun which darted its burning shafts between the tree-trunks he felt a kind of dizziness and a pain in the pit of his stomach. It might only be due to the fatigue of hunger, of long marches, and of warfare which, for the past three months, had formed the fabric of his life; but the pain might also have come from the memory of what he had experienced when, hidden among the trees, he had seen her approach, a strange, disquieting spirit, decked in her flame-coloured cloak. It had given him a horrible sensation in which he thought he had recognized fear and uneasiness at some strange, new thing that defies understanding.

Hunger made his head swim slightly, giving him a supernatural and sublime insight. His mind became detached from his body and floated before him. His spirit was like an intoxicated bird that went before him, wailing in despair. This must be how the lost souls wailed. His soul wailed because of the everlasting temptation created by the Palefaces, the eternal seduction that brought the Indians to the feet of those treacherous, coarse brutes, with the ever-living hope that this time it would be He, the Ancestor-with-the-white-face, bearer of the torch of glory, whose coming was foretold by every Indian priest and by the most ancient legends of the Cult of Birds.

How much longer must you go on, before you realize that it is not He, that it never is He?

Instead it is the False Messiah, as the Black Robe would say. The Ancestor-with-the-white-face did not exist, he would not come.... What weakness was it that brought Swanissit back to the feet of an illusion, there to seek greatness, strength, victory, and protection, and to receive nothing but poison?

Have you not received enough musket shots, O Indians, have they not let you swill enough of their fire-water that destroys the forest? But Swanissit the wise man, Swanissit the hero, still hopes against all evidence, and against all experience. He still hopes in the Man of Thunder.

And Outakke himself, making his way to spy on the Paleface outpost, did he not hope too? He too, alas!

To escape from the temptation of the Palefaces one would have to kill them all, to kill their soul. But they had no soul! Their soul was a beaver skin. . . .

The sun was beginning to go down, shooting great golden shafts between the trees. The Iroquois stopped, and sniffed the surrounding air.

He hid behind a tree and soon caught sight of two Abenakis. They were Patsuiketts, members of a tribe that had come from the upper reaches of the Connecticut, who had tricked their way into the land of the Children of Dawn. They had long noses, protruding rabbit teeth, and short chins. Their skin was the colour of red clay, they wore their hair in plaits, and their topknots were so badly tied that it was hard to know where to grab them to 'do their hair' for them.

The Iroquois stayed hidden, looking at them with scorn as they passed by a few paces from where he stood. Their long hooked noses were inclined towards the ground; they were following a track.

That track would lead them to the place where the five Iroquois chieftains had recently held their pow-wow. Although Tahoutaguete had taken care to destroy his tracks from time to time, the Abenakis would undoubtedly see them, for they were even better trackers than coyotes, probably thanks to their long noses. The two men would find the place where the pow-wow had been held, and would certainly notice the scent of their enemy.

The Iroquois glided after them like a furtive shadow, slipping from tree to tree, and, when he had come up behind them, stove their heads in with two blows of his tomahawk, so perfectly aimed and so deadly that the two redskins fell to the ground without a sound, their skulls split open. Heedless of their bodies, even of their scalps, the Iroquois went on his way.

As he reached the approaches to Fort Katarunk, the sunset was casting a red, powdery light across the open space that men had wrested from the forest, at the river's edge.

He heard the neighing of horses and was so startled by the

unfamiliar sound that a great shudder ran through him, shaking him to the roots of his being. He stood there for a long time, as if in a trance, listening to the distant sounds through which he could now make out a new one.

Without ever having seen him, he hated the Paleface who had just come, for he was yet another to hold out to the Indian people the promise of support and hope, a new venture that could be their salvation. And yet he knew all that was nothing but a mirage.

How could he reach the soul of the Paleface, if he could not get rid of him by force, before he deceived them yet again?

At the risk of being discovered by one of the Abenakis, or a Huron, or of being dislodged from cover like some common animal by the dogs that stood yapping over there at the river's edge, the Iroquois remained where he was, as if under some spell.

This was where he had seen the white woman kneeling among the sweet-smelling plants, with her hair flying free like feathers in the shades of the night.

'Oranda! Oranda!' he murmured. He was calling to the Supreme Spirit who lives so closely intermingled with created things and communicates his strength to them.

He could hear the stream sobbing and the heat intensified the warm scent of the mint.

Then he reached his decision :

'Tomorrow I shall come back here. I shall call the white woman, and when she comes, I shall kill her.'

CHAPTER TWENTY

A HALT HAD been called to the exodus of the Indians. A message had been drummed out, telling them that two Patsui-ketts had been found in the forest, their skulls split open.

There was no doubt that an Iroquois was responsible.

Nicolas Perrot waxed eloquent in an attempt to prove to the Hurons and the other Algonquins that the affairs of the Patsui-ketts were no concern of theirs. They were not even Abenakis like the others, he explained, for their name meant those-who-have-come-by-trickery. They were in fact strangers, who had come from the other side of Connecticut, and had infiltrated among the Children of the Land of Dawn to raid their hunting and fishing grounds.

Let them sort things out with the Iroquois, he told them. Their numbers were so small that there was no point in the fearless warriors from the north setting out to chase the offenders on their behalf. The Iroquois themselves were lying low at present, not daring to attack the powerful tribes gathered together at Katarunk. It was not even worth digging up the war hatchet that had been buried by Onontio, the Governor of Canada, for the sake of a handful of squabbling Iroquois and Patsuikett scum.

As he orated, poor Perrot could not help having an uneasy conscience with regard to the Patsuiketts; for they were in fact the best fighters and best Indian converts in the whole of Acadia. Although to some extent intruders, they were nevertheless one of the tribes that showed the greatest devotion to the Catholic missionaries.

Count Peyrac had spoken to Loménie and told him that the Iroquois were in the forest asking for a safe passsage across the Kennebec.

But the incident of the two murdered Patsuiketts put the whole issue in the balance again.

Nevertheless, Peyrac's orders were categorical :

'Let the Patsuiketts fight it out with the Iroquois farther down the river if they want to avenge their dead. As far as I am concerned, I don't want Katarunk involved in anything, neither my own people nor the others who are here at the moment. The French have a deplorable habit of getting involved in the endless inter-tribal quarrels of the Indians with disastrous consequences to their schemes of colonization,' he told Loménie, who was still hesitant.

Loménie agreed, and confined himself to sending a small group of Etchimins south in case Father Orgeval required any help.

All the white men made the most of the hatred the other Abenakis felt for the Patsuiketts, and towards the end of the afternoon the atmosphere had grown less tense. Laden with gifts, the Indian chieftains decided to go home, leaving the Patsuiketts and the Iroquois to their fate.

Only Baron Maudreuil disagreed and wanted to launch an attack on the enemy.

'And what if Father Orgeval and his catechumens are attacked?' he asked passionately.

'The Iroquois have said that if we allow them to cross the river without hindrance, they will undertake to return to their own lands without causing any trouble among the people they encounter on the way,' Peyrac replied.

'And to prove it they've started by killing two Patsuiketts.'

Peyrac had to admit to himself that he could not explain this act of violence after the conversation he had had with Tahoutaguete on the previous evening.

'You'll get to know them,' said Maudreuil sarcastically. 'There is nothing but double-dealing and treachery in the mind of an Iroquois.'

Loménie called him to order. The Canadians were too prone to forget that their Governor had signed peace treaties with the Five Nations. . . .

'Treaties mean nothing to scum like that,' the other man replied.

And he went on, his blue eyes flashing: 'War, war to the bitter end! There can be no other solution between the French and the Iroquois.'

In spite of all this the army of redskins went on witn their plans for embarkation, and in the evening the women and children who had gone off to hide in the woods in preparation for the fighting, returned to the camp and hung their stewpots over the fire for the evening meal.

It was then that someone noticed Madame de Peyrac's absence.

They searched everywhere for her, hunting high and low through all the buildings and the compound. They shouted her name across the burnt-off clearings and along the banks of the river.

A sense of disaster seized upon them all.

Angélique had disappeared.

CHAPTER TWENTY-ONE

THE FEELING had crept over her in the strangest way when she had been alone in the cottage; an uneasy feeling that weighed heavy on her heart.

Then she had suddenly felt an urge to go back to the hillside behind the fort and pick some mint.

She had to put the persistent feeling out of her head several times, then in the end she began to fell a little better.

She had nothing special to do and seemed incapable of settling down to any particular task so she leaned up against the window and looked through the little parchment panes, although she could make out nothing but hazy shadows coming and going across the courtyard.

She was thinking about her younger son Cantor's character and his moods, for he had been in a sulk with her ever since she had thrown the bucket of water over him. It had never been easy to know what he was thinking, even when he had been a curly-headed cherub. But now that he had grown into a strong, sturdily built young man, with that healthy, somewhat rustic good looks that she had known in some of her brothers, he had become still more difficult to deal with.

Angélique tapped her fingers automatically against the small parchment squares as she remembered the way Cantor had looked at her. His eyes were those of a girl set in the body of a young athlete.

'What is wrong, my son? What is wrong, young man?' she said softly to herself. 'Have we already nothing more to say to each other? Do we mean nothing to each other any more, although we are still mother and son?'

This thought echoed a question which she had often asked herself without knowing how to answer it, ever since she had found her two sons again in Gouldsboro.

'Of what possible use is a mother to two grown lads of fifteen and seventeen, who for so long have learnt to do without one?'

There was a loud bang on the door followed by the appearance of a happy, smiling, and sun-tanned Florimond.

Angélique, whose hand had leapt to her heart, asked him whether he remembered that he had been the best-mannered page boy in Versailles, and if he could not manage to adopt less military habits when he came to see a lady, even if only to spare her pointless distress.

A bang on the door so often meant soldiers and heaven knows what, bringing nothing but trouble to people.

Florimond agreed good-naturedly that his travels, and in particular his life as cabin-boy on a merchant vessel had rapidly put an end to the good manners of drawing-room and court which his tutor the Abbé had inculcated into him. It was not his fault; he always had been a scatter-brain.

And if the manners he had encountered in New England had been more formal than on board ship, they still lacked grace.

Here at least people didn't add to life's difficulties by silly bowing and scraping. He pointed out shrewdly that the thickness of the wooden doors in a forest outpost made it impossible for one to scratch with one's little finger nail like a well educated damsel brought up according to the principles of honourable civility, because one would risk having to stand on the threshold for a very long time before being heard.

Angélique laughed and agreed with him. She watched him with pleasure as he moved back and forth through the room, thinking what a splendid lad he was now, and remembering all the worries she had had about his delicate health when he had been small.

He had done his hair like Romain de I'Aubignière and Baron Maudreuil, and wore it long, held by a pearl-studded headband, topped with feathers and fur tails, which suited him extremely well.

He too was handsome, as handsome as Joffrey de Peyrac would have been had he not been disfigured by a sword-cut in his youth.

Florimond was almost as tall as a man now, but his smile was still the smile of a child.

He told her he had come to have a talk about Cantor. He admitted that his brother was pig-headed, but that he was kindly and plucky, and that just at present, he was 'having difficulties'. Florimond did not elaborate on this point.

Angélique felt touched by the concern showed by Florimond both for his brother and herself.

She assured him that she had nothing whatever against Cantor, but that they must both try to reach some kind of understanding.

After this they had a friendly chat together and Florimond told her of the plan he had in mind. He said he wanted to take advantage of the advance his father had made into the hinterland of America to take an expedition still farther towards the west where he hoped to discover the China sea passage for which men had been searching for so long.

He had his own ideas about the matter, and had not yet mentioned it to his brother.

It was better to wait for the spring.

Evening was falling. As she began to prepare the lamp and fix candles in the candlesticks, Angélique went on talking with her son. Then suddenly the memory of the dream she had had in which the Iroquois had stood brandishing his tomahawk over her, came back to her so vividly that she thought she was going to faint.

Seeing her grow pale, Florimond stopped short and asked her what was wrong.

She admitted that she did not feel well, she felt stifled. She would go out for a bit and enjoy the cool of the evening air. She would go and pick some mint up there by the spring, for soon the frost would blacken the delicate leaves and they would be no use for making potions. Angélique spoke like one in a dream. It seemed essential to pick the mint and she was surprised to find that she had forgotten to do so, and only to have remembered it at this late hour.

She threw a woollen cloak over her shoulders and picked up a basket.

On the threshold, she had a feeling she had still forgotten something, and stood looking at Florimond for a while, who, quite unperturbed by her abrupt departure, was pouring himself some beer.

'Florimond, would you lend me your cutlass?'

'Certainly, Mother,' he replied, with no sign of astonishment.

He handed it to her; it was a blade as well cared for as you could hope to find in the possession of a boy of seventeen who already considered himself an experienced hunter and practised trapper.

The double-edged blade was razor sharp, and its polished handle, the grip of which was carved, fitted comfortably into the hand.

'I shall give it you back presently,' Angélique said, and she hurried out of the room.

When they began to search for her a little later, Florimond was playing the flageolet in the kitchen, and watching Monsieur Malaprade making a cake with wheat flour, sugar, and vanilla, a cake such as he had not tasted since his childhood. A bit of elk fat had to be used instead of butter, which was something unknown in these parts.

When Florimond was questioned he told them that his mother had gone to pick mint up on the hillside near the spring, and that she had borrowed his cutlass.

He was surprised to see his father give a start and look at him in horror.

'Quick,' he said to Nicolas Perrot. 'Let's get up there. I am sure she is in danger.'

CHAPTER TWENTY-TWO

ANGÉLIQUE HAD climbed up the hillside between the rows of felled trees.

She had crossed the de-forested zone and continued on up the grassy slope.

Then at last she saw the spring. It was just like in her dream, as the sun was still shining brightly up on the slope.

And she knew that there was a presence there, as there had been the day before, still invisible, though undoubtedly there, even though on this occasion she could see nothing between the tree-trunks. The undergrowth hummed with swarms of flies, the stream babbled and everything was calm.

But the Iroquois was there.

She also knew that it was too late to turn back and that her dream must become reality.

The slightly strained feeling of nerviness that had brought her this far now left her, and she felt an old familiar strength welling up inside her, the strength that came before the fight. Many a time had she felt it, particularly when she had had to defend her children, dagger in hand. She had experienced on these occasions such a sense of inner calm that afterwards she would remember these moments as some of the most exalting in her life.

She took Florimond's blade in her hand, and, hiding it in the folds of her skirt, went on to the edge of the stream, where she knelt down.

And the hidden watcher, seeing her with her back towards him, apparently unsuspecting, had not expected to see her suddenly turn to face him as he leapt forward.

She saw him, a dark shadow, thrown into relief against the setting sun, with tomahawk raised, his tuft of hair transformed into a brilliant crest like that of a huge bird of prey, immense and silent as he plunged down upon her. She twisted out of his path and he tripped, missed his aim, and fell heavily into the leaves at the edge of the stream, brought down by her hand on his ankle. His tomahawk fell from his hand and almost immediately he felt the sharp point of the knife against his throat.

All this had happened with such extraordinary speed, without a sound, without even a noticeable change in their breathing.

Yet, as she was on the point of killing him, Angélique hesitated. Her full weight bore down on the prostrate Indian, and through the slanting slits of his eyelids his brilliant black eyes were witness to his incredible astonishment.

The Iroquois could not understand how so strong so skilled, and so invulnerable a warrior as he could possibly find himself at the mercy of a woman, and a white woman at that! The spirit was utterly knocked out of him, and only began to revive when he considered the possibility that it was not a real woman, but a superior, doubtless a divine being. Then he began to breathe again, for in this case he could admit his defeat, which was no longer a disgrace.

His voice came hoarse and low:

'Woman, spare my life!'

During her moment's hesitation before slitting his throat, he could have attempted to struggle, but he seemed to have given up all idea of doing so.

'If I spare your life, you will take mine,' she murmured.

Her soft musical voice trembled and went straight to the savage's heart. He was overcome by an almost mystical feeling of jubilation.

'No,' he replied fervently. 'That I swear by the Great Spirit. If you are an incarnation then your life is sacred, and henceforth no one can destroy it.'

She noticed that their exchange of words had been in French.

'Are you not Outakke, the chief of the Mohawks?'

'It is even so.'

Then Angélique released her hold on him and stood up slowly. The Iroquois rolled slowly over on to one side, never taking his eyes off her, then he too stood up, as supple as a cat. He made no attempt to pick up his tomahawk, but stood there empty-handed, motionless, looking at her.

'And you, you are Tekonderoga's wife, are you not?'

And, as she appeared not to understand, he went on:

'The Man of Thunder. The man who blows up mountains, the man the outpost of Katarunk belongs to?'

She nodded in affirmation.

'Then take me to him,' he said.

The men who strode swiftly up the hill, guns in hand, rushing to Angélique's rescue, saw two silhouettes coming towards them, not very clear at first, for night was falling on that mountain.

They recognized the young woman, but their feeling of relief was rapidly mixed with suspicion of the man who accompanied her. They stood still, alert and wary. Many of them experienced that strange feeling of fear and awe that men must have felt, in days gone by, who witnessed some legendary saint returning from the mountains trailing behind her some monster, some dragon, some Tarasque in chains, finally rendered harmless.

For it was evident that the man who followed her was no common creature; there seemed to be in him the daunting heat of the vanquished monster.

It was indeed the breath of the fire-breathing, all-devouring dragon that swelled his tattooed chest and made his dilated pupils glow like red-hot coals.

And the scent of the savage that emanated from him, the reek of the lair and of guilt seemed more pungent and more stifling by contrast with the lithe figure of the woman who walked before him. Some of Peyrac's men, for all that they were hardened sea-dogs, started back in dismay. The Metallak Indians, who had joined the party, turned on their heels and ran off as fast as their legs would carry them to seize their weapons and position themselves for an ambush. Back at the camp, the women, warned of his approach, snatched up their children, cooking-pots, and food, loaded them on to their shoulders and made off once more for the forest, with their dogs, which did not even bark.

'This is Outakke, chief of the Mohawks,' said Angélique, introducing him. 'He is alone and wishes to parley with you. I have guaranteed his personal safety.'

They stood in silence looking at the indomitable leader of the Mohawks.

Outakke wanting to parley. . . . This was inconceivable.

But those who had already met him, recognized his thick-set body, that seemed to be inhabited by a fierce, controlled passion giving an impression of vast strength.

It was indeed he.

They recognized him by his way of making his hair and plumes quiver spasmodically, as if they had been set on end by a series of terrifying lightning flashes, and were as stiff and hard as the fur of an enraged or terrified animal. Outakke the Mohawk always created an atmosphere of drama around him.

Young Baron Maudreuil spoke a few words in Iroquois, to which the Indian replied with a grunt. Maudreuil gave a start:

'He says that Swanissit is with him. . . I thought as much. I followed his tracks. There's no mistaking the smell of that fox. We've got them at last, these Indian savages!'

'Hold your tongue,' Nicolas Perrot snapped, 'you are forgetting that you must never insult a plenipotentiary.'

'Him, a plenipotentiary! Not him, he's God's worst enemy about to enter our camp, and I would not trust a single word from his mouth.'

The Iroquois remained impassive, then he spoke, and they were surprised to hear him express himself in guttural but almost perfect French.

'Where is Tekonderoga, the Man of Thunder? Is it you?' he asked, turning towards Peyrac. 'Yes, I recognize you. I, Outakke, chief of the Mohawks, greet you. Swanissit, the Seneca, chief of the Five Nations, wishes to have peace with you. I have come in his name to ask for your alliance, and to ask you to prevail upon the French to allow us to cross the Kennebec.'

Count Peyrac raised his hand to his hat, whose black and red plumes were bending in the wind, removed it, and bowed low to the savage as a token of respect and welcome.

'I knew,' Outakke was subsequently to relate, 'that the Pale-faces reserved that kind of greeting for their King. And yet that was how this white man greeted me, and my heart began to glow as if the fires of friendship had been kindled within it....'

Some hours later Outakke set off again, bearing proposals for an agreement to Swanissit. If the party of Iroquois were allowed to cross the river without hindrance, the chiefs must undertake not to molest any of the Abenaki or Algonquin peoples they might encounter on their long journey home.

'But why should you Frenchmen be concerned about those red foxes?' the Mohawk asked scornfully.

Maudreuil remained adamant, and even the two lieutenants Pont-Briand and Fallières wholeheartedly supported him when he protested :

'You'll see, they will give undertakings, and will keep none of them.'

The allied leaders were also displeased.

'We came to make war,' said the Huron chief, 'and now that the enemy is at hand, there is talk of nothing but treaties.... What will our people say when we return without a single scalp?'

Loménie stood firm. To obtain an undertaking from the Iroquois that they would go home without causing any devastation on their way was far better than letting one easy victory reopen the series of bloody feuds which had been going on for nearly a hundred years and which Monsieur de Frontenac had been very anxious to see ended.

'Don't forget that the hatchet has been buried between Outakke and the Five Nations,' the Colonel repeated.

'We do not forget it,' the Iroquois replied. 'We have not attacked the French for a long time now.'

'But you have attacked the tribes friendly to us....'

'We have not buried the hatchet with any other tribes than the French,' the Indian replied craftily. 'What concern is it to the French?'

When the men had begun to parley, Angélique had wanted to withdraw, but the Mohawk chief had lifted his hand to stop her.

'Let her remain !'

His tone was peremptory, angry, insistent. No one could guess what prompted him to demand the presence of the white woman at the war-council. There was some mystery here, and people were left wondering whatever could have happened up there on the hillside, and surreptitious glances were cast in Angélique's direction, with more than a hint of trepidation in them.

She was beginning to think that things were getting complicated and that on balance she would have preferred to stick to her cooking and household tasks. A sick headache throbbed in her temples and she ran her hand over her forehead in a vague kind of way. She could not begin to see how she would explain to her husband what lay at the origin of her encounter with the Mohawk chief.

Occasionally her eyes fell on Outakke's tomahawk, which now hung from his belt, and the sight of this terrible weapon which had been raised against her made her shudder in retrospect with a fear she had not felt at the time.

When the Iroquois had gone off in the direction of the forest, she went to her own room; for she did not wish to join in the buzz of comment on what had happened; there she got into bed and fell into a deep sleep.

When she woke the following day, she felt better.

She saw that her husband had slept beside her, but he had already gone. She had been totally unaware of both his arrival and his departure. She still kept wondering what she would say to him, coming first to the conclusion that she should say nothing and then that she should ask him to give her the benefit of his experience in an attempt to understand all the strange and disturbing things that had happened. After seeking to kill her, why had the Mohawk manifested this sudden desire for loyalty and alliance that had led him to follow her.

As soon as she was ready she went out and ran to the small corner bastion from which one could survey the surrounding countryside while remaining in the cover of the palisade.

The gates of the outpost were closed, but as soon as the arrival of the Iroquois was heralded by smoke signals from the neighbouring hills, they were opened again, and both Count Peyrac and Loménie-Chambord went out on to the esplanade with Peyrac's soldiers and armed men behind them.

Their Indian allies came out of the forest where they had been hiding, armed with bows and tomahawks, and gathered round the outpost, but in silence, like a reddish tide.

The Jonases and the children had joined Angélique on the platform, where they all stood looking with interest between the points of the rough-hewn stakes.

At last the Iroquois appeared round a clump of willows beside the river. There were six of them, half naked, and they moved slowly along the stony bank, apparently heedless of the armed throng that awaited them; then, when they reached the beach, they lined up in front of the outpost. They were the Iroquois chiefs.

Angélique had no difficulty in recognizing Outakke the Mohawk with his earrings made of inflated bladders painted vermilion.

Beside him stood an old man. His hair was grey and full of eagle feathers. His body was spare and his strong muscles stood out like strands of knotted rope beneath his leathery yellow skin. His long face, with its little wrinkles round the eyes and mouth, wore a haughty, intimidating expression. Innumerable tattoo marks outlined his ribs, his breasts, and his collar-bones.

Angélique guessed that he must be Swanissit, chief of the Senecas, the supreme leader of the Iroquois league. They moved forward a little, then all sat down on the ground beside the water, except Outakke, who began to climb slowly up towards the Paleface outpost.

When he reached Count Peyrac and Count Loménie he stopped, lifted both his arms and handed them something that looked like a kind of fringed scarf, close-set with tiny beads embroidered to form geometrical designs in purple on a white background.

After the presentation of the scarf, he laid it on the ground, then, taking a red stone pipe decorated with two black feathers from his belt, he put this down likewise beside the scarf. Taking two steps back, he crossed his arms across his chest and stared fixedly just above the heads of the assembled crowd, remaining as motionless as a stone statue.

By now everyone seemed to be perfectly calm, even the Abenakis and the Hurons, and even Maudreuil, who wore a vague smile, his hair, like that of an archangel, blowing freely in the wind.

Nicolas Perrot once more acted as interpreter.

He conducted the pow-wow according to the time-honoured ritual. Lengthy, solemn sentences were accompanied by broad gestures to indicate the sky, the earth, this person, or that, and every question and answer patiently repeated. Angélique was astonished at the subtlety of the Iroquois in confusing his interlocutor. But Nicolas Perrot was no easy game. He knew every lakeland tribe and all their dialects; he had acted as go-between hundreds of times in their wars and during the French military campaigns. Besides, he had spent a year as a prisoner among the Oneiouts. Not a single subtlety in the speech of the Iroquois escaped him.

There came a moment when the Iroquois warrior lost his impassivity and let slip a somewhat sharper remark, which brought a noisy and hilarious response from his Canadian interpreter.

'He says that had he known that I was here, he would have preferred not to come, but to have grabbed his tomahawk instead.'

After a while Chief Outakke returned to the lakeside among his own people and the Europeans went inside to talk things over. The sun shone high in the sky and the time had come for a drink.

Angélique noted in passing that the officers seemed anxious, and she went forward to greet them.

'Monsieur, how do you feel things are going?' she asked Loménie. 'Are you pleased with your parleys with the savages? Shall we be able to avoid fighting as Monsieur de Peyrac hopes?'

'What am I to say? It's always the same with these Iroquois,' said Loménie. 'Even when they are outnumbered ten to one they always consider they are doing their enemies a favour in suing for peace. This alone seems to them to justify every sort of concession from us. In the present instance, they are unwilling even to undertake not to molest other tribes, arguing that if they withdrew under those conditions, everyone would regard it as a defeat and scorn them for it.'

'Let's charge and exterminate them all,' urged Maudreuil fervently.

Pont-Briand was quiet, for he was watching Angélique, unable to take his eyes off her pure, perfect profile.

Joffrey de Peyrac was also silent. He looked at each of them in turn but no one could read his thoughts. Loménie-Chambord turned towards him:

'And you, Monsieur? Are you not afraid they are laying a trap? Supposing all their protestations about wanting to make an alliance with us are nothing but duplicity. Once we have gone, they will swoop down on your outpost and ransack it – and as for you and your people. . . .'

'I'll take that risk. . . .'

'We don't even know how many there are of them. . . . There may not be enough to stand up to all of us, but there may be plenty to deal with you and your party.'

'Don't be so concerned about my fate,' said Peyrac, while a subtly ironic smile lit up his eyes. 'Suppose I were backing the wrong horse in counting on the good faith of the Iroquois. Well, that ought to be a welcome prospect to those who, only yesterday, would have liked to see the end of me! But for the moment that is not the problem. We have to decide whether hostilities are to be reopened between New France and the Five Nations, whether violence is necessarily the answer, and whether you are prepared to accept responsibility for it.'

'I say, look who's coming!' said Fallières.

The Mohawk chief reappeared in the doorway. To come to them like this before they had finished their deliberations could hardly be regarded as according to the rules.

'Did you forget to transmit some important message to us?' Perrot asked.

'You have guessed aright! My brother Swanissit instructs me to tell you this. In the forest not far from here my braves have a child of your race, who is your sister's son, your nephew,' he said, turning to Romain de l'Aubignière. 'The great Notable of the Senecas is prepared to hand the child over to you if the French and their allies agree to allow us to go on our way towards the valley of the Mohawks without molesting us.'

Surprise was on every face.

'Little Marcelin, my nephew!' cried L'Aubignière. 'So he escaped the massacre!'

'The dirty swine!' Maudreuil growled. 'He must have realized that there was opposition among us and that his mission had failed. They have decided to play their last card.'

Turning towards Loménie, L'Aubignière entreated:

'Monsieur le Comte, we must do all we can to save the child! We must get him back from these wretches who are bringing him up to hate God and his ancestors!'

Loménie bowed his head gravely.

'I think we must accept,' he said after a glance at Peyrac.

Then, turning to the Iroquois, he went on:

'So be it; give us back the child and you can proceed without hindrance across the Kennebec.'

Young Baron Maudreuil contained himself until the messenger had gone, then he exploded.

'No, they can't! Those miserable wretches can't leave this region with impunity. Let it never be said Swanissit had come so close to me and that I had failed to get his scalp....'

'Do you care so little for my nephew's life, and the saving of his soul?' shouted L'Aubignière, seizing him by the scruff of the neck.

'It wasn't Swanissit who scalped your family! He's here and I can't let him get away alive. I have promised his hair to Our Lady....'

'Quiet now, you two,' said Loménie as he separated the two young men.

With a wild glint in his eyes Eliacien de Maudreuil dashed off to his hut to pack his kit.

These young men were decidedly hot-headed, and Angélique found herself admiring Loménie all the more with every day that passed, for managing to retain his graciousness of manner in spite of so long a stay in Canada.

Realizing that it was necessary to get rid of young Maudreuil, who was a man of the region, the Colonel made no objection to his departure.

He summoned him, gave him something of a dressing down, and then decided to turn the young baron's impulsive action into an official mission. First he gave him a message for Father Orgeval, then a letter for Baron Saint-Castine who was Governor of the outposts of Pentagoet at the mouth of the Penobscot river. The long journey would calm Maudreuil's ardent Canadian temperament.

'The outpost of Pentagoet is near the Gouldsboro post where Monsieur de Peyrac has settled a party of recently arrived French Huguenots, and I want to give the Baron instructions concerning them. If, when you arrive there, you find one of the company's ships which hopes to reach Quebec before the ice sets in, get aboard her; if not, you are to spend the winter at Pentagoet with Castine. One last thing. Don't take any Hurons with you, or you will work one another up with ideas of vengeance. I shall give you my Outane friend, Massonk, as a travelling companion.'

CHAPTER TWENTY-THREE

THE SURRENDER of L'Aubignière's nephew took place early the following afternoon.

This time the Iroquois came by the river. They appeared downstream, paddling against the current in some reddish canoes they must have stolen from the river tribes. They disembarked on the gravel shore and walked up towards the outpost.

As on the previous day, the Palefaces stood in a group round the entrance, the Hurons, Algonquins and Abenakis standing to one side in a compact, silent mass. Angélique stood slightly behind the others with Honorine and the two other women. True, the spectre of war seemed to have been averted, but such was the reputation of the Iroquois that their appearance invariably caused considerable apprehension.

There were only some ten of them and they carried no firearms, advancing in a scornfully off-handed way, and pretending not to notice the other natives, whose hatred of them found expression in angry grumblings.

The wampum necklace placed half-way between the river and the outpost guaranteed the safety of the enemy spokesmen.

At their head came Swanissit and Outakke with a little boy of seven or eight trotting between them, holding their hands. His clothing consisted of a single band of leather between his legs and a pair of moccasins on his feet. Although his hair was plastered with grease, they could see it was as golden as corn, and the eyes that looked out from his sun-tanned face were as limpid as lakewater. There was no doubt about his likeness to the trapper with the mutilated fingers; they were certainly kith and kin.

The sight of him wrung Angélique's heart with pity and apprehension, and she clasped Honorine to her. Elvire, the young widow, looked at her two boys sitting quietly on the grass a few yards away. The same thought struck both of them: would fate ever cast their children into the hands of these barbarous Indians, to live half naked in the forest? They had before their eyes living proof that such things could occur, and the two women were moved by pity and distress at the sight of the unfortunate little boy. Their minds were already busy planning the bath they would give him, in a few hours time, when at last he was restored safe and sound to his own people.

That day the two parties sat facing one another across the wampum necklace. The negotiations did not go off without incident.

'Why,' asked Nicolas Perrot, 'why have you not brought your peace-pipe with you? Have you come with your minds made up to reject any possibility of peace?'

'We have come for the sole purpose of exchanging the child in return for your promise of a safe passage. We shall smoke our peace-pipe later with Tekonderoga, the Man of Thunder, when you others have gone and we are sure that he has not betrayed us to the other Frenchmen, and above all to the jackals who are with you,' Swanissit replied bluntly.

'Why did you take a young child like that on a war-party with you?' Romain de l'Aubignière asked in turn.

The Seneca screwed up his eyes craftily.

'Because I love him, and I am all he has in the world. He did not want to leave me.'

'Shouldn't you rather say you wanted to have him with you if things turned out badly for you, when you found that the time of reckoning had come for all the crimes you have committed among our people and the friendly tribes. . . ?'

Florimond went backwards and forwards, keeping the ladies informed of what was going on. At last he was able to tell them that it looked as if a general amnesty was about to be declared. The French seemed willing to state that they were not interested in this wretched band of Iroquois who had allowed themselves to be cornered between the river and their way back to their native valley. Onontio, who had been Governor of Quebec since the treaty of Michilimackinac, was prepared to treat the Iroquois as his children, and the French here present would forget their grievances, following the example of their father Onontio, remembering only the satisfaction Swanissit had given them by handing over the little boy.

A barrel of brandy which Romain de l'Aubignière himself handed over to Swanissit put the seal on his new era of peace as well as on the transfer of the tiny hostage.

It was then that things began to go wrong.

They were all standing now and Swanissit and Outakke

brought the child to within a few paces of his uncle. Then, letting go his hand, they called out: 'Off you go!' with a sweep of the hand that returned him to his own people.

But the little boy, after glancing in terror around him, began to howl, and rushed back to Swanissit, clutching the chief of the Senecas round his long skinny thighs, and looking up at him with tear-stained face as he whimpered, terror-struck, in Iroquois.

Consternation seized the Iroquois braves forthwith; their impassiveness vanished and their tattooed faces revealed their dismay and perplexity. They crowded round the child, entreating and admonishing him volubly.

'What's going on?' Angélique asked anxiously, turning to old Macollet who stood smoking his pipe in the shade of the palisade as he followed the scene with ironic gaze.

He shook his red woollen cap.

'What was bound to happen, heavens above! The lad doesn't want to go to his uncle and refuses to leave the savages! Ha! Ha! Ha!'

Then, still laughing, he gave a fatalistic shrug.

'What was bound to happen, after all. . . .'

The bawling of the child continued to rise over the general uproar.

With their high-pitched voices, and their eloquently onomatopoeic words, and the swaying of their feathered headdresses, the Iroquois looked like a group of delirious parrots.

Without the slightest thought for his dignity, Outakke knelt down to be at the same height as the child so that he could explain things to him better, but the little French boy clung to him as well, with one arm round his powerful neck and the other grasping the leather straps Swanissit wore round his hips to hold his loin-cloth.

The French, extremely vexed, took council.

'We must stop this!' said Count Loménie. 'L'Aubignière, go and fetch your nephew whether he likes it or not, and get him away from here quickly. Put him somewhere where we can't hear him crying any more, otherwise we'll end up with everyone in a fine state.'

L'Aubignière walked over to the Iroquois with the intention of firmly grasping the object of dispute, but no sooner had he put out his hand than the savage braves turned menacingly towards him.

'Don't touch him!'

'Looks like trouble,' Eloi Macollet muttered to himself. 'Well, couldn't expect anything else! Couldn't expect anything else! They say that everyone knows the French are cruel to their children, but that no one's going to lay a hand on this particular child.... You've got to be patient, they say. That'll get us a long way. If the lad's as pig-headed as his uncle L'Aubignière, we'll still be here tomorrow. In any case, all the L'Aubignières are as obstinate as mules!'

Angélique moved forward a little, and approached her husband.

'What's your impression?' she whispered.

'That things could take a very nasty turn.'

'What shall we do?'

'Nothing for the moment. Just be patient! That's what these Iroquois gentlemen wish us to do.'

He remained calm, apparently standing aside from these negotiations which did not yet directly concern him. Angélique realized as he did that it was essential to keep calm, but tempers were growing frayed.

The child was purple in the face and bawling louder than ever, with eyes tight closed as if refusing ever to accept the terrible fate that awaited him, that of leaving the savages and returning to these monsters with pale faces! His nose was running and his eyes streaming.

Angélique was seized with pity for the child in his despair and felt she must do something. She went back into the fortress and ran over to the storehouse, where, feeling her way, she managed to find what she was looking for – a loaf of white sugar from which she broke off several lumps. Then she dipped her hand into a barrel of prunes, grasped a handful and ran back to the scene of the trouble.

Loménie had called his lieutenants to one side.

'Let them go off with their insufferable brat, then we'll fight it out with them, get him back, and have them at our mercy.'

'Supposing they killed him to get their own back,' said Pont-Briand.

'They wouldn't, they're too fond of him.'

Peyrac intervened.

'If we were to break off negotiations at this stage, we should have to face not only the difficulties we have been trying to avoid but still worse ones. I beg you to keep calm and be patient.'

Angélique bent down to talk to Honorine.

'Look at that poor little boy who's crying over there; he's frightened by all these grown-ups he doesn't know. Take him a piece of sugar and some prunes and then take his hand and bring him back to me.'

No one ever appealed to Honorine's kind heart in vain. Completely fearless, the little girl made straight for the Iroquois, whom she seemed to regard as familiar friends.

She looked like a little doll who had stepped straight out of a picture-frame, with her broad pleated dress and her green linen pinafore. Her green bonnet, from which her copper-coloured curls escaped, shone bright in the sunshine. Her feet were shod in moccasins, their turnovers embroidered with beads. An Indian woman had brought them to her the day before as a gift from Lieutenant Pont-Briand.

In a sweeping, spontaneous gesture, she held the offering out to the little boy. Swanissit and Outakke immediately joined in the game, enthusiastically singing the praises of these wonders that Honorine was offering to their young charge, who, for all his despair, actually managed to open his eyes. He sniffed spasmodically as he examined the presents. Had he ever seen white sugar before? He preferred to grasp the prunes, which were more familiar to him, but his eyes stayed glued to the piece of white stuff they told him was edible. Then Honorine took the little child by one hand and made her way slowly back towards Angélique.

All nations held their breath.

That short distance covered by those childish feet would decide between peace and war.

Angélique knelt down, and watched the child's approach, taking care not to make any movement that might frighten him.

When he reached her, she spoke softly to him.

'It's sugar! Taste it. You'll see.'

He could not understand her but seemed to like the sound of her voice. He looked up at her with his big blue eyes in a kind of fascination that seemed to make him forget his fear or even where he was. Did this white woman's face, with her fair hair held back in a coif, remind him of the young Frenchwoman who had been his mother and who had been scalped one terrible night? It almost seemed as if he was trying to remember something.

She went on talking reassuringly to him. Then old Macollet came to her rescue and, speaking as gently as his gruff voice would allow, repeated what Angélique was saying in Iroquois.

'It's sugar. Taste it. . . .'

The child made up his mind to lick the piece of sugar, then he took a great bite of it, and his dirty little face lighted up in sudden wonder, and he broke into peals of clear laughter.

Everyone breathed a great sigh of relief.

The Iroquois delegation relaxed again and everyone crowded round Angélique and the two children.

Angélique had called Elvire's two boys to her.

'Haven't you anything in your pockets that might interest him?'

It was a wise guess. Any self-respecting seven- to ten-year-old boy has pockets full of hidden treasures. Bartholomew found two agate marbles, left over from the last game he had played in the streets of La Rochelle.

They were all that was needed to win the little boy over completely.

The women and children formed a tight group round him and managed without any trouble to get him into the compound, then over towards the house. At last they found themselves with their captive safe behind a closed door.

Angélique was afraid that, once he felt himself shut in, he might begin to scream again. But after glancing at the walls around him and giving an almost imperceptible start of surprise, he seemed to resign himself somewhat unexpectedly and went over and sat down on the hearthstone in front of the roaring fire. She felt sure that his surroundings must have reminded him of happy days gone by in his Canadian farmhouse. He was being worked on by the memory of things he knew, and he nibbled at his piece of sugar as he watched Bartholomew rolling his marbles across the floor. Occasionally he would say something in Iroquois, so, to win him over completely, Angélique sent for the old trapper with the red cap, and settled him too before the fire with a glass of brandy.

'Do me a favour, Monsieur Macollet, and act as "go-between", as you call it here, for this young savage. I am worried in case he grows impatient if he feels that we don't understand him. . . .'

She gave each of the children a lump of the precious sugar

by way of thanks for their help.

'Without your help, children, we should have been in trouble. You were very useful.'

And that was also Monsieur de Loménie's opinion, when he came over in person a little later to thank Madame de Peyrac.

He informed her that the Iroquois had left peacefully, satisfied that their charge was in good hands.

'We owe you a thousand thanks, Madame. Had it not been for you and your charming children, we should have reached a deadlock. We soldiers forget all too easily that there are certain situations which only a woman's tact can handle. We should have all got ourselves massacred over this bit of a lad, whereas all you had to do was smile. . . .'

Then, turning to the children, he added imprudently :

'I want to give you something to thank you. What would you like?'

The youngsters, intoxicated with success and a week spent in the open air, showed no hesitation. Bartholomew was the first to speak

'I want some tobacco and a pipe.'

'I'd like a gold Louis,'[1] said young Thomas who still retained his Old World sense of values.

'And I,' said Honorine, 'I'd like a scalping knife . . . and to go to Quebec.'

The Count showed considerable astonishment at the variety of their wishes.

'A scalping knife for a young lady? And who are you going to scalp?'

Honorine hesitated. Angélique was on tenterhooks.

But fortunately Honorine decided that she did not yet know and that she would think about it.

'And you, my lad, what do you want to do with a pipe?'

'Smoke it of course !'

Count Loménie laughed heartily. He gave Thomas his gold piece, and told Bartholomew he would get his pipe but only to blow bubbles with.

'And as for you, Mademoiselle Honorine, before I give you the knife, I shall wait till you have decided who your enemies are. But I can already say on behalf of his Lordship Governor Frontenac that he extends a most cordial invitation to you to visit his worthy city of Quebec.'

[1] French twenty-franc piece.

CHAPTER TWENTY-FOUR

REALIZING WHAT a trial this complete change in his way of life would be to a small child, Angélique gave up all idea of trying to bath her new charge.

'But he smells absolutely awful,' Madame Jonas and Elvire protested. 'And look at his hair! It must be full of vermin.'

'Yes, I can see. But we might scare him if we put him in the bathtub today, so let's be patient and hope that perhaps tomorrow we may be able to attempt this delicate operation.'

Things began to settle themselves, and for the rest of that day the child was only difficult for short periods. He would occasionally cry and Eloi Macollet managed to calm him very effectively.

'I've told him that, if he is good, Swanissit and Outakke will take him off to hunt and fight tomorrow.'

Later, when he saw the other children splashing about happily in a tub of warm water, the little boy decided to join them. But the women only managed to get the top layer of filth off him, since the bear-grease and dust together had formed a resinous coating all over his skin.

Angélique managed to get him to take a warm drink to which she had added a few drops of some poppy-seed decoction which she had found in the rather unadequate medicine cupboard of the outpost.

O'Connell the Irishman could hardly have been ill very often, and whenever such a misfortune did befall him, he must have treated himself with brandy. She thought of all the bags of herbs she had left behind in La Rochelle, of the ointments, the syrups, and the elixirs that it had given her such pleasure to make for the Berne family, using recipes she had learned from the witch Melusine and the good advice she had received from Savary the apothecary.

All these would have been very useful here, but it was already too late in the season to pick the plants she needed most ... even supposing they could be found in this new hemisphere. Still, some of the bark and the rhizomes she needed might still be available during these later autumn months. She would see about it tomorrow.

That evening, Romain de l'Aubignière came over to see how his nephew was.

The little boy was just going off to sleep, rolled in a blanket on a litter they had prepared on the floor, as he had refused to be put into a bed.

The trapper looked glumly at him.

'I know exactly how he feels,' he murmured, shaking his head. 'I too was a prisoner of the Iroquois, over there in the valley of the Mohawks. How can I ever forget that time? How shall I ever forget that valley?'

'But in heaven's name,' said Angélique with a certain impatience, 'are the Iroquois your friends or are they your enemies? Did you enjoy the life you led with them or was it intolerable? For goodness sake make up your mind!'

He seemed surprised. Like Perrot, he saw nothing illogical about mingling his nostalgic feelings with his bloodthirsty intentions. He agreed:

'Yes indeed, I was happy with the Iroquois. But I still cannot forget that they slaughtered my entire family and Maudreuil's too. My sworn duty is to scalp them and scalp them I will. I know we have just reached an agreement with them today, and that that was the price of my nephew's life. But, never fear, we shall meet again face to face!'

She asked him softly:

'What do you intend to do with this little lad?'

'I shall send him to the Jesuits! They have a seminary in Quebec for orphans and Indian boys they want to train up to be priests.'

Angélique looked again at the sleeping child. With his funny little face all smudged with dirt, and his pouting expression, he seemed so innocent and vulnerable. What would the walls of a seminary in Quebec seem like to this forest-bred child? Like a prison, she guessed. She lifted her head to tell young L'Aubignière of her doubts.

Had it been worth setting such store by the child's freedom, if it were only to shut him up again? Their sole concern seemed to have been to snatch him away from the savages in order to save his soul. A worthy motive no doubt, but she wondered whether any thought had been given to the child's happiness and well-being.

As she was about to open her mouth she noticed that the

trapper had vanished. These trappers came and went like shadows.

In the next room Elvire was helping the other children prepare for bed. Monsieur and Madame Jonas were in their room, busy tidying things away. Eloi Macollet had gone off to fetch some tobacco. Angélique was alone for a few moments beside the child's bed in the main room. He kept on moving and giving sudden moans, and seemed to be looking for something beside him which he could not find. To calm him, Angélique gently stroked his filthy, unkempt hair.

Then she softly drew the cover up over his thin naked shoulders.

There was no sound in the room save the crackling of the fire.

Yet, as she went to stand up, she discovered the two great Iroquois chiefs, Swanissit and Outakke, standing so close behind her that the fringes of their loin-cloths brushed her shoulder.

She looked up at them in stupefaction. How had they got in? The Mohawk chief's hand rested at about the height of her own eyes on the handle of his polished wooden tomahawk, tipped with a great, pointed, shining ivory spike. A single blow from this weapon would cleave a skull through to the brain, and especially when held by such a hand, equally broad and smooth, an amber-coloured hand with prominent muscles.

Angélique had to make an effort to avoid giving a visible start. Outakke's eyes were no more than two black almost invisible slits, and the great Seneca was not looking at her but watching the sleeping child.

After a few moments, he leant forward and laid a little bow and quiver containing some arrows on the makeshift bed, the weapons the French boy had learnt to use under his tutelage.

Then he pulled himself together and appeared to recover his self-possession. He began to pace round and round the room, followed by Outakke, looking here and there with an insolent stare, touching everything, and still pretending not to notice the young woman. They went into the next room.

Angélique heard Madame Jonas cry out in terror at the sight of the two grimacing, feathered men, as she stood up after poking the fire. The two Iroquois burst into noisy laughter. So far they had been silent, but now they began to talk volubly, exchanging impressions in a mocking tone. Madame Jonas

187

cried out a second time when they laid their dirty hands on a
lace scarf which she had just spread out on the bed to get the
creases out. What a pity the poor woman had chosen this day
of all days to take out her precious things!

The two chieftains made a great hullabaloo in the children's
room, and while Elvire huddled in a corner shaking from head
to foot the children looked on them as if they were masked
figures from a carnival. Disappointed at not finding anything
interesting, the visitors went into Angélique's room, where
their curiosity seemed at last to be satisfied. They opened the
boxes, took out clothes, and seized books off the shelves,
thumbing through them before putting them back again in
complete disorder.

Angélique had followed them, trying hard not to lose her
patience. She prayed to heaven someone would come and get
them out of the place, someone who knew their language.

It seemed to her that Outakke's feelings towards her were
questionable. While Swanissit had apparently come to take a
last look at his adopted son, it seemed clear that the other
wanted to try to pick a quarrel with her, the woman who had
humiliated him.

'Should I throw them out?' the watchmaker whispered to
her.

'For goodness' sake don't! You'd get your head split open.'

Although they had spoken so quietly, the two savages suddenly swung towards them as if to catch them out in some
guilty secret; but they could read nothing but calm in Angélique's expression as she leaned against the door-frame.

They were visibly amused by the frightened Europeans. And
they left everything higgledy-piggledy around them, like over-
excited children.

Then Swanissit suddenly discovered Angélique's dressing-case
full of precious things. He seemed dazzled, and began to handle
the comb, the brush, the candlestick and the seal, finally
settling his attention on the hand mirror, in which he pulled
funny faces, guffawing with laughter. But the gold and tortoise-
shell frame and the handle made of the same precious material
delighted him even more than the clear reflection in the
glass.

Outakke did not seem to share his enthusiasm, and made
some rather sharp remark. Was he reminding the chief of the
Senecas that the Palefaces were not lenders, that their gifts had

to be bargained for, and that this woman belonged to the same tight-fisted race?

Abruptly Swanissit became the great chief again, cold and hostile. He froze, tall and thin in his leather loin-cloth, and put the looking-glass back into its case. With lowered head, he fastened on Angélique the grim gaze of a wounded eagle. His furrowed face wore a sombre frown, as it had earlier, when he had stood looking at the little Canadian boy. Then he seemed to change his mind and reach a decision; a flash of triumph lit up his face, and he grasped the mirror again, tucked it into his belt with a possessive gesture and throwing a defiant glance in Angélique's direction. But his look was very much that of a naughty boy, crafty and provocative.

Angélique went over to him, looked in the dressing-case and took out a red silk ribbon. She lifted the mirror out of Swanissit's belt, placed it against his chest just below his bear-tooth necklace, and, tying the red ribbon round the handle, added this new and exotic ornament to his barbaric finery. The two chieftains had followed her every movement, intrigued.

'You can speak and understand the tongue of the French,' she said to Outakke; 'will you translate my words to the great Seneca. I, wife of Tekonderoga, in the name of my husband, make him a present of this looking-glass he likes so much.'

Outakke repeated her words with a certain reserve. Swanissit looked down at the mirror which now glittered on his breast, and spoke rapidly:

'Does the white woman seek to deceive the great chief of the Senecas?' Outakke translated. 'Swanissit knows that the Pale-faces reserve such beautiful objects for the service of their God alone. Black Robe has already refused to give him the mirror in which he looks at himself every morning and which he kisses with his lips, even though Swanissit has offered him a HUNDRED beaver skins in exchange....'

'What can they mean?' Angélique asked herself. 'I suppose the Jesuit father must have refused to give them his paten or some other object used in religious services; how can I explain to him that it is not the same. Oh well, never mind!'

'But why does the great chief of the Senecas fear that I am deceiving him?' she asked aloud. 'Is this object not worthy to grace the breast of the Great Considerable of the Five Nations?'

And she felt certain that Swanissit understood the meaning of her words, for an almost childish jubilation shone from the eyes of the grey-haired Indian. He radiated pride and joy, but in a heroic effort to regain his human dignity snapped out a few abrupt words which Outakke managed to make sound still more scornful.

'The Palefaces do not know how to make gifts. They are a vile race of merchants. What is the white woman seeking in exchange for what she has done?'

'The white woman has already received payment for her gift,' she replied, 'by being honoured by the visit of the great Swanissit, chief of the Five Nations, to her house.'

'Was the Frenchwoman not frightened by the visit of these fierce Iroquois,' Swanissit went on through his interpreter Outakke.

'Yes, I was frightened,' she replied. 'The arrival of the great Iroquois warriors took me by surprise. I am only a weak woman ... quite unable to use arms in my defence.'

As she spoke, she looked Outakke full in the face, thinking that he would be the only one to understand the jibe in her remark, but Swanissit must either have had an inkling of the misadventure that had befallen his second-in-command – nearly having his throat slit by a white woman – or he must have been psychic, for he burst into peals of noisy, offensive laughter, slapping his thighs and casting mocking glances at the great chief of the Mohawks. Angélique feared she might have gone too far in humiliating Outakke and decided to pacify him by offering some kind of explanation.

'You see, once I had a dream,' she said. 'I was standing beside the stream up on the hill, towards the setting sun, while an enemy lay in wait for me and rushed out to strike me. So the following day, when I awoke, I armed myself with a knife before I went up the hill, for dreams are often a warning. . . .'

At the mention of dreams, they had grown serious again. All trace of hatred, irony, and distrust had left them.

'Tell us!' Outakke said in a hoarse voice. 'Speak, O white woman, tell us your vision.'

And they drew closer, leaning towards her like children awaiting the continuation of a fascinating, terrifying story.

At that moment, the door burst open with a crash, and a group of trappers and soldiers appeared on the threshold, led by Nicolas Perrot, Pont-Briand, Maupertuis and Three-Fingers. They looked at the floor and Angélique had the distinct impression that they had expected to see her lying there dead, her skull split open. Seeing her standing, alive and well, and apparently on the best of terms with the two redoubtable Iroquois, they stood aghast.

'Madame!' stammered Pont-Briand. 'Are you not? Have you not?...'

'No, I am not dead,' Angélique replied. 'What do you want?'

'We were told that Swanissit and Outakke were seen coming in here.'

'Yes indeed, and here they are; they came to see how their young ward was faring and to bring him his weapons. It was a thoughtful action that has made a very favourable impression on me.'

Nicolas Perrot gave a shudder on seeing her standing there so calmly with the two grim and revolting braves close beside her.

'You!' he exclaimed. 'You have never ceased to astonish me ever since the day I met you in La Rochelle. But never mind! Since all is well, we shall not be angry with them for breaking in so brazenly.'

He spoke to the two chiefs in their own tongue and Angélique vaguely understood from their gestures that he was inviting them to feast with the Palefaces. But they shook their heads.

'They say they will feast only with Tekonderoga, and only when all the French from Quebec have left,' Perrot translated. 'They give you their greetings and say that they will return.'

Then, with great dignity, the two chiefs allowed themselves to be escorted to the door and over to the gates of the fortress.

The gates were closed behind them.

CHAPTER TWENTY-FIVE

'WILL THEY leave? Will they all leave? When can we be alone again, alone with the silence and the wilderness?'

Angélique would not be happy until the welcome time came when she could be alone for a brief moment with her husband far from the eyes of strangers. Then she would let her head fall on his shoulder and would clasp him convulsively to her, avidly drawing strength from him to sustain her in her weakness; for she sensed that he was calm and free from anxiety. Anxiety was something he had never or hardly ever known in all his life, even in the hour of death or torture. Face to face with trials or dangers, he would summon up his strength to fight or bear them. He would never refuse to face the dangers of a difficult situation and would, as far as possible, take action to avoid them; but that which belonged to the future, or to the realm of the imagination, never had any power over him. All that mattered was the immediate tangible fact. During those difficult days Angélique discovered the secrets of a manly way of looking at things which her sensitive woman's mind found it hard to appreciate.

This discovery made him almost a stranger to her, but a comforting stranger; for, at the height of the storm, he remained truly, deeply calm, while she felt that, if this intense activity, this straining of every nerve and swift alternation of hopes or disaster that came and went like capricious gusts of wind, continued any longer her nerve would fail.

Ever since she had brought back chief Outakke from the mountain, nothing had been quite the same for her. The others behaved differently towards her.

Now she felt she was at the centre of things, deeply involved in lives and events that had hitherto been a closed book.

She began to realize that, little by little, she was becoming part of the New World, that she was becoming involved in its loves and its hates.

'They are going,' Joffrey de Peyrac repeated in so confident a tone that the matter seemed to be already settled. 'They are all going, and we shall be on our own in Katarunk.'

Gradually groups of canoes pushed off from the bank in ever-growing numbers.

Then the day came when Count Loménie-Chambord himself departed, the last to climb aboard the last vessel of the French expeditionary flotilla.

Things had not gone as they had expected when they had borne down on Katarunk to beleaguer it, but the Knight of Malta was not sorry.

He watched the couple standing on the shore and began to see them as the symbol of something he himself could not have been, but that he had always hoped to encounter.

In the distance the horses were cropping the grass, and the chirping of crickets filled the air.

'I am leaving you on your own,' said Count Loménie-Chambord.

'Many thanks.'

'And what if you don't manage to convince the Iroquois of your good intentions and they succumb to the temptation to fix your hair for you and carry off your possessions before they go back home?'

'Inch Allah!'

Count Loménie smiled, for he too knew the Mediterranean. 'Allah Mobarek!'[1] he replied. As he rounded the bend in the river he was still waving his hat.

CHAPTER TWENTY-SIX

SUDDENLY SOLITUDE descended upon them, and their own adventure was about to begin.

They were alone, they belonged to no nation, they represented no king.

When the Iroquois came to seek alliance, they would negotiate with Joffrey de Peyrac, as if he were a king, speaking in his own name.

Hardly daring to believe it, they looked around at the outpost that was theirs once more.

That evening they held a joyous 'family' celebration to mark their victory and their independence. Goblets of wine were raised to Joffrey de Peyrac in honour of his skilful leadership, which once again had rescued them from a tight corner.

And that night Angélique experienced new bliss in clasping in her arms the man who supported them all and had not betrayed their confidence in him, feeling the urgency of his lips as they drank hers as if, now that the danger was past, he was seeking to take his revenge on fate.

To meet the Iroquois delegation, Joffrey de Peyrac put on his red velvet doublet, embroidered with flowers and black onyx beads. He had silver spurs on his black leather boots. With one hand resting on the silver hilt of his sword, he stood waiting in front of the fort.

[1] God is great.

The six Spaniards who formed his armed guard stood rigidly to attention on his left, wearing flashing armour and morions and holding their halberds; while on his right six of his sailors also stood to attention, dressed in a kind of uniform of dazzling colours their jackets were half yellow and half scarlet, their breeches were scarlet and their leather boots fawn, a uniform he had had made by a tailor in Seville for his household livery.

It was a rare occasion indeed when he ordered his men to put on their full dress uniform.

The New World, except for the territories under Spanish rule, was no place for the pomp and ceremony of the Old. More often than not, men landed in the northern territories on hands and knees, with their shirts as their sole possessions, and poverty forced austerity on them for long periods.

Such was the case of all those who had fled from religious persecution, like the English Puritans or the French Huguenots, and the Jonases had trundled the same modest pack containing all their worldly goods all the way from La Rochelle.

Joffrey de Peyrac had come over with ships after he had grown rich diving for treasure in the Caribbean. He was therefore able to give his colony a more sumptuous turn, and even among the necessarily small amount of baggage they had brought from Gouldsboro he had seen fit not to leave out his soldiers' dress uniforms.

As they climbed up towards the outpost, the Iroquois wondered what could be the significance of all this brilliance, sparkle, and glitter that stood awaiting them, adding its splash of colour to the autumn setting. The purple foliage of a giant maple beside the entrance to the outpost seemed to stand in welcome to them, like the escutcheoned banners which had been set up on the hillside as if to line a triumphal way.

The breeze was sharp and brisk, flattening the straw-dry pearly grass that bowed down and rose again as the wind whistled softly across it.

Swanissit was carrying his gun with the mother-of-pearl butt across his arms.

There were five of them: Swanissit, Outakke, Anhisera, Ganatinha, and Ouasategan. Their breasts were bare, their stomachs empty, and their simple leather loin-cloths flapped in the wind.

Ouasategan was chief of the Onondagas, Ganatinha one of the bravest chieftains of the Oneidas, and Anhisera was spokesman for the Cayugas; for he was brother to their chieftain, although he himself was a Seneca. . . .

These men were therefore among the most important representatives of the Five Nations of the Valley of Maize, come to make alliance with the Man of Thunder. They had taken this risk for the sake of their peoples, but in their hearts there was more than a hint of suspicion, which they attempted to disguise beneath an attitude of arrogance.

Angélique wondered as she watched them advance from the top of the rampart what those wild hearts really felt, and she thought she could sense their suspicion, anxiety, and sorrow. For Swanissit had told them : 'The Five Nations are no more what they once were. Now we must try to make peace with the Paleface.'

The fate of the Iroquois was becoming more and more subtly bound up with Angélique's existence. Was it because she had held Chief Outakke's life at the point of her dagger, or on account of that business with the tortoise that there still seemed to be a barrier between them ?

That morning she and Honorine had sorted out the best of the beads from among the shoddy merchandise used for bartering.

'These are to give old Swanissit, if he comes to visit us again. He is a man worthy of great respect.'

'Yes, I like him too.' Honorine declared; 'he was nice to the little boy. Why did the little boy go away with the Frenchman ? He could have taught us to use a bow and arrow.'

Angélique would also gladly have kept the Canadian child, but the question had not arisen.

Half-way up the hillside the Iroquois found the gifts Joffrey de Peyrac had had placed there for them with a wampum sash of considerable value that he had taken from one of his chests.

When Swanissit and the others had worked out the meaning of the message drawn in white and midnight-blue porcelain beads, they appeared pleased, looked at one another, nodded and said : 'This is good ! This is valuable !'

Swanissit reminded the others that the necklace had once been part of the treasure of the Mohicans. The fact that it had come into Count Peyrac's possession was an indication of the importance of his alliances and showed in what high regard he was held by the southern tribes. But the mere thought that he should present it to them made their hearts beat faster. They were feverishly excited at the idea that they might take it home with them, and Swanissit could already see himself entering the cities of the Long Houses, bearing the precious strip of wampum on his outstretched hands. The thought of his people's excitement when they saw it made him quiver inwardly like the skin of a tambourine beneath a merry musician's fingers.

They laid down their arms, their bows and arrows, the musket with the mother-of-pearl butt and the red stone peacepipe. There was only one of these, a rather crude specimen, whose stone had grown cold from not having been smoked for many a long month....

They laid it down and gave a sigh when, among the gifts placed there by the Palefaces, they noticed some brown plaits of tobacco neatly set out on tanned hides; it was the best tobacco, from Virginia, and its delectable smell filled their nostrils.

How good it would be to have a smoke soon, sitting round the fire, with all the pleasure of promises exchanged.

But they must not succumb to the temptation of these pleasures and neglect the ancient complicated rituals of so important a pow-wow on which hung the whole future of the Iroquois League.

On this occasion Angélique had asked her husband if she could be excused from assisting at the ceremony. In spite of the part she had played, however unintentionally, in preparing the ground for this interview, she did not consider that her presence was necessary. This she deduced from what Nicolas Perrot had told her, namely that, in Iroquois society, although the women and above all the mothers have a right to be heard, their views are made known to the council of men only through their secretaries, who were usually chosen from among the young men. Besides since that morning she had been suffering from a terrible migraine and could not bear the idea of spending several hours listening to the noisy cackling of the Indians, and enduring their overpowering smell, their belches and snuffling noses, wiped with their hands or their hair. Joffrey de Peyrac agreed that, if the chieftains did not insist on her presence, she was free to stay away. Deep down she felt apprehensive at the thought of facing Outakke, the chief of the Mohawks again. She felt happier about the idea of seeing Swanissit and, by way of excuse for her absence, she got

Nicolas Perrot to take him the collection of Venetian beads she had sorted out for him.

When she saw that the exchange of greetings was over and the parley about to begin, she retired to the cottage, feeling slightly chilly, and spent the afternoon with her friends and the children.

From time to time somebody would come over and tell them how things were going.

Out of conscientiousness and vanity, and because he was terribly hungry and the delicious smells coming from the outpost courtyard made him long to cut short some of the oratory, old Swanissit prolonged his speeches well beyond the limits of human endurance. But Count Peyrac seemed to be able to stand anything.

Swanissit exclaimed at great length that if there were only five of them today, this was because they had left Tahoutaguete in charge of the braves still in the forest and those who were beginning to cross the river a little farther down. There were a great number of them, a very great number, possibly a thousand of them, far more than the departed French had ever thought possible.

If he, Swanissit, had any reason to believe that the Man of Thunder had been trying to lull his suspicions, or that his promises had been false, and that he merely sought to weaken the Iroquois by making them bury the hatchet so that he could then help the French to deceive the Five Nations, let him beware, and straight away load his guns, for, before returning to their own lands, the Iroquois would derive much pleasure from roasting alive some of these impudent, deceitful Palefaces. There were some handsome heads of hair among them. Yours, for instance, Tekonderoga, and those of your sons. And that of your wife as well. 'Although I should not be the one to scalp your wife,' the elderly chieftain commented, as if seeing himself already faced with this situation. 'For I tell you, and I repeat, that never in all my life have I killed or scalped a woman or a child. I shall die before I ever take the life of a woman or a child, according to the ancient traditions of our people.

'But I cannot say the same of the new generation of braves,' he went on, with a scornful glance at the three other chieftains, although they were mature men; 'for they have learnt from the Palefaces no longer to respect those that give life, those

197

that ensure our future, and they have hung women's hair on the doors of their wigwams. Ugh! The men of my nation will soon have become creatures as vile and ignoble as you Palefaces. But all the same I must defend them and lay the foundations for their future.'

Peyrac, calm and dignified, took little notice of Swanissit's remarks or threats, and managed to calm the suspicions which were apparent beneath this foretaste of ill-feeling. It was a lengthy process, and they would all have been there still at dusk if the weather had not suddenly clouded over. The wind dropped and a thick mist rose with astonishing speed from the river and the lakes, enveloping everything as it swept in like an irresistible sea over the tops of the fir-trees and the mountain crest.

So they had to gather up their gifts, their wampums and their peace-pipes, and shut themselves up in the outpost, where these humans made a refuge of heat and light that shut out the Land of Shades and the melancholy Kingdom of the Dead. They lighted two enormous fires in the hearth of the great hall, and there they feasted on fat meat, sweet-smelling maize and sour berries. They grew tipsy on tobacco, blue smoke, and colourless alcohol.

This paradise was only for those whose capacity for absorption and resistance had been proved by long experience of native banquets or piratical orgies.

Florimond and Cantor, among others, were sent off to the cottage, to eat their meal with the children, the womenfolk, those who preferred to keep sober and those with delicate livers.

Angélique was vastly amused at their discomfiture. The young Breton lad Yann had joined them too, explaining frankly that he did not enjoy drinking a great deal, nor eating endless boiled bear, and that the horrifying drunkenness of Indians made him feel sick.

Enrico Enzi, the Maltese, also sought their hospitality. He was the one with the delicate liver, which had been the shame of his life, but since he also had a reputation for being handy with a knife, scarcely anyone ever mocked him any more when his skin turned a shade more yellow and he refused a glass of wine or spirit.

The women helped to make the evening pass gaily. Someone played the guitar, and someone the fife, and they all sang. They ate fritters and aniseed-flavoured sweets that the children had made with sugar on the hearthstone.

Master Jonas told them all a story of a werewolf from the province of Saintonge. It was a very long time since he had last told it and he would occasionally lose the thread of the story. This was not because his memory failed him; on the contrary, he remembered the story very well, but he had not told it since his two little boys had been carried off one fine morning by the Jesuits of La Rochelle and had never been found again.

He went on pluckily to the end and was pleased to see how much they all liked the tale. Florimond and Cantor were not the only ones to ask him for another story.

Then they all went off to bed. Angélique suggested that the two boys should sleep there, since, if they went back to the hard mattresses in the other house where they usually slept, the noise of the festivities would keep them awake. So they rolled themselves up in blankets and lay down in front of the fire.

The fog made everyone sleepy without realizing it. It bore down on the world with a soft woolly pressure, its opacity shot through with damp, confused sounds, and heavy with an uneasy silence.

Sentries stood on the platforms at the four corners of the palisade, vainly attempting to catch any sight or sound, trying to make out the significance of the drips, the rustles, and the lapping sounds that came to them as if dulled, more like sighs, woolly echoes sent back from the swirling fog. They could hear the croaking of frogs coming in from the riverside, the call of nightjars and the hooting of owls in the forest.

The absence of the Metallak and Naraandsouak Indians who had left the camp made the night seem even darker. Had they been there, even through the fog one could have seen the glow of their fires, one could have smelt smoke as it seeped through the birch-bark wigwams, and one could have heard their babies whimpering.

But tonight there was nothing.

The outpost of Katarunk lay in the depth of the night like a wreck in the midst of the ocean.

CHAPTER TWENTY-SEVEN

AT THE outpost of Katarunk there was mist outside the walls, and mist within. Icy mist outside and warm mist within. Outside the light made the mist look grey, and it sparkled with frost, whereas inside it was the blue mist of tobacco smoke. Outside it was the mist of the great open spaces with their stale, cold tomb-like smell, which came creeping across the dark land like a fearsome beast trying to thrust its way into the shelters of men; whereas in the hall it was a sweet-smelling mist, that rose in delicate spirals from the bowls of many pipes as men sat smoking to their hearts' content, their bellies full and their minds empty.

Swanissit was happy. The old Seneca had eaten fit to burst. He had not drunk much; for he dreaded the frenzying effect of brandy, and had never taken to it. He had likewise refused the beer and the wine they had offered him, whereas the water, with its earthy taste, drawn from a deep well, he had found delicious, and had washed down many a full bowl of 'sagamité' or maize mush. This excess of food and tobacco after a long fast, added to the weariness of warfare, had the same effect on him as alcohol, and he was every bit as drunk as the others. He thought of the band of wampum he would carry in his two hands before the Council of Mothers and Elders. He thought of the gifts they had received and the promises they had exchanged.

He thought of the great hunting-grounds that awaited the gallant brave when he reached the other side. There were certain festive evenings when the heart revelled in delight. And although he was still in this world, he found it easy to imagine that the pleasures of the elect must be similar to those he felt that night. There was nothing missing. And even, oh wonder of wonders! he suddenly caught sight of Baron Maudreuil, another child he had adopted once, standing before him, his teeth bared in a broad grin as he brandished his cutlass. . . .

CHAPTER TWENTY-EIGHT

TOWARDS THE end of the night, but when it was still dark, the horses neighed.

Someone outside shouted :

'Bears !'

Joffrey de Peyrac stood up and hurried over to the door. In spite of his splendid powers of endurance, he was none too sure of himself as he made his way as best he could past bodies lying in a drunken stupor.

No matter what one's capacity may be to endure the manifestations of hospitality, there is no more gruelling experience than that of honouring an important treaty signed with Indian chieftains, and especially with the Iroquois. Their appetite for speeches, food and drink is such that one begins to despair of a halt ever being called.

Fortunately his patience had long since passed its tests, and he could at least say that in a single night his knowledge of the Iroquois language had grown enormously.

The cold hit him like a blow. He was surprised not to be able to hear his own footsteps as he walked across the compound towards the fortress gates. He heard someone cry out again in a hoarse, strange voice and recognized it as that of the Spaniard Pedro Majorque, one of his sentries.

At the very same moment someone struck him a violent blow on one shoulder that sent him reeling. Actually the blow had been intended for his head, but an instinctive reaction had saved him. He had felt the blow coming and had moved to one side. Other blows followed, falling at random through the thick fog. Feeling his way, he grasped some slippery limbs, twisting them in one of the deadly holds he had learned in some oriental port, and heard the crack of bones. But whoever his attackers were, they seemed possessed of boundless energy, constantly renewed like the hydra with a hundred heads. Another blow – from an axe this time – almost struck him full on the forehead, but he dodged it once more and it just grazed his skull a little above the temple. The wound began to bleed and he tasted something sticky and salt on his lips.

He gave a bound and wrenched himself free from the knot of serpents that held him prisoner and sought to kill him.

He ran off through a strange silence he could not understand. His eyes were growing accustomed to the blackness, but he knew he could not see as well in the dark as the Indian. Nevertheless, seeing a silhouette coming towards him, a shadowy figure made still larger by the thick fog, he was first to hit out this time, striking the man full in the face with the solid silver butt of his pistol. The shadow fell, and disappeared from his sight, but through the darkness of the night still more shadows appeared, surrounding him in an attempt to seize him.

His wound was weakening him, and he ran towards the river to escape them, heading straight for the water. As soon as he felt the edge of the bank beneath his feet, he dived in.

This dark and icy haven seemed familiar to him, and he let himself go in the water, scarcely breathing, all thought suspended; and for a time, he knew not how long, he seemed to be reliving his escape into the waters of the Seine, fifteen years back, when he had slipped over the edge of the boat into which the King's musketeers had thrust him more dead than alive.

He struck against something, and stopped, clinging to some branches and wedging himself against some roots.

A cold pink light made his eyes ache, and he had the impression that someone was sending up fireworks in his direction. But then he realized that it was the pink sky of dawn and the glow of the rising sun. The air about him was full of tiny drops of gold and diamond, and a dazzling whiteness had replaced the black curtain of night; although he had not thought he had lost consciousness, he realized that he must have fainted for a time after clambering out on the bank.

Then he remembered... : Angélique... ! Over there in the outpost. What had happened... ? She was in danger! And what about the children?

His mind instantly became lucid and, in spite of the blood he had lost, the fury that filled him gave him a terrible strength. He was immediately ready, on the alert, with that kind of empty feeling that overcame him whenever the time to fight had come, a feeling that left him deaf and blind to everything that was not an essential part of the battle and an element in the peril he was facing.

Even the thought of Angélique was wiped from his mind now, and he was nothing more than a creature defending himself with all his skill, instinctive and acquired; his enemies had learned at their expense just how formidable a man in this state of mind he could be, even when he stood alone.

Slowly he got up and looked around. He was under the cover of a willow-tree, whose dangling leaves, golden beneath the snow, glittered like precious earrings.

It was this layer of snow everywhere that explained the dazzling whiteness, the silence, the sudden stifling of sounds and footfalls. Stealthily it had fallen in the middle of that night, mingling with the mist. It was characteristic of these very dry lands that, with the first shaft of sunshine, the thick veil of fog had disappeared as in a single breath, restoring the countryside to its dazzling clarity.

Count Peyrac realized that he was some way from the outpost : he could see the dark rampart of the palisade at the top of the hill, and spirals of smoke rising lazily from two chimneys, leaving a trail across the morning sky as white as the snow itself.

Carefully he came out into the open, holding his pistol by the barrel, ready to strike. His sharp eyes scanned the countryside, but he saw no human form. A little way up the hill he encountered some footprints, visible in the fresh snow, which led along the shore. As he drew nearer to the outpost, there were more footprints, going off to the right and left. They must have surrounded the outpost before attacking it.

Attacking it? No, it seemed more as if they had entered the fort without difficulty, for he had been struck in the compound.

Then as he began to climb up the path that led from the river's edge to the main entrance of the fortress, still just visible beneath the thin layer of snow, he saw a human form spreadeagled on the ground.

He went up to it carefully and turned the body over. The Indian's head had been battered in, and his brains and blood poured from the gaping hole.

It was the man he had struck during the night with the butt of his gun.

He examined the man carefully.

Although Joffrey was not under cover and would have been an easy target for any enemy, he at once realized that he need have no fear of an immediate attack.

The Indian was one of those who come in the night and who make off with the dawn : one of those who do not fear to die in the dark since their souls thus escape their ancestral curse, those who alone dare. . . .

There was only one kind of Indian who would do this, and Joffrey de Peyrac's suspicions were confirmed as he leaned over the dead man. Something shone round the Indian's neck, and Peyrac gave a sharp tug to break the chain that held the amulet. After a quick glance at it, he slipped it into his doublet. Then slowly he continued on his way towards Katarunk.

CHAPTER TWENTY-NINE

ANGÉLIQUE HAD been a long time getting to sleep. Her migraine gripped her temples and her eyes ached.

During the night some Abenaki tumblers whom Nicolas Perrot had persuaded to entertain the Iroquois chieftains with a little music had begun to shake their little tortoise-shell bells, to beat their drums and to blow their six-holed oak whistles. The fires cast pink dancing lights across the parchment of her little window.

Angélique was in a state of permanent anxiety lest threatening shadows appear at that window. The Indians were dancing in the compound with short, syncopated tread, and in the big hall she imagined their leaders and the Palefaces making merry together, passing round bowls full of Indian corn, steeped in bear-grease and sunflower seeds, hunks of boiled meat, and many a goblet of brandy.

Every now and then a raucous cry would go up, rising above the piercing strident sounds of the music, and Angélique would shudder uneasily.

She missed her husband's company and felt frightened.

'Oh, how I wish you were here,' she thought like a child. 'I do so need you. . . .'

Then everything had grown hazy, and deep silence had engulfed her, the silence of the grave.

When she awoke the same silence reigned. The daylight had the special quality of light from an alabaster lamp.

Outakke the Mohawk was standing at her bedside. He was naked and deathly pale like a yellowed marble statue. He bowed his head as he looked at her and suddenly she noticed red blood running down from his shoulder or his chest, she could not quite tell which.

He spoke in a whisper :

'Woman, grant me my life !'

She leapt out of bed, and this sufficed to make the mournful shade of the Mohawk vanish. There was no one in the room.

'I am going mad,' she told herself. 'Am I going to start having visions too, like everyone else round here ?'

And she ran her hand across her face in bewilderment.

Her heart was beating a wild tattoo. She listened carefully. What did this brooding silence mean ? She knew it must be the result of something that had happened.

Something had happened !

Swiftly she dressed and, in her haste, seized the nearest cloak to hand, which happened to be the purply-pink cloak she had worn across her shoulders the other evening to go to the banquet. Little did she realize that this unpremeditated gesture would help her to save a life. . . .

In the next room her two sons still slept the deep sleep of youth; after putting her ear to the Jonases' door and to that of the children's room, and hearing the light sound of sleeping people breathing, she began to feel easier.

But she still felt that the dead silence was very strange.

She walked quietly over to the main door and unlocked it, and was dazzled by the white light which, seeping through the tiny opaque panes that morning, had so intrigued her when she woke.

At the same moment an icy blast struck her and her dazzled eyes blinked as she stifled an exclamation.

SNOW !

Snow had fallen during the night, early, unexpected snow, which had fallen softly, enveloping the fortress in a fleecy mantle, stifling the noise of shouting, the rhythmical beat of chanting, and the crackling of fires, burying all life, sound, and movement beneath it.

When morning had come, the snowflakes had ceased their stealthy dance, but the impression of surprise remained.

The wooden buildings seemed darker, more shut in under their immaculate white roofs. A rainbow-tinted mist hung about the edge of the palisade, softening its outlines and making them fade into the ghostly landscape. There was not a soul in sight, although the white-carpeted compound bore traces of many recent comings and goings.

Angélique saw that the porch stood wide open, and she could

see something dark that looked like an outstretched body lying inside. ·

She was about to run over to it when a swirl of mist, thicker and lower than before, unfurled itself behind her, from over the roof top, in smoky grey rolls, dimming the light of the sun and plunging her almost instantly into a dense world of silence.

A strange piercing cry came from somewhere, but she could see nothing. She had to grope her way along the palisade to the gate, and once outside, she no longer knew in which direction she thought she had seen the outstretched form.

She shouted. Her voice echoed dully and did not carry.

Then, almost as suddenly as it had descended, the fog began to lift again, and became a watery mist, heavy with dazzling droplets. Above her on her right a tall scarlet form began to take shape. It was the solitary maple that stood near the entrance to the outpost. The snow had not managed to cover its glorious foliage. An edging of snow only served to heighten its scarlet splendour, while the diffused sunshine, struggling through the mist, glowed through the purple leaves as through stained glass.

Slowly the fog rolled away back to the river's edge.

A human form was climbing up the hill, from the river, through this first velvety snow that had flowered precociously, ready to melt as soon as the heat of the day touched it.

He was handsome and radiant like the Archangel Michael himself, that morning, little Baron Eliacien de Maudreuil. His golden hair shone beneath his Indian headdress of feathers and beads. His bare chest was visible through the open neck of his doeskin jacket, and three medallions hung there, shining and glinting from time to time, like the blade of the long cutlass he held in his raised fist.

He climbed the hill with his head held high, the snow deadening his footsteps. His blue eyes were filled with the dream of paradise.

What he saw through the mist, under the red maple with its stained-glass colours, was a vision of supernatural beauty, with a halo of light, a face as white as a lily flower and the most wonderful eyes.

She was waiting for him, watching him coming, serene and earnest, draped in the folds of a pink cloak.

Overcome with emotion, he fell on one knee.

'O Blessed Lady,' he murmured, his voice broken. 'O Mother

of God, blessed be this day! I knew that I should see you in my hour of victory!'

Where he knelt, scarlet stars spangled the snow. It was blood! Blood falling drop by drop...!

In his raised fist he brandished something black, and damp, trickling with pinkish droplets.

'Here is the demon's hair! Here is the spoil I promised you, O Mother of God...! Here is Swanissit's scalp.'

A cloud blew across, wrapping them both around in cold mist and hiding the kneeling man from Angélique's gaze.

Once again she heard him cry out in the voice of a man demented:

'Swanissit is dead! Glory to God in the highest!'

Feeling her way, she backed away from him, seeking something to guide her. She walked in a kind of limbo across the compound, trying to find the main hall where they had all been feasting that night.

Suddenly she caught sight of the door a few paces from where she stood; it gaped like a black hole opening on to cold shadows. The heavy wooden door creaked on its leather hinges as the wind moved it back and forth.

A terrible fear gripped her heart.

'The banqueting hall!' She reached the threshold.

There were only four men sitting at the table. She saw immediately her husband was not one of them. They were the four Iroquois chiefs, Swanissit, Anhisira, Ouasategan, and Ganatinha. They lay with their heads on the table, and seemed to be sleeping off their wine. There was a stale smell in the room where the fog had penetrated. The fires had gone out. Angélique noticed a sinister sound that sent shivers through the roots of her hair. It was the sound of something dripping slowly, like the trickling of slimy waters in the depths of a dark cavern.

What did it matter if the open door let in the cold and the fires had gone out! Those who sat there had no further need for warmth, for they lay there in a pool of blood, scalped. And the sound Angélique heard was the sound of their blood dripping from the table to the ground.

She suddenly felt sick.

And even her anxiety about her husband's fate seemed to give way to a sensation of sheer horror, the unspeakable shame of the sight before her.

The Iroquois chieftains had been scalped as they sat at their host's table, under Joffrey de Peyrac's own roof.

A shadow stirred behind her, and she wheeled round, grasping the butt of her gun.

She saw Nicolas Perrot, rubbing his head through his cap, staring vaguely at her. He too was looking at the scene in the room, and his lips mouthed oaths which he had not the strength to utter.

'Monsieur Perrot,' Angélique asked almost in a whisper, 'have you any idea who did this?'

He indicated that he knew nothing.

'Where is my husband?'

'We are looking for him.'

'What happened?'

'Last night we were all pretty drunk,' said Perrot. 'When I went out into the compound, someone knocked me out and I have only just come round.'

'Who struck you?'

'I don't know yet. But I'll wager it was that Sagamore Piksarett with his infuriated braves the Patsuiketts.'

'And Maudreuil...! I saw him just now near the gates.'

Perrot looked at the Iroquois and said dully :

'One of them's missing.'

He counted the dead men.

'One of them's missing. . . . Looks like Outakke. He must have got away.'

'But how could they have got in and taken you by surprise?'

'Someone opened the gates from inside. The sentries thought the French had come back.'

'And Joffrey? Where can he be? I'll go and tell my boys.'

Angélique crossed the compound once more; the dull grey fog had transformed it into a desert in which she might run into an enemy with every step she took.

She recognized the storehouse and stopped there, leaning against the wall with her pistol raised, thinking she had heard a slight rustle.

She heard the sound again, and something heavy slithered off the shingle roof in a shower of snow.

A body fell heavily at her feet. Outakke lay there motionless on the white snow; his body had the pallor of wax.

A moment passed and, seeing that he did not move, she bent over him. He was scarcely breathing. His open palms had lost their grip on the ridge of the room, from which he must have hung, wounded, for many a long hour.

The Iroquois opened his eyes, flashing a glance at her. His lips moved, and she guessed rather than heard the words he had already said once to her beside the stream and had repeated in her dream:

'Woman, grant me my life!'

She grasped him under the armpits, tugging and dragging him along. He was heavy, and Angélique's hands could not get a grip on his slippery skin.

She hunted through the pocket of her dress for the key to the stores, unlocked the door, pushed it open with her elbow, dragged the wounded man inside and placed him in a corner, covering him with a few old sacks to keep him hidden.

Then she went out and shut the door.

Behind her someone had come out of the fog and was watching her.

When she turned round she gave a violent start. An Indian stood before her and she recognized the tall chieftain with the bearskin whom she had seen a morning or two ago beside the gilded wooden altar. He was gigantically tall but very thin. His heavy greased topknot had the wooden beads of a large rosary plaited into it, and on either side of his face wisps of braided hair were held in position by clasps made from the feet of red foxes.

He wore around his neck several rows of medallions and little crucifixes that hung on his tattooed chest.

He was watching Angélique, head on one side, his eyes screwed up in malice.

Slowly he came towards her.

He bared his teeth in a silent grin: they were white and pointed like those of a rodent, and his two protruding upper incisors made him look like a mischievous squirrel.

She could not think why but she felt no fear.

'Are you the Sagamore Piksarett?' she asked him.

Since all the Abenakis came into contact with the French, he must understand a little French even if he could not speak it.

He nodded his head.

She slipped between him and the door of the storehouse, determined to prevent him from getting in. Yet she did not want to kill him, only to send him away, to prevent him finishing off the wounded man, to strike a bargain with him.

She slipped her big purple cloak from her shoulders.

'Take this cloak.... It's for you.... It's something for your dead....'

The Indians had been dazzled by the cloak, news of which had already travelled far down the banks of the Kennebec. They dreamed of it, for ever obsessed with the problem of finding a shroud worthy of the bones of their ancestors. Many a Catholic priest had been martyred for refusing to give them his chasuble.

She had made the only gesture capable of diverting the Sagamore Piksarett's attention. He looked at the proffered garment in ecstasy as it lay there glowing like a piece of the dawn cut straight from the sky.

He made a grab at the cloak, spread it out, draped it around himself, then rolled it up into a ball and clasped it to his heart.

He looked once more at the closed door, then at Angélique, then at the cloak.

At that moment the sun, triumphant at last, spread abroad its rays, and the houses became visible again, and the palisade, while the snow began to melt in a whisper.

Nicolas Perrot, who was standing at the other end of the compound, saw Piksarett beside Angélique.

He ran over towards them. But the Abenaki took to his heels and, still clutching the cloak, bounded over the far wall of the palisade like the huge squirrel that he was, and vanished.

It was at this moment that Joffrey de Peyrac reached the outpost and entered the compound. Angélique ran towards him and threw herself into his arms, fearful to see him wounded, but wild with joy at finding him safe.

'God be praised! You are alive,' he said, clasping her to him. 'Are you hurt?'

'It's nothing. What about the children and the boys?'

'They're all right. I don't think we have any dead to mourn. At least, no one of ours.'

Peyrac's eyes had already lighted on the open door to the main hall, where some of the men had begun to form a crowd, and he went over, overcome, as Angélique had shortly before, by a premonition of the tragedy he was to discover.

He stood on the threshold and looked at the waxen figures, grown stiff in an attitude of sleep or inebriation, with their blood-soaked heads reclining among all the dishes.

Then a wild anger shone from his black eyes, and he swore; teeth clenched:

'Damn them! Damn them! Accursed be the man to whom we owe this.' His fists were clenched and his blood-streaked face, framed with wet, mud-spattered hair, struck fear into them.

'It must have been the Patsuiketts,' said Nicolas Perrot.

'I know. I know who it was who came and betrayed us under cover of the night. I saw their sign.'

And from his soaking doublet he drew the object he had torn from round the neck of the dead Indian, and they saw a small gold cross glittering in the palm of his hand.

'The cross,' said Peyrac bitterly. 'Is there no place on earth where I can undertake anything without someone hurling a cross between my legs to trip me up!'

'Monsieur, I beg you, do not blaspheme!' Nicolas Perrot cried out, growing pale.

'What does blasphemy matter! It's actions that count!'

He looked darkly at them. Smothered violence made his voice shake. These blasphemous words he longed to utter, not one of the men standing round him, not even his brothers, his companions, would understand them. No one but her. For she had suffered with him, as he had, and for the same reasons. He put one arm round her and clasped her to him, passionately, looking with desperate intensity into her lovely face with its blue eyes.

She, like him, had been rejected by the world of believers and just men, and her love for him had branded her, when she was still only twenty, for ever to be cursed; and now, he realized in a flash, she had become his double, possibly the only person on earth who was like him.

'This must be the Patsuiketts' doing,' Maupertuis, who had now joined them, repeated, feeling he must say something. 'They can't set eyes on an Iroquois without getting their teeth into his throat. I suppose when they saw that these were going to get away from them ...'

'Yes, it was them. It takes a fanatically Christian Indian to risk fighting at night. Fanatical and fanaticized. The Patsuiketts are the only ones like that. Their faith is strong enough for them no longer to believe in the superstitions of their race that say that a brave killed at night will roam for ever in the outer darkness. They have been so successfully hypnotized by Black

Robe that they trust in his mystical power when he tells them that the death of an Iroquois or an Englishman is a sure passport to heaven.'

'Are you referring to Father Orgeval?' Nicolas Perrot and Maupertuis asked. 'That's impossible, the man's a saint!'

'He's a saint fighting for his God. I've known all about him for a long time. The Pope and the King of France sent him to Acadia, for the sole purpose of encouraging the Abenakis to fight a Holy war against the English heretics and anyone else who might be considered an enemy of the Catholics or France.

'It was he who sent for reinforcements from Quebec and got them to occupy our outpost. When he saw that I was beginning peaceful negotiations with Count Loménie, he believed Loménie had gone back on his word, and decided to strike a final, irreversible blow. This is not the first time he has sent the Patsuiketts out to fight on his own initiative.

'And now,' Peyrac went on, in a hoarse, broken voice, 'and now, through his fault,' and he looked down at the glistening gold cross in the palm of his hand, 'through his fault I have the blood of treachery on my hands.... Perrot, do you remember what Tahoutaguete said when he came here as a messenger. He had his doubts, for Outakke had told them that it was impossible to make an alliance with the Palefaces. But the Iroquois still clung to the hope of finding a Paleface who would not betray them. And now, what can I say to them? My house has been stained by an unpardonable crime!'

His voice trembled as he spoke, and at the same time, Angélique, whom he was still clasping to him with one arm, had the impression that this last phrase had, as it were, suddenly lighted up something within him, enabling him to catch a glimpse of a possible solution.

He grew calmer, regaining his habitual self-control.

He repeated softly:

'My house is dishonoured.'

He stared fixedly before him, as if in a dream.

'Outakke got away,' said Perrot.

'That only makes things worse! He will go back to his braves beyond the river and in a couple of days if not tomorrow they will be here. All we shall be able to do is to kill them down to the last man or be killed ourselves. Where are the sentries who were on watch last night?'

Jacques Vignot and two of the Spaniards stepped forward.

The Parisian related how at about two o'clock in the morning, as they were about to finish their watch, he had heard a French voice asking for the gates to be opened for Monsieur de Loménie-Chambord, who, the voice claimed, had been forced to turn back.

Reassured by the memory of their friendly leave-taking from Loménie's expeditionary force, the sentries had believed they were doing the right thing in opening the gates and letting him in. The foggy night was as black as pitch. No sooner had they opened the gate than they were knocked over the head and trussed up.

It was not Colonel Loménie. It was Baron Maudreuil at the head of a small party of Patsuikett Abenakis.

The cry of 'bears' having brought running outside those who, towards the end of the meal, were still sufficiently lucid and able to stand on their feet, the Indians took advantage of the darkness to knock them all out too.

It was then that the realization of a disturbing fact came upon Peyrac and his company : during the swift, silent scuffle in the night, not a single white man in the Count's service had been killed or even seriously wounded.

Some had been knocked out, most of them had seen nothing, for they had been sleeping either the sleep of the just or the sleep of the intoxicated.

It looked as if categorical orders had been given to spare the lives of the Europeans in the outpost. It seemed as if Maudreuil and Piksarett had been after the Iroquois scalps and nothing else.

The Patsuiketts had not reckoned with Count Peyrac's desperate fight to defend himself nor with his prodigious strength. One of them had been killed.

While Joffrey had been fighting in the compound, and plunging into the river to escape the blows of his assailants, Don Juan Alvarez, Maupertuis, Macollet, Malaprade, and those who were not already snoring, had witnessed the sudden appearance of Baron Maudreuil and Sagamore Piksarett.

'I realized what was going on straight away,' old Macollet explained, 'but what could I do? I couldn't get my backside off the bench. And even if I had ... bit of a delicate situation, wasn't it? There's Maudreuil, a young lord, reeking holiness and money, and me, just a penniless old pagan. And the lad was right to come for Swanissit's scalp, since he had killed all

213

his folk. When Swanissit saw them, he realized what it meant too, but he had gorged himself so much he couldn't budge. Anhisera and Ganatinha were equally incapable, and Ouasategan didn't see a thing as he was already snoring. Outakke was the only one to get up. And he fought like a devil before escaping through the window after smashing the frame with his fists ... look.'

Joffrey de Peyrac ran his hand over his brow. He touched the sore spot and made the troublesome wound bleed again. This was the first blood he had spilled in his conquest of the New World. This wound would be called Etskon-Honsi, the Black Robe.

And it would not be the last.

The order to spare the Europeans had only been given for appearance sake.

They had been condemned all the same. For what primitive people, what people of any kind, could accept the outrage of these treacherous murders without seeking vengeance. From now on Katarunk would be an object of everlasting abhorrence to the Five Nations.

In spite of all the efforts made by Loménie and Count Peyrac, in spite of their reason, their wisdom, and all the patience and shrewdness they had exerted as men of honour to banish the spectre of a pointless war, it stood before them now, crazy, stupid, and inevitable.

CHAPTER THIRTY

ANGÉLIQUE SLIPPED into the storeroom and stood motionless with her back to the door, listening for the slightest sound in the shadows.

Was the wounded Iroquois still alive? Was he dead? Was he about to spring on her? Anything was possible.

She waited. Nothing stirred.

She knelt down and crawled slowly over to where she had dragged him. The pile of old sacks she had thrown over him did not seem to have moved.

Shortly before, when someone had remarked that Outakke the chief of the Mohawks was not among the dead, she had chosen to say nothing yet. Before informing her husband they had a hostage, she must make sure that he was alive.

She ran her hand under the sacks and her fingers encountered a rigid body. He was still there, he had not moved, but had remained in the position in which she had left him, face downwards on the beaten earth floor. But Angélique felt that his flesh was warm and supple.

With a sigh of relief she got to work.

She had brought a lamp with her which she stood on a box and lit. She also had a flask of brandy, some ointment, and some pieces of lint she had found in the inadequately stocked medicine cabinet of the camp, and a calabash full of water freshly drawn from the well.

She removed the dusty sacks she had thrown over the wounded man to conceal him in the event of a search, and in the yellow light of the oil lamp his whole body was revealed, inert and marble-like. She turned him over flat on his back and held up the lamp.

Her practised eyes scrutinized him – the way he held his hands, the folds of his lips, the hollows of his closed eyes, and the pinched look about his nostrils.

It took her only a moment to decide that he would live. For she had nursed many a wounded man in her lifetime, both in Morocco and during the Poitou wars. She put down the lamp, and began to examine him more closely to discover the wound that had plunged him into this deathlike sleep.

When she laid her hand on a sick or wounded man, it was as if his body had become transparent. Invisible signs were revealed to her that lay beyond the sense of touch. She searched for her answer, her whole mind intent, scarcely touching him. Gently her fingers moved forward across the tattooed flesh. So light was their pressure that he remained unconscious, unaware of her presence. Then the Mohawk opened his eyes, and saw the white woman's profile with her hair hanging loose about her head, kneeling there in the light, like a moonbeam. He saw her lowered eyelids, and the grave line of her lips which gave her face an expression of utter absorption. And he felt the shock of her hands on him and the warm magnetic current that seemed to flow from those slender fingers with the glistening nails that shone like shells, and spread through his body to bring him to life again.

Then suddenly he saw her stiffen, like an Indian who has

come upon the track of an enemy, and he heard her give a brief exclamation.

Then she nodded several times. She had lifted his bloodstained loin-cloth, and had discovered a wound on his right thigh, which extended almost up to the groin. A lance had been aimed at his stomach but the blow had been turned aside.

A piece of whipcord had been bound tightly around his thigh to stop the bleeding. As soon as he had broken out of the hall, Outakke had tied it himself, to prevent his blood leaving a track to show which way he had gone. It had been an effective though dangerous treatment; for the edges of the wound and the leg itself had already swollen in an ugly way, and could have caused a fatal blood clot.

Angélique picked up the lamp again, and examined the wound with still greater care. She loosened the cord a little with great caution, and a small trickle of blood appeared. It was red, and should have gushed out in spurts. She could not understand it. The blood had stopped flowing. Within this rigid body, an impossible task of healing had already been accomplished. By what miracle, by what occult powers could it have happened? She looked up at the wounded man's face and shuddered to see that he was staring at her. Some strange power! Yes, indeed. Did she not know that Outakke, the chief of the Mohawks, had greater powers than any other? She had given much thought to the impulse she had felt the other evening to go up to the spring where he was lying in wait to kill her, and now she was sure that he had drawn her there by a spell.

She guessed that he must be capable of stopping his own blood from flowing and forcing death back step by step, by some supernatural yet acquired skill of which he held the secret. For all those hours while he had waited motionless for the white woman to return to help him, he had held death at bay as it tried to snatch him from life, by the sole strength of his secret, controlled willpower.

She began to examine him suspiciously. His catlike smell made her feel sick, and once again she had the impression which she had experienced several times in his presence, that she was not dealing with an altogether human being, but rather with a kind of animal, from an unknown world, and was almost surprised as she looked at him lying there naked and abandoned before her, to find that he had hands, feet with toes, protruding ribs, a navel, and sex organs like any other man.

She began to staunch the blood, cleaning the wound with fresh water and covering it with an ointment made from the emollient roots of the costus.

She fixed the dressing on tight hoping that the ointment would take out the swelling, and that this, coupled with the great Outakke's robust constitution, would turn his mortal wound into nothing more than a memory.

That was how the Iroquois were.

He knew that she knew. He also knew that he could harm her, but he had learnt that she was strong enough to frustrate his plans. He had 'called' her to the stream, but she had come with a dagger. She was a match for him. And it was probably because she too was on friendly terms with the Spirit of Dreams. But although it might not be a contrary power, at least it was a different one from his that animated this foreign woman, come from distant lands, and he had felt a strange shudder when she laid her hands on him.

Thus it was that Angélique and the Mohawk exchanged thoughts with each other through their glances. She wanted to convince herself that he was unconscious, and that in spite of that slanting glint that filtered from beneath his eyelids, he could not see her. She accused him of being an embodied spirit, dangerous, possessed, and diabolical, and he on his side thought the same of her. And with every look, the things they learned about each other's powers, strength, and character made their exchanged glances grow more and more fierce, but at the same time more and more understanding.

It was a magical duel, but a duel in which both sides were equally matched.

Who would have guessed it to see this white form kneeling at the side of a dying savage?

All they would have seen would have been a nobly born European woman devotedly tending a wretched wounded Indian, whereas they were really two creatures of equal strength, of close affinity, who were, without knowing it, embarking on an incredible adventure. . . .

With puckered brow, Angélique tied the last bandage, gave a last angry glance at the wounded man and stood up. She went across to a bale of merchandise and drew out three of the blankets intended for barter.

Trying hard not to disturb the body too much – it was as heavy as stone – she managed to slip one of the blankets between it and the ground. Then she covered him up from his feet to his chin with the second, and, rolling the third into a ball, placed it under his head.

Finally she allowed herself to look at him with satisfaction. Now at last he looked like a wounded man, like a well-behaved patient. Summoning up her courage, she slid one hand under his head, into the resin-impregnated hair of his bristling topknot, and tilted his head up a little as she held a calabash full of water to his lips. The Mohawk's impassive features came to life; he gulped the water down greedily like a child, and a deep sigh rose from his breast.

When she laid his head back on the pillow, his eyes had closed and she thought he had died, then realized that he was fast asleep.

CHAPTER THIRTY-ONE

ANGÉLIQUE HAD to wait till the evening for the opportune moment. Her husband was outside the camp for some of the day talking with Nicolas Perrot and Maupertuis, who, after some initial hesitation, seemed more and more disposed to agree with the ideas he expounded to them. One thing worried Angélique, which was that he did not seem to be feverishly organizing the defence of the outpost.

There was every indication that they could expect the Iroquois to appear any day, if not any hour. Yet the gates stood open, and Peyrac's men moved about the compound with no sign of haste. There was the old brief discussion, a few orders were given and some of the men went off to carry them out. Some holes were dug outside the fortress on the hillside and beside the river, but they scarcely looked like fortifications.

Angélique found Florimond in one corner of the compound busy filling some stout cardboard tubes with powdered sulphur, potassium chlorate and copper oxide.

'What are you making there?'

'Fireworks.'

'Is this the moment to be thinking about fireworks?'

'Father told me to.'

'What for?

'I don't know. Some idea of his.'

Angélique looked around. The snow had melted in a few hours, leaving a layer of shimmering moisture on the ground and the leaves, which made the sun's rays even more dazzling.

'Florimond, what is your father up to? The gates are wide open, although the Iroquois may appear at any moment.'

'Father has sent out scouts to reconnoitre and warn us about what they are doing and when they draw close.'

'What is he thinking of doing?'

'I don't know. But don't worry, Mother. I know our position is serious, but with our father things always work out.'

This was the magic formula they all used. 'With our father, with our leader, things always work out....'

When they saw certain expressions on Joffrey de Peyrac's face, his men and his sons knew that they must no longer ask any questions, but simply obey.

Well, she, Angélique, had learned the hard way that things didn't always work out easily, even with him. She had learnt at her expense that life is above all a snare set in the path of the human quest for happiness, and that, more often than one hoped, one falls into the trap. Deep down, she still found it impossible to forget or forgive the memory of the one and only time Joffrey de Peyrac seemed to have under-estimated his enemy, or at least his swiftness to strike. Of course that enemy had been the most discreet, the most urbane, the most powerful King of France. Louis Deodatus, the fourteenth. It was also true that Count Joffrey de Peyrac had ignored the councils of prudence that warned him to escape immediately, in order to spend one last night with her, his wife, Angélique. And Louis XIV had struck like lightning. And both their lives had been shattered.

Even now there were still times when she felt she could only trust in her own strength, and how often, alas! she had found that strength wanting!

When something untoward happened, she found it easier to see the danger than to see what part chance or skill could play to turn it aside.

She mistrusted chance while Joffrey de Peyrac looked on the bright side and affirmed that there was always a way out from even the worst situations.

This quality in him made her envious, even a trifle jealous. He remained calm.

But he nearly lost his calm a second time in one day, when

she at last caught him alone and told him that the Mohawk chief Outakke was alive, that she had saved him and nursed him, and that, far from being capable of rallying his brothers and urging them on to vengeance, he was at their mercy, in their hands.

'Why didn't you tell me about this earlier?' he exclaimed, almost banging his fist on the table. 'It seems to me it's pretty important news! This can greatly influence my plans! It strengthens my hand and makes me almost certain they will succeed.'

'What plans have you in mind?'

'That's my affair.'

'Do you intend to defend the fortress? Shall we have to fight?'

'Yes. . . ! Perhaps. As a last resort. We are well armed and we could win. But if we wiped out this particular war-party it would be the end of our prospects in Upper Kennebec. Sooner or later we should be forced to depart as the Iroquois would never leave us in peace. I would prefer to try another way.'

'What way?'

'I can't talk about it yet.'

'Of course, I am too stupid to understand!' Angélique burst out. 'You seem to forget that I too led men in war. . . ! But you want to send me back to my saucepans. You never tell me anything, it's infuriating!'

'And what about you!' Peyrac shouted. 'Are you so free with your explanations about what you do and what you feel? Did you ever tell me what it was, what piece of folly you committed to get hold of Outakke the other day, and bring him back, the dread enemy of the Palefaces, as if he were on a lead. . . ? Do you think there's nothing extraordinary about that? Do you think that calls for no explanation, really? You come, you go, you risk your life just as it pleases you, you do fantastic, crazy things! And do you think it has nothing to do with me, your husband? Then today, after saving the Iroquois' life, you keep quiet about it for hours on end as if I were an unapproachable stranger. And what about all those Frenchmen staring at you the other evening, and the way you twisted them round your little finger. Do you think I enjoyed that? Do you think it's easy to have you for a wife!'

They glared angrily at one another, standing face to face and glowering.

Then suddenly their features began to quiver and relax, and they both burst out laughing.

'Oh, my love!' said Peyrac, drawing her to him. 'Oh my love, forgive my violence. I love you too much, that's the trouble. I am frightened of losing you and that some imprudent action of yours could be the end of you. You must admit that if you find me secretive, you give me as good as you get. But with every day that passes, I realize just how precious you are to me.

'Take this morning for instance! I would have choked with anger had you not been there, beside me, close to me. I could see in your eyes that you felt exactly as I did. It may be that you inspired me. We are very close, my love, much closer than we think, and I think we are very like each other. But I am still not going to tell you. Not yet, little lady...! I can only ask you to be patient. It's a shot in the dark, and a gambler needs to be alone and to concentrate his full attention on what he's doing. I have two wise advisers, Perrot and Maupertuis, to support me, and they approve of what I am attempting to do.'

He took her face between his hands and gazed into her eyes.

'Trust me, will you, my love?'

And such was the power of his loving, masterful gaze that all she could do was lower her eyelids as a sign of assent, and yield to his will.

Outakke opened his eyes. He saw two silhouettes standing beside his bed, in the bright frame of the open doorway. A man and a woman leaning against one another. Then he shut his eyes again in despair, for he already knew that his hatred would break against this rampart.

'My greetings to you, Outakke,' Count Peyrac said in even tones. 'I bring you news. Take courage, my brother! Swanissit, Ouasategan, Anhisera, and Ganatinha were killed last night, struck down by the dastardly tomahawks of the Patsuiketts.'

'I know. I saw it.'

'Outakke, I remember the words that Swanissit told me in confidence. You are his heir. I therefore salute you as chief of the Five Nations.'

The Indian remained silent for a long time before replying in a dull voice:

'You invited us into your fortress, you made us enter your palisade and treachery awaited us behind those stakes!'

'But who was it who struck the blow? Tell me! Who was it who struck, since you saw it all?'

'It was Baron Maudreuil and his cursed allies, the Patsuiketts, children of Black Robe.'

'So you know it wasn't me. So you know that those who entered my fortress to strike you betrayed me too!

'Don't try to make my brow redden with shame, for it is already red with the blood those same Patsuiketts shed with their blows. Look!'

And he pointed to the bandage round his head.

Outakke seemed to hesitate, then raised himself up on one elbow, and a bitter grimace twisted his inscrutable features.

'What do I care about the Palefaces' quarrels,' he remarked disdainfully. 'They all stand by one another and I regard them all as one single enemy.'

'You are talking deliberate nonsense, Outakke, or else the fever is confusing your mind. I for one would never blame an Iroquois for a Huron's treachery, although Hurons and Iroquois are members of the same race, as I myself am a Frenchman.'

He was silent for a considerable while to give the Indian time to consider the comparison. Then he went on in persuasive tones:

'Outakke, take heart. Consider what I have said and, before you make up your mind, think about the fate of your people.'

'We have left braves on the other side of the river,' the Mohawk replied, 'and Tahoutaguete is in the forest. Soon they will learn what has happened, soon they will be here.'

And he fell back.

'You can kill me, Tekonderoga, but you will never prevent the Five Nations from avenging their dead.'

'And whoever said that I wanted to prevent them doing so,' the Count replied quietly. 'Yes, people of the Long House, come to Katarunk! Come, Five Nations of the Iroquois League! Come and avenge your dead...!'

And he went off, taking Angélique with him, leaving the chief of the Mohawks puzzled and anxious.

The air was so dry and clear that the echo of the fierce battle between the Patsuiketts and the Iroquois lower down the river near Mobedean seemed to carry all the way to Katarunk.

They heard later that almost all the Patsuikett braves had

222

been massacred. A few of them managed to escape and Piksarett was the last to remain.

Father Orgeval was struck in the side by an arrow. Piksarett, seeing him alone, lifted him on to his back and ran off into the thicket, where, although the Iroquois pursued him, they were unable to catch him. He carried the missionary to the Penobscot, where there was a French outpost on the island of Novumbega. It was a long time before anyone discovered what had happened to Maudreuil.

The victorious Iroquois, after setting fire to the village, roasted alive two Abenakis they had managed to seize.

And the following day they set out for Katarunk, where they had learned that their chieftains had met with an ignominious death.

CHAPTER THIRTY-TWO

ANGÉLIQUE WAS kneeling, dressing the Iroquois' wound, as he lay on a pallet in the main room of the cottage, when an indefinable noise, both piercing and rumbling, rose up into the clear sky, grew until it drowned everything, then suddenly died away.

Angélique glanced out of the open window, looking for some sign of thunder or storm. But the sky was blue.

Outakke had sat up, his eye a-glitter.

Then she understood, and a shudder ran down her spine.

What she had heard was the Iroquois war cry.

But once again all was silent, and not a musket shot was fired in reply to the terrifying din.

Angélique finished dressing the savage's wound. She carefully tidied away the medicines and the lint, placing them all in the bundle she had prepared, for they had been told without further explanation to keep a small pack ready in case of need. Her pack contained one dress, a change of underwear, her tortoise-shell-and-gold toilet case, now lacking the mirror she had given to Swanissit, and Honorine's box of treasures.

There were moments when she began to suspect how Peyrac hoped to save their lives and still keep his influence in the area intact. Then she would shake her head, for it seemed impossible to manage such a thing without a terrible battle.

She checked that her pistol was ready on her hip. They all had to be armed; Madame Jonas stood holding a musket in her arms as if it were a child. On hearing the noise they had left their room and gathered with the children around Angélique, whose composure reassured them. There they waited with their weapons and their luggage, looking down at the Iroquois at their feet as if he was a poisonous beast.

When instructed, they were to cross the courtyard and leave the fort without showing any signs of fear. That was all they had to do. They had absolutely no idea of what was going to happen.

Maupertuis and his son came in, grasped the Mohawk under the shoulders, stood him on his feet and supported him so that he could remain standing.

Then Count Peyrac came in, magnificently dressed in scarlet.

'Your brothers are here,' he said.

Slowly he drew on his leather gloves with their silver-tooled gauntlets, and almost seemed to be smiling.

'They're here! Nicolas Perrot is watching them from the top of the hill and they are watching him. They don't know whether to pierce him through with their arrows, and they are waiting for you to come and tell them what to do.'

'What are you trying to get me to do, Tekonderoga,' asked the Indian with a shudder. 'You know very well that if I open my mouth it will be to call my brothers to vengeance.'

'Against whom?'

'It was in your camp, beneath your roof that the treachery took place. . . .'

'I know. I shall wipe out the shame. That's my business. But what about you? You asked the white woman of Katarunk, my wife, to grant you your life, and she granted it. That alone ought to tell you we do not seek the death of the Iroquois. But there is more. . . .

'Remember, Outakke, why it was that Swanissit died. He risked everything to come here, and become my ally. Now you are the chief of the Five Nations. Where will you lead them? Towards peace, or extermination. . . .'

He stood towering over the Indian and, just as the other evening he had bowed before him, now he did his utmost to dominate him. It was scarcely conceivable that he would be able to win over this restive soul. But it was a question of life or death.

All their lives depended on this flickering flame:

'Extermination,' cried Outakke. 'Yes! But you shall die first.'

'So be it, we shall all die!' said Peyrac philosophically. 'Monsieur Macollet,' he said, turning to the old Canadian who had entered the room with him, 'you know what you have to do. I entrust these ladies and their children in your care. Get yourselves in a position where you cannot lose sight of Nicolas Perrot. If he signals to you, as we have agreed, you will know that you must bring them back immediately into the shelter of the palisade and prepare for battle.'

'I'll keep my eyes open,' said the old man.

Peyrac looked at the Iroquois chief whom Maupertuis and his sons were holding erect.

His trump card! Thanks to Angélique....

'Give him a swig of rum,' he said, 'to help him to stand up! Then come along, everyone.'

As he strode across the compound he tore the dressing from the wound on his forehead, and blood began to trickle slowly from it again.

Yann le Couennec was waiting for him, holding his black stallion by the bridle.

Peyrac leapt into the saddle, galloped off towards the open gates of the outpost and disappeared through the sunlit opening.

As he appeared, the Iroquois gave their war cry a second time and Angélique stopped short, her heart gripped with fear. But once again no shots were fired in response to their bellicose roar.

'Come along now!' said Macollet. 'When you are acting a part you must act it to the bitter end, ladies. Nothing will stop a wild beast in its tracks so effectively as a surprise, something it doesn't understand. Some of those savages have never even seen a horse...! And don't forget, ladies, if you feel a trifle anxious, that you never had, nor will you ever have again, a gentleman in attendance who's a patch on me.'

He went on in this vein and by the time they reached the gates of the fortress they were almost laughing.

There stood Nicolas Perrot, hands behind his back, the fringes of his doeskin clothes and the point of his fur cap flapping in the wind, as he looked out calmly down the hillside towards the river and the Iroquois army.

Joffrey de Peyrac was prancing up and down on his restive

horse, and seemed to be inspecting his assembled men, who held banners in their hands.

The Spaniards' black breastplates sparkled in the sunshine.

Maupertuis and his son, supporting Chief Outakke, went and stood beside Nicolas Perrot.

A dull roar rose up from the foot of the hill.

Angélique looked in the direction from which it had come and felt the blood drain from her cheeks.

Both sides of the river and the beach were thick with a throng of filthy, feathered, blood-stained savages. The water was covered with canoe-loads of braves and more kept arriving in an endless procession.

Seen through the cloud of dust they raised as they disembarked, they formed a busy, moving mass, brandishing their bows and tomahawks, yet remaining almost silent.

They were all looking up towards the outpost.

They were looking at Nicolas Perrot, whose moccasins had so often trodden the secret valley and who had sailed across the five lakes of the Five Nations. In their eyes he was almost an Indian...! They looked at Outakke, and no longer understood, for they had been told that all their chiefs had died at Katarunk...!

And the sight of Count Peyrac on that black, fabulous animal quite clearly filled them with superstitious dread.

They went on congregating at the foot of the slope, but remained expectant.

Joffrey de Peyrac dismounted from his horse and took up his position towards the front beside Perrot and Outakke.

His cloak billowed in the wind, which likewise blew his hair, his lace jabot, and the streaming ribbons that hung from the shoulders of his doublet.

Angélique clasped Honorine's little hand in hers. She looked around for her sons, and saw them standing very straight, slightly back from the others, each holding one of the great banners embroidered in red, blue, and gold, with their pennants flapping in the wind.

She did not know what the banners represented; she must ask them one day.

Everyone seemed so calm that it did not seem possible that anything terrible was likely to occur.

'What's going to happen?' Angélique whispered to Macollet.

'Well, for the moment, they're just looking at one another.

Summing one another up! Counting the odds! They hadn't expected to find Outakke alive, and, what's more, those chaps there are frightened of palisades and open land. Then when in addition they find all the Palefaces gathered outside, waiting for them, they don't know where they are any more.... They wonder what they should do! Look, some of them have begun to dance to give themselves courage. They are behaving like a cat trying to frighten a mouse. But at the moment no one knows who is the cat and who is the mouse. Careful now! They are going to give their war cry again. Don't move.... Don't show you are frightened....'

An inhuman bellow rose from their hoarse throats and open mouths.

Madame Jonas and Elvire huddled close to Angélique, who held on to the frightened children saying: 'Don't be upset, it's only because they are all shouting together that it makes such a noise!'

The youngsters hid their faces in her skirt.

This time there was an answer. Two violent explosions were heard, one coming from the shore, not far from the spot where the advance guard of the Iroquois army was standing, and the other from the cliff behind the outpost.

Huge lumps of rock were hurled into the air, falling back to earth again with a crash multiplied many times by its echoes.

A breath of panic swept over the Iroquois, who began to waver in all directions.

A number of them surged back to the clumps of willows where they took cover while others hastily took to the water again. The bravest among them tried to form up again, lifting their arrows to their bow-strings. But a succession of explosions distracted them and they did not know which way to turn.

'What is it?' asked Outakke who had turned pale.

'Your brothers greeted me with a shout,' said Peyrac. 'That is my reply. Have you forgotten that I am the Man of Thunder...?'

And he added ironically:

'What are you frightened of, Outakke? What are they all frightened of? It's only some stones falling.'

The Mohawk chief stared fixedly at him.

'What do you seek from me?'

'I want to discuss the question of blood-money with you and your people.'

'What blood-money could ever pay for our chiefs?'

'Let us discuss it and you will hear.'

Outakke turned towards his braves and began to abuse them. But his voice had grown weak and did not carry. Perrot relayed his message for him and, with his hands cupped round his mouth, insulted them up hill and down dale on behalf of their chieftain.

'You dogs! You jackals! Come back! Show yourselves! It's only some stones falling. Let the chiefs come forward. We are going to discuss blood-money....'

Eventually the braves calmed down and seemed to have decided to agree to a pow-wow, to discuss the question of blood-money.

They had already gained a respite.

The dictates of tradition were now going to allow enemies to sit down together with all the appearance of friendship, and meet the Indians' impulsiveness with a barrage of arguments, proposals, and sober thought.

The leaders stepped forward. At their head stood old Tahoutaguete with his dark, hideous, pock-marked face. But the other Indians also climbed the hill behind them, settling in dense masses on the slope in reclining or sitting positions. In the sunshine the smell of these naked bodies rose in great waves, and hundreds of black, inscrutable eyes formed a kind of magic circle around Katarunk.

'They've not left us much of a retreat,' said Macollet. 'But never mind! Let's sit down too, ladies. We are in a good position here. If Perrot signals to me, it will mean that things are going badly and that there is no more hope. Then we shall have to take cover as quickly as possible, and hey ho for the big bangs.'

'What a lot there are,' said Angélique.

'Pooh! No more than a hundred. Their weapons aren't up to much and they're tired. You can see it. They must be war parties who agreed to meet here after their campaign. With weapons like ours we shall easily get the better of them.'

'My husband hopes thing will be settled peacefully.'

'And why not? In this country, Madame, until you are actually dead, you can never say that the situation is desperate. Of course, this time we mustn't lose sight of the fact that four of their big chiefs have been killed. But we can always try.'

And he waved a hand in the direction of one of the Iroquois

who was seated not far from him, and called out something as he half lifted his red woollen cap.

'I told him there was no point in trying to scalp me, because it had been done already. Ha! Ha! Ha!'

'And you can laugh about it!' Madame Jonas said with a sigh, looking at him in admiration.

'That's the way it is here. You must always laugh, even if you're tied to the torture stake.'

Meanwhile Outakke, the two Canadians, and Count Peyrac had seated themselves opposite the Indian leaders. Peyrac's other men had likewise taken up their positions behind him, and seemed calm, even casual, but Angélique, who was secretly keeping an eye on them, noticed that they were all on the alert, that each one had his allotted task. And their concentration never faltered for a single moment. Occasionally someone would enter or leave the fort, and everything that was done that day was done so efficiently, with such perfect discipline, that Angélique came to the conclusion that the men Peyrac had brought with him, although to her some had appeared unexceptional though not without use, had in fact been hand-picked.

In spite of all their faults and failings, when danger threatened they turned out to be as cunning as serpents, unquestioningly loyal, and unfailingly brave.

Count Peyrac began, through his interpreter, Nicolas Perrot, by reminding the Iroquois braves of the agreements they had reached with Swanissit before he had been treacherously murdered.

From where she sat, Angélique had no difficulty in following their gestures; she could hear bursts of conversation, as Nicolas Perrot tirelessly translated the French point of view to the Iroquois, and the lengthy speeches of the Iroquois which he repeated without leaving out a single word, even when these consisted solely of a flood of invective and threats to Peyrac.

Then Peyrac stood up, displaying his dazzling clothes, and fixed them with a fiery stare, so that he added the full weight of his personal magnetism to that of his eloquence.

He reminded them of the approaches he had made to the Five Nations and how Swanissit had thought them worthy of consideration. And how the other evening he and the wary old chief, who for more than twenty years had led his braves on the warpath, had made a peace treaty – there were wampum necklaces to testify to this – a treaty that covered all the Pale-faces under Peyrac, or his allies, in fact all those who claimed the protection of his flag or of an alliance with him.

A secret sign would allow them to mingle with the Iroquois people with impunity, regardless of their nationality, whether they were French, English, Spanish, or Flemish, that is to say Dutch.

In return Peyrac and his people would undertake never to take up arms against the Iroquois, even if asked to do so by their French compatriots from Quebec or by the Abenakis, or the Algonquins, with whom they had signed peace treaties.

He had also added a promise, which the old chief had particularly insisted on, not to sell brandy to the people of the Long House, and not to encourage trade in beaver skins, thus preventing them from hunting the deer and the moose, or planting crops.

The old Seneca had been like a father to them until the moment of his death, seeking to protect his people from the two great temptations, fire-water and trading, that might bring about the rapid downfall of his people through degeneration and famine.

For, urged on by the white traders for ever to hunt beavers, and still more beavers, the Iroquois had ceased to hunt for food or grow crops, and a harsh or lengthy winter would wipe out whole tribes, who had not managed to gather enough food to see them through. The third temptation, the most crucial for the Iroquois people, was war, as Swanissit had explained to Peyrac. And here again the old chief had tried to save his people from this mortal danger by forcing them to live in peace with at least one Paleface, namely the Man of Thunder and his tribe.

To support these undertakings and to serve as a reminder in years to come to whose who might be tempted to forget them, Count Peyrac had promised to make a gift each year to each of the five chiefs of the Five Nations, of a long-barrelled flintlock gun, to which he would add two barrels of gunpowder and two barrels of lead shot for hunting, five fishing nets of English fibre, ten scarlet blankets of English wool, five scarlet or blue jackets according to choice, which would not lose their colour either in the rain or the sunshine, two hundred and fifty knives, two hundred hatchets, five saws for felling trees, five barrels of saltpetre, which is the wonder dust that makes the maize grow. And in addition a few of the cooking-pots which are known as cauldrons, of varied sizes, from Iron Mills, the best foundry in Massachusetts.

Should such agreements, so advantageous for the Iroquois people, be revoked without having given them a trial, if only for a year?

Tahoutaguete shouted something and Nicolas Perrot's voice repeated it after him.

'It is you, Paleface, who went back on your agreements even before they had been tried out. For we have never seen your gifts; but treacherous death and your attack, those we saw. It was you who provoked war between our peoples as soon as we had decided to set warfare aside.'

Peyrac showed no sign of dismay, but replied through Nicolas Perrot that Tahoutaguete was mistaken.

They would shortly be able to see all the presents Swanissit and his plenipotentiaries had received when they concluded the agreements, but first he would ask Outakke to give his brothers an account of the attack and tell them of the circumstances under which the Iroquois chiefs had met their deaths.

The Mohawk grudgingly agreed to do so.

Perrot, Maupertuis, and all the other Palefaces who knew the Iroquois tongue listened carefully to what he had to say. Twice they forced him to admit that he had seen, with his own eyes, Peyrac's men struck mortal blows by their assailants; and he told how Baron Maudreuil and the Patsuiketts had used treachery to enter the outpost, and that afterwards the white woman, Tekonderoga's wife, had saved him from Piksarett who was hunting him down to kill him.

Then Peyrac threw back his hair to show them his red wound, and reminded them that it had been an Abenaki tomahawk that had caused it.

It was an exhausting duel of words. Not so much a duel in fact as a single-handed battle which he had taken on with the assistance of interpreters. As far as the savages were concerned, the matter was already settled. He was to die. But the sight of the blows he had received seemed nevertheless to impress them.

It was very hot.

The discussions had been going on for hours. From time to time someone would walk down to the river to have a drink or to cool off. Angélique remembered that she had prepared a few slices of bread with a piece of fat pork and that she had them with her in her baggage; so she handed them out to the children to keep them happy.

They were all so exhausted that they had ceased to be frightened. Then suddenly things rose to fever pitch again and Peyrac's Spaniards imperceptibly moved in the direction of their weapons, ready to fire.

Outakke's statements had greatly disturbed the savages.

The fever of battle and of revenge was slow to subside in the heart of an Iroquois.

They all sensed that the savages had come to kill, and that they had no intention of being deprived of their pleasure, for incalculable pleasure it was to avenge a hundredfold the death of a brother, and still more so if he were a beloved and venerated chief. They were grief-stricken at the mere idea that they might not be able to assuage their thirst for blood, and they kept on muttering restlessly.

A young brave, more impatient than the rest, went up to Florimond, lifted his thick hair, and drew a circle in the air round his head with his knife. At the sight of this dumb show, Angélique found it hard to suppress a cry.

Florimond, imitating his father's composure, did not blench, and the Iroquois went off again, abandoning all attempts to frighten him. Angélique was full of admiration for her elder son. His delicate brown profile stood out like a medallion against the blue sky, and she thought with a quickening of the pulse that he was Joffrey de Peyrac's son. And because long, long ago, on the banks of the Garonne, under the star-spangled sky of Aquitaine, Joffrey had taken Angélique in his arms and had made her a woman, the sterling qualities that were his flowed through the veins of this young man. It was like discovering something quite new. But it had never seemed so clear before, and she thought : our son... !

She was not really frightened on Florimond's behalf, but she considered Cantor too young to be exposed to danger like this, although he stood his ground pluckily and never flinched, banner in hand. Sweat was pouring down his round face, and she would have liked him to come and sit beside her with the other children, but he would never have forgiven her.

She also felt some anxiety for 'her' patient, Chief Outakke. How could a man, wounded as he was, stand up to so many hours of wrangling and agitation?

'Don't worry about him,' said Eloi Macollet, to whom she confided her anxiety. 'I know those critters, I tell yee. They've got several lives to spare, and so long as he can talk his head off he'll be all the better for it.'

'Couldn't you take him something to drink?' Angélique begged him. 'If he went and died there, right in the middle of the Council, that wouldn't do us any good.'

The Canadian did as she suggested and took a calabash of water over to the survivor of the Abenakis' bloodbath. This considerate gesture seemed to please him.

The murmurs had died down. The Iroquois were chewing over the account of the attack they had been given and their vivid imaginations could picture every twist and turn of it. From time to time they threw out a question then went back to their thoughts once more.

At this juncture, Joffrey de Peyrac stood up and began a long speech, which he interrupted at frequent intervals to allow Nicolas Perrot, who had stood up also, to translate his words in all solemnity so that they could be heard by those farthest away. 'Now hear me, all of you. I know that the sacred laws of vengeance forbid you to touch any food whatsoever before avenging your dead. You have attacked the Patsuiketts farther up the river and have killed and dispersed them. You might well consider that your duty towards your dead chiefs has been fulfilled, for the Patsuiketts alone are guilty. But I also know that your hearts are full of hatred towards me. Nevertheless, considering myself an ally of Swanissit, even beyond the grave, I shall treat you as friends. I welcome you without fear, as you see, since I do not wish to insult Swanissit by treating his sons as enemies before they themselves have given any sign of their hostility.

'I have therefore prepared a fitting welcome for friendly braves. Here are three piles containing the things I intend to give you.

'First there are supplies. You will not touch them until your hearts have grown calm and you have felt within you that your honour has been appeased. Then you will eat your fill. There are twenty earthenware jars of maize, four of moose meat, two of bear along with some vegetable marrows and some dried berries to give savour to your "sagamité". This will serve to strengthen the bodies of braves grown weary from a long campaign, to the point of giving way to the weakness of blind rage rather than thinking of the future of their race.'

Someone stood up and protested violently, but his neighbours reduced him to silence. It was evident that they were curious to know what gifts lay in the second pile.

'Hatchets and English knives to defend yourselves, two barrels of gunpowder and two of shot, three muskets and one flintlock gun.'

'You gave Swanissit a gun too. . . .' someone shouted.

'And it shall not be taken from him. He will take it with him into his grave, so that he may catch his game the more easily in the Happy Hunting-ground. As for the third pile you can make use of that immediately. No, do not make the sign of disdain and refusal, braves of the Five Nations. It is tobacco from Virginia, and there is no discredit in smoking before making up one's mind between peace and war, for tobacco will help you to act wisely when your spirits have been cheered.'

Outakke and Tahoutaguete consulted each other and agreed.

The temptation was too great for the exhausted Iroquois, who were swept by alternate waves of exhaustion and frenzy.

Nicolas Perrot, Maupertuis and Pierre-Joseph, the half-caste, handed out the strings of dried tobacco and a few pipes to be passed around from man to man.

'I'll be leaving you for a moment,' said old Macollet to the ladies, 'I must just go and chum up with them ruffians. Things look as if they've gone off the boil for a bit, and we'd better make the most of it.'

He went and sat down among the Iroquois, lighted his pipe from one of theirs and began to chat with them on the friendliest of terms. Maupertuis and his son, the half-caste Huron, went right down to the river's edge, noisily greeting those they recognized, and Angélique shuddered at their daring as she saw them alone and unarmed in the midst of these hostile savages.

The Iroquois smoked avidly. Thick blue wreaths of smoke rose from their lips and it was apparent that indulgence in the fragrant weed was calming their turbulent hearts and exchanging their grief and anger for a brief period of lethargy.

An hour went by almost in silence, occasionally broken by the cry of bustards or wild geese from the river's edge, whose V-shaped flight across the whitening sky was watched dreamily by all the savages reclining on the parched earth.

Fine dust mingled with the smoke and everything around them took on a hazy appearance through which colours glowed with heightened intensity.

Angélique felt a hand on her arm. Old Macollet had come back and was pointing to the sun, which had begun to descend towards the horizon.

She looked at her husband and saw him cough twice. For hours on end he had never stopped talking, and his aching throat must be torturing him.

She wished with all her heart that she could be close beside him, enveloping him with her tenderness and her passionate devotion. For hours now he had been fighting, he had been carrying them all on his outstretched arms. When, oh when, would victory be granted him?

Tahoutaguete rose suddenly and began to speak with great emotion.

'This is what Tahoutaguete says in the name of the Five Nations,' said Nicolas Perrot:

'Man of Thunder, do you think your gifts can bring our beloved chiefs back to life again? We have received presents and food, but they have received nothing but shame and death.'

A wave of commotion swept over the savages as he spoke. Once again Joffrey de Peyrac turned to face them. He seemed to be gathering all his strength together and spoke with such persuasive passion that he communicated it to Nicolas Perrot, whose voice rose firm and strong, alternating with Peyrac's.

'That is where you are wrong, braves! Iroquois braves! Your chiefs will not have received nothing but shame and death here, for, let me tell you, ever since the Sacred Valley took the Iroquois peoples into its bosom, not one of your chiefs has ever gone to his grave accompanied by so many riches and gifts and honours as these.... In your hearts you are saying: "They died far from their villages, and we are unable to drape their bodies with gowns and furs, neither are we able to give them cauldrons, nor weapons to use in the Happy Hunting-ground!" Well, look upon these things!'

And the armed Spaniards who had been standing in a close-knit group slightly in front of the outpost towards the left, solemnly drew apart and revealed what it was that Count Peyrac had wished to keep hidden up till now from the Iroquois army.

The moment had come.

At the foot of the great red maple sat Swanissit, Ouasategan,

Anhisera, and Ganatinha, cross-legged, their weapons in their arms, heads erect and eyes closed.

Magnificent plumed and tufted headdresses hid the ignominious sight of their scalped heads and a skilful hand had traced festive lines in ochre and vermilion across the cold livid skin of their dead faces. This too had been the work of the two Canadian trappers, who, bending low over the Iroquois faces, had recalled their memories of life among the Indians. These memories had been so closely woven into the fabric of their Paleface hearts, so inextricably bound up with their lives, that it would have been impossible to tell just how much of the Indian and how much of the European their hearts contained.

Maupertuis's thick finger had reverently outlined Swanissit's cheekbones in red while Nicolas Perrot had drawn a long yellow line across Anhisera's cheek, in memory of the first wound he received as a young brave.

When they had finished they had decked the Indian chiefs in sumptuous cloaks of fur or figured silk which Count Peyrac had brought with him in his coffers. They had driven a stake into the ground behind each figure and tied each by the neck and the back by way of support, enabling them to sit erect before their people; and these stakes had been decorated with ribbons and plumes that danced in the wind.

When the Iroquois saw the chieftains a muffled lament went up on all sides. Far from their own valley, in enemy territory, they saw their dead chiefs before them, and saw that the robes they had been decked in and the honours that had been bestowed on them were far in excess of anything their own people could have given them had they been slain in war.

They stood up and surged forward.

'Speak to them,' said Peyrac, laying an imperative hand on Nicolas Perrot's shoulder. 'Speak to them quickly...! Say anything to them! Show them the gifts the dead men have received!'

And Nicolas Perrot's voice rose up calm yet firm, dominating them because it was a familiar voice, as he began to run through the items like a merchant in a bazaar.

He held their attention, drawing their thoughts away from the horrible reality that faced them, the reality of their dead chiefs, and distracting them from their grief with all the skill of a medieval jongleur. He showed them the four silver bows with their multicoloured arrows encrusted with shells in leather quivers embroidered with thousands of beads, the scarlet blankets, rolls of tobacco, the ermine skins sewn together and the white bear skins, lynx and wolf skins which were to be thrown into the grave for the dead men to lie on. He counted out the jars of maize and rice, fat and meat, one for each dead chief so that he might eat during his long journey to the Happy Hunting-grounds. He explained the symbolic meaning of four unfamiliar objects, that looked like a kind of yellow flower and resembled touchwood; these were for wiping away their tears, for these huge light objects, known as sponges, came from distant islands, and were able to absorb water.

He took a calabash and demonstrated what the sponge could do.

Just as the pure water had suddenly vanished on contact with the sponge, so would their tears of shame and despair be wiped away, he told them.

He described the message inscribed on the two magnificent wampums, while the Iroquois' tears trickled down their smooth faces and they passed the damp sponges from one man to another, wiping the warpaint from their gaudily painted cheeks.

For the newly arrived Europeans, it was a strange sight to see the savages weeping and wiping their eyes with sponges, a grotesque spectacle, moving and tragic, a spectacle that brought laughter to their lips and tears to their eyes at the same time. Nicolas showed them the famous necklace the Pale-faces had received as a token of faith from the Abenakis, a priceless treasure, ancient and venerable, showing a rising sun in blue on a white background and a procession of fish and sea-lions hand in hand – or flipper in flipper – a matter of personal opinion – two of the most handsome necklaces in all the treasures Tekonderoga possessed, which Swanissit could present to the Supreme Spirit by way of reparation for the treachery on the part of the Abenakis of which he had been a victim.

Then, growing still bolder, he described to them in detail the magnificent costume Swanissit was wearing, heavily embroidered with gold and silver threads, the very same costume that Hiawatha, the great founder of the Iroquois league, had told them should be worn by him who was to carry on his work, by saving the Iroquois people from perpetual warfare, and keeping them at peace, to the benefit of their hunting and harvests alike.

The braves crowded round to look at and touch the magnificent gifts that had been made to their dead.

They were jostling one another with growing excitement, and they were dangerously close. While most of them manifested sincere admiration, it was obvious that some of them had grown covetous, and were casting glances towards the fort and arguing among themselves.

Angélique felt the change in the atmosphere; they had reached a turning-point. This was the moment at which Peyrac would either win or lose.

She noticed that those of Peyrac's men who had been standing farthest back, carrying the banners, had begun to slip away surreptitiously into the darkness.

Others, under cover of nightfall, had led the horses away into the forest, and Yann came over to Angélique and whispered that she and the other women and children were to move away too, and make their way quietly down towards the river-bank without making their movements too apparent.

The Spaniards covered the silent retreat, for they had loaded and prepared their weapons without the slightest sound.

'Look after Honorine for me, will you, and go down with Yann,' Angélique told the Jonases. 'I'll join you in a moment.'

Nothing could have induced her to leave until she saw her husband out of danger.

She noticed that the Iroquois were creeping up and peering through the gates at the interior of the outpost.

The bluish shadows grew thicker while a great red patch in the western sky continued to cast a coppery glow over everything.

She went up to the group of men which included Joffrey de Peyrac, Nicolas, Maupertuis and his son, Eloi Macollet, and a few of the men from the *Gouldsboro*, such as Malaprade and the Maltese Enrico Enzi who were standing guard behind their master.

Outakke stood in the midst of them, leaning on Pierre-Joseph Maupertuis's shoulder, but by now they were completely surrounded by Iroquois, who were growing progressively bolder and wanted to take a closer look at the fort.

It was not Joffrey de Peyrac that Angélique looked at, but Outakke. She stared so intently at him that, bit by bit, as if by some attraction, the Mohawk turned his head slightly to one side and his fearless, lustreless eyes met those of the young white woman.

'I granted you your life the other evening, by the spring,' her eyes cried out to him. 'When you were wounded I saved you from the hands of Piksarett who was after your scalp...! And now, you save him, save him! You who are able to, I beg you to save him!'

It was both an order and a supplication that flashed from her pale, staring eyes, and a wave of indefinable emotion swept over the Mohawk's yellow face.

A group of braves had drawn close to Peyrac and were talking to him insolently.

'And what about the firewater, the precious drink of the Paleface, where is it? We noticed that you refused to give any to our chiefs...!'

Their self-appointed spokesman sniggered as he casually balanced his tomahawk on the end of a brown hand.

'The brandy and the rum are inside the outpost,' the Count replied. 'They are gathered together in a single lot, which has been set aside as a tribute to the Great Spirit, and they are not for you.'

The man let out an ironical exclamation and shouted something in a mixture of rage and triumph.

Nicolas Perrot suppressed a grimace but translated in unfaltering tones:

'He says: we shall take it ourselves without your permission, Tekonderoga, you ally of the traitors who killed our chiefs.'

On hearing these insulting words, Peyrac took a step towards the man until he almost touched him, and stared fixedly into his eyes.

'And what is thy name, thou who darest to lay claim to something that has been offered as a tribute to the Great Spirit?'

The Indian leapt back a pace and raised his tomahawk but Peyrac neatly avoided the blow that whistled over his head then, standing up again, brandished his pistol and struck his adversary on the temple with the butt.

The Indian reeled backwards and collapsed stunned among his companions. Angélique's cry was lost amidst the roar that rose from the Iroquois.

But a still more imperious cry hushed the tumult. It was Outakke.

One arm raised, he placed himself in front of Peyrac, protecting him with his own body. Silence fell again, and all lowered their weapons. Outakke made a sign to a young brave to come and help him to stand, then, turning towards Peyrac, he spoke softly to him in French.

'I do not wish your death, Tekonderoga. The spirit of justice required me to grant you your life, for it is true that if vengeance is one of the laws of our people, that of gratitude takes precedence, and I would be false were I to forget that your wife Kawa, the Fixed Star, has twice saved my life.... Yes twice.... But will my braves agree to leave you alone and to retire without a fight? That I cannot answer! Nevertheless, I shall try to persuade them ... and you will give me credit for trying, even if I fail.'

In moments of great stress, incongruous thoughts always seem to flash across one's mind. Angélique later remembered that the thing that had struck her above all at that moment was that the Mohawk, just like the Canadian trappers or lords he had mixed with in his youth, spoke French in a highly polished manner, and that nothing could have been more startling than to hear such choice phrases rippling over those barbarous lips.

'Our hearts are not quick to forget insults,' he went on. 'My authority will be weakened if I ask them to spare you.'

'I am not asking you to forget,' Peyrac replied.

Angélique could bear it no longer. Now she knew that even if Outakke intervened he could not save them. Only one thought remained to her, to take refuge inside the fort, to barricade the heavy log gates and to seize the muskets. Enough of this! She could no longer bear to see Joffrey exposed as he was, in constant danger of being killed....

But he seemed in no hurry to leave, neither did he appear to be unduly wearied from the tensions of the day.

'I do not ask you to forget,' he repeated more loudly. 'In fact I intend to make it impossible for you ever to forget what has taken place at Katarunk. You are all busy asking yourselves: "If we spare these Palefaces, who will wipe out the shame that the renown of the Iroquois has suffered here?" And I reply: "I will...."

'Perrot, translate please....

'You think that the pow-wow is over. But it isn't! Things are just beginning. You have seen nothing yet, heard nothing yet,

240

men of the Iroquois nation. For it is now that I am about to speak. Listen well! For I want my words and my actions to sink like arrows into your hearts, for only then will you be able to leave this place without bitterness, your hearts satisfied. It is not true, my brothers, that the heart of the Paleface and the heart of the Indian are incapable of sharing the same feelings. For my heart, like yours, is filled with horror when I contemplate the outpost of Katarunk. Like you, I cannot help thinking that this place has seen the foulest of murders, the most loathsome of treacheries that I have ever seen committed in my many long years...! Like you, I believe that this place of treachery bears forever an indelible mark, and that the sight of it perpetuates that memory, and so all just men would wish to see it wiped out.... Moreover, are those who in future years might come to this outpost to say every time they come here: "That was where Swanissit was scalped, beneath the roof of his host, the Paleface Tekonderoga, the Man of Thunder"? No...! No...! That I could not bear!' cried Count Peyras with a depth of violence and anger that awed them, and which on this occasion – Angélique could sense it – was not feigned. 'No, I could not bear that. Rather let everything be wiped out.... Let everything be wiped out...!'

He coughed after shouting these last words.

Nicolas Perrot slowly repeated what he had said, with a kind of exaltation: 'Let everything be wiped out...! Let everything be wiped out!' And now it seemed as if every eye in the dusk was glued to those two upright figures, the trapper and Count Peyrac, in his storm-coloured clothes, as they stood there still just visible in the last glimmer of the sunset.

'I know,' the Count went on, 'there are some among you who are thinking: "There are some good wares in that outpost!" Some of you would like to satisfy your greed and your desire for vengeance! May those jackals cease their growling and sniffing around and go away, their tails between their legs. For I am telling you that from henceforth everything inside this fortress belongs to the shades of your ancestors. Thus, and only thus will they be satisfied!

'You have received your gifts. They are valuable gifts. And when you come to load them on your backs, you will realize that they are considerable gifts.

'But that which lies within this fort of Katarunk you have no right to take, any more than I have the right to make use of it.

I have given it to the shades of your dead chiefs, in compensation for the treachery they suffered.

'Harken to me, and remember my words : in this fort lies food for several months, possibly enough to last years, venison, moose, and bear meat, dried and salted cod, salt from the sea, ten barrels of sunflower-seed oil, whale oil and sea-lion oil. There is maple syrup and sugar from distant islands. There is rum and wine for the Palefaces and the Indian chiefs. There are twenty bags of wheat and maize flour. Two hundred tresses of Virginia tobacco. A hundred tresses of Mexican tobacco. Fifty bales of Dutch cotton goods. Ten bales of silk from China and the East. There are cloaks of wool and Egyptian cotton, carpets, guns, shot, and powder. There are fifteen traps for wolves, bears, foxes, or lynxes. There is ironware : needles and scissors.... There are furs. None of this belongs to you, neither does it belong to me any more.

'All this belongs to your dead chiefs.

'You who say : "They have nothing but shame," this is what they possess. Everything except the barrels of brandy and wine, which I know that Swanissit would not have wanted and which has been set aside for the Supreme Spirit, who alone has the power to cleanse them of their harmful properties.

'And now, draw aside ! Outakke, order your braves to go back as far as the river if they want to avoid being wounded or killed.

'I am going to make thunder !'

A stupefied silence fell on the assembled company after he had spoken. Then slowly the great throng of savages began to flow back towards the bottom of the hill to the bank of the river.

Their superstitious fears were mingled with avid curiosity. What did he mean to do, this Paleface with the clever tongue who claimed a better vengeance for them than that their arms could obtain?

Count Peyrac gave a few more orders to those of his men who were near him then, noticing Angélique, he put an arm round her waist and drew her away.

'Come quick ! We must not stay here. Maupertuis, would you check that all our people are down at the river-bank and that there is no one left inside the compound !'

They found themselves mingling with the Iroquois on the river-bank where the evening mist was beginning to rise. Angélique felt Peyrac clasp her close against him before releasing her and quietly taking a tinder-box from a leather pocket on his belt. The Indians jostled one another like children at a play, for everyone wanted to see Peyrac and to know what he was about.

Angélique looked around for Honorine, the Jonases and her sons. It was impossible to see any more, but Maupertuis came and told her that everyone was there, gathered together beside a small coppice under the protection of the armed Spanish guards.

Yann Le Couennec came down the hillside unwinding a hempen fuse as he went. Under cover of the dark, some of Peyrac's men went back to the outpost, hastily laid the Iroquois chiefs in the prepared grave, threw their gifts in higgledy-piggledly after them, and rapidly shovelled the earth on top of them.

As they were finishing their task, the harsh sound of a bugle rose into the air, they broke up, and ran down to the spinney beside the river where the women and children had gathered.

Then for a second time the bugle rang out.

Then Count Peyrac took his tinder, struck a spark, and bending down lit the end of the hempen fuse which the Breton had unrolled to where he stood.

The flame caught on, swift and lively, and sped up to the hilltop, threading its way through the tree-trunks, the grass and the stones like a swift golden snake.

It reached the gate of the fortress and then they could see it no longer.

For suddenly a tremendous explosion burst up into the dark sky.

The whole outpost began to burn fiercely with vast flames fanned by the wind. All the woodwork of the houses and the palisade had been previously impregnated with oil and rum and sprinkled with saltpetre. It literally exploded.

In the dry parched atmosphere of the end of summer, the whole outpost immediately became a roaring furnace, devouring everything, wreaking destruction amidst ferocious convulsions. The spectators had to retreat to the river-bank, scorched by the fierceness of the blaze.

Suddenly visible once more in the red glow from the fire, the upturned faces revealed both admiration and terror, horror and delight, that mingling of complex emotions which man feels in the presence of the unleashing of natural forces in all their splendour and indomitable power.

After a long pause, a voice rose up from the oppressed, panting crowd, the voice of old Tahoutaguete. He was asking a question.

'He would like to know,' said Outakke, 'if you had any beaver skins in your fortress?'

'Yes yes! there were,' cried O'Connell the Irishman, tearing his hair. 'Thirty bales of them! At least ten thousand pounds' worth of them in the loft. Oh! Monsieur de Peyrac, if only you had told me what you were going to do, if only I had known. . . ! My beaver skins. . . ! My beaver skins. . . !'

Such was the despair in his voice and so comical was he in the expression of his grief, that the Iroquois burst out laughing.

Here at last was a Paleface who spoke from his heart! A Paleface like the others. . . . A true son of that race of merchants. They were back on familiar ground again. . . .

'And what about that skin there?' said Peyrac, pinching his great fat cheeks as they shook with grief. 'What value would you set on that? Ten thousand pounds, twenty thousand pounds? And that scalp they have left you with,' he went on, grasping the unfortunate trader by his red hair. 'How much for that? Thirty thousand pounds. . . ?'

The braves laughed even louder. They clutched their sides as they mimicked the Irishman's gestures, pointing at him the while.

Their great bursts of terrifying laughter rang out like an echo to the noise of the flames.

'Are you laughing with us, Swanissit?' Outakke suddenly cried out, turning towards the blazing top of the hill. 'Are you laughing with your braves? Are you consoled by the riches and the presents they have left you?'

Then suddenly, like some fantastic answer to his appeal, a blueish white streak of light rose up from among the roaring scarlet wreaths of flame, higher and higher into the black sky, where it exploded several times and fell back again in a shower of silver stars.

No sooner had the shouts of surprise and fear left their lips, than another long red serpent unleashed itself across the blackness, bursting into a sheath of stars, which, in their turn, exploded into diadems of rubies that slowly disintegrated, liquefying themselves and dripping like blood across the dark panoply of the sky.

The Indians fell to their knees. Others recoiled and tumbled into the river.

They were thrown into a state of utter confusion among themselves which mirrored the confusion in their minds.

Yet even those who found themselves splashing in the waters of the Kennebec were unable to take their eyes off this magical spectacle.

Now plumes of sparks and dazzling trails of fire seemed to fly in all directions in a display of fireworks that overwhelmed even the crackling of the last walls as they fell. The sky was full of green, red, and gold, falling back to earth as flowers, garlands, domes, long coils that crossed and recrossed, chasing one another through the darkness, forming weird figures, the shapes of animals, that would go out or vanish the very moment when they seemed about to leap. . . .

During an odd moment of silence, Angélique heard the children's delighted shouts. All fear had vanished in the general wonder, and with it hatred, anxiety, and suspicion. . . .

And Florimond, who had made the fireworks, received the acclamations as if intended for him.

She heard his youthful voice saying: 'Well . . . what do you think of my skill. . . ? It's every bit as good as Versailles!'

And Captain Alvarez and his men for a moment almost forgot the orders they had received to remain on the alert, one finger on the trigger.

But there was no longer anything to fear. The fearsome Iroquois stood there with raised heads, in utter fascination, like children. Their hearts were filled with delight. The intoxicating visions before them were like dreams, making them forget the reality of their bodies and the reason for which they were standing there on the banks of the Kennebec.

An immense emerald caterpillar fell squirming towards them. A fiery butterfly flew off into the darkness, and a giant glowing pumpkin exploded. . . .

When the last of the fireworks had flung their coloured powders out into the night sky, the outpost of Katarunk had vanished. Its ramparts had collapsed in showers of sparks and the place where it had once stood was nothing more than a vast glowing wound growing slowly darker as the minutes passed.

CHAPTER THIRTY-THREE

THEN THE moon rose, a late moon rising towards the middle of the night. And its serene light, mingling with the shifting glow of the dying conflagration, gave a surprising brightness to the scene.

They waited. In the mingled darkness and brightness the half-naked braves were awaking as from an incredible dream.

Through the silence the murmur of the river at their feet grew louder.

Slowly Outakke came to himself once more; his glance, half-hidden between his long narrow eyelids, fell on the Paleface couple who stood before him, and he seemed to see them in a new way. There they were, a man and a woman supporting each other, waiting for him, a Mohawk, to give his verdict of life or death.

Then his heart swelled within him, carried away by the passionate, poetic incantations which so often swayed him, and he spoke privately to the man before him, the man who had mastered him.

'Are you the Ancestor foretold to us by the Bird, who is to come back to earth in the guise of a Paleface? I do not know ... I still do not know who you really are ... but I shall never forget what I have seen at Katarunk ... never shall I forget it. ... Speak, you ...' he said aloud, turning to Nicolas Perrot. 'Repeat what I am about to say to my braves. I do not know who you are, Tekonderoga, but never shall I forget what I have seen at Katarunk.'

Nicolas repeated what he said, and the braves responded with a long-drawn-out cry that seemed to echo down the dark valley.

'Never shall we forget. ...'

'I have also seen that you are not a Frenchman like the others, Tekonderoga,' Outakke went on in French in a voice that grew in clarity and firmness. 'I see that you are no Frenchman from Quebec, neither are you from the King of France. You really do stand alone and speak in your own name. Did it really mean little to you to lose all those beaver skins?'

'Of course I minded, but what I minded even more than losing the beaver skins was losing the instruments I had that enabled me to discover the secrets of nature, to see invisible things. I could talk to the stars, but now Swanissit and your dead captains will use my instruments and will learn the secrets of the stars.'

'And happy may they be,' the Iroquois murmured.

'And as for you others, you know where their grave lies. It is in front of the fort, beside the ashes. No one will ever build here again, and you will be able to return here without shame and without grief to wash their memorable bones.'

'And you, Tekonderoga, what will you do? You have nothing but these horses and these clothes. The forest lies all around you, it is night, and the winter cold is drawing near.'

'That matters little since my honour has been retrieved and I have paid the blood-money.'

'Will you go back towards the Ocean?'

'No. The season is too far advanced and the journey too fraught with danger. I shall go into the mountains, and join forces with my four men who have a hut up there. May I tell them that you are still our allies?'

'Yes, you may. When the Council of Mothers and Elders has approved my decision I will send you a necklace of porcelain. Tekonderoga, do you really think you will triumph over all your enemies?'

'The result of a battle is in the hands of the Supreme Spirit. But I have made up my mind to fight and to win.'

'You have great courage and great cunning, and I foresee victory for you. But take a care, Tekonderoga, for you have many enemies still, and your muskets cannot vanquish the most terrible of them all, Etskon-Honsi, the Black Robe. He speaks for his God, he speaks for his King. He is invincible. Many a time have we sought to kill him, but he has always survived, he CANNOT die, do you understand? He wants to sweep you from his path, and he will hound you ceaselessly, for you come from the other side of his life. You belong to this world while he belongs to the world of invisible spirits, and for him the earth is unbearable. . . .

'I fear for you, now that you are my friend. I know he seeks your downfall. I know it, I have seen it – how often have I seen it in my dreams, seen his blue eye glistening! And I, a brave, I trembled, for I know of nothing on earth more terrifying than that eye. When he used to look at me like that when I lived with the French, I felt my soul and my spirit go out from me. . . . Beware, Tekonderoga,' he repeated in urgent tones, 'and take care, for you possess a treasure, you who possess nothing else, and that one last treasure he will try to snatch from you, especially that one.'

He pointed to Angélique.

'His hatred is already upon her. He will try to separate you. Will you be able to resist his powers? He is very strong, you know, and he cannot be killed.'

Suddenly Outakke seemed to have grown fearful.

And perhaps it was at that moment that Angélique's heart opened to love for the Indians.

It was a feeling that went beyond fear, beyond any repugnance one might have felt for these wild men, it was a feeling that took root in all the feelings of friendly, fraternal, and motherly love she felt for others.

Now she saw them naked, credulous, defenceless, with only their arrows to face the deadly fire of muskets, with no other defence against the mystical power of the Jesuits than their crude magic. Pity and respect for them made their way into her heart.

The broken voice of this Iroquois who, after so many words of hatred, was now offering them advice, revealed to her the human characteristics of these cruel people.

With all the passionate changeability of primitive creatures, here they were desperately concerned about the plight of those whom they had sought to massacre a few hours earlier, and for whom, since they had become friends, they now felt more concern than for their own fate.

Joffrey de Peyrac went up to Outakke and spoke to him confidentially.

'I shall tell you something you can understand. My own guardian spirits are such that they fear neither the evil spells of the Redskin nor those of the Paleface. And Etskon-Honsi, in spite of his powers, remains a Paleface. Like me . . .'

'That is true,' the Mohawk conceded, apparently reassured. 'You are a Paleface, and you can understand him, whereas our heads sometimes become confused, I understand. You will know how to get the better of him just as you knew how to outwit us when we sought your death. That is good! May you remain strong, Tekonderoga. We need your strength. And now, go where you will. However far you may wander, you and yours, if you meet a brave of the Five Nations, he will sing for you the song of peace. I have spoken! Farewell!'

CHAPTER THIRTY-FOUR

THE NIGHT wind blew over the ashes, and everything had grown dark and silent. The moon had vanished into the distant mist, leaving a faint diffused light that revealed the dark shapes of forest and mountain.

Joffrey de Peyrac was walking slowly along the river-bank. He was alone, and from time to time he halted and looked pensively towards the top of the hillside where, only a few hours before, the outpost of Katarunk had stood.

Angélique was standing some distance from him and could see him as he stopped, then took up his meditative pacing once more.

She too had returned to the same place, as if by some irresistible attraction.

The children had fallen asleep beside a fire in the cave to which, the previous day, the Count had had their blankets and some food taken. Most of the adults were exhausted and slept like children. Angélique had left them and had gone off quietly into the night where, for the very first time, she no longer felt afraid. The evil spirits seemed to have left the place, scattered far and wide by some tempestuous, tragic wind.

Now she found herself walking in the heart of a friendly forest, and every sound that reached her ears took on a new significance. They were merely the echoes of a living world, a world coming to life again under the branches, a tiny animal world, preparing for winter, busying itself with final tasks, singing its final song, nothing more. Mosses perfumed the air for the last time, squirrels scrabbled to bury their last nuts, and far, far away, beyond the ravines, like the blast of some melancholy horn, she heard the bellow of a moose.

Angélique no longer felt afraid. In doing what he had done, Joffrey de Peyrac had freed her from her anxiety.

It had been a crazy gesture! But it had been the only possible one. To burn down Katarunk. He was the only man who could ever have dared such a thing and carried it out. The idea must have occurred to him when he had said: 'My house has been stained by an unforgiveable crime!'

It was then that he had known what he must do. It was then that he had grown calm once more.

From now on no evil would come to them from the land of

America. The holocaust had been consummated.

At first Angélique had felt something vaguely, then it had come to her like a revelation. And now she walked on through the trees, her heart light within her, for she felt that the rites had been accomplished and this gave satisfaction to her soul, steeped as it was in Christianity.

The sacrifice had been a good one not only because it had saved their lives, but also because it would bring them happiness. And the words that she had often murmured during the Mass came back to her: *Hanc igitur oblationem* ...

'This is what we offer up to you, O Lord, we your servants, and our entire family with us. Graciously accept our sacrifice, O Lord, and dispose our days in Thy peace. . . .'

The land of America would no longer be hostile to them. Joffrey de Peyrac's sacrifice had touched its fiery heart. The Iroquois would never forget. But still more, Angélique thought of the utter destitution in which they both found themselves, and from her heart rose up the serene prayer: 'Dispose our days in Thy peace, O Lord. . . .'

Everything had gone up in smoke! What was left for men to strip them of now? Nothing remained save one marvellous secret treasure, their love. This must have been what fate had intended in giving them back to each other, so that they should recognize its value and not underestimate it. They had had to be able to recognize it without confusing it with other values. The pure love of a man for a woman, and of a woman for a man, two flames in one, burning in the arid desert, in the icy wastes, two hearts burning through the night of the universe, as at the time of the Creation. . . .

She stood and watched from afar as Joffrey de Peyrac's shadow moved meditatively along the river-bank.

The smell of fire still hung about the landscape, and in spite of the cold she still caught whiffs of the crowd that had so thoroughly trampled the ground here; now by contrast everything was so quiet that Angélique was overcome by a sense of well-being.

From afar she watched the lonely man who stopped from time to time and raised his head towards the hillside where the wind on occasion stirred the ashes to a red glow.

Then she walked towards him, without haste, sure she would find him in the night. When she was a few paces away she stopped once more. He caught sight of her, the shape of a woman standing out in profile against the blue shadows, her face a bright patch, then, after looking at her for a moment, he came towards her. Joffrey de Peyrac's hand touched Angélique's shoulder and she drew close to him as if to a source of warmth, placing her palms on his chest, then slipping her hands round his body and huddling against him as he tightened his grip round her body and drew her to him, gathering the folds of his cloak around her to cover her, and drawing her ever closer and closer to him until they stood intertwined, clasped in each other's arms, feeling no passion, no other desire than the primitive need to be close, like two animals which fall asleep resting their heads on one another's necks, seeking mutual warmth and the reassurance of the other's presence.

Joffrey de Peyrac began to say something, but he refrained. What was there to say, he thought, that was not utterly banal? 'Were you frightened? Are you cross with me for burning down the house you already thought of as your home? For facing you with endless difficulties?'

These were banalties he could have said to any woman. But this woman, this woman who stood quivering against him, it would have been an insult to speak like that to her. She was far above it. She was far above anything he could ever have imagined her to be.

And he rubbed his cheek against her delicate skin as if to reassure himself of the presence of this living creature, warm and gentle, who was there in his arms and who was his wife.

She too had been on the point of saying something and telling him some of the thoughts that flooded her heart: 'How I admired you today, my love! Your courage saved us all! You were inspired....'

But these words all seemed inadequate and did not exactly express what she wanted to say. Nor did she want to tell him what she had just discovered, that the sacrifice had been accomplished, that the gods were satisfied.... 'You and I are alone on earth, my love, you and I, penniless and alone ... and I am happy....'

But this he knew as well as she did. So they both remained silent. And they clasped each other still closer, in silence and in joy.

And from time to time she would throw her head back to seek the light of his eyes, that shone like two stars above her, and she guessed that he was smiling at her.

CHAPTER THIRTY-FIVE

TOWARDS THE north there lies a place where the waters spread out to form a vast silvery desert. Dead forests, their roots drowned beneath the waters, thrust their branches up into a pearly sky, like spiky candelabra, white as bone. A thin cloud of mosquitoes and sandflies lies like a haze along the shifting shores. The land is unsure and treacherous. But here and there, islands covered with black fir-trees standing up like so many distaffs, cast their long reflection across the unfathomable mirror of the waters.

This is the Lake Megantic region.

When the French soldiers reached it a few days after leaving Katarunk, autumn seemed to be much further advanced than on the other side of the mountains. Dry moss, the colour of old gold, covered the ground, and the leaves were falling from the sparse trees. They could already sense the atmosphere of Canada in the icy air they breathed and the wild desolation of the region. The soldiers, the Hurons, and the Algonquins all felt it and agreed among themselves that, on this side of the hills, they felt more 'at home'.

All they had to do was to get their canoes back into the water, to cross the lake, and there they would find the good river Chaudière, which would lead them easily down to the Saint Lawrence, into which it flowed opposite Quebec.

For the last few miles, they would make their way past villages with vast stone farms built on the river's edge, while from the hillside the peasants, busy bringing in a late harvest of wheat, or picking a few apples, would wave their caps to greet the return of the war party. The white pointed spire of Levis would come into sight round the bend and then suddenly they would find themselves beneath the walls of Quebec.

Then they would look up to greet the lofty city, perched on the rocks, and the city would reply with all the bells of its myriad belfries.

Then it would be goodbye to the vast open spaces, goodbye to savages, to bowls of tasteless 'sagamité' and stewed dog. And heigho for Calvados, rum, and brandy brought over by ship, for wheaten bread thickly buttered, for juicy steaks and ham cooked with cabbage, for cheese and red wine, and the pretty girls they would meet down town at Janine Gonfarel's....

At Lake Megantic the sun shone dazzling and brilliant in a pale sky, the water had a metallic sheen, the trees were dead, and winter stalked the countryside.

The birch-bark canoes slid swiftly over the surface of the lake, hunting through the monotonous archipelago for the source of the Chaudière, for one had to know the area well to find it among all the islands and the endless meanderings of the water channels.

The Marquis of Loménie remained on the bank and watched his troops embarking. Fallières, L'Aubignière and his nephew, and one group of Indians were already far off, while others kept on arriving, their canoes on their heads, along the portage track.

An Indian, who had run the full length of the column of men, dashed up to the officer with one arm raised in brief salute. He was a foreigner and Loménie-Chambord recognized him as the Panis slave, Nicolas Perrot's inseparable companion. He blurted out something, but nobody understood him for he belonged to a distant tribe, beyond the freshwater seas, a small group of Indians known as the Panis who had been dispersed and had then disappeared. He claimed not to understand any of the dialects of the Indian nations present, but agreed to use his lamentable French.

With the help of Pont-Briand, the Colonel managed to piece his message together. It appeared that at Katarunk, the Iroquois chiefs had been scalped by Maudreuil and the Patsuiketts. The Iroquois braves were marching on Katarunk to seek vengeance, and Count Peyrac and his family would be massacred.

'We must go! We must go straight away,' exclaimed Pont-Briand. 'We must go back. There are not enough of them to hold out against those hordes....'

Loménie made no comment but immediately ordered those still with him to turn back. Most of the Hurons and Abenakis agreed to accompany him along with half the soldiers. There were always volunteers when a chance offered of having a go at the Iroquois.

When, a few days later, they found themselves beside the Kennebec again, they listened hopefully for the sound of shooting, which would have shown that those defending the fort were still holding their own. But the silence was unbroken, and the whole region seemed dead. Loménie was also concerned about the fate of Father Orgeval. Pont-Briand was plunged in gloom as if suffering some inner torment.

Before rounding the last bend which would bring them to the river-bank opposite Katarunk, the two officers halted the flotilla and ordered the men to draw the canoes up on to the shore among the willows. Each man loaded his gun in silence. Loménie and Pont-Briand climbed the rock face in order to take a look without themselves being seen. The air was clear and yet it had a tang of cold smoke. As soon as they reached the top and looked through the leaves they realized what had happened.

Katarunk no longer existed.

Before them lay an area blackened with ash and gutted tree-trunks, where once the outpost had stood.

And at the foot of the hill the Kennebec flowed on, its vivid, almost dark-blue waters rolling between the banks of scarlet sumacs, mountain-ashes, and wild cherry-trees.

Not a human trace anywhere.

Pont-Briand gave a dull groan, and banged his head several times against a tree-trunk.

'She is dead,' he cried, 'she is dead; how can I have the courage to go on living. . . ? You see, she was no devil. . . . She was only a woman! A beautiful, weak woman. . . . An adorable woman! Oh, my God, why must I remain here on earth now?'

'Tush, you are talking nonsense,' said Loménie, shaking him by the shoulder.

Then suddenly he too closed his eyes and bitter grief flooded his soul. Once again he saw the horseman in the black mask, surrounded by his oriflammes, facing Katarunk. And beside him the man's wife, such a lovely woman!

His heart was rent with pain and a searing sense of loss. Then he came to his senses again, thinking that it must have been Father Orgeval's hand that had planned all this. For was this priest not guided by God, for whom he had already spilled his blood? When Loménie had come from Quebec a month earlier at the head of his men, the Jesuit had given him an order.

'Get rid of them at all costs! Destroy them if you must, it will make things easier!'

He had been attracted by the strangers and had swerved from his duty. Heaven had taken a hand in the affair.

'Mission accomplished!' he thought.

And his heart flooded with bitterness. He stayed for a long time with Pont-Briand, unable to tear himself from the place. Then he gave orders to head north again.

When the French had finally departed, the Panis slave left the forest and he too came down from the mountains to the river-bank. His long black hair floated behind him in the wind. He moved stealthily down to the river-bank, stooping towards the ground as he walked. After following the shore to the little launching point, he climbed the hill to the charred area, wandered round the destroyed fort then returned to the river.

He had read on the ground the tale of an astonishing adventure.

Then he raised his head again, seemed to sniff the wind, and set off resolutely in a north-easterly direction towards the heart of the mountains.

Angélique

'The intrepid, passionate and always enchanting heroine of the most fantastically successful series of historical romances ever written.'
DAILY HERALD

ANGELIQUE I : The Marquise of the Angels	8/–
ANGELIQUE II : The Road to Versailles	6/–
ANGELIQUE AND THE KING	6/–
ANGELIQUE AND THE SULTAN	6/–
ANGELIQUE IN REVOLT	6/–
ANGELIQUE IN LOVE	6/–
THE COUNTESS ANGELIQUE I : In the Land of the Redskins	5/–
THE COUNTESS ANGELIQUE II : Prisoner of The Mountains	5/–

These novels by SERGEANNE GOLON comprise a tremendous saga of 17th-century France, tracing Angélique's career from childhood through a series of strange marriages and amorous adventures, perils and excitements, unequalled in the field of historical fiction. Translated into most European languages, a sensational runaway success in France, Angélique is one of the world's most fabulous best-sellers.

The most ravishing — and surely the most ravished — heroine of all time.